The
Book
of
Silver Linings

Nan Fischer

Berkley
New York

BERKLEY
An imprint of Penguin Random House LLC
penguinrandomhouse.com

Copyright © 2023 by Nan Fischer
Readers Guide copyright © 2023 by Nan Fischer
Excerpt from *Some of It Was Real* copyright © 2022 by Nan Fischer
Penguin Random House supports copyright. Copyright fuels creativity,
encourages diverse voices, promotes free speech, and creates a vibrant
culture. Thank you for buying an authorized edition of this book and for
complying with copyright laws by not reproducing, scanning, or distributing
any part of it in any form without permission. You are supporting writers
and allowing Penguin Random House to continue to publish books for
every reader.

BERKLEY and the BERKLEY & B colophon are registered trademarks of
Penguin Random House LLC.

Library of Congress Cataloging-in-Publication Data

Names: Fischer, Nan, author.
Title: The book of silver linings / Nan Fischer.
Description: First edition. | New York: Berkley, 2023.
Identifiers: LCCN 2022054531 (print) | LCCN 2022054532 (ebook) |
ISBN 9780593438718 (trade paperback) | ISBN 9780593438725 (ebook)
Classification: LCC PS3606.I7666 B66 2023 (print) |
LCC PS3606.I7666 (ebook) | DDC 813/.6—dc23/eng/20211206
LC record available at https://lccn.loc.gov/2022054531
LC ebook record available at https://lccn.loc.gov/2022054532

First Edition: August 2023

Printed in the United States of America
1st Printing

Book design by Nancy Resnick
Title page photograph by Agnes Kantaruk/Shutterstock.com

Praise for
Some of It Was Real

"Fresh, surprising, and compulsively readable, *Some of It Was Real* sucked me right in with its rich characters, sparkling wit, and captivating story arc. This debut is more than a page-turner; it's an unflinching exploration of identity, trauma, and transcending the past, and it kept me riveted all the way up to its jaw-dropping conclusion."

—*New York Times* bestselling author Andrea Bartz

"*Some of It Was Real* had everything I love—characters I was rooting for and an intriguing premise that kept me guessing. The ending had me turning the final pages at breakneck speed. You will simply love this book."

—*New York Times* bestselling author Tracey Garvis Graves

"The perfect blend of mystery and love story, *Some of It Was Real* kept me guessing and turning pages way past my bedtime, all the way to its shocking denouement. An absolute must-read."   —*USA Today* bestselling author Colleen Oakley

"*Some of It Was Real* by Nan Fischer is an addictive mixture of several genres—magical realism, mystery, family drama, and romance—and is the perfect distraction for summer's dog days."

—*The Augusta Chronicle*

"Fischer has a natural touch for plotting and clever dialogue, and her fresh, delightful plot charms and entices. Women's fiction readers will devour this."   —*Publishers Weekly*

Titles by Nan Fischer

Some of It Was Real
The Book of Silver Linings

This novel is dedicated to Henry
À la maison pour toujours
Je te retrouverai encore et encore . . .

Chapter One

Yoga speed dating? You can't be serious!" I hold out the bright red flyer, awaiting my best friend's reaction. Now I understand why Mars told me to dress casually. She was too smart to suggest yoga clothes—those who *can* stretch do. I can't and don't and prefer adrenaline sports that do not require an instructor or navel-gazing.

Mars takes the flyer back then tugs me down the sidewalk. "Remind me again, when was your last date?"

I've been on two dates in the past six months. On the first, my date asked the waitress out when he went to the bathroom. The second guy took me to a strip club so I could *make it rain* dollar bills for the scantily clad performers. I hop over a crack in the pavement. "Fine. I'll go."

"Of course you will," Mars says and bumps my shoulder. "You never say no to any of my ideas."

We pass an unhoused man camped out in the doorway of a closed Gap. A mutt in a blue rain jacket, his face sugared with gray, lies beside him. I dig into my backpack for the plastic bags I always carry and hand the man one. Inside there's a granola bar, a travel-sized toothbrush and toothpaste, a pair of wool socks, and a grain-free dog biscuit.

"Bless you," the man says while his dog happily munches the treat.

"Seriously? You've added socks?" Mars mutters once we're well past the two of them.

She doesn't begrudge the guy socks. She's just concerned because I live on a tight budget. I glance back. The man has wrapped a sleeping bag around his dog to keep him warm. We get frequent visits from the unhoused at the animal shelter where I volunteer. Most of the time, they take better care of their dogs than themselves. Unconditional love is priceless, something I witness often when our animals find their forever home.

"Watch out!" I drag my best friend around a ladder set beneath a sign for Chestnut Street Doughnuts.

"What do you actually think would happen to us if we walked under it?" she asks.

Mars has always been the voice of reason in my life. "In the old days people believed you'd face death by hanging." I can't help but share the historical origins of the superstition with her. "But my mother thought that the spirits of people were trapped in the triangle beneath the ladder. Walking under it is like asking them to haunt you."

Mars snorts. "And you believe in haunting?"

I giggle. "Maybe."

"Good to know." Mars drags me forward. "Almost there."

"I seriously doubt my perfect match will be at yoga speed dating," I say under my breath.

"I'm sure there will be some old shoes in the studio."

Mars knows I'm looking for comfort and durability in a relationship, like a perfectly worn-in pair of sneakers. While she's game for stilettos, sparkly cowboy boots, flip-flops, even ten-inch platforms.

"If you're not up for it, you could go hang out at the shelter you love so much, all alone with your unwanted fur-balls," Mars adds.

"They're not unwanted! They just haven't found their forever home. *Yet*. But point taken—we're doing this."

"Look on the bright side," she says with a cheeky grin, "men in yoga clothes leave little to the imagination."

"Oh. Lovely."

"Remind me again why we're best friends?" Mars teases.

But she knows the answer. Destiny. We met the first day of freshman year at San Francisco State when I walked into a generic dorm room and saw a striking girl with high cheekbones, wild brown curls, and a smiley face T-shirt seated on a red plastic suitcase . . .

"Are you Martha?" I asked.

"I've changed it to Mars. What should we change your name to?"

"It's just Constance. Why would you change your name?"

Mars gave me the hard blink that always punctuates her irreversible decisions, then said, "I know what being Martha is like—a mom who's on her fourth husband and weekends working at the bowling alley spraying disinfectant in smelly shoes. I have no idea what life as Mars will be, but I plan to make it epic." She held up a box of pink hair dye. "Join me?"

I set down my duffel. "Sorry, I've got to run. I'm on scholarship and they're handing out jobs. I want to make sure mine doesn't interfere with the classes I've already chosen."

"Well, *just* Constance, I'm on scholarship, too, though I haven't considered my schedule yet. What're you studying?"

"Biology. I've lined up a job for the next three summers at an animal hospital. After graduation, I'll spend a year in research then apply to veterinary school."

"Any room for fun in that plan?"

I knew she was teasing me and blushed. "Sure. If there's time."

Mars winked. "There's always time. I'm a chemistry major. You're looking at a future plastic surgeon. But *my* plan is to balance studying with *tons* of good times. You only live once."

That night I let her dye one lock of my dark blond hair bright pink while I organized our small closet, but kept my name. We became best friends despite her kicking me out to sleep in the lounge a few times a month so she could have privacy with a momentary crush. I'd never had a close friend before, mostly kept on the periphery of the cliques in high school for fear of being judged, and Mars's steadfast loyalty was a revelation that resulted in a deep trust between us.

In the end we both ditched our professional dreams to play the hand we were dealt but remained best friends despite the fact that she's a firefly everyone wants to catch so they can bask in her light and I'm more of your everyday moth.

Mars, her hair now a shade of purple that complements her light gray eyes, leads me inside the yoga studio, a spare space with white walls and a gleaming wood floor dotted with red yoga mats. Despite the yoga part, a trill of excitement rolls through me. Mars has always pushed me out of my comfort zone. And if my best friend wants my company, I'll do pretty much anything for her even if I'm not suited for it . . . like the time Mars made me sign up for hip-hop class for the physical exercise credits we needed freshman year of college. I couldn't find a beat if it hit me over the head and was mortified for an entire semester but also had never laughed harder.

Five minutes later twenty-six barefoot women stand in a line on the wooden floor facing twenty-six men while our "guide," a lady with long gray hair in a crimson and gold maxidress, walks between the rows and explains how yoga speed dating works.

"Hello, my name is Sara and I'm here to help all of you open yourselves up to new experiences and connections. You're here because swiping based on first impressions and meaningless hookups has left you empty, yearning for deeper bonds."

I glance at Mars and she wrinkles her nose.

"We'll start with a yoga warm-up. Then you'll be given a series of exercises to do with a partner, each lasting five minutes," Sara says. "When I ring this bell, it's time to move down the line to the next person. Each of you has a one-letter name tag and a piece of paper. If you like your interaction and want to know more about your partner, write down their letter. I'll compile your lists at the end of the night and if there are any matches you'll be connected via email."

Sara holds her hands up in a prayer pose. "For your own sake, the next time you meet build upon your initial connection in a meaningful way, open up your soul, and share your life force, your heart energy. Make something beautiful together."

I whisper to Mars, "My heart energy wants to run for the door."

Sara stops in front of me. "Tonight you're being asked to shed the skin that hasn't worked for you; to expose your true self. Are you up for the challenge?"

Her eyes are so earnest I want to support her. "Sure."

"What's the number one thing you want out of a relationship?" Sara asks me.

That's easy. "Someone who stays."

"And you?" Sara asks Mars.

My best friend grins. "I also want someone who stays . . . at least for the night." The room erupts with nervous laughter and Mars now has all of the men's undivided attention, which she already had the minute she walked through the door because she's tall, striking, and wears a crop top and leggings that showcase all her curves while I'm barely five-two and sport a T-shirt with a red dog on the front pocket and leggings that have lost most of their elastic. An old boyfriend told me that I look like the actress Michelle Williams but with none of her style. I have more of a "vintage" (meaning thrift store) vibe, favor clothes with flowers or animals on them, and usually wear my wavy dark blond hair swept into a ponytail despite Mars's best efforts to give me a more put-together *look*.

After a handful of Down Dogs, Warrior, Baby, and Tree poses, Sara rings her silver bell. "Let's begin," she says. "Remember, you are free to say no to any exercise that makes you uncomfortable, but I encourage everyone to give it a try. Your first challenge is to take a step toward the person across from you, place one hand on their chest, and gaze into their eyes. Let your mind open like a flower and drink in their sunlight . . ."

I stand for five minutes with my hand over the heart of a shirtless man with the letter B stuck to a chest matted with black hair that climbs from his belt, covers his shoulders, and carpets his back. Meanwhile, his own hand is sweaty and partially soaks my T-shirt. We look into each other's eyes for what feels like an eternity. When the bell rings, I don't write down the letter B nor does he scribble down the N stuck to my T-shirt.

The next guy, D, and I are supposed to tell each other our biggest secret. I stick with something safe—"I wish my career had gone in a different direction."

D smiles, revealing a mouthful of crowded teeth that match his sallow skin tone. "I wish I was a vampire."

I can hear Mars and her current partner laughing, and the room is filled with the gentle buzz of people getting to know each other. I notice several people writing down initials on their pad. Squelching my discomfort, I ask, "So what attracted you to being a vampire?"

"Mostly the sunlight thing, but also the biting," D shares.

When the bell rings I'm relieved to escape without a puncture wound and then incredibly uncomfortable when I have to hug Z for a full five minutes while listing all the things I love.

I start. "I love spending time with animals."

Z pulls me in tighter. "I love human contact."

Mars is right. Yoga pants leave little to the imagination.

When the bell dings, I can't get away fast enough while I notice Mars is still locked in a hug and only moves on at Sara's request. She blows me a kiss, clearly in her element.

I go through an exercise mirroring my partner's movements, then hold hands with another to share our energy. K's hands are freezing and mine are clammy so there's that. Plus, he smells overwhelmingly of patchouli, an earthy scent that makes me sneeze repeatedly.

When I'm partnered with C, we're asked to share our first jobs and what we loved about that experience while balancing on one foot and supporting each other if we wobble.

"I was a lifeguard and I loved working on my tan and hanging with girls in swimsuits," C says with a wink.

"I worked for a telemarketing company making phone calls." What I loved was the anonymity but instead I say, "I liked connecting with people."

"Didn't they curse you out sometimes?" C asks.

I laugh, wobble, and he grabs my arm. "Definitely, but there were also the old folks who just wanted someone to talk to and it was cool to make their day a little less lonely." C doesn't write my name down when the bell rings.

When I'm asked three guys later to release what I've been holding back while my partner intones "and it is so," I release work stress, worry about the dogs and cats who have been at the shelter over a year, concern over my grandfather's health, and the fear that I might never meet the right guy because if past choices predict future success I'm in trouble.

My partner, P, releases his fear that he won't get a promotion, that his brother's leukemia might return, and that women won't want a guy who's bald. Instead of intoning Sara's *and it is so* I tell him that Jean-Luc Picard is one of the sexiest men in the world. But P has never heard of the *Star Trek* captain and dislikes science fiction. Before that, I'd considered writing down his letter. But I draw the line at a guy who doesn't appreciate the starship USS *Enterprise*.

Three men later I'm instructed to list all my deepest wounds. I opt out of that one and notice Mars does, too. There's actually a lot of reasons we're best friends. One of the biggest is that we don't see a point in dredging up trauma from the past. I can't help but notice that only a few of my partners have written down my initial while I've written several of theirs down, mostly because I don't want to hurt their feelings.

When I sit across from X, we're told to massage each other's feet. Neither of us seems comfortable so I suggest we just talk. His name is Ryan and his tight black T-shirt reveals a tattoo sleeve down one arm. He's in ripped jeans so my guess is that yoga isn't his thing, either. "Did you get dragged here by a friend, too?" I ask.

Ryan laughs and points at a guy at the end of the line. "I'm playing wingman for my brother over there—letter Q. So why'd you agree to come?"

After an hour of discomfort, I'm too tired to scrounge for a witty or flirty response. "My best friend's idea, but the truth is I'm tired of dating and I'd like to find my person."

"You said to our *guide* you're looking for someone who stays?"

My cheeks grow warm. "I guess that doesn't sound very romantic."

"Why's that so important to you?"

I consider cracking a joke at my own expense, but opt for a version of the truth. "Both my parents were gone too soon. When that happens, it leaves a lot of empty space. I want the chance to fill in what's missing." A flush creeps up my neck. "What about you?"

Ryan runs a hand through his shoulder-length brown hair and shrugs. "It'd be cool to find someone who likes listening to live music and doesn't mind my dog—he's a mastiff and slobbers on everything. It's truly disgusting."

I laugh. "Dogs are some of my favorite people."

"Me, too, but I don't think we have the same vibe. I'm not looking for forever right now. I'm hoping to match with your friend, though. I think we'd have a good time."

He's Mars's type—sexy and uncommitted. "No worries," I say with an overly bright smile.

My final exercise is with O, whose real name turns out to be Oliver. He looks young, with soft brown eyes. We're supposed to lie down facing each other with our bodies inches apart, and see if the air between us becomes charged. It's incredibly awkward.

"I didn't want to come tonight," Oliver shares.

"Why did you?"

"All of my buddies are coupling up."

I ask, "Are *you* interested in a committed relationship?"

"I'm only twenty-two and to be honest, I just want to date around. But sometimes it's really lonely. I wish there was someone in my life to go for a run with on the weekends, watch a movie or go camping—but is that enough of a reason to have a serious girlfriend?" Oliver sighs. "Why does commitment matter so much to people?"

"I guess everyone has a different reason."

"What's yours?" he asks.

Not that I'm going to tell him this, but it would make me feel like there's a path to follow into the future instead of being in uncharted territory.

The bell rings and I get up to leave, then turn back to Oliver. "Were you serious about wanting someone to hang out with?"

He grins. "Are you offering?"

"I don't think we're a match. But do you like animals?"

"As a kid, I had a French bulldog named Atticus. He was my buddy."

"Why don't you swing by the Mission Animal Shelter? We have a bunch of dogs that would love the company and could go camping or watch a movie with you. There's one in particular, a Weimaraner-Lab mix named Boone, who lives to run but is also a great cuddler. I think you two could be best friends."

Oliver's eyes light up. "I'll come by next week."

Chapter Two

B lueboy hears my key in the lock and bounds down the hallway. I end up beneath the seventy-pound shepherd mix and
he bathes my face in wet kisses. I kiss him back, then extricate
myself from beneath the mutt before calling out, "Hayden?"

"Back porch."

The dog follows me through the kitchen my boyfriend re-
modeled, past white granite and stainless appliances, and out
French doors onto the porch, which this morning was wide open
to the backyard but is now entirely screened in. Samson, the
blind tabby we're also fostering, is curled on the wide railing.
Her nose flares as the smells from the yard and garden waft along
a light breeze. Even from a distance I can hear her motorboat
purr.

"What's going on out here?" I ask.

Hayden looks like an oversized kid in a flannel shirt, work
pants, and a baseball hat, his hazel eyes bright. He pounds a
few more tacks in to secure the last screen then turns. "It's not
safe for Samson to go outside, so I wanted to bring the outside
in to her . . . as much as I could."

A rush of gratitude floods my body. "Have I told you lately that you're the best?" I kiss him then breathe in his scent—wood chips—he must've taught shop today in addition to his AP English class.

"My pleasure," Hayden replies then sneezes three times.

He's allergic to animal dander, but still lets me foster long-haulers, turned his xeriscaped backyard into a lush garden, and even planted a border of my favorite flowers—red poppies and fuchsia sweet peas and a giant buddleia with deep purple blooms to attract butterflies. His house is on a triple lot, unusual and valuable in Potrero Hill. Realtors and developers constantly call because there's enough land to build three houses, but Hayden values his shop, and now a yard for my foster animals, more than money.

I grin. "How'd I get so lucky?"

"I ask myself the same question all the time." Hayden hugs me and whispers, "You're my constant Constance."

My smile slips a tiny bit. "That makes me sound kind of boring."

He pulls back and looks into my eyes. "I hate surprises. Seriously, Constance. I feel incredibly fortunate. It's not every woman who would be okay with a guy who doesn't want to be a master of the universe, especially in a city like San Francisco. *I'm* enough for you. And that means the world."

When we kiss, it feels like a promise.

It's hard to believe how far we've come since we met at a Scrabble night at a bar called Delilah's. Mars didn't want to go that night but agreed to be my wing woman, despite failing to make me wear something sexier than Levi's and a wool poncho. She waited for me at the bar, while I sat down across from a stranger in a comfy fisherman's off-white cable sweater and jeans, with brown hair and a neatly trimmed beard.

After introductions Hayden gave the tiles waiting in the box top a mix and we picked. I went first and my best option was the word LOVE. "It's not a great opening," I said with a blush.

"It's a fantastic word. Underrated, actually," Hayden remarked with a lopsided smile that made him look a bit like Jake Gyllenhaal. He added an R and spelled RING off my word.

A sense of being in the right place washed over me. Mars doesn't believe in premonitions, but my mother swore by them, along with the predictions of 1-800-psychics. She even knew how she was going to die.

"What do you do for work?" Hayden asked.

"Paralegal for a big law firm."

"Favorite part of the job?"

"The structure. In law, there are clear rules to follow. What do you do?"

"I'm a teacher. I won't ever be able to afford a seat on Elon Musk's rocket ship"—he laughed—"but I love working with high school kids."

I played the word FATE.

Hayden asked, "Hobbies?"

"Well, I grew up in San Rafael and like to bike on Mount Tam."

"Your parents still live there? In San Rafael?"

I heard the echo of a cell door clang shut, but my lie came easily. "No. They've passed. What about yours?"

"My big sister was the golden child. When she died we kind of fell apart."

There was an awkward silence. I blurted, "I volunteer at an animal shelter."

"I'm pretty allergic. Couldn't even have a pet as a kid. Just a turtle named Orvis." Hayden quickly threw down the word LIAR before the timer ran out.

"What do you like to do when you're not working?"

"Build furniture, tinker on old cars, and cook, especially homemade pasta."

I joked, "I can boil water and scramble eggs."

"Maybe I could teach you how to make a few meals sometime?" Hayden offered.

My face flushed. "I'd like that." I spelled RENT, not really trying anymore.

"So where do you live in the city?"

"That's complicated," I admitted. "Up until last week I lived with a roommate in the Castro. But sometimes I bring home long-haulers—animals from the shelter where I volunteer a lot that need extra love. The last one, a terrier mix named Chewy, ate three pairs of my roommate's shoes. She kicked us both out. So I'm on my best friend Mars's couch until I find a new place."

"Okay, this is kind of weird, but maybe it's kismet," he said with a nod at the board. "I rent out a studio apartment over my garage. The grad student who's currently in it moves out soon. Rent is $800 a month and that includes utilities. The place isn't huge, but it's modern and there's a shared backyard, for the occasional long-hauler."

"But you're allergic."

He scratched his beard. "They aren't going to be in my

house. Outside in the yard shouldn't bother me. The garage and the apartment are on the alley. So you'd have your own entrance and a small parking spot."

"Where's your house?"

"Potrero Hill. It's nothing fancy. I bought it in a foreclosure sale nine years ago and slowly renovated it." .

I paid $975 for my last place and shared the bathroom. "I'd love to check it out."

Hayden scribbled down his contact information along with the name and number of the grad student currently renting the place and an email for Brig O'Neill, his school's principal. "So you can make sure I'm not a creep," he said with a shy laugh as he handed over the napkin.

Our fingers brushed and I felt something in that moment. Not a spark exactly, not quite, but a definite warmth. The buzzer rang signaling the end of our thirty-minute game and Hayden moved on to play a winner while I played another loser.

"Was it everything you dreamed?" Mars asked me on the walk home.

"I met a nice guy named Hayden and he has a small apartment over his garage for rent. You could have your couch back."

"Was that the first guy you played?"

I nodded.

"That sweater, beard, and scuffed leather boots were too curated. He could be a serial killer."

"He gave me references."

Mars arched one brow. "Did you give him any references, Constance *Sparks*?"

I ignored the good-natured ribbing. "I'll give him Trudy's email at the shelter and someone from work if I like the place."

Mars grunted. "Did you tell him you're determined to save every dog and cat on earth?"

"Well . . . he's allergic to animals."

"I can see by the twinkle in your eye that you're interested in the guy. But if he's allergic to animals, it'll *never* work," Mars said with a dismissive wave of her hand.

We reached the corner and a cold wind off the San Francisco Bay plucked open my coat. When I shivered Mars gave me the side-eye. In the past, I'd told her a chill meant the spirit world wanted you to do their bidding.

"Do you seriously think a ghost has any interest in a thirty-two-year-old woman looking for romance at Scrabble night?" Mars demanded.

She doesn't believe in anything mystical, but the superstitions ingrained by a mother who was always following signs, which led to a pretty unstable home life, still haunt me.

"He offered to teach me how to cook," I said.

"You hate to cook!"

As we waited for the light to change, the words played in my game with Hayden rolled through my mind—*FATE-LOVE-RING.* "I could learn to like it."

"Ready?" Hayden now asks. It's game night at the place we first met. We leave Blueboy and Samson on the porch to enjoy the night air and hop on my Vespa, joining a steady stream of cars. Hayden's hands rest on my thighs and a sense of comfort envelops me. Is Hayden the one? Mars is still *positive* that he's not. There's no rush, I remind myself. *Time will tell.*

When we walk into Delilah's the scent of whiskey tickles my nose. We've brought our Scrabble board same as the rest of the crowd, but since we're late, they've already been randomly paired and begun. That means our first match will be against each other. Shouts and waves from the regular players greet us as we make our way to the last open table. Hayden pulls out my chair and I go to the bar to buy two beers while he mixes the tiles.

"Don't be too hard on our Hayden tonight," Bunker calls over. He's a retired ferry captain and started game night here.

Hayden pushes the box top containing the tiles toward me and I pick seven. I'm shocked to see I have a seven-letter word right out of the gate. ANXIOUS. That's 14 points on a double word score, plus 50 for using all my tiles. Hayden gives me a high five. "I used that same word," I muse, "in the last game Grandpa and I played before I left for college."

"Were you anxious?" Hayden asks.

"Very. Grandpa thought I was afraid to leave home for the first time, but he was already becoming more forgetful. He'd left the stove on all day, spaced on the electric bill, and twice he'd forgotten to turn off his car *in the garage*."

Hayden plays off my tiles then asks, "Did he want you to go?"

"No one in my family had ever gotten a scholarship, let alone gone to college, so yeah, he really did." He wanted better for me than what was waiting if I followed in my parents' tracks.

"We have that in common," Hayden says. "Struggling for something different." He squeezes my hand. "I'm excited to get to know your grandfather."

I haven't introduced them yet. Grandpa has dementia and goes in and out of clarity. I'm afraid of what he'll say in front of my boyfriend. Plus, there's the name thing.

"Constance? Your turn," Hayden says.

I find a spot to play my M. Hayden misses an obvious three-way score, then sacrifices a Y to spell YOU in a move that opens the board. I garner another high score. Hayden spells ME for measly points. He continues to miss obvious moves and his forehead speckles with perspiration. It's warm in here, but he doesn't usually sweat. Hayden plays off my Y to spell MARRY. The bar goes totally silent. When I look up, Hayden is watching me and so is everyone else. "What's going on?" He points to one of the words he played early in the game, WILL, then to another, YOU, then to the last one, MARRY, and finally to one of his lowest scores, ME.

My first thought is, how'd he get those exact tiles?

Hayden picks up an M and holds it out to show me. "I filed notches in the letters I needed."

My heartbeat has started to pound so hard it's distracting. "What if I'd picked one of those tiles?"

"Once I mix you always pick from the tiles closest to you. While you were getting our drinks I made sure the ones I needed were on my side of the box. Figured I'd find opportunities to make them work."

Bunker holds up a bottle of champagne, hands poised to pop the cork. "Well?"

I turn back to Hayden and there's an open blue velvet ring box on the Scrabble board. Someone in the crowd whistles. The ring is exquisite—a square diamond set in platinum and held in place on the sides by delicate flowers made from rubies. I never would've chosen anything this elaborate, but absolutely love the design.

"Will you?" Hayden asks.

The silence in the bar is deafening. We haven't even known each other a year . . .

Hayden says, "I love you and want to be your safe place to land, and to commit to share our lives, build a family together."

My heart swells. I think back to how during the first game of Scrabble we played together, the words LOVE, FATE, and RING were on that board. I've never had any sort of success in finding love for myself and always hoped that the universe would lend a hand. Hayden and I are meant to be. I meet his eyes. "Yes."

We kiss to cheers. One of the regulars, Molly, catches my eye and raises her glass with a little smile. I raise mine in return.

"Way to go," Bunker says as he shakes Hayden's hand. "How many times you two been married?"

"Never," Hayden and I say in unison.

"Engaged?"

We both shake our heads. It's something we've talked about—how Hayden only wants to ask a woman to marry him once.

Bunker looks at us like we're unicorns. "My advice, don't spend a lot of cash and don't wait to tie the knot."

"Works for me," Hayden says. "How about May twenty-eighth?"

It's his birthday and only two months away. I joke, "Did you pick that day so you'll never forget our anniversary?"

Hayden grins. "I picked it because I can't wait to marry you. And, we're both thirty-two, old enough to know what we want."

I feel off-balance, like my life is running on fast-forward, but I'm also beyond excited to plan our future. "May twenty-eighth it is."

Chapter Three

Y ou are wanted." I kiss Lucy's wet nose and get a return lick
on mine.

Trudy taps her silver cane on the cracked concrete floor. She's
eighty with jaw-length white hair and perfect posture. "You say
that to every animal at the shelter."

Gently I turn Lucy in the oversized sink and rinse the suds
from her fur. She's part dachshund with white ears that drag on
the floor and was found outside the Fred Meyer employee exit.
With each passerby she ran through her litany of tricks—paw
shake, spins, and body rolls—to prove her worth. Luckily a new
family has realized how wonderful she is and is picking her up
this morning. Trudy heads to reception to greet them while I
towel Lucy off.

"Ready?" Lucy gamely limps after me past the cat area.
Thankfully, her new owners plan to get her hip fixed. We stop
by the dog pens so she can say goodbye to her roomie, Growler,
a dark gray terrier-Lab mix with a white blaze on his chest and
major behavioral issues, hence his name. The two touch noses
between the pen's bars and Growler's head hangs low, like he
knows this is goodbye. "You can be next," I tell him.

"I doubt it."

A burst of adrenaline needles my skin as I spin to face Trudy's youngest son, Ellis. He's dressed in jeans and a forest-green fleece that matches eyes ringed with long lashes. At six-foot-four with an athletic build and wavy dark hair, he has the confidence and looks of a pirate.

"They can't all have happy endings," Ellis points out.

He's divorced, forty-one, and Trudy thinks I'd make a good wife number two, probably because I'm her most dependable volunteer. But Ellis has always grated on me. "That's pretty cold," I say.

"Not cold, just realistic," he replies with an apologetic half shrug.

"Wow. I hope you have a better bedside manner with your patients," I half joke.

"I'm a surgeon so a quick conversation usually covers it."

I smile sweetly. "I'm sure they appreciate that."

Ellis chuckles. "Ouch."

"FYI, Growler is losing his best friend. That might not mean anything to you, but being with Lucy is probably the only time in his miserable life that he felt loved." It's a small consolation to watch Ellis's grin slip.

Lucy and I head toward the front office. Ellis follows us. "What are you doing here anyway?" I ask.

"My first surgery was canceled so I'm helping out for a few hours. Mom's ticked at me so maybe this will get me back on her good side."

"What'd you do?"

His dimples peek out. "Typical family stuff."

Maybe Trudy has asked him to help more. She created the

shelter and it's her passion, but what keeps the lights on and our rescues fed is the dog boarding and training side of the business that's run out of a separate building on the property. It's a lot for Trudy to manage. We leave Ellis behind and walk past walls lined with Polaroid photos of dogs and cats in the arms of their new owners. The Freemont family waits beyond the door that opens into the reception area. "You're going to your *forever* home," I tell Lucy, then open the door.

Trudy stands alone in the bright orange and yellow room. When she sees me the corners of her mouth droop. She raps her cane on the floor with each word. "They changed their minds."

Her words land like a punch. I scoop Lucy up and hold her close, wet fur soaking through my blouse. "Why?"

"The kids loved her but decided they'd rather have a puppy."

A memory slithers out of the dark . . .

I was seven. My dad had missed Christmas then showed up two days later with a gift—a small locket with the inscription *I love you, Becky.* I asked if he'd stay with us this time.

Dad crouched so we were eye to eye. "Here's the deal. You can love somebody, but not want her. Don't be like your mother and make me feel guilty about it."

Trudy reaches for the sparkly blue goody bag she sends home with each adopted animal—a stuffed lamb, handmade crocheted blanket, chew toy, and organic treats she bakes herself. She holds out the lamb and Lucy gently takes it in her mouth. "Go ahead and take her back."

If I had the money to fix her hip, I'd adopt her right now. But she needs a family that can afford to take care of her. With me, she'd just get more pain pills. "We'll find a better home," I croak. "Promise."

Trudy twists her cane in tight circles. "Want to foster her for a bit?"

I'm already fostering two animals. "Sure."

I carry Lucy to the parking lot, wedge my backpack into one of the Vespa's hard saddlebags, and then slide the dog into the other one. "Don't move around, okay?" There isn't time to drop her at the house, so she'll have to hide under my desk at work. If she's discovered my boss, Brock, a senior associate at Hollister, Duckwall & Berger, won't fire me. I'm his ninth paralegal and the only one who hasn't asked for reassignment.

"Drive carefully," Trudy calls after us. Ellis is now by her side, probably judging that my heart is made of mush.

Halfway down the block, I glance over my shoulder to make sure Lucy isn't too scared. Her head is out of the saddlebag, ears flapping in the wind. She smiles at me. How could her family have ever ditched her? I push the rush of sadness away. Things don't always work out the first time, but that doesn't mean it's the end of the story. Lucy can still have her happily ever after.

Mars is already at her desk when I arrive at the office we share as fellow paralegals. In her tight pencil skirt and mock turtleneck she looks like one of those stylish women from *Mad Men*. I adjust my white silk blouse from T.J. Maxx. There's a water splotch on the front that has puckered the cheap silk. I hide it in the waist of the black pleated pants I wear three days a week. Mars thinks they do nothing for my figure, but for me, function and saving money always win over style.

"You're late. Brock has been in here three times looking for you," Mars warns.

"Dang." Lucy pokes her head out of my backpack.

"What the hell is *that*?" Mars demands.

"Lucy. Her forever home fell through so I'm fostering her until she gets over the disappointment. I didn't have time to take her home."

Mars frowns. "She better not pee on the rug."

I make a bed under my desk and the little dog obediently curls on it, then I fire up my computer. Every morning I open an Excel spreadsheet to plan the day. Mars thinks it's excessive, but reviewing yesterday's work and allotting time for each of today's tasks helps me stay on track. And it's the only way to efficiently keep up with Brock. He takes on more cases than any other associate in the office. The average age at the firm for making partner is fifty and Brock is only forty-three but determined to prove he's ready *now*, even if the workload buries both of us. Sometimes I feel sorry for his wife, Reagan, and their kids. I've fielded too many evening calls from Reagan, annoyed that her husband isn't home yet. When his last paralegal got tired of Brock's workload, late nights at the office, and covering for him, she complained to HR and was assigned to a new associate. Unfortunately that meant Brock asked me to work for him.

Mars swivels in her chair to face me. "You didn't have to say yes."

My stomach flips. Did she already see my ring? I took it off to wash Lucy but slid it back on after I left the shelter. Now it's twisted on my finger so the diamond faces inward because I wanted more time to figure out how to share the news with her. I nibble my lower lip. "What are you talking about?"

"Brock—your boss? I told you working for him was going to be way too much. And now that he realizes you're brilliant but also a pushover, he'll never let you go. Maybe in your next life you'll learn to say no."

"So reincarnation is my only hope?" While I'm superstitious and do believe in ghosts, reincarnation is a step too far, even for me.

"Constance?" The man's voice comes from the intercom on my desk.

Mars waves. "Later, alligator."

Brock waits in the small conference room, files spread out on the polished table. He's a good-looking guy with a dimpled chin and intense, amber-colored eyes. He's also an impeccable dresser and has great manners—the product of some fancy boarding school then Yale followed by Cornell Law. Behind his back the younger paralegals in our office call him Mr. Wonderful because he brings in chocolate from Vosges once a month. It's an obvious ploy, but it works for him.

"There's my most valuable player," Brock says. "Have a seat."

My boss has a way of making me feel we're a team, even though he's the only one who financially benefits from our hard work. I've been a paralegal for eleven years and my salary is capped unless I move to Alaska, where the firm pays double because employees must endure perennial winter darkness. Not an option. I'm a big fan of sunlight.

"New case. Not our usual type but it's a favor for a partner's wife's friend. Laura Tarroway is being sued for divorce. Her husband, Martin, is a high roller. She'll be here Monday morning for a meet and greet. All I know is that she married very young, is now thirty-nine, has three minor children, and there's infidelity."

Our law firm specializes in representing high-tech companies, corporate takeovers, and land rights battles. Our clients are the Goliaths and can pay way more than their adversaries.

Regardless of whether or not they're clearly on the right side of the law, the firm usually wins. That's the part of my job that doesn't sit well. "What do you need?" I ask.

"Call Mrs. Tarroway and ask her to pull together what she can ASAP—net worth; salaries for both of them if she works; bank, brokerage, and retirement accounts and benefits; assets; credit card bills going back at least three years. Also ask if she signed a pre- or postnup and get a copy."

"Anything else?"

"Find out their relationship story. That includes domestic violence, if there were any police reports, child endangerment, and basic misconduct—meaning who did her husband screw and how often."

"How do you know he's the one who cheated?"

"That's what happens more often than not."

"So much for happily ever after," I murmur.

"You have a boyfriend, right?" Brock asks.

A fiancé. "Hayden."

My boss leans forward. "Is he *the one*?"

I keep my left hand in my lap—Mars needs to know first. "He's extremely trustworthy and there's no roller coaster of emotions like in past relationships where it always felt like I was proving over and over again I was worthy of love." I flush at how much I've just shared.

Brock chuckles. "So he's perfect? 'Cause Mars mentioned she's not sure about your guy."

"Pretty darn close to perfect," I say with a smile that covers mild annoyance. Why is Mars discussing my love life with Brock?

Of course there are little things that niggle at me in our

relationship. I wish Hayden would share more about his sister. As an only child I have a fascination with siblings. But it's clear when I bring her up it's painful for him to talk about so I don't push. And if anyone can understand not wanting to talk about the past, it's me. Hayden only knows that my parents are gone. No details, besides the ones Mars helped me create—my mom died of a heart attack, which is true but we leave out the part preceding that, and Dad passed away from an aneurism when I was a teenager. For the past eight months I've been afraid Hayden will discover the truth and decide to move on—that he doesn't want to deal with my emotional baggage. Now that we're engaged, I'll have to tell him *everything*. My mouth instantly goes dry.

"Hayden is a lucky guy," Brock says. "You're a prize."

Heat creeps up my neck. I don't get attention from the Brocks of the world. That's Mars's territory. Sometimes I worry that her admirers are starting to take away a little bit of her shine. Their adoration used to feed her but now it's feeding on her.

Brock turns back to the files in front of him. "How's it going on the Chimes case?"

"Draft of the correspondence is in your inbox."

Brock looks up with a tired smile. "Con, what would I do without you?"

Inside I wince a tiny bit at the nickname. In middle school there was a boy named Puck whose father was a cop. He told his son about my dad and Puck changed my name to *Con*. His buddies used to chant it on the playground. "Anything else?"

"Don't tell anyone, especially those busybodies in HR, but I'd kill for a double espresso with a splash of nonfat vanilla soy?"

"Sure," I reply.

The rest of the morning goes by in a flurry of work. I almost skip out on lunch with Mars, but know I have to tell her that Hayden proposed. *What am I so afraid of?* But it's obvious. Other than Grandpa, Mars is the only other long-term constant in my life and losing her love and friendship would be like tearing off a limb. At noon, we head to Chez Luc's—a cheap and cheerful bistro with butcher-block tables and a French countryside vibe. It's not my favorite restaurant, but Mars is addicted to the onion soup and I want her to be in a good mood. My left hand rests in my jacket pocket, even after our food arrives.

As Mars digs into her soup, twisting strands of melted cheese around her spoon, she says, "There's a new band playing at the Bottom of the Hill on Friday night. Come with?"

"Can't. Hayden and I are doing an MG road rally at sunset and after there's a dinner."

Mars makes a disgusted face.

"Hayden goes on bike rides with me," I point out.

She scoffs, "When was the last one?"

Mars still hasn't budged from her early assessment of my boyfriend. Fiancé. It's partially my fault. As we got more serious, he took over my weekends and free nights. That left less time for Mars. When I'd invite her to join us, they mixed like oil and water despite Hayden including her on some of our date nights. Eventually I gave up on trying to bring them closer, which felt rotten. But in the past, Mars has all but disappeared for months at a time, caught up in a romance. She'd always text, and I still do, too, plus make sure we grab lunch and dinner when possible. But this is the first time in our long friendship that *I'm* the one who isn't as available. That's hard for her. I try to make it up to Mars whenever I can, but it never feels like enough.

Mars sighs theatrically. "I just wish you'd slow things down with him."

My dream that she'd be happy for me deflates. I haven't touched my food, afraid to use my left hand. "Says the woman who flew to Paris for a weekend with a guy she'd only known one day; took a cruise with a blind date on a dare; spent a week in Bali with a pro surfer who—"

"Point made," Mars snips. She toys with the straw in her iced tea. "But in my defense, I was never looking for forever with any of them. Whereas you're determined to settle down, play house, with anyone who asks."

No one has ever asked before. Gently I say, "Hayden doesn't have to be the right fit for *you*."

Mars doesn't understand how effortless our relationship has been. When I moved into the apartment over his garage, Hayden invited me over every few nights to try out new recipes. I started looking forward to those cozy evenings, conversations about his students or a Scrabble game. A few weeks after I'd moved in, we went to Farley's, a neighborhood coffee spot, and Hayden asked me about what I wanted in life. We weren't dating so I told the truth. "Children—as many as my husband and I can handle—and a partner who is kind and won't leave, regardless of the challenges we might face."

Hayden said, "That's what I want, too. And someone who shares my passions."

We had our first kiss. It tasted like the sweet mocha lattes he'd ordered us. From that moment on, I was all in. Hayden went biking with me and opened his home to foster animals. First a fat cat in need of a diet and then a boxer mix who'd been surrendered because he ate cushions. A month into dating, he taught me how to use his table saw and we made a kitchen table together out of bird's-eye maple. After our first dinner on it—homemade ravioli—he invited me to crawl under the table with him.

"What are we doing down here?" I asked.

Hayden pointed to the words he'd carved in the wood: *Constance, I love you.* "I know it's fast," he said. "But it's true . . ."

Mars's eyes glitter at me as she prepares to pounce. "Answer me this. How's the sex?"

My face warms and silently I curse being the girl who easily blushes. "Not everyone is interested in using the Kama Sutra as a guide." Why does she hate him so much?

"I don't hate Hayden," Mars says, reading my mind.

"Well, that's a relief." My pulse sprints as I take my left hand from my lap and hold it up. The stone catches the light and sends rainbows across our table.

Mars shouts, "WHAT IS *THAT*?"

Chapter Four

I cringe as the lunch patrons at Chez Luc's stare at us.

Mars splutters, "Did you—? Did he—? Hayden? Seriously?"

"He asked me last night." I watch her gray eyes ice over and my appetite disappears.

"And you said yes?"

I slide my hand free. "Of course." Mars sits back and waits. She used to do this in college whenever I started dating someone she didn't approve of, or right before a breakup, or senior year, when I visited my dad after he was remanded without bail. I consider waiting her out, but I always break first. "Say it."

"You barely know him."

"I know enough."

She taps her long nails on the table. "How'd he ask?"

"He spelled it out on a Scrabble board."

"Of course he did. Do you even know if he's been married before?"

Mars recently dated a woman who'd been married four times and it didn't end well. She said she'd never date someone with that much baggage again, even though Mars always chooses people who are too complicated to ever work out. I say, "Hayden hasn't been married or even engaged before."

"We could track down past girlfriends, ask why they broke up? Seriously, Constance," she repeats, exasperated, "you don't know him well enough to make a lifetime commitment!"

Mars always asks me for details about Hayden and his life before me. But he and I rarely talk about that. The truth is that neither of us wants to look back. "How about you just accept that Hayden is an incredible person," I say. "He loves teaching, and we have fun together, even when we're cooking or driving around in his MG."

Mars takes a bite of quiche then jabs her fork in my direction. "Sounds like a friend. Speaking of which, have you met any of his?"

"No, but we spend all of our free time together." I push my plate away. "Please be happy for me. Please?"

Mars wipes her mouth then crumples the napkin and tosses it on the table. "What about his family?"

"I haven't met them." Worry creeps forward. "His sister died. He won't talk about it, so I don't know what happened. After that, his family fell apart. But I'm sure they'll come to the wedding."

"And Gary?"

She's talking about my dad. He's currently a guest of the California Department of Corrections at San Quentin. My experiences in elementary and junior high, combined with a brutal breakup after I told a boyfriend I desperately loved about Dad and he bailed, made me realize that no one wants to date the daughter of an inmate at San Quentin. Mars agreed and we created both stories about my parents.

"Maybe we should've stuck with the truth," Mars now says.

I shake my head. "It could've ruined things before they began."

Unfortunately, Dad's arrest did derail my plans to go to graduate school for veterinary medicine. I needed to help him and also start making money as quickly as possible. Mars decided to join me at paralegal college. Her goal was to save until she had enough money for medical school. Neither of us ever made it to that next stage. The thing about putting off your dreams is that they recede each year until the distance to reach them becomes too far.

"Your dad is going to get paroled, eventually," Mars says.

She's right. I have to tell Hayden about him. But what's a good time to tell your new fiancé that your dead dad is actually alive *and* he's in prison for second-degree murder? Dad was up for parole four months ago and denied. He'll have another shot in three years.

"If Hayden is such a wonderful guy, he won't care." Mars blinks hard to underscore her point.

"He *is* a great guy." But he doesn't like surprises. "I'll tell him."

"When?"

"Soon."

Two men in business suits walk by. One whistles at Mars and she crooks her finger, invites him over to our table. Sweetly she says, "You do know that whistling indoors summons the devil?" He quickly moves on.

"So my superstitions do come in handy," I point out.

Mars nods at my ring. "Sorry to say, but it can't be real."

"I know." Hayden makes a decent living as a teacher but that doesn't go far in a city as expensive as San Francisco and we live on a budget. "It doesn't matter. Look, it has wildflowers on the side." I twist the ring to show her the red stones. The fact that Hayden found a ring with my favorite flowers matters way more to me than a cubic zirconia.

Mars asks, "Why didn't you tell me sooner?"

I throw up my hands. "It just happened last night and Brock had me racing around from the second I got to work."

"You could've called. It's *huge* news." She locks eyes. "Are you sure you want this?"

"Yes, of course I want to do this. Hayden and I are getting married May twenty-eighth."

Mars pushes back her chair and scowls. "His idea or yours?"

"The sooner the better for both of us." I stand. "Now you and I need to get back to work."

"You get this one, I'll get the next?"

Mars is an incredibly generous person with her time, attention, and energy, but she's always short on cash, stashing it away for her next impromptu adventure. "No worries."

As we leave the restaurant, Mars tugs me in the opposite direction from our office. I pull my arm free. "What? I have a meeting with Brock in an hour."

"We'll be back in time," Mars promises. "But first, let's find out about that diamond."

She leads me toward Arnett's, a very expensive jewelry store I've never dreamed of stepping inside. At the glass double doors I pull my arm free. "I am not doing this."

"Constance, if that ring is actually real you'll need to get it appraised and insured."

She has a point. And she knows it's my nature to button things up when possible. "Fine."

A buzzer rings and the door to Arnett's unlocks. We step inside the store and the street noise instantly disappears. There's plush green carpet beneath our feet, the air smells of lilacs, and glass cases filled with sparkly things line the walls. I don't belong in here. I grew up in a sagging ranch house in San Rafael. My grandpa did his best when Dad would disappear or do time, but there was no expensive jewelry, new clothes, or school trips. The car only ran because Grandpa was a mechanic who knew how to give our piece of junk, named Sanford, life support.

An elderly man in a black suit and pale blue tie approaches. "Welcome to Arnett's. My name is Jonathan. What can I do for you ladies?"

"My friend just got engaged," Mars explains. "And she wants to know if her diamond is fake—"

"So I know if it needs to be insured," I interject, my face beet red. "It might not. Need to be."

"Ah," Jonathan says and picks up a black velvet square. "Let me take a look."

I hesitate then slide the ring free, place it on the pad. As he heads to the rear of the store, stopping on the way to show a younger employee in a black skirt and white blouse the ring, the muscles along my neck screw tight. Being parted from my engagement ring for the first time is physically uncomfortable.

"How will you feel about Hayden if it's a fake?" Mars quietly asks.

A rivulet of sweat slips down my spine. "I told you, it doesn't matter."

The woman who spoke to Jonathan approaches us. "Ladies, I'm Ebony. Who is the owner of that engagement ring?"

I'm transported back to the elementary school cafeteria as I handed my meal voucher to the cashier and the kids around me snickered. "Um. Me."

"I used to work at Westcott and Sons Antique and Estate Jewelry," she says. "I'd recognize that mine-cut diamond anywhere. It came from the estate of Olivia and Louis Arnaud."

A tremor rolls through my body. I quickly glance around the store. Mars snorts.

"Olivia was once a local socialite who married a French man and moved to Paris," Ebony continues. "They were childless so the ring was sold by a distant relation."

"What's mine-cut?" Mars asks.

"A square diamond with curved edges popular in the eighteenth and nineteenth centuries. Old stones were cut and polished by hand. Each is *utterly* unique."

Mars's forehead wrinkles. "But the stone, it's not *real*, right?"

Ebony replies, "Of course it is. As are the rubies."

"And the value?" Mars asks.

"Approximately twenty-seven thousand," Ebony says.

"Dollars?" both Mars and I exclaim. Ebony laughs then nods.

Jonathan returns with my ring. "Ebony has certainly shared that your ring came from Westcott's. It is, indeed, real and measures a bit over three carats. I called and they've already had it appraised for your fiancé. He must love you very much to buy such an extraordinary engagement ring."

In a daze, I slide my ring back on. "Thank you."

We head back to the office. As we wait for the elevator Mars says, "I just worry that even if you wanted to, you'd never say no to Hayden."

"That's not true!"

Mars rolls her eyes so hard it's amazing they don't get stuck that way. "Please," she huffs. "We went to college together. You say yes even when a stranger asks you for a favor. And when you know someone, it's way worse."

"You're exaggerating," I say as we step onto the elevator.

Despite the elderly woman in the back corner, Mars continues, "I am not exaggerating, my friend. Don't forget, I witnessed your catastrophic turn as a residence hall adviser—those kids chewed you up and spit you out. Then there were the guys."

"Hal wasn't that bad," I quip.

"He stole your mattress!"

"Not exactly." I agreed he could have it after he took it.

"What about Marcus?"

I took pole-dancing classes, twisted my moderately flexible body around cold metal just to impress him. "I'll give you Marcus."

"And Nate?"

"Hey, you're never supposed to say his name."

"Whoops."

For his birthday Nate wanted a threesome. "I only agreed to *one* night," I remind Mars. It was horribly awkward for me, but Nate was thrilled and said he wanted an *open* relationship. When I came home crying, Mars called Nate, told him in a very creative way where to stick his open relationship, and broke up with him for me.

It was the first and only relationship in my life where I did the breaking up, at least by proxy. While Mars never has trouble ending her relationships, I've always stayed, even when things went south. We both had turbulent childhoods, but her takeaway was to embrace change while I crave stability. Everything is different, though, with Hayden. For the first time in a relationship I can actually relax. We're *both* totally committed. I love him and, unlike my past choices, our relationship and marriage are meant to be.

The woman gets off the elevator with a backward, pitying glance at me.

"I'm happy for you . . . if you're sure," Mars says as we walk to our shared office.

"I am sure." But I know what she's thinking because I'm thinking it, too. How could Hayden afford such a valuable piece of jewelry?

Chapter Five

Back at my computer, there are ten emails from Brock and a summons. I smuggle Lucy out for a quick bathroom break and short walk. Once she's curled beneath my desk, I race to Brock's office. Upon my return, arms filled with more work, Mars's head snaps up like she's been caught doing something wrong. She lowers her laptop screen as I pass.

"What is it?" I ask.

Mars *never* blushes, but there are bright red circles on her cheeks. "No way. You'll be mad at me."

My insides churn. "I won't. Swear." We hook pinkies like we're back in college. An email pings as I take a seat at my desk. It's from Mars and a little voice inside my head tells me not to open it. But I do anyway . . .

The wedding announcement was published ten years ago in the *Sacramento Bee* . . .

Amanda Benson of Sacramento, California, is pleased to announce the engagement of her daughter, Lydia Elizabeth, to Hayden Carrington Whittaker, son of Whit and Grier Whittaker of Brooklyn, New York. Lydia is a graduate of California State, Sacramento and works at Wyden &

Knopf Advertising. Hayden attended the Lawrenceville School and Stanford University and is employed by the San Francisco School District. The wedding will be held at First Presbyterian Church in Napa Valley, California . . .

"You said Hayden told you he'd never been engaged before." My mind scrambles, then pivots. Hayden *Carrington*. I didn't know that was his middle name. It sounds so . . . formal. And he was married in a church? He told me he's an atheist. I reread the announcement. "What's the Lawrenceville School?"

Mars slams both hands on her desk and Lucy lets out a startled yip. "Who the hell cares about that?" she demands.

Despite my best efforts, I return to the biggest part of the bomb Mars just dropped. "Hayden told me that he only wanted to ask a woman to marry him once," I admit. "And he told Bunker at game night that this was his first engagement." Hayden was married before? I shake my head to clear it. "There has to be a good reason he never told me."

Mars's jaw drops, like she can't believe what she's hearing. "Seriously?" she asks. "So who's Lydia?"

My chest squeezes. "He's never mentioned her. How long were they married?"

"There was no wedding announcement, and no court record of a marriage license for Hayden and Lydia Whittaker, so it must've been called off."

Relief slowly eases the knots from my muscles. "That's probably why he didn't mention it."

Mars wheels her chair over to my desk. "But he *lied*. Come on, Constance, even *you* can't ignore this."

"What do you mean, *even me*?"

"I know you want this," Mars says slowly, like she's carefully choosing her words, "but you have no idea what other lies he's told. And the ornate engagement ring seems . . . unlike him to say the least."

Last month I read an article about bushfires in Australia, and how the biggest danger is from an ember attack—moss or bark fragments that become airborne and carry the fire to a new area. That's what Mars's words feel like—a dangerous attack that could burn the life I want, the life I thought I had been building, to ashes. I shuffle the files on my desk, too upset to look at my best friend. "We all have secrets," I say. "We're allowed to bury the things that hurt us. Hayden has that right. So do I. You do, too."

"And if he's lying about more than a broken engagement?"

I knock on the underside of my desk. "He's not."

"Then why did you knock on wood for luck?" Mars shakes her head and adds, "He's *always* struck me as a phony."

I snap, "Good thing *you're* not marrying him."

She gathers several folders and a rush of irrational fear that she won't come back, that I'm going to permanently harm our friendship, strikes me. "Where are you going?"

"To work in the conference room." At the door she stops. "I wish you could see what I see."

"Meaning?"

"You're not some abandoned animal desperate for a home," Mars says. "You're Constance Sparks—quirky, smart as hell, adorable despite your questionable style sense and wacky superstitions, and beyond kind. But this is what you *always* do. When you can't handle reality, you make excuses, look for distractions, or bury your head in the sand."

I blink back tears. "Mars, I love Hayden and really want this marriage to happen. I need your support. Promise me that you won't do any more digging. He's a good guy. I swear."

"Are you going to confront him?"

We both know I won't. "Promise me?"

Mars scowls but then nods. "I promise."

After she's gone, I nervously spin the engagement ring on my finger, then open a browser and skim the information I find about the Lawrenceville School:

Founded in 1810, Lawrenceville is one of the oldest preparatory schools in the United States, located in Lawrence Township, Mercer County, New Jersey, with an endowment of $487 million . . . and the highest tuition in New Jersey, $69,420 per year . . .

I click on the school's website and there are photographs of gorgeous brick buildings, a language lab touting myriad options, and extensive athletic facilities, all set in a wooded campus that outshines most universities. It doesn't make sense. When I told Hayden about my conversation with Grandpa before college, how I was the first one in my family to attend university, make something different of myself, he said that we had that in common. But the Lawrenceville School makes it seem like we're from entirely different worlds.

"Stop," I mutter and close the browser. So what if Hayden went to an expensive private school? Obviously he was on scholarship. And I was one of the poor kids, too. I don't talk about it—I try to forget the experience. Hayden's private boarding school is not a red flag. But he was engaged . . . I feel like a mouse lost in a maze, desperate to reach the reward at the end.

Come on, Constance, even you can't ignore this.

"But I can," I mutter. It's an engagement, a marriage that never happened, not an evil plot. But now that I know about it, do I tell him? What if he dug into my history and unearthed the truth about my dad before I had the chance to come clean? And what if I tell him what I know, then start asking too many questions, and it changes how he feels about me?

I delete Mars's email with the engagement announcement from Hayden's past and open the file Mrs. Tarroway has already sent. There are folders inside—Prenup, Life Insurance, Vehicle Policies, Estate Planning, Bank Accounts, Trusts, Brokerage and Real Estate Holdings.

I start with the prenup. It's pretty draconian. Laura Tarroway isn't entitled to any of the property or cars in Martin's name (*everything* but their current home is in his name) and alimony is set at $80,000 per year for five years plus limited child support until the kids are eighteen. Back when she was younger, more naive, and never thought they'd get divorced, she probably didn't even pay attention to the amount. But now she's almost forty with three children. Brock will fight to break the prenup, but it'll be a long, uphill slog that will cost a lot of money Mrs. Tarroway doesn't have and may never receive.

I print out all the credit card bills, including the ones Laura sent from Martin Tarroway's American Express Black Card. The Amex charges go back three years. Red pen in hand, I start going through them, looking for any inconsistencies that might help our client, but I'm not too hopeful.

Mars pops in to get a file. "You want to grab a drink after work?" I ask.

She wiggles her brows. "I have a date."

"Is *she* or *he* or *they* hot?"

"*He's* older and mostly unavailable. That makes him smoking hot."

My heart slumps a little. Her mom's marriages really did a number on Mars. There were a few guys who were actually good stepdads, but when the marriages broke up they dropped Mars, too. That left a mark. She doesn't believe long-term is possible, let alone a real happily ever after.

Mars stops at the door. "I'll cancel if you want to grab dinner?"

"I promised Hayden I'd be home early to start planning our wedding. Another time?"

The light in her eyes dims. "Whenever."

I should get back to work, but my ring catches the light and tugs at my attention. I want to know more about its history and look up the number for Westcott & Sons Antique and Estate Jewelry. After the answering machine picks up, I leave a message with my name and number, then pivot. Olivia Arnaud was originally from San Francisco. From past land rights cases I know that the public library has files of old newspapers. Since my ring is valuable, and Olivia was a local socialite, her family was probably prominent enough to warrant a wedding announcement. I send Brock a text that I'll be at the library for an hour to do research pertaining to Mrs. Tarroway's case. He sends back a thumbs-up emoji.

For a second I feel bad about the little lie, but the firm doesn't pay nearly the overtime I work, and what harm can it do to find out a little more about my ring? Plus, the library is one of my favorite places. As a child libraries were my refuge whenever things were difficult with my parents, and the hushed atmosphere, impeccable orderliness, and the fact that everyone who works there is welcoming still gives me a reassuring sense of solace and peace.

But the real truth, the one I'd prefer to deal with later, blaring beneath the calm surface I showed Mars, is that I'm spooked and need a distraction.

Chapter Six

The Old San Francisco Library never fails to impress. It's housed in a Beaux Arts–style building with a white granite facade. A massive, modern skylight illuminates a five-story atrium in the entrance, and bridges connect floors across light wells. One of my favorite touches is a wall installation with hundreds of authors' names beside the four-story staircase. I come here at least once a week to do research for the firm, and each time I enter the almost three-hundred-thousand-square-foot building, I take a moment to let the stillness that's only found in libraries settle around me.

Today, I cross a thick wool carpet to the information desk. Molly, in a slightly wrinkled pale pink blouse and tan pants, looks up and offers a smile. The freckles across the bridge of her nose are lost in little wrinkles that remind me of kitten whiskers.

"Hey, Constance."

"Hi, Molly."

"What a game night," Molly gushes. "Congratulations. Hayden is quite a catch. Word to the wise, though. Don't let him know that you know."

I have no idea what she's talking about. I have noticed that when Molly comes to game night solo, she angles to play against Hayden and flirts during their games. I don't think Hayden notices, but, having lost two boyfriends to women who were "just friends," I have.

"I was wondering where I'd find *San Francisco Chronicle* newspapers from the 1920s?"

Molly points. "Second floor. The Kirby Room. Unfortunately anything from the late 1800s to 1930 is on microfiche. I hate those readers, they always give me migraines." She nods at my ring. "It's gorgeous. Family heirloom?"

I shake my head. "But you're right, it's antique."

After some help from a librarian, I sit down at the reader with a stack of microfiche from the *San Francisco Chronicle*, each filled with grid images. Pretty quickly, I learn that in the early 1900s wedding announcements in the newspaper appeared on Sundays under the heading "The Proposal Post." I start with 1918, scan for the names Olivia and Louis Arnaud. Once I know where to look, I can move through the weekly paper fairly quickly. Thirty minutes later I have a dull headache but find what I'm looking for in January 1920.

Miss Olivia Harriet Edwards, daughter of Mr. and Mrs. George V. Edwards of San Francisco, California, will be married to Mr. Louis Arnaud, son of Helene and Francois Arnaud of Paris, France, at Saints' Episcopal Church of Nob Hill on May 3. Miss Edwards is a graduate of Linden Hall and Brillantmont finishing school in Switzerland. Mr. Arnaud is a graduate of the Sorbonne in Paris. Mr. Arnaud proposed with a family heirloom—a round yellow canary diamond of six carats.

Miss Edwards's maid of honor will be her best friend, socialite Elizabeth Vanderpool. Mr. Arnaud's best man will be his brother, Claude Arnaud. In honor of Miss Edwards's brother, James V. Edwards, deceased, the couple will donate all wedding gifts to the French organization Les Veuves de la Grande Guerre (Widows of the Great War). The couple will honeymoon on the *Île de France* cruise liner and then make their home in France.

I study the diamond on my finger. It's not Olivia's. So how did she end up with this ring? And how could my fiancé afford to buy a piece of jewelry that once belonged to a socialite? "Stop," I mutter. My phone buzzes and I jump, then quickly make sure I'm alone in the room before answering it.

A computer-generated voice says, "This is a call from inmate number 12759 at San Quentin State Prison. Do you accept the charges?"

"Yes." There's a series of clicks.

"Hey, honeybunch."

"Hi, Dad."

"Why are you talking so softly?"

"I'm at the library."

"Ah. Our library is pathetic, and nobody whispers in there or anywhere else in this madhouse."

"How are you?" I ask.

He chuckles. "Other than being locked up for thirteen years and counting? I'm dealing, but every day I wish the trial had gone down different."

When Dad was arrested for a robbery gone wrong I was about to graduate from SF State. I had a biology research position lined up with one of my professors and planned to apply for veterinary school in a year. But Dad begged me to get my paralegal degree so I could help with his defense and expenses. Grandpa tried to talk me out of it, but I couldn't say no.

The experience of working with Dad's lawyer on his case was difficult. There was an eyewitness in the convenience store who saw him brandish a knife and demand money. The terrified young clerk pulled out his phone. Dad jumped over the counter and launched into him. When the clerk's head hit the floor it killed him. Dad finally admitted it happened but wasn't intentional. We tried to get him to plead out in the hope for a lesser sentence. He refused. But the jury didn't believe that the clerk's death was an accident, and because there was a knife involved in the crime the judge gave my dad the maximum sentence.

"I have some *amazing* news." Dad clears his throat. "Due to overcrowding and my *exemplary* behavior, I'm being given another parole hearing!"

My insides freeze. "What? When?"

"May twenty-fifth!"

"That's less than two months from now." And it's three days before my wedding. "Wow."

"You don't sound happy," Dad says.

"That's not it," I quickly explain. "I'm just stunned. I thought you'd have to wait another three years after the last denial."

"Me, too. But the sooner I get out, the sooner I can make up for not being there for you."

"You did the best you could."

Dad sighs. "We both know that's not true. I was an addict. But I'm determined to do better once I'm out. I'll never leave you again and always put you first, okay?"

Despite how much my dad's parole might complicate my life, hope rises. "Okay."

"I need your help with this, honeybunch. You've been so great visiting, despite your busy life, and always taking my calls, but can you come next Saturday so we can go over my statement? Figure out ways to make it better?"

"Well . . . okay."

"And could you write another letter? I'll ask some of the guys what we missed saying last time."

The parole board asks for character witness letters detailing how an inmate has changed and why he should be paroled. While Dad's crime was reprehensible, most prisoners eventually get out. My hope has always been that by remaining in touch and being his link to the outside world, I'll motivate him to be a better man. And in the past few years he's made some positive changes. "Of course."

"You are the best daughter in the world!"

"I love you, Dad."

"Love you, too, honeybunch. So tell me what's going on in your life. Anything new?"

Every nerve in my body fires a warning. But I have to tell Hayden before we marry. And Dad could be out soon. They are going to meet. "I'm getting married."

"That's so wonderful! Oh, man, I wish I could be there to walk you down the aisle. When's the wedding?"

"The end of May." Even if he's paroled he won't be released in time.

"This May? Can you wait a month? I could be there!"

The lie comes too easily. "It was really hard to find a venue, so we're locked in."

"Well. You'll be such a pretty bride. Who's the lucky guy?"

"His name's Hayden. He's an English teacher."

"Well, he must have a real kind soul. Tell him I don't mind that he didn't ask me for your hand, given my situation, but I hope to meet him *really* soon."

My brain goes numb. Thankfully the operator intones that we only have twenty seconds left.

"See you next week?" Dad asks.

"I'll be there."

I hang up then rest my cheek on the cool table. My ring catches the light and I slide it off, study the very real diamond and rubies. There's an inscription inside I hadn't noticed: *À la maison pour toujours.* I put it into my phone for translation. It means: *Forever home.*

Hayden has become my safe place. But given what Mars found out, do I really know him well enough?

I make a list of everything I do know about Hayden.

- Loves me
- Always kind
- Very considerate
- Accepting of my shelter work
- Allows foster animals in our home
- An inspired teacher
- Loves to cook, build things, work on his car
- Never mean, loud, or violent
- Does what he promises
- Wants to get married and commit to a life together
- Excited to have children, create a family
- Will stay even when things get tough

So what *don't* I know about Hayden?

- I've never met his parents
- No details about his sister's death
- Should I worry he'll change once we've been together longer?
- Why didn't he tell me about boarding school?
- Why did he lie about his past engagement?

I reread the list. What I don't know is definitely important, but the pros here outweigh the cons. My ring catches the light and a trill of anticipation runs through me. Hayden is a great guy, regardless, and I'm excited about my impending marriage.

Next, I refocus on the engagement announcement from 1920. How did my ring wind up in Olivia's possession if Louis didn't propose with it? My eyes are drawn back to the old wedding announcement—I'm a dog with a bone when there's a mystery to solve.

I Google Olivia Edwards's maid of honor, Elizabeth Vanderpool, since the engagement announcement said she was a socialite. Beyond a small oil portrait donated to a museum in Pennsylvania, there's little information. The only other name in the announcement is Olivia's brother, James. I do a search on James V. Edwards and a Wikipedia page appears.

James V. Edwards, born 1891 in San Francisco, California, died October 24, 1917, in France. During his time as a volunteer driver for the American Ambulance Field Service, he wrote letters from the front to his sister, Olivia. Following his death, she compiled them into a book, *Letters from*

My War, now in the San Francisco Public Library's Special
Collections.

The yellowed black-and-white photograph on the Wikipedia
page shows three men in baggy uniforms and helmets. They
stand beside an old-fashioned truck with a compartment on the
back. A thick white strip along the top of the compartment has
a cross in its center. James is the man on the right. He's tall,
broad shouldered, and has dark brown hair. When I try to blow
the image up, his face goes out of focus, but there's something
compelling about the line of his jaw.

Chapter Seven

When I tell Molly what I'm looking for, she directs me to Special Collections and Mr. Sumner, the librarian in charge. I'm astonished, once I've entered the department through a glass door on the second floor, to find a two-story wood-paneled library *within* the library complete with a spiral staircase leading into stacks of ancient volumes, photographs, and maps.

Mr. Sumner is in his midfifties with receding ginger hair twisted into a bun. He adjusts a plaid bow tie and asks from his seat behind a desk with a roll top, "How can I help you?"

"Mr. Sumner? I'm looking for a book titled *Letters from My War* compiled by Olivia Edwards Arnaud."

"Call me Colin. I can help you find that volume, but first let's go over the rules of Special Collections. I'll need to see your library card and then I can help you find whatever you desire. When you finish for the day, just bring me the materials you've used so I can log the return and ensure that it's put back in the proper place."

"Got it."

"In addition, you'll need to leave your purse or backpack in an open locker at the front of the room and take the key with

you. Apologies if that's an inconvenience, but we've had disappearances of valuable works in the past. You are permitted one
pad of paper or notebook and a pencil. Absolutely no pens allowed. We can't risk having the collections damaged by ink.
When handling the materials here, we ask that you wear the
white gloves in the basket by the lockers. Please drop them off
as you leave so we can launder and reuse them. Special Collections is open from eight a.m. to seven p.m. seven days a week.
No matter who's manning the desk, you'll follow the same pro-
tocol."

Colin finds *Letters from My War* on an iPad then walks me
by a massive oak table in the center of the room. Many of the
twenty seats are occupied and a few of the people look up and
nod, silently welcoming me into their club.

"Historical nonfiction collections are in rows 1 through 16,
sections D, E, and F. Can I ask your interest in this specific
book?" Colin asks.

"I just got engaged. My ring is an antique from the early
1900s and purchased from the French estate of Olivia and Louis
Arnaud. But it wasn't Olivia's engagement ring and they didn't
have any children. She did have a brother, James V. Edwards,
so my hope is that there may be some reference to my ring in
the letters he wrote to his sister during World War I. Maybe it's
a family heirloom or their mother's or an aunt's . . . Truthfully,
I'm grasping at straws."

"That's how the best discoveries are made."

I laugh. "I don't even know why it matters to me."

"Sometimes these things are more about us than the actual
mystery," Colin remarks.

My cheeks warm as he uses a step stool to pull the book from a high shelf. "Thanks." I take a seat at the table. The researcher to my right is in his midtwenties, wearing a gray Berkeley sweatshirt, giving off a surfer vibe including flip-flops and shaggy, sun-kissed blond hair. Across from him is an older woman with gray pigtails and beside her a middle-aged man with an impressive paunch. A twenty-something guy to my left studies a hand-drawn map with writing scrawled in the margins. When he glances up my insides spin—he's a dead ringer for the Duke from that show *Bridgerton* Mars was so obsessed with that she watched the entire thing three times.

The Duke whispers, "I'm Chester," and nods at the map in front of him. "I'm reading the diary of a ship's captain from the 1800s to learn about my ancestors. You?"

"I'm trying to find out the history behind my engagement ring." I slip on the gloves Colin provided, then open James's book. The smell of old vellum wafts up and itches my nose. After sneezing into the crook of my arm, I carefully turn the pages. Each one has a sleeve with an airmail letter in it. The same faded address is on every envelope.

Miss Olivia Edwards
Number 1 Hastings Street
San Francisco, California USA

I turn back to the foreword and a window to the past cracks open . . .

Dear Reader,
My brother, James V. Edwards, was the light of my life. He was handsome at six foot two, with brown hair and eyes the color of spruce

pines. James was passionate about literature and the horses he helped raise with our stable-master, who loved him like a son and was his refuge from the immense burden of family expectations. James also adored the majestic mountains he climbed with friends and was known by all as honest, devoted, and compassionate.

Our family was pleased when James announced his engagement to Kristina Poole, the daughter of Father's law partner. Kristina would have made a wonderful wife and a devoted mother to their children had she not tragically drowned in a sailboat accident on Lake Tahoe. Her death changed the trajectory of all our lives.

James abandoned Harvard Law and joined the American Ambulance Field Service in France just after the United States formally entered the Great War. He risked his life at the front to transport wounded soldiers to hospitals and rail stations, witnessed horrific brutality, discovered a depth of bravery men find only under threat of death, and met the one true love of his life.

Only 126 Medals of Honor were awarded to United States soldiers during the Great War. James V. Edwards was posthumously awarded the Medal of Honor for gallantry and bravery and risk of life above and beyond the call of duty. James deserved a much longer life, but so did all the young men and women on both sides who perished in that terrible war.

Sincèrement,
Olivia Edwards Arnaud

The scent of tobacco smoke prickles my nose. But there's no smoking in the library so clearly I'm imagining it. Returning to my task, I carefully withdraw James's first letter to his sister and begin to read.

May 1917

Dearest Olivia,

I know that Mother and Father are deeply upset with my decision. But Kristina's death has made me question everything. Our betrothal was a very good match, but I do not know if I ever truly loved her or if I was trying to meet everyone else's expectations and fulfill my own desire to be loved, be married, and create a family.

The truth is that Kristina and I had little in common beyond our backgrounds. She did not share my appetite for books, the outdoors, horses, or my desire to address the social woes of our time. And I did not share her passion for the opera, dinner parties, and museums. Perhaps we would've still had a happy home life and family. But as our wedding date approached, many times I wondered if our union would leave me wanting for a more sympathetic partner.

Olivia, I am also unsure if I love the law, or want to join Father's firm. I have known from the time I was a boy that this was expected of me—to carry on the firm's work and continue to make it more prosperous. Just as you are expected to marry well and in a way that ensures the continuation of your social standing and brings honor to our family. But just because something is expected, must we always acquiesce?

I have traveled a great distance in the hopes of being useful and finding clarity. Wish me well and please keep me in your prayers.

All my love,
James

The urge to share my feelings so honestly with someone, as James once did with his sister, presses heavy against my chest.

But if I talk to Mars about my fears, she'll insist again that Hayden is wrong for me; that I must break off the engagement. And I can't burden Grandpa with any of my concerns. He's more and more fragile. Maybe Trudy could give me some advice, but when she interviewed me years ago for the shelter volunteer position, she told me my biggest weakness was uncertainty. I'd be embarrassed to prove her right these many years later.

And Hayden? He'd be so hurt that I'm having any doubts about our relationship—shocked that I'm not his constant Constance, and upset that Mars has been digging into his past. He did lie to me . . . but I'm sure he has to have had a good reason for the deception. If I bring up Lydia, Lawrenceville, and all the other little doubts that are cropping up he'll feel like I don't trust him. I could lose him.

A headache gathers like a storm and I massage my temples. Everyone tells lies. I'm the guiltiest of all. But I can't seem to let this go, shake my fears. I hesitate then slide a scrap of paper from my notebook, a pencil from the container on the table, and write . . .

I am engaged to someone. Reading this letter has brought my own worries to the surface. I'm afraid that I don't really know my fiancé. I've discovered several lies. Some are small, like the fact he attended an expensive, private boarding school, and others larger—he was previously engaged but said I was his first proposal.

I am unsure if these things matter. Finding my person, being loved and married, is everything I've ever wanted but never thought I'd have. And now that my dream is about to come true I'm afraid to do anything that might jeopardize it.

In addition, my best friend believes I have been too quick to give pieces of myself away. She sees me as smart, kind, and quirky, and doesn't support my engagement. But the truth is that I'm nothing special. I have a pretty dull job as a paralegal, volunteer at an animal shelter and foster dogs, and used to love mountain biking but now am trying to learn how to cook. That's me in a nutshell—but someone finally thinks I'm worthy of commitment and marriage.

My fiancé is a really good man who is dedicated to the students he teaches, has many talents and hobbies, and is kind and considerate. If I tell him what I've discovered, it will hurt him and he may see me differently, even break things off. I don't want to lose him.

It's a relief to finally put my fears in writing. Maybe it's the first step to letting them go, embracing all that's right with my relationship and focusing on the future. With a few minutes remaining before the manuscript room closes, my fellow researchers gather their books. I rest my hands on the old volume of letters then impulsively scribble *Dear James* at the top of the note I've just written and *Sincerely, Constance* at the bottom. I fold the note and when no one's looking slip it into the sleeve with James's first letter.

As I close the book, a heavy quiet descends over me. It reminds me of the moment before a summer lightning storm, when the sky is painted like a bruise, the air thick, charged. I draw in a breath, waiting for . . . something. But of course nothing happens. What was I expecting? Telling a long-dead man my worries carries no risk or repercussions. Hayden will never find out and it's not like James will ever read this confession. This is just a silly way of getting my fears out, leaving them behind.

A puff of cold breath hits the back of my neck. I spin around, but there's no one there.

Chapter Eight

At the end of the day, I make a quick stop by the shelter to pick up more pain meds for Lucy. She's asleep in my saddlebag so I leave her while I quickly run inside. Growler snarls from the back corner of his pen when he sees me. He was discovered beneath an abandoned building and showed signs of abuse. When he first came to the shelter he wouldn't let anyone near him, but he and Lucy instantly hit it off, played, then curled up on a bed together. Her presence allowed Growler to grudgingly accept ours. I crouch by the gate. "I'll bring Lucy back in a few days," I promise. Growler tips his head sideways at her name. "But she *will* eventually get adopted. Even with her bad hip, she's the kind of small dog that finds a home. So you're going to need to trust someone, okay?"

Growler's response to my question is a low growl. We're a no-kill shelter, which is why we're filled to capacity, but that definition is misleading. Trudy does everything she can to rehabilitate dogs with behavioral issues, but when it's not possible, they're euthanized. She believes it's a mercy. No animal should live its entire life in a cage. She's right, but giving up on them still feels wrong. Growler doesn't have much more time left.

"I know you're afraid," I tell the dog, "and I can't make up for what happened to you in the past, but please let me help you." I toss a treat into his pen. He doesn't move to get it, but as I walk away I hear the click of his nails on the concrete. It's not much, but Growler usually won't eat when any of us are around. Trudy thinks it's because he's afraid we'll take his food away. Whoever once owned him must have been a terrible person. The sound of Growler crunching the treat while I'm still in sight gives me a little hope.

When I reach Trudy's office, Ellis is seated behind his mom's battered metal desk, head bent over a laptop. He must've come from work because he's still in blue hospital scrubs. I knock on the door. His green eyes flash in recognition and he smiles. My breath catches, but he's just a good-looking guy who knows it.

"Ah. It's the girl with cardiomegaly."

"What's that?"

"An enlarged heart."

I ignore the joke. "Is Trudy around? Lucy was extra sore today so I wanted to pick up more pain medicine." Dr. Yang, the vet who takes on most of our animals' needs pro bono, keeps the shelter's drug cabinet stocked with pills that are still good but recently expired.

"Mom's at an appointment, but I can help. Unless the meds are for you?"

I bristle. "What?"

He chuckles. "I'm kidding—bad hospital joke. We get *frequent flyers* looking for drugs."

"Arthritis meds?"

"Anything they can use to get high." Ellis grabs a ring of keys from the top desk drawer and heads to the locked medical cabinet in the corner of the office. "What's Lucy on now?"

"Vetprofen. She needs hip surgery. Her new family promised they'd do it, but then they decided they wanted a puppy instead."

"Can you blame them? They're going to put a lot of time, energy, and love into a dog and the parents probably want one for their kids that'll be around for more than a few years."

"Lucy isn't old," I snip. "And just because she's not perfect, she's still worthy of love."

"How do you really feel about it?" Ellis asks with a grin.

Clearly I'm overreacting. Why does he get under my skin so easily? Breezily, I say, "The dogs and cats that have gone through the toughest times make the best companions. They're grateful. But I wouldn't expect you to understand."

"Meaning?"

"It doesn't seem like you've lived a hard life."

Ellis winks. "I'll take that as a compliment."

If I didn't have any self-control, right about now I'd stamp my foot in frustration. He unlocks the cabinet, roots around, then hands me a green pill bottle. "This is Gabapentin. How much does Lucy weigh?"

"Twenty-five pounds."

"Give her one pill a day. If she has stomach upset, break the pill in half and give her half in the morning with food and half at night." He tosses me the bottle.

"Thanks."

"If that doesn't work we can talk about steroids, maybe an injection of cortisone into the hip."

"That sounds expensive." The shelter doesn't have any extra funds and my salary barely covers all my monthly expenses. But maybe I can swing it. I turn to leave.

Ellis says, "Hang on. Can I ask your advice?"

I tense, unsure if it's a trap to embarrass me again. "I guess."

"I have a patient, a little girl who's five. She's terrified of me. Cried today when I did the presurgery consultation, hid behind her parents, clutching her stuffed bear like I meant to torture them both. Her surgery is in a few days."

"Is it a big one?"

"Yes."

"Maybe there's another surgeon who could help?"

Ellis frowns. "I'm the head of general surgery at UCSF—youngest ever appointed to that position. People come to *me* for help, not the other way around."

A little smile tickles my lips—I got under his skin for once. "O-kay. See ya."

"Wait. I'd just like a way to stop the kid from leaking tears on surgery day. It's annoying."

I hesitate. "You can't have one of your PAs take care of her?"

"That's not how I roll."

I consider the problem. "If it was a dog, I'd try to show her that she'd be okay . . . and give her a high-value treat." Ellis doesn't make a snarky comment so I go on. "Ask the parents to bring you her stuffed bear. Before you see her on surgery day, put stitches over the same spot where she'll get them, preferably in a fun color, like pink, and then explain how her stuffed animal is doing great and she will, too. It wouldn't hurt to promise her a lollipop as soon as she's able to have one—one of those giant, swirly kinds. Dogs need to see their incentives, so maybe have it there, so she can see how cool it is."

Ellis chuckles. "That's an *interesting* idea."

It *was* a trap. My face is hot as I stride to the door.

"Hang on. Maybe I'll try it. In the meantime, let's grab a drink. I'm just about done with my work."

"I need to head home to my fiancé."

Ellis whistles. "When'd that happen?"

I hold up my left hand. "Last night."

"You're not married yet. C'mon, it'd make Trudy so happy if her favorite volunteer went for drinks with her favorite son. She's been telling me for years to ask you out."

"But instead you dated lots of women and then married one and divorced her."

When Ellis smiles a dimple forms in his left cheek and despite his arrogance it's easy to see why women are drawn to him. "One drink," he implores.

I wave goodbye with my left hand and hope my ring catches the light.

When I get home, I give Lucy her meds along with kibble from the bin in the front hall, then plant a kiss on her nose. "That was from Growler." Samson joins us—she's figured out the layout of Hayden's house and uses all her senses to avoid Blueboy, who insists on licking her until she's soaked. I scratch behind the cat's ears and she purrs.

"Hayden?" I call.

"Kitchen," he responds.

I pet the top of Blueboy's head then wander into the kitchen where Hayden sits at the table working. It smells like fresh bread and there's homemade soup cooking on the stove. I peek into the pot. It's lentil. "My favorite. Yum."

Hayden looks up, sees Lucy, and cocks one brow. "Who's this?"

"Lucy. Her adoptive family bailed today and she needed a little extra TLC."

His forehead creases. "You don't think we've got our hands full with Blueboy and Samson?"

I should've called to ask him. "She was so sad. I couldn't say no."

Hayden chuckles. "And that's just one of the things I love about you."

"So Lucy stays?" I ask.

"We can make a second dog work for a bit."

Appreciation washes over me. "I have a fiancé!" I say and kiss him.

Hayden grins. "How'd we get so lucky to find the perfect match?"

His absolute trust makes me a little queasy. Hayden chews on a piece of the red licorice he's addicted to and scribbles something in the notebook in front of him. "What are you up to?" I ask.

"Wedding stuff," he says.

My belly does a little flip. "Let me see." He hands over his list . . .

Location—winery, restaurant, park?

Food—appetizers, buffet or plated?

Wedding cake—include other options—cupcakes,
        cookies . . . ?

Guest list—people, dogs, kids?

Music—live band, DJ, or—?

Attire?

Given the time frame, I figured we were going to keep things super simple. I consider suggesting we pop all of this into an Excel spreadsheet but stop myself. I don't want to encourage Hayden to get more elaborate. "Um."

"What's on your mind?"

Despite my fears, I have to tell him about both of my parents. But given what he said about accepting him *as is*, there's something I need to get out of the way first. I pull my chair closer to his and then hold out my hand. "My ring."

Hayden's smile goes out like a candle in a puff of wind. "You don't like it?"

"I love it! But, Hayden, it's much too expensive."

"It wasn't that bad."

My face flushes. "Mars insisted I find out if it needed to be appraised."

Hayden recoils. "If?"

"I told her I didn't care about my ring's value but agreed it'd be a good idea to get it insured."

"I already did."

"Great!" I barrel ahead. "There was a woman at the jewelry store who recognized my ring, told me a little about its history . . . and also the price." Hayden frowns. "We shop at Costco, cook at home most nights, and play board games for entertainment— why would you think I'd need a ring like this . . . and how could you possibly afford it?"

Hayden finally smiles. "Here's the deal. I wasn't planning on buying such an expensive ring, but when I saw it, well, I just knew it was meant for you; that you *had* to have it."

"Why?"

Hayden's eyes are earnest. "You've always reminded me of an old soul, so an estate piece seemed right. And it has the red flowers you love. Plus, and I know this doesn't make sense, but I was drawn to it in the jewelry case. Once I held your ring, I just had to buy it." He chuckles. "And yes, it's really freaking expensive, but this ring is a symbol for the rest of our lives of how much we mean to each other."

"But *any* ring you give me, even a string on my finger, would symbolize that."

"And that's another reason I love you." Hayden hesitates then adds, "Look, we don't talk much about our pasts, but I've made mistakes, okay? This time I want to do everything right."

Is he talking about Lydia? Maybe if I open that door he'll walk through it, tell me about her. "Is there anything you want to ask me," I fumble, "about my past, or prior relationships?"

"None of that matters to me," Hayden says then frowns. "Why?"

Anxiety pricks sharp needles along my skin. *I'm pushing too hard.* "No reason." I stare at the ring. "I do love it."

"Then it's settled." Hayden kisses my palm. "So. Tux or suit?"

"I don't even know what I'm going to wear." Just that it'll come from a secondhand store.

"What about location? I've heard that it's hard to find a venue on short notice."

I have next to nothing in my checking account and zero savings. He's my fiancé—I should tell him that I don't have the money to help pay for an expensive wedding, or even one that's not expensive. Hayden does know that I supplement Grandpa's care, but I'm sure he assumes that leaves *some* money. Unfortunately, what's left at the end of each month goes into Dad's prison commissary. Given that I'm an extremely responsible person, the lack of savings really bothers me, but there's nothing I can do to change it.

The weight of my secret bears down on me. It's time for me to come clean. I clear my throat. "There's something I have to—"

"Why don't we hire a justice of the peace and get married in the backyard?" Hayden interjects.

"The backyard works great. But—"

"Food?"

I consider the most cost-efficient option. "How about Jack's taco truck?" It's cheap but delicious. "We could get take-out tacos and I could mix sangria to go with it?"

"Brilliant."

He's so easygoing and unpretentious. "I told Mars."

Hayden sucks in a nervous breath. "And?"

"She's happy for us." Hayden gives me a look. "She will be happy for us, eventually."

He forces a smile. "She'll be your maid of honor?"

I hadn't even thought about that. Some women imagine every aspect of their wedding. But despite the dream of finding my person, I never considered the details. "Definitely."

"I promise I'll do my best to win her over. Does she like homemade tiramisu?"

I'm not sure that will be enough. I lean in and kiss Hayden. His lips taste like strawberries. "She loves any dessert. Who's going to be your best man?"

"Austin Wilmers."

"Is he a teacher at your school?"

"Nope. We went to high school together."

My scalp tightens. "I don't know any of your friends."

Hayden shrugs. "Most live on the east coast."

It makes sense. Out of sight, out of mind. "I'll stop by Grandpa's tomorrow before work to tell him."

"I already did," Hayden says.

The ground beneath me gives way. "You did?"

"I went by last week to ask for permission to marry you. I wanted to do things the right way."

I'm both touched and totally freaked out. I've talked about my grandpa a lot, but never brought Hayden to meet him. He's been so muddled the past few years and might've let it slip that Dad's alive *and* in prison. Plus, there's the name thing.

"Given the dementia," Hayden explains, "I went in the morning so he'd be more with it."

"What'd he say?"

"That you're a wiz at Scrabble."

I actually laugh. "He taught me everything I know."

"He's a lovely old guy. I can't wait to spend more time with him." Samson leaps onto Hayden's lap. Gently, he deposits her back to the floor, wipes his palms on his pants, then asks, "One thing that confused me, though. Your grandfather said he's your *father's* dad, not your mother's, so why do you two have different last names?"

Cold seeps into my body. This is my chance to tell Hayden the truth . . . but a shameful lie comes instead. "Grandpa isn't my biological grandfather. He married my grandmother when Dad was in his early teens, adopted him, but Dad didn't want to change his last name at that point." But that's not the truth. Too many people Google potential dates. When that happened one too many times after college with disastrous results, I legally had my name changed to my mother's maiden name.

"Got it," Hayden says with an easy smile. "Guest list?"

Slowly the warmth returns to my hands and feet. "I probably have fifteen people between college friends, work, and the shelter. What about you?"

Hayden sneezes. "Same—some teachers, friends from volunteer work, some of our buddies from game night."

"What about your parents?"

"I'm not going to invite them."

I shouldn't push—at the very least it's hypocritical. But . . . "This is their son's wedding. It might help your family reunite." Hayden doesn't answer. Again I'm a mouse in a maze looking for the way out. "They do know about me?"

"The last thing that you and I need is my parents involved in our relationship."

They don't know about me. I shove aside all my childhood hang-ups and focus on being supportive. "That bad, huh?"

"Trust me."

I wait for more, but Hayden picks up a pen and doodles along the side of the page. It's his decision. I'm already getting a guy who loves me. Wanting his family to be part of the package is greedy. "What about invitations?" I ask.

Hayden considers. "Given the short time frame, how about Evites?"

"Perfect."

"Now my favorite part. The cake!"

My fiancé has a much bigger sweet tooth than I do. Right now he looks like an excited little boy. I slide onto his lap. "Anything you want—the more icing the better." Hayden slips his hands to my hips and pulls me closer. Just as we kiss, the theme from *Jaws* rings on my phone. It's Mars—*she* picked the ringtone. "Hold that thought," I tell my fiancé and walk onto the screened porch. Lucy limps after me.

"Hey, Mars." I sit down on the wicker couch and lift Lucy onto my lap. Out here the sound of crickets fills the night air—it's serene.

"What are you up to?" Mars asks.

"In the midst of wedding planning."

An owl hoots somewhere in our backyard and my mom's voice rasps, *In Egypt they believe hearing an owl is a warning of terrible news.* Anxiety pinches, but I hold Lucy closer and ignore it. "Big question. Will you be my maid of honor? I promise you don't have to wear an ugly dress. You can wear anything you want."

"Anything?"

"Yes."

"Then of course. But once again my BFF underestimates her power. I would've worn one of those hideous mauve taffeta dresses for you."

Mars's laugh sounds off. "You're home early from your date. Is everything okay?" I ask.

"I'm fine. But *you* sound a little weird."

I lower my voice to a whisper. "Dad's up for parole again. May twenty-fifth. He's asked me to help him prepare and to write another letter to the parole board."

"You can't seriously want him out!" Mars shouts.

I wince then glance beyond the half-open door. Hayden is scribbling away and didn't hear her. "Maybe we could finally get to know each other, have a *real* relationship, outside of prison."

Mars presses, "Explain to me how that'd be possible."

I get why she's pressuring me, but my heart tugs hard in the opposite direction. "He's clean now, so he could be an entirely new man."

"Constance, you need to live in reality."

My knee-jerk reaction is to defend him. "Dad's been on the right track the past few years."

"That doesn't mean . . ." Mars trails off. "Better tell Hayden soon or things could get messy."

I unclench my fists and blow out a breath. "Thanks, Captain Obvious."

Mars chuckles.

"I will tell him. And I love you for caring enough to push me. 'Night."

An ambulance races by as I end the call and the wail of sirens hangs in the air. Even as a child, ambulances always filled me with dread. When they'd pass, I'd imagine the people inside and ask Grandpa if they'd be okay. He'd just hug me. I knew that meant he didn't know, and even though they were strangers, sometimes I'd cry.

"Ready for dinner?" Hayden calls.

"Sure."

We eat, plan a bit more, then head to bed. He falls asleep first, his arms wrapped around me. But even though he's holding me tight, I feel unmoored.

Chapter Nine

The sun has barely risen when I pull up to the small bungalow in San Rafael where Grandpa now lives. I tried to find
an assisted living facility in the city but they were all too expensive and the state-run one was dingy and depressing. He now
stays with a nice couple, Rosa and Marcio, who care for two
other elderly people in a similar situation. The government pays
for a little over half, and I make up the rest. Grandpa took care
of me when Dad left. I want to do the same for him.

Rosa, in a blue tracksuit, her salt-and-pepper hair swept into
a high ponytail, answers the door and ushers me inside. "I was
just getting ready for my online Zumba class."

"Don't let me keep you." I follow her down the hallway. The
house smells both sweet and spicy and is filled with worn, comfortable furniture and photographs of Rosa and Marcio's four
kids, now all adults. Grandpa, in a brown terry cloth robe, drinks
coffee at a red table in the kitchen. His mug reads: WORLD'S
BEST DAD. I brace myself—it's never a given that he'll recognize
me and it always hurts if he doesn't.

A smile lights his grizzled face. "Constance!"

Happiness bubbles. It's a good day and despite his dementia

I cherish these times when it feels like nothing has changed about our rapport. I kiss his forehead and sit down. Rosa brings me a cup of coffee and then leaves with a wave to dance her way to fitness. "How are you, Grandpa?"

His tangled gray brows knit together as he frowns. "I'd be better in my own house."

We go through this every time I visit. At first I corrected him, told him we'd sold the house to help pay for medical bills (that money ran out years ago). Each time he realized he was never going home, Grandpa would get angry, but the next time I visited he had forgotten and we'd go through it all again. Rosa finally pulled me aside and suggested I tell a white lie, that Grandpa would get less agitated that way. For a while I resisted. But she was right. Some lies are a kindness.

"Your house is getting renovated," I now explain.

"Will I go back soon?"

"Yes."

Grandpa smiles. "Good. My old place isn't much, but it's home. And every inch you grew is marked on the kitchen wall." He drinks his coffee. "When do you leave for college?"

At least he recognized me. "Pretty soon."

"You scared?"

"A little."

"Don't be, sweet pea. All the kids will love you. And if any of them call you that nickname, kick 'em in the shin. I'll deal with their parents." He reaches over and touches my cheek. "You're the thing I'm most proud of in this life. I'm just sorry I couldn't give you more."

"Grandpa, you gave me everything that matters."

He pulls a Kleenex from the pocket of his robe and wipes wet eyes then blows his nose. He never used to cry, but now he gets teary every visit.

"Do you have time for a game?" he asks.

"Of course." I find the box in the living room and set it up on the kitchen table. Grandpa only picks five tiles instead of seven. When he's not looking I put two more on his wooden stand. He opens with GOOD. And I add LAD to spell GLAD.

"I bought your first Scrabble board."

"I remember."

"At night, after you'd gone to bed, I'd read the dictionary and make lists of words for the next game. Never was much of a student, but I wanted to help with your vocabulary." He shuffles the tiles and adds, "I met your young man."

I'd always hoped that Grandpa would be around to see me fall in love. "Hayden. What'd you think?"

"He drives a Chevy Volt. Those electric cars are going to put me out of business."

As a former auto mechanic, Grandpa resents all electric cars. "Hayden also has an MG convertible he found in a junkyard and restored. It's *constantly* breaking down."

"That's better," Grandpa says.

I hold out my hand to show him the ring. "Hayden asked me to marry him and I said yes. Will you walk me down the aisle at our wedding?"

Grandpa shakes his head. "That's your dad's job."

"Dad can't be there." Grandpa doesn't always remember that he's in prison.

"Hope they never let the SOB out. Only good thing he ever did was create you, and that was an accident."

A timer buzzes and Rosa dances in to take blueberry muffins out of the oven. She puts two on a plate for us with some butter then dances back out. I cut Grandpa's muffin in half to let out the steam then butter both sides. I do the same with mine.

"I don't know who that woman is," Grandpa says with his mouth full, "but she loves to bake. If I stay here too long, I'm gonna get fat."

"Rosa and her husband, Marcio, are family friends."

Butter dribbles down his chin and I wipe it off. Grandpa pushes back his chair when he's done and shuffles toward the door that leads into the TV room. Sadness nibbles at me. I guess our visit is over. When he reaches the dimly lit hallway, he turns around. His face is in shadow, but I can see the gleam of his eyes.

"Your dad is a liar. Hayden's one, too. When he asked for permission to marry you, I told him no."

That doesn't match the way Hayden described it at all. He said they had a lovely talk. Did Hayden not want to tell me that my grandfather doesn't approve of our engagement? *It must be the dementia.* "I love you, Grandpa."

Grandpa waves one hand and then slips into a recliner to watch *The Price Is Right.*

Chapter Ten

Man overboard," Hayden shouts.

On Saturdays we stay in our PJs, an oversized shirt for me and flannel PJ bottoms for him, and eat breakfast together before I head to the shelter to walk dogs. Today I decided to make pancakes. Everything went well until I tried to flip them with the pan like Hayden does. Now Blueboy is happily scarfing my masterpiece.

Hayden takes over while I cut up some fresh fruit. When we first started dating I always felt in the way in the small kitchen, but now we move around each other seamlessly. There's a comfort to that I really appreciate. "What's on your agenda?" I ask.

"The MG is running rough so I'm going to give her a tune-up."

I toss a strawberry and he easily catches it in his mouth. With the last pancake flipped, we sit and Hayden smothers his breakfast in maple syrup while I put a dollop on mine.

"New teacher joke," Hayden says.

His students tell jokes for extra credit. If Hayden laughs, they get five points on their next test. He *always* laughs.

"Why did the teacher go to the beach?" Hayden asks.

I chuckle at his enthusiastic delivery. "No idea."

"To test the water!"

"Not that funny."

Hayden takes a bite of pancake dripping in syrup. "I know. I only gave Kyle three out of five points for it."

"Sounds fair." Lucy curls at my feet, one paw on my toes to make sure I don't leave her behind. I plan to bring her back to the shelter in a few days, before Growler's bad behavior starts getting on Trudy's nerves.

Hayden blows his nose. "I should buy stock in Kleenex. Hey, could we consider building a small kennel next to my shop?"

I take a bite of fruit. "It wouldn't be the same for them."

"I know. But keeping the animals outside the house while we're at work and then playing with them in the yard would be better than the shelter, right?"

It's hard to swallow, but it's clear that I'm being incredibly selfish. "You're right."

Hayden kisses my cheek then says, "So fill me in on your week."

"We have a new divorce case. Husband cheated and now he's trying to hold his wife to a brutal prenup."

He takes another bite of pancake. "But she signed it, right?"

A wave of irritation seizes me, but maybe I'm not explaining this well. "She was *really* young and didn't know better."

"Still seems cut-and-dried."

"Her husband took advantage of her naivete."

"Maybe it's not entirely fair, but a prenup *is* legally binding, right?"

I shrug off my annoyance. We don't always have to agree. "I did go to the library to do some research on my engagement ring. I wanted to know the story attached to it."

Hayden rubs his hands together, instantly dispelling the dark cloud gathering overhead and returning to the supportive guy I love. He wriggles his brows. "What'd you find out?"

"Well, it was bought in Paris from the estate of a couple named Olivia and Louis Arnaud—Olivia was a San Francisco socialite before she moved to France to marry—but it wasn't Olivia's engagement ring. I thought I'd hit a dead end, but she had a brother named James who wrote her letters from World War I—he was a volunteer ambulance driver. So I'm hoping there might be a clue in those letters about the ring. And I also left a message at Westcott and Sons to see what they know, but they haven't called back yet. We'll see. Maybe it'll always be a mystery."

"Then we'll create our own story," Hayden suggests. "That'll guarantee it has a happily ever after." He clears our dishes, his back to me as he rinses them at the sink. "You said Olivia was a local socialite? Maybe you could find her old home? Poke around for leads?"

I grin. "That's a great idea!"

Hayden chuckles. "Happy to help. Hey, how about cutting short the shelter time today and we can give the MG a spin after I work on her and then have lunch in Sausalito?"

For a second I feel like a little kid whose favorite thing might be taken away. But that's not true. Hayden loves how devoted I am to the shelter. He just wants to spend more time together. "I'd love to," I reply, "but Trudy counts on me to walk dogs on Saturdays."

"I get it. It's just our weeks are so busy, it'd be nice to spend more of the weekend together."

The house suddenly feels too warm. "Today I'm committed, but I'll talk to Trudy, see what I can work out in the future."

When I walk into the shelter I find that Ellis, dressed down in jeans and a gray flannel shirt, is already there.

"Can I join you on the walk?" he asks.

I shrug. "Okay."

Ellis takes Helen, an Australian shepherd with different-colored eyes, out of her pen. She was too high-energy for her original owners. I put my hand on Growler's gate, consider trying to get him out to walk, but he lets out a low grumble. He's never bitten anyone, but he's clearly not in the mood. I open the package of string cheese I brought. He watches, still growling, as I peel off a big piece and toss it through the wire. He eyes the cheese—it's a high-value treat. I leash his neighbor, Happy, a Lab-pointer mix whose owners had a baby and realized they couldn't deal with a dog, too. As Ellis and I head for the exit I glance back. Growler has crept forward and eaten the cheese. Now he watches me. "Good boy," I call out and he scoots back to his corner.

Ellis chuckles. "You're as hardheaded as my mom." We head down Transom Street toward a small dog park so the dogs can feel grass under their feet.

"Is Trudy still mad at you?"

He laughs. "That'll take time." The light changes and he grabs my arm to keep me from walking into traffic. "Hey, I wanted to thank you."

Ellis hasn't let go of my arm so I slide it free. "For what?"

"Your idea—about the teddy bear. I felt like an idiot suturing its belly. But the stitches and a very expensive artisan lollipop did the trick. No tears, even when she was wheeled into the OR."

"I'm really glad it worked." We cross the street. There's a crack in the sidewalk and I skip over it then cringe as Ellis walks right on it.

"What?" He looks at the bottom of his shoe. "Did I just step in poop?"

I laugh. "It's not that."

"Then?"

"It's just, you stepped *on* that crack."

His mouth falls open a little. "Are you telling me that you believe if I step on a crack I'll break my mother's back?"

Do I? "My mom believed that cracks were the connection to hell and that if you stepped on them you released bad things into your life."

Ellis chuckles. "Charming. What else did your mom believe?"

That it was okay to walk out on an eight-year-old kid. I force a smile. "That two mirrors in a room facing each other invites the devil. If you laugh when a hearse passes you'll be the next to die. Oh, and then there were the death crowns."

"Death crowns?"

I explain, "If you tear open a pillow and there's a hard clump of feathers inside, quills all pointing inward, it means someone died sleeping on that pillow. In order for them to get to heaven, the crown has to be framed and put on display."

"Do you actually believe superstitions are valid?" Ellis asks me.

"Best not to tempt fate," I hedge. Happy tries to dart for a squirrel and I ask him to sit and chill out before we continue. Ellis probably thinks I'm too strict. That shouldn't matter to me, but I still change the subject. "Did you always want to be a surgeon?"

"I thought I'd be an oncologist, but after Dad's cancer I decided there wasn't enough control in that field. I'm better suited for surgery. In a lot of ways it's less complicated."

"So you prefer your patients anesthetized?" When Ellis laughs I notice a tiny chip on his front tooth that makes his smile even more charming.

Helen spies a miniature poodle across the street and barks. Ellis asks her to sit then treats her to regain control. He's good with dogs. We walk on, both dogs heeling at our sides.

"I was so sorry about your dad."

"Thanks. He was a complicated man but we loved him."

"I'm glad Trudy has the shelter. It's kept her going all these years."

Ellis watches a red Porsche whiz by. "My attending during residency, Dr. Garvey, used to tell us a story about a guy he knew, a serious weight lifter. He'd won dozens of competitions. But by the time he was sixty he'd had nine neurosurgeries. Still, every morning he'd use a walker to hobble down to the gym and lift. Mom's that weight lifter. She's eighty, has six grandchildren, but instead of spending time with them, she's at the shelter seven days a week."

"She loves the animals."

"And she's done great work. But it's time to move on. Unfortunately, she can't let go of the shelter as her identity. I know it's just human nature, even if it hurts us."

"Maybe you're projecting and you're the one who's tired of being a surgeon but it's *your* identity," I challenge.

"Hardly. There's something very addictive about the license

to cut a human being open, solve a problem. And I'm not eighty. What about you? Is being a paralegal everything you dreamed it'd be?"

I snort a bit too loud. "No. I took the job because I needed to make the most amount of money possible after college."

"Student loans?"

"Yes. And my grandpa has dementia." Of course that's half the truth. I skipped the part about having a parent in prison.

"Sorry to hear about your grandfather. Are you close?"

Ellis's gaze is intense. I look away. "He mostly raised me."

"Where were your parents?"

The lie comes easily. "They both died young."

Ellis waits for more details. When I don't offer them, he says, "Tell me more about *your* job."

"This week I wrote a brief for a case involving a high-tech firm suing another high-tech firm and started work on a divorce case."

"Do you like the case with the Goliaths duking it out or the divorce stuff better?"

"You ask a lot of questions," I say.

Ellis smiles. "I'm interested in your answers."

"I like the cases where we're helping people who *really* need us."

"Cool. What do you like to do for fun?"

I'm suddenly aware that we're walking very close together and create more distance. "Lately I've taken Thai, tapas, and pasta cooking classes."

"Wow. You must love to cook."

"I think it's important to share my partner's passions." I ignore the face Ellis makes. *I'm* engaged and *he's* divorced.

We watch a couple, hand in hand, cross the street. Both of the women are in their early twenties. Ellis nods at them. "When you're that age, you can't fathom ending things with the person you once said you loved more than anyone else."

Helen wraps her leash around Ellis's and my legs in an attempt to chase a bird, pulling us tightly together. We laugh as we extricate ourselves, but I'm absurdly aware of the brush of his warm skin against mine. "So why'd you get divorced?" I ask when I'm a safe distance away.

"The grass looked greener in a different park."

I'm disappointed, even though it doesn't matter to me. "So you cheated?"

"She did, with my best friend."

"I thought it'd be you."

Ellis bursts out laughing. "Clearly I've made a fantastic impression. Lizzie and I were great on paper—similar backgrounds, she's also a doctor, and our families got along well. But if I'm honest, something was always missing. I guess she found it with Aaron."

We enter the park's gate and let the dogs off leash then sit at a picnic table. "So. You have a fiancé," Ellis says.

"I do."

"That's quite a ring."

"It's from the early 1900s." I find myself telling Ellis about researching my ring, the letters James wrote home to his sister from the front, and how breaking with his family led to finding his true love. I'm taken aback that Ellis seems truly interested; that talking to him is so easy.

"I'm fairly obsessed with reading both fiction and nonfiction accounts of wars, expeditions to far-flung places, and death-defying adventures. But the rest of it?" he says with one brow cocked. "Do you actually believe in true love?"

There are blue splinters in his forest-green eyes that seem to draw me in. I focus on the dogs.

"FYI, the answer should be an immediate yes," Ellis says. "You just got engaged."

I snip, "FYI, I love my fiancé."

He smiles easily. "I didn't say you don't."

"Look, I just don't buy into the whole starry-eyed, bodice-ripping romance thing. But I do believe people can have a long-term, happy, and fulfilling relationship when they want the same things."

"Bodice-ripping?" Ellis teases.

My face reddens and I turn away. The day has warmed and I gather my hair into a ponytail then unzip my sweatshirt. Beneath it I'm wearing a blue T-shirt with a possum in sunglasses in the center. Mars gave it to me as a gag gift for my last birthday, but I love it.

"Great shirt," Ellis says.

I'm not sure whether or not he's making fun of me so I just nod. After a circuit of the park Happy comes over and rests his blocky head on my thigh, tail wagging. "Life's pretty simple for them," I note.

"Has my mom told you yet?"

"Told me what?"

Ellis runs his long fingers through his hair, messing it up. "The lease is up on the shelter and the owners have decided to sell the entire property. It's being auctioned on May twenty-eighth."

It's a gut punch that leaves me gasping. "What? No! Trudy

will be lost without the shelter—it's her life's work. And what about the animals?" This means Growler is doomed. No other shelter will take him. "That's two months from now." And it's my wedding date. "There's no way we can rehome all of our dogs and cats before the sale." I don't say the rest—that more animals than Growler will be euthanized. My brain scrambles for a solution. "Maybe we can hold a fundraiser, buy the land and shelter building for Trudy?"

"A full city block, with four other buildings on it pulling in rent, that's zoned for apartment buildings or condominiums? It'll probably go for nine or even ten million." He nods at my ring. "Maybe your fiancé can buy it?"

"Hayden is a public school teacher." Helen comes over and jumps up on Ellis's lap, licks his face. "Take Helen home and one of the cats? She's good with kittens."

Ellis gently deposits Helen back on the grass. "Wouldn't be fair. I work long hours. That was one of Lizzie's reasons for having the affair—neglect. And apparently I wasn't a good communicator."

He rests his hand near mine. The urge to move my hand closer hits hard. But that's a normal reaction to a good-looking guy—I'm engaged, not dead. I pretend to need my hand to adjust Happy's collar.

"So how long have you and Hayden been dating?" Ellis asks.

"Eight months."

He meets my gaze with serious eyes. "Have you told him yet that you're having doubts?"

Panic ricochets through me. "No, because I'm not. Hayden is everything I've ever wanted. He's considerate, caring, and supportive. And we both want a family."

"And the whole starry-eyed, sexual chemistry thing?"

My cheeks burn. "We're fine in that department. But I'm not even sure that's what lasts in life. Hayden is perfect for me."

Ellis hesitates then says, "Got it. But one thing I've learned in both medicine and life? It's what people *don't* say that tells their real story."

My carefully constructed life suddenly feels like it's made of straw, and Ellis is the wolf about to blow it apart. "Let's head back." I slide off the table and quickly walk away.

Ellis gets a call just as we return to the shelter and thankfully has to leave for an emergency surgery. The next few hours are quiet, just me, and dogs that are grateful to play in the grass. And every time Ellis's comment about *what people don't say telling the real story* returns I shove it away. When I finish a few hours later, I pull out my phone and type "1 Hastings Street" into Google Maps. It's on Nob Hill, an area high above the water that has expensive hotels, old mansions, and stunning views of the bay.

I should head right home, see if Hayden still wants to go for a drive, but instead pilot my Vespa into the hills and easily find Olivia and James's old family mansion. It's an enormous Victorian made of wood and stone, asymmetrical in shape with cylindrical turrets, a wraparound front porch, curved windows, roof towers, and a slate-tiled roof. The sign out front says it's now the Mark Hotel and closed for renovations. Clearly no ancestors of the Edwards family remain, but still I climb the sweeping front steps. Olivia and James once ran up these stairs. I close my eyes and can almost hear their footfalls, the sound of children's laughter. I peer through glass front doors into a darkly paneled foyer. Beyond it I can see ladders, paint cans, and drop cloths.

"Can I help you?"

I almost leap out of my skin. The older man beside me didn't make a sound as he approached. His face is worn and only sparse tufts of hair cover a head speckled with age spots. Gray coveralls hang from a slight frame and he sports heavy work boots.

"Sorry to trespass," I say. "I was just doing some research."

"Hmm." He pulls a cigar from his pocket, lights it, and draws in the smoke, his face collapsing into a mass of wrinkles with the effort. He blows out perfect rings that hang in the air between us then asks, "'Bout what?"

"The family that used to live here in the late 1800s. There was a son and daughter who both ended up in France. Olivia and James Edwards."

"It's a hotel now—just changed owners. New ones plan to brighten up the place," he says. "Good, that. These old mansions were dark, dark, dark. Kinda creepy, if you ask me, despite the money those railroad barons and fancy doctors and lawyers that built here had." He rubs his narrow-set eyes. "Too much money makes people rotten inside. They think they run everything, get to decide who does what and when. All that matters is *their* happiness. Life is too short to live someone else's dream. You get that?" he asks, dark brown eyes glinting.

"Um. Sure."

He takes another pull off his cigar and the smoke slowly leaks out and billows around his face. "New owners are going to turn the stables out back into some kind of bistro. Those stables were a place of joy. A refuge. Shame to destroy that. We all need a safe space to be our true selves."

He forms another smoke ring and it hangs in the air between us.

"Off you go now," he says.

I give a little wave then descend the stone steps. When I glance back over my shoulder the porch is empty, save for a solitary smoke ring. I shiver. But it's broad daylight, he's a contractor helping to transform the old house, and I have a wedding to plan. I take the steps two at a time and speed back to Hayden.

Chapter Eleven

M y Monday morning meeting shows up right on time. Mrs. Tarroway has shoulder-length blond hair with artful highlights and wears a perfectly tailored blue blazer over a white shirt and jeans. She's still got her wedding ring on— emerald cut with a matching band of brilliant square diamonds. I usher her into the small conference room.

"Where's Brock?" she asks once she's settled in a leather chair.

"I'm here to get additional background information. Brock will read it, along with what you've already sent, then he'll call to talk over the particulars and once he's developed the best strategy we'll meet with your husband and his lawyer." What I don't say is that Brock is easing her into having her entire life ripped open by using a female paralegal to make her more comfortable.

She pulls out her phone, taps in a note, then says, "I'll email you possible dates." She sets the phone down and takes a deep breath. "Okay. Let's do this."

Since she's done a good job with the financial portion and I've followed up with the specifics I need her to collect, I focus on the personal. "Mrs. Tarroway, can you tell me how you met your husband?"

"Please, call me Laura. Martin and I met at casino night at

the country club. He saw me and handed over all his chips." She rubs her forehead hard enough to leave a pink splotch. "Stupid me thought it was cute."

"How old were you?"

"I was nineteen, a sophomore at SUNY Empire State College in Manhattan, working part-time to pay my way through college as a nanny for a family who belonged to the club."

I'm reminded not to judge a book by its cover. "How old was Mr. Tarroway?"

"Martin was forty and already a master of the universe in finance. The people I worked for told me to steer clear. Martin had been married twice and had a reputation for dating young girls on the side. But he swept me off my feet. I was a small-town kid from Corning, New York, struggling to make it through school and looking at a decade before I could possibly pay off my loans.

"Martin introduced me to a new world, taught me about wine, took me for my first fancy dinner, surprised me with helicopter flights over the city, trips to Saint Bart's, and expensive gifts. I dropped out of college because he wanted us to spend more time together. He proposed during a weekend in Paris. Cliché, right?"

"It sounds romantic."

Laura winces. "It was, actually. I thought I'd been transported into a fairy tale. Martin was my prince."

"When did things get off track?"

"When I gave up my education. Hindsight," she says. "The day I agreed to live his life was the day I lost control of mine."

I shift in my chair. "What did you study in college?"

"English literature. I wanted to be an editor at a publishing house." She takes off her wedding ring and spins it on the polished table. It settles with a hard *plink*. "Martin insisted we wait to start our family until I was thirty—he wanted me all to himself and available at a moment's notice. He had an affair when I was eight months pregnant with Maisy. I kicked him out of the house. But I was about to have my first baby, with no money of my own. So I forgave him and he promised to be faithful.

"The second affair was right after Britt was born. Martin told me it was partially my fault for gaining seventy pounds. My OB had put me on bed rest for the final trimester. The third affair started during my first trimester with Idabelle. I had hyperemesis gravidarum—extreme nausea. At one point I was hospitalized. Martin never visited. He was mad at me. We'd learned Idabelle was a girl and he'd desperately wanted a son. After her birth the doctor said that having more children would be dangerous for me so I had my tubes tied." She sighs. "You must think I'm a fool."

"I don't. Not at all."

Laura fidgets with the Rolex on her wrist. "When my parents divorced I was seven. My dad started a new family on the other side of the country. It made me feel . . . replaceable. I never wanted that for my children."

"How long have you been married?"

"Eighteen years, as of three days ago."

"What precipitated your husband suing for divorce?"

"Martin has been sleeping with our nanny, Sigrid."

"How'd you find out?"

Laura puts her ring back on. "Idabelle was playing with her dad's phone while he was in the shower. She asked Siri to call Daddy's girlfriend. I thought it was romantic and sweet that my husband still had me in his phone as his girlfriend. But *my* phone didn't ring. Sigrid was making dinner for the kids, and her phone rang. I thought it was a very poorly timed coincidence, but she made no move to answer it." Laura grimaces. "When I picked up her phone, I saw my husband's number. Sigrid had put him under the name *Big Daddy*." Her laugh is brittle. "It's appropriate—he's old enough to be her father."

"I'm very sorry."

"Yeah. Me, too. It didn't take much to get the truth out of Sigrid. She even cried. I actually felt sorry for her. They'd been screwing for seven months. A week later, Martin announced that he was leaving me for her and wanted a divorce. I'm sure he's hopeful for the son I never gave him." Laura blinks rapidly to keep from crying.

"Just to double-check, you signed your prenup?" I ask. Some men will forge their wife's signature.

"Yes. I was young and an idiot. And I watched Martin sign the postnup."

"How did that come about?"

"After the first time Martin cheated I made him sign one. He still loved me enough back then to do it. It was pretty basic. If he had a child with another woman while we were together, then he had to give me half of *everything*." She exhales. "I was trying to protect our children. But Martin is a brilliant man. He wasn't stupid enough to get someone pregnant. If he did, he would've made her terminate."

Laura's eyes flit down to my left hand. "You're engaged."

I blush. "Yes."

"Have one of your firm's lawyers draft a prenup that says you get every dollar if he cheats," she says. "Hire a private investigator to unearth any skeletons before saying *I do*. And talk to his exes. It might save you from becoming a cliché like me."

My mind flits back to Lydia. I have no idea where she is now. But I suppose I could try to find out. She might be able to put all my fears to rest.

Laura clears her throat. "Anything else?"

I flip through my notes. "Child custody? What's your best-case scenario?"

"I'd like primary, but my guess is that he'll fight me on it. Martin doesn't have the time, but he's a control freak and he's still got Sigrid to look after the girls."

As I escort her back through our lobby, a question pops into my head from her file. There were charges on Mr. Tarroway's card that didn't fit in with his usual expensive lunches, world-wide business trips, and high-end hotels. "What is Snips and Snails?" I ask while we wait for the elevator.

"It's an expensive children's store," Laura replies.

"Do you go there often?"

"The name is a play on the old rhyme, how *girls are made of sugar and spice and everything nice* while *boys are made of snips and snails and puppy dog tails*. I have three very girly girls, but it's a great place for gifts."

"Did you—"

"Don't let my situation scare you off marriage," Laura interrupts. "The truth is that somewhere deep down I knew Martin was no prince. I just wanted to be rescued."

"Would you take it back and do things differently if you could?" I ask.

"Absolutely not. I adore my children. I just wish I knew then what I know now."

"About Martin?"

"No, about myself," Laura admits. "I had a lot to offer, even though he was the successful one. I sold myself short because I was afraid I couldn't succeed on my own."

Back at my desk, I get a call from Trudy. The family that originally wanted Lucy have changed their minds again. They're willing to sign a contract, something Trudy demands from anyone who has waffled, and also commit to getting her hip surgery. They want to pick her up from the shelter tomorrow morning.

Brock keeps me so late there's no time to swing by the library and continue reading James's letters or to retrieve the silly note I left in the book.

When I step through the front door of our house that night, the smell of chili and fresh corn bread fills the air. A sense of calm envelops me. My mom rarely had groceries in the fridge and many nights dinner was a box of cereal with milk that had soured. Dad fed me fast food when I was with him. Grandpa did way better, but sometimes had to work late. That left the option of frozen dinners. So I really appreciate that Hayden plans out weekly meals that are always nutritious and delicious.

I greet the dogs, snuggle Lucy for an extra-long moment. "You're going to a forever home after all," I whisper in her ear so Blueboy won't hear and be hurt. In the kitchen, Hayden sits grading papers at the table. I sink onto a chair. "Dinner smells incredible. Thank you for cooking."

"My pleasure," Hayden replies with a grin.

"Guess what? Lucy has found a home." My smile falters. What's going to happen to Growler?

"That's fantastic! So why are you frowning?"

"I wasn't ready to talk about it over the weekend, but the

shelter lease is up, and the property is going to be auctioned. All our rescues will be scattered—some to kill shelters. And it's going to happen on our wedding day." I wait for his reaction, hope he'll suggest we push back a week so I can support Trudy and help with the animals.

Hayden hugs me. "I'm so sorry, honey. I know how much you love the shelter and Trudy. Is there anything I can do to help?"

I consider asking if we can switch our wedding date. "No, but thanks," I say.

"I have some fun news," Hayden offers. "Your research on the ring inspired me to add a new poem to our curriculum. It's called 'In Flanders Fields.' Written by a Canadian surgeon named John McCrae, who volunteered, just like your James did—"

"He's not *my* James," I quickly correct.

Hayden kisses my cheek. "I'm kidding. McCrae volunteered to help the war effort. He wrote the poem after his best friend was killed." Hayden shuffles through his papers and pulls out a page. "I think it'll make a real impact on my students."

I take a seat with Lucy curled on my lap and he reads the poem aloud.

In Flanders fields the poppies blow
Between the crosses, row on row,
That mark our place; and in the sky
The larks, still bravely singing, fly
Scarce heard amid the guns below.

As Hayden reads, I'm transported to a graveyard. Weak sun warms my skin. I watch the birds dive and envy their freedom high above the battlefields while the noise of bombs exploding only a few miles away mingles with the sound of gunfire.

"Sweetie?" Hayden pulls me onto his lap for a long hug. "I didn't mean to make you cry."

I brush the salty tracks away from my cheeks and try my best to compose myself. "It's just been a long day." But the truth is, that poem made me feel like I was actually there. I could smell the funk of wet earth, hear birds, see the crosses, and it made me unbearably sad.

Once we've eaten and tidied up the kitchen, we play a quick game of Scrabble. I suspect Hayden throws a few rounds to make sure I win. We go to bed early and when he traces the freckles on my right shoulder, his overture to sex, I almost pretend to be asleep. But then I hear Ellis's voice telling me that *my answer should've been immediate*, and roll over, tell Hayden how much I love him. Sex, for us, is like following a worn map. We know exactly where the road leads, but it's still fulfilling to reach our final destination. I do love him and I'm going to marry him. Slowly I drift off . . .

I walk through glass double doors that lead into what was once James and Olivia Edwards's childhood home. Inside the entryway, the walls are paneled in dark wood, the air is warm, and dust motes float in beams of light that filter through narrow windows reminiscent of the ones in the prison where Dad is incarcerated.

Feet bare, I step into a two-story foyer. "Hello?" I call out. There's no answer.

A massive chandelier rocked by an invisible breeze gently swings overhead, crystals lightly tinkling. I step from the polished wood boards onto a crimson-colored runner that's stained brown in spots and rough where something organic has dried and spiked the fibers. I hear a dog's muffled bark, the scamper of toenails, but no animal appears. My pulse quickens. Is the dog hurt? Should I look for him?

Sudden gunfire erupts and I crouch, cover my head, heart jammed in my throat. Two champagne flutes set on a polished table at the foot of a massive staircase shatter. In the distance, cannons boom. More artillery rattles the house and glass shards dance along the floor. Then silence descends . . .

When I look up, the old man I met on the porch at the Edwardses' old home appears at the top of the curved staircase and slowly descends. Gone are the ratty coveralls. He now wears an old-fashioned black tuxedo with silk lapels. The end of his cigar glows orange as he draws in the smoke. When he reaches the landing he stops and looks down at me.

"You can't get married," he says with a smile that reveals crowded yellow teeth. "Or you'll be as dead as they are."

It feels like my lungs are about to collapse. I claw at my neck, desperate for oxygen, and wake up in the dark, Hayden fast asleep beside me.

Chapter Twelve

I bring Lucy to the shelter the following morning. The Freemont family is waiting and instantly surrounds her. When their little boy cuddles her in his arms she rests her head on his shoulder, eyes still trained on me. That will change. Lucy has found her forever home. The experience reminds me of the reason I volunteer at the shelter—happily ever after is possible.

"She'll do well with them," Trudy says as the family drives off in the SUV.

"And Growler?" I ask.

"I think we both know the answer, but let's give him a little more time anyway."

"Ellis told me that the shelter lease is up."

Trudy gives a sharp nod. "Did he give you the details?"

"Just that the owners want to cash out. Can't you call and ask them to consider renewing the lease?"

"I've tried. They want to sell. Truth is, I've been holding them off for years. Even if they did renew my lease, the number would be too high to afford."

Reality settles like lead in my stomach. "I'm so sorry."

Trudy sniffs. "Me, too." She squares her shoulders. "I better get to work trying to find homes for as many of our rescues as possible."

I visit Growler for a few minutes, this time with a small piece of chicken. He creeps forward while I'm still near his pen, eats it, hesitates, and then grumbles as he slowly backs away. "Good boy."

With thirty minutes left before work, I zip to the library to remove the note I left and, if there's time, read another letter. I do want to find out more about my engagement ring but the jeweler who sold it to Hayden still hasn't returned my call. Before I enter the library, I leave another message at Westcott's. Maybe someone famous designed my ring, and going down that avenue will yield more results than visiting the Edwardses' childhood home or my research.

In Special Collections, a different librarian, this one as ancient as some of the books in the room, is quietly going through the room's rules with two women, several new people have their noses buried in books, Chester is in the same spot, as is the surfer guy still wearing the same gray Berkeley sweatshirt, and the woman with the gray pigtails sits beside him.

I flash my library card, lock up my backpack, snag gloves, retrieve Olivia's compilation of letters, then take a seat across from Chester. Resting the book on my lap so no one notices me retrieve the silly note I left behind, I discover that it's gone. In its place is a blue slip of paper. My heart punches against my rib cage as I slide the handwritten note free and start reading.

Dear Constance,

I cannot speak of your fiancé or whether or not you know him well enough to marry. I can only give you my perspective.

Love is a reflex for most people—they say the word to partners they hardly know, to children they might abandon, and spouses say it again and again yet still deceive each other. The word "love" has little value to me and I look to someone's actions to know their heart and my own.

Your fiancé's lies could have been ones of omission, or they also could be something more serious. The context does matter and I encourage you to find out more. If your fiancé is the right man for you, you can talk to him; share your fears and give him the chance to allay them. If you can't do that, how will you grow together? Not just grow old, but push each other to expand horizons and face new challenges?

As for you being nothing special, I disagree. You volunteer to help animals the world has forgotten and who have no power or voice. That means you're compassionate. Think about how when you were a little girl, you didn't tell anyone the time that neighbor dog bit you. Instead you worked to gain the animal's trust and became his only true friend. That is a spectacular thing. And if you are, indeed, quirky as your best friend says, then you make the world a more interesting place.

Why do you think so little of yourself? Was it something you were told as a child? Or did things happen in adulthood to you that took away your confidence?

In regard to your best friend and her concerns . . . I can only share this advice: You must not give up the things that are important to you in order to be loved. Life is a long road best traveled with someone who shares your passions or at the very least makes room for them, sees your light, and helps it shine even brighter.

My pulse beats like a hummingbird's wings. No one knows about Axel, the Doberman our neighbors kept on a thick chain in their backyard with only a thin plywood doghouse to protect him from the rain and cold. I was ten the first time I tried to pet him and he bit me in the thigh. I went home, cleaned the punctures, and never told Grandpa. Then I made peanut butter sandwiches each morning, cut them in tiny squares, and for the next month threw that treat to Axel as I passed. I was scared but somehow knew that Axel needed a friend as much as I did. Each time I stood a little closer until one day he ate the treat out of my hand.

From that moment on I spent as much time with him as possible. I'd sneak out on cold nights, find him shivering in his doghouse and cover him with a blanket, use my own body heat to help him get warm. During the hot summer, I made sure he always had fresh water in his bowl and if he looked too thin, I'd share my lunch. If the neighbors, a couple who fought so loudly some nights Grandpa called the police, noticed, they never said a word. And then one day he was gone, his chain strewn in the yard, spiked collar empty. I knocked on the neighbors' door and they told me Axel had bitten the mailman and they'd *put him down*. It felt like a piece of me had been torn off and thrown away.

My hands are trembling as I reread the note. How in the world could the letter writer know about Axel? I *never* told a soul. Invisible fingers brush a lock of hair from my cheek and a tremor rolls through me. Despite my efforts to remain tethered to reality, my wildly spinning brain makes the leap. Could this note be from James?

Mars's voice cuts in. *Constance, there's no way.*

But the note I'm holding *isn't* a figment of my imagination. It's real and so is the charged current dancing through my body. It's the same otherworldly presence I once felt as a child when I woke to see Grandma Hazel seated on my bed. She had glossy dark hair, a smile that looked like a secret, and when she kissed my forehead, my body felt electrified . . . the same as it does right now.

Ridiculous, Mars reiterates.

Quietly I tear a piece of notepaper free and write back anyway . . .

Dear J,

    I haven't thought about Axel in many years. He was truly my best friend when I needed one, and I've always believed I let him down by not being there to fight for his life before he was euthanized. It's one of the reasons I volunteer at an animal shelter—to be an advocate for animals who have no voice.

    You're right that actions speak louder than words. My fiancé makes me feel loved, safe, and wanted—that's what I've always needed. But beyond the lies I've discovered, I don't know any of his friends or his parents and he's evasive about their relationship. I worry there's more I don't know . . . and I guess I don't entirely trust my perceptions. In the past I have not been a great judge of character.

    You've asked why I think so little of myself and I've never really considered that question. Perhaps because it involves dredging up the past, which is something I try not to do . . .

Memories of my mother, always lurking in the back of my mind, jump to the forefront of my thoughts.

Why do you think you're so special, she rasps.

I was eight, waiting for my dad to take me out to dinner for my birthday. He never showed, but I refused to take off my scratchy party dress and demanded to know where he was . . .

over and over again. Finally, Mom yelled, *If you ever want to be loved, then shut up, take off that ugly dress, and go to bed!* She walked out on our family a few months later. Then Grandpa took over when Dad couldn't handle solo parenting.

I return to writing my note . . .

> I think my self-perception has to do with my mother and her abandonment. But I don't want to blame who I am as an adult on things from my childhood. Shouldn't I have gotten past that by now?
>
> I will think about what you've said, about giving up the things that are important to me in order to be loved. I believe my fiancé would want to help me shine brighter if I give him that chance. Maybe I haven't done so because I, too, am guilty of keeping secrets.
>
> I hope you'll write me again. I very much need someone who's not involved that I can trust to confide in.
>
> Sincerely,
> Constance

Folding the note, I wait until no one is looking and quickly tuck it into the first sleeve. Will James write me back? I desperately hope so. The air-conditioning in the library kicks up a notch. I untie the gray sweater covered in daisies that's wrapped around my waist and slip it on. My fingers shake a little as I button it. Still rattled, I take in the room to settle my nerves. Sunlight filters through the elegantly curved windows at the far end and makes the brass on the rectangular overhead pendant lights gleam. I slowly inhale and hold in the calm of muffled voices and the solidity of floor-to-ceiling shelves filled with neatly ordered books. Finally calm enough to continue, I pull out James's next few letters.

Dearest Olivia,

I arrived in Paris and now work in a giant building constructing the ambulances my fellow drivers and I will use to transfer the wounded. I toil alongside soldiers, but also a French nurse named Anna who has eyes the color of the Pacific . . .

An old boyfriend once said my eyes were the color of a starless sky. I'm not sure it was a compliment, but maybe they're similar to Anna's? Impatient, I move on to the next letter.

Dearest Olivia,

I have learned so much more about Anna. Her mother cleans homes and her father is a road worker, so far from my own life of wealth and privilege, yet I'm drawn to her. In the evenings Anna and I wander down cobblestone streets where purple wildflowers cascade down low rock walls and the fragrance of rosemary, a note in the perfume she wears, scents the air . . .

When I close my eyes, I can smell the rosemary and feel the cobblestones underfoot.

Dearest Olivia,

Being with Anna has a gravitational force. Last night, we kissed beneath a cherry tree laden with white blossoms and my whole world exploded and then began anew . . .

I trace my lips. They feel bee-stung, like I've been kissing someone for hours. The way James writes, how he expresses himself, makes me feel like I've stepped into his world.

"I'm Veronica," a woman near me whispers.

I recognize the older woman with the gray pigtails. "I'm Constance."

"Chester told me you're researching that gorgeous engagement ring by reading letters from a volunteer ambulance driver to his sister for clues."

"I am. Nothing about my ring yet," I say and stand, my knees slightly unsteady. "But James, the ambulance driver, met a French nurse named Anna. She showed him how to shape braces for the ambulances they're building, worked at a forge right beside him."

"Impressive," Veronica notes.

"James wrote that despite their different backgrounds he's never been so taken with a woman."

"Have they kissed?"

I nod. "He said his *whole life began anew.* He hopes they'll be stationed together, so they can *truly* know each other despite the uncertainty of war."

Chester looks up. "Holy hell. Even I think that's romantic. So the hunt continues?" he asks.

"I'll be back," I agree. "How's your search going?"

"It's really freaking depressing," he admits. "Every night when I get home my girlfriend asks if it's worth it."

"Is it?" I ask.

Chester runs a hand along his jaw. "I was adopted and I've always felt a bit adrift. My hope is that learning about my ancestors and where I came from will help give me more of a sense of belonging."

"Let's grab coffee sometime," Veronica suggests. "We can share stories from our research, cheer each other on."

I can't recall the last time I hung out with anyone new. Almost all of my free time, when I'm not at the shelter, is spent with Hayden or Mars. "That'd be nice." Suspicion wriggles under my skin. "Hey, have either of you read any of *Letters from My War*?" I ask then hold my breath. When they shake their heads, I'm absurdly relieved.

Mars interjects, *Come on! Do you actually think James's spirit is reaching out from his grave?*

Do I? Despite wracking my brain, I can't come up with another plausible explanation. No one knew about Axel . . .

I race to work, fill Mars in on my ring research but skip the part about James's note and writing him back. It's the biggest secret I've ever kept from her, but embarrassment about what she'd say stops me. There's a stack of work waiting for me, and I lose myself in a mountain of tasks that Brock continually adds to. Despite my desire to return to the library, he keeps me well past Special Collections' closing time. Once home, I give Samson some love, play a quick game of catch with Blueboy in the backyard, and then sit down with Hayden to a late dinner.

"Good day?" Hayden asks over a rotisserie chicken and red potatoes.

"The usual," I reply.

If your fiancé is the right man for you, you can talk to him; share your fears and give him a chance to allay them.

I push around the food on my plate and work up the nerve,

starting small to test the waters. "You went to high school on the east coast, right?" I ask Hayden. He nods as he chews. "Was it a good experience?"

He takes a sip of water. "The same as yours, I'd guess."

"Mine was pretty limited. We could only learn Spanish. I'd always been drawn to French, but my school couldn't afford two language teachers. And you had to pay extra if you wanted to take music lessons or be in club sports. Did yours have team sports?"

"A few."

A fault line zigzags through me. From what I read, Lawrenceville taught French, Spanish, German, Chinese, Russian, and Japanese and had teams ranging from fencing, lacrosse, and squash to water polo in their own Olympic-sized pool. Why is he lying to me right now? I'd planned to ask about his past engagement next, but can't bear the thought of him lying about that, too. My stomach burns. I'm such a hypocrite. My lies are far worse.

"What do you think about skipping the pizza cooking class next week and going mountain biking instead?"

Hayden laughs. "Are you trying to kill me before our wedding?"

He fell twice during our last ride and hasn't gotten back on a bike for months. "We could ride a much easier route, or even the waterfront trail then over the Golden Gate Bridge to Sausalito?"

Hayden polishes off his chicken. "The pizza workshop is being taught by Ken Forkish. It's a once-in-a-lifetime chance to learn from a master. And you love pizza, right? This way we can learn together how to make a great pie."

I do love pizza and we can always go biking some other time. Still, disappointment patters down like rain. I remind myself that Dad used to say he was a wild stallion and Mom wanted to put a bit in his teeth. Concurrently she blamed him for getting her pregnant and anchoring her with me. Trying to force people to do what you want only shoves them away. I clear our dishes, my back to him. "No worries. It was just an idea."

He asks, "Have you come up with your guest list yet?"

"Not yet." I return to the table. Samson winds around my ankles and I pick her up. She curls on my lap. Fear about what will happen to her once the shelter is closed pushes away my other concerns. Who will want a blind cat?

Hayden hands me a sheet of paper with his guest list—twenty people but I only recognize nine names. "Who's Kenneth Jones?"

"Another buddy from high school. He lives in Palo Alto."

"Sara Gold?"

"Habitat for Humanity."

I make a quick list—fifteen people and Hayden has either met or heard me talk about each one. Hayden sneezes three times and I put Samson back down on the bed she shares with Blueboy. He happily licks her face. Maybe I can find someone willing to adopt them together.

"Anything more about the origin of the ring?" Hayden asks.

"I checked out the Edwardses' childhood home. It was a dead end."

"That's too bad."

"I'm not giving up," I add.

"Of course you're not," Hayden chuckles. "I'm covering for Gareth while he's on paternity leave—he runs the robotics club.

Between my own class and being there for his I don't have a lot of bandwidth left, but I could work in some time to help with your research, if it's important to you?"

My nerves jitter. "It's no big deal. There's probably not much else to find anyway." I feel ashamed at his willingness to support something that matters to me while I'm sharing details about my life and fiancé with a ghost. And how can I expect Hayden to come clean about his past if I'm unwilling to share mine? It's time. "Hayden, I have to tell you—"

"Hey!" He spins to face me. "I forgot to mention what happened at work today. You know the student I told you I was worried about—the one who's seven months pregnant? She's decided to give her baby up for adoption."

I sit back in my chair. "And that's a good thing?"

Hayden nods. "She's only fourteen with little parental support. Now both she and the baby will have a better chance."

A question slips out. "If I'd had a baby at fourteen, given her up for adoption, and hadn't told you, would you call off our engagement?"

Hayden's mouth drops open. "I'd hate that kind of surprise, but absolutely not. Did you?"

"No. But I guess everyone has a line in the sand?" I venture.

"Well, you'd have to have done something *truly* unforgivable for me to break it off with you."

"Like what? Rob a bank?"

"No. That's a crime of desperation and a thief can be reformed. Like killing someone. Taking a life is indefensible."

Invisible fire ants sting my skin. "Sometimes families actually forgive the murderer."

"Ridiculous," Hayden scoffs.

It's hard to breathe. "Even if it was an accident?"

"An accident isn't murder. I'm talking about an intentional, aggressive act. Going after someone and killing him." He shrugs. "Anyway, it doesn't matter. We don't have to worry about it."

We go to bed early and when Hayden traces the freckles on my right shoulder, I pretend to be asleep. A few minutes later, he's lightly snoring. I whisper, "My mom abandoned me and my dad's in prison for murder. I support him because he needs me." Hayden doesn't stir. Earlier he cut me off and I wonder if subconsciously he knows I'm going to say something that might blow us up. Writing about my mother's abandonment to James has given me the courage to say the truth aloud. Maybe next time I'll even do it when my fiancé is awake. "Hayden loves me," I murmur.

Unable to sleep, I tiptoe into the kitchen and open my computer to get a jump start on tomorrow's tasks. But instead of working, I do a search for Lydia Elizabeth Benson. The first thing that comes up is her engagement announcement to Hayden *Carrington* Whittaker. I type "Lydia Elizabeth Benson Marriage" and two links appear. First, there's a wedding announcement in the *Chicago Tribune* in 2013 to a stockbroker named Caleb Barnes. Clearly that didn't work out because the second link is an announcement in the *San Francisco Chronicle* in 2015. Lydia married Ari Sproule, CEO of Sproule Enterprises.

I put "Lydia Benson Sproule" into LinkedIn. She worked as a sales rep for a TV station and then in marketing for an advertising agency. Her profession since 2015 is listed as *Influencer*. I grab my phone and put her name into the search bar on Instagram. I have an account to post photos of the animals at the shelter up for adoption. Over the years I've placed a lot of animals.

Lydia's Instagram bio reads: Influencer based in San Francisco. Loves high fashion, mimosas, ALL dogs, and spa weekends.

She has 1.5 million followers. I scroll through her photos. Most show Lydia wearing cute outfits by the pool, in a park, on an old cruiser bicycle, with stores and prices listed for every shirt, skirt, purse, or pair of sunglasses below the glamorous shots. I magnify her image. She has wavy, shoulder-length strawberry blond hair that's reminiscent of the style worn by old movie stars and is striking in a put-together way I could never pull off. Why would Hayden ever want someone like me?

Laura Tarroway's warning boomerangs back to me.

Talk to his exes. It might save you from becoming a cliché like me.

I slip into Lydia's DMs and write: Starting a campaign to place shelter dogs and cats. Looking for an influencer with a BIG heart that LOVES animals. Please DM!!!

Chapter Thirteen

The remainder of my night's sleep was restless. I dreamed of walking through a rocky field dotted with rows of simple wood crosses and stopped at one bearing James V. Edwards's name, a single red poppy sprouted from clotted earth. The dream morphed into a cavernous warehouse where men and women in uniform worked side by side building ambulances. When I opened the door to one of the trucks, it turned into a garden gate and I stepped into a field, the cool night air perfumed. A man reached for my hand, drew me close, found my lips, and desire pierced me. When I pulled back to see his face, it was Ellis. I tore free and found myself in a stark gray cell, dressed in prison blues. Hayden locked my cell door with a harsh clang and walked away. I gripped the bars, screamed after him to love me anyway.

This morning, I desperately need something familiar and comforting to get me through the day and head to the shelter before work. "Hang on," I call out when I catch Trudy struggling to lift a large bag of kibble into the red wagon she uses these days to move anything that weighs more than ten pounds. I take the bag and she follows me from pen to pen dishing kibble into the dogs' bowls. A corgi spins in circles before eating his breakfast—a trick learned from his owner, who loved him but died on her eighty-seventh birthday. "You're wanted," I tell him before moving on to a sweet vizsla named Gordie, whose face has gone white with age. "Eat up, your forever family's coming to get you tomorrow." Trudy's smile matches my own. We both love it when the older dogs get adopted.

"I forgot to inquire, did you and Ellis have a nice time walking dogs over the weekend?" Trudy coyly asks.

I flush, the memory of kissing him in my sleep still all too vivid. It was just a dream. "You do recall I'm getting married really soon?" Trudy's reaction to the news was supportive but a tad underwhelming.

She shrugs one bony shoulder. "You can't blame a mother for wanting her son to date a young woman who'd make him a better person."

"That's flattering," I say, "but he already saves lives. Why does he need my influence?"

"Everyone can use a little help understanding what's most important."

"Like you once said, I'm not his type."

Trudy grins. "You don't think he actually came on Saturday *just* to walk the dogs?"

Flustered, I focus on giving Houdini, a dachshund who somehow manages to escape every enclosure but never goes far, his food. I'm not interested in Ellis that way, but the idea that he's *actually* interested in me sends curls of heat through my body. I remind myself that being in love and engaged to Hayden doesn't just shut off desire when there's an annoying but hot guy around.

"I wrote to an influencer," I tell Trudy.

"A what's-it?"

"An influencer. That's someone who has a large social media following." Trudy gives me a blank look. "Influencers are paid to post photos of places, jewelry, clothing, or services and those posts are followed online by people—"

"Why?"

"They present an image that other people find appealing in order to sell stuff."

"And why would a young woman with a good head on her shoulders, and I mean you, contact someone who has the compulsive need to brag about her life through pictures and sell crap nobody really needs?"

I'm afraid I might not really know my fiancé and I need to talk to someone from his past to find out why he's kept so much hidden from me. "The right influencer might be able to help us place more animals before we're shut down."

Trudy lifts a patchy brow and the Band-Aid stuck above it from her last dermatologist visit crinkles. "Tell me more."

"The influencer I DM'd—that's 'direct-messaged' on Instagram—is named Lydia. She lives in San Francisco, loves dogs, and has over a million followers. Influencers need content," I explain. "Lydia can use photos of our animals that need homes *and* push whatever romper or pair of overpriced sunglasses she wants to sell. It's a win-win for her and the shelter."

"Has she written you back?"

"Not yet. But she's worked in sales and marketing so I think she'll recognize a great opportunity." The bigger question is whether or not I'm going to tell Lydia that I'm engaged to her ex-fiancé and try to find out what went wrong between them. It's an invasion of Hayden's privacy. But can I actually marry him without knowing the truth? Maybe I could've . . . before J wrote me. But now I'm not as sure.

I follow Trudy to the front office. "Where will the animals we can't place go?"

"They'll be divided between all the shelters in the city and the surrounding suburbs."

"But some of the dogs in the bunkhouse that depend on their companions will be separated."

Trudy nods. There's nothing she can say to make the situation any better.

When I get to work, Mars points out the circles beneath my eyes. I share that I've been dreaming about some of the things I've read in James's letters to his sister.

"Sexy dreams?" Mars asks with a wicked grin.

I tell her about the graveyard and warehouse but don't mention the kiss with Ellis or the prison cell—any sign that I might subconsciously be having doubts about Hayden will give her more of a reason to question him. "It's like I'm there," I admit.

"You've always had an overactive imagination," Mars points out. "Lately, because of your engagement ring and its connection to World War I, you've been thinking about the war, right? Not to mention all those old movies you made me watch in college."

I went through a war movie phase when I took a history course sophomore year. I made Mars watch *A Very Long Engagement* four times—about a young woman who travels into the dangerous no-man's-land during World War I in search of her lost fiancé. We also watched *The Officers' Ward*. It detailed the gruesome facial wounds in World War I that for some reason fascinated me, and surgeons' innovative techniques to give disfigured soldiers some sort of future. Neither of us understood

French so we had to read the subtitles, which drove Mars up the wall. Soon after, she turned me on to *Star Trek* and all its iterations.

"Do you ever get bored being right?" I now ask my best friend.

She grins. "Never."

With the wedding and news about the shelter's impending sale, it's true that my mind has been all over the place. I consider what I wrote to J, about why I don't feel special, but how it's unfair to blame it on the past, my mom. Mars's mom wasn't sure who her dad was and Mars never tried to find out. He didn't show up for her so Mars figured why bother. And with each of her mom's subsequent relationships and marriages, Mars's belief in happily ever after was chipped away until there was nothing left. But neither Mars nor I believe in playing the blame game. Mars would say *it just is what it is.* And I've come to agree with her.

"Do you think that if we'd grown up in more normal families we might see love differently?" I ask.

Mars twirls a pen around her thumb, considering. "Maybe. But that wouldn't change reality. I respect that you want to be married and I hope it works out. But love gets stale. People move on. It's easier for me to accept the truth and just enjoy the moment."

The idea that Mars will never give long-term commitment a chance worries me. I don't want her to be alone. When I look over at her she blinks hard, twice. The subject is closed. "Lunch at the food truck of your choice, my treat?" I offer.

"Nope. I have a much better idea."

Mars skips out of our office with the kind of wink that signals trouble. Some of her past surprises led to jumping out of a plane, getting a body piercing (I took my belly button ring out the next morning), and a flight to Mexico that neither of us could afford.

The intercom on my desk buzzes and I head to Brock's office.

"We need to get ready for the Tarroway meeting," Brock says before I even take a seat.

"Have you figured out a way to break her prenup?"

"She's screwed unless we go to war, and even then I'm not sure we'd win," he replies with a grimace. "I hate loser cases. Most I can do is try to up her child support. Don't feel too bad for her. She'll end up with more than a lot of women do in her situation—a car, enough to buy a little apartment in the city once the house is sold and she gets half the proceeds, and five years to figure out how to make a living before her alimony runs out."

"I still do feel kind of sorry for her. She's supported Martin for almost two decades and given him three daughters. *Girly girls . . .*"

"Constance?"

The conversation I had with Laura while we waited for the elevator zings through my brain.

"What is Snips and Snails?"

"It's an expensive children's store."

"Do you go there often?"

"The name is a play on the old rhyme, how girls are made of sugar and spice and everything nice while boys are made of snips and snails and puppy dog tails. I have three very girly girls, but it's a great place for the occasional gift . . ."

I started to ask her whether she and Martin went there to-gether to buy gifts for friends' children, but got interrupted. Breathless, I say, "I need to run an errand. It's about Mrs. Tar-roway's case."

"Care to share?"

"I will, if it pans out."

I run back to my desk, pull out the Tarroway binder to look something up. Twenty minutes later, I park my Vespa in Pa-cific Heights and walk through the doors of Snips and Snails. A woman in her early twenties, wearing a pair of bright green overalls, hair in braids, practically bounces over to greet me.

"Welcome! I'm Bonnie. Can I help you find something?"

"I'm here for my boss, actually, Martin Tarroway." I know from his credit card receipts that he bought $1,800 worth of clothing here in January. Over the past three years, there were at least thirty other charges at this store.

"Do you need to make an exchange?" Bonnie asks.

I scramble. "No. But he'd love me to get a few more color options."

"Of which item?"

"All of them. But he didn't give me a list. Busy guy," I ex-plain with an eye roll. "Could you look up what he bought? He was here on January second."

"Sure thing!" Bonnie goes behind the register, pulls out an iPad, and does a search. "Aha! I remember him now. They got some great items."

I throw a Hail Mary, gambling on Mr. Tarroway's arrogance and vanity. "Did he have Martin Junior with him?"

"Yes! Such a cute little boy—the spitting image of his dad."

My inner cheerleader leaps into the air. Gotcha.

"And his wife was stunning. Amazing body—I could work out for ten years and never look like that—and thick brunette hair I'd kill for." Bonnie taps her temple. "Her name's Rebecca, right?"

"Great memory," I say. Sigrid is the nanny he's marrying. So who's Rebecca? I reach into my bag, pretend to get a text. "So sorry, but it's the boss. I've got to run."

"Do you want me to pull the clothes, have them waiting?"

"Thanks, but we can do it together when I get back." I race out before she can ask more questions. Back at the office, I tell Brock what I've found, give him the name Rebecca and a description, and he makes a call, hires a private detective.

"How'd you know?" Brock asks.

"I didn't. But there were enough charges over three years on Martin's Amex from a shop called Snips and Snails that it caught my attention. When I asked Laura about the store, she said it was a boys' clothing shop. That she only goes there for the occasional gift."

His eyes spark when he gets it. "She has girly girls!"

"Exactly. I forgot to follow up—there's been a lot going on in my life. Sorry."

"Don't be. You came through in a big way." Brock rubs his hands together. "Their postnup says Laura gets half of everything if Martin had another child while they were married."

"She thought he was too smart for that. But he's always wanted a son."

"Way to go, Constance. You're a star."

A sense of accomplishment stretches my smile until it's too big for my face. "Thanks."

When it's time for lunch, Mars leads me out of the building

then left on a narrow street between Nordstrom and the Shoe Gallery that I've never walked before. She makes me close my eyes and takes my hand, forcing me to stumble along until we finally stop.

"Open your eyes," Mars commands.

We're standing before an enormous plate-glass window filled with stunning wedding gowns. Crystal bodices and jeweled veils twinkle beneath overhead spotlights. The name of the shop is etched in gold on the door: THE BRIDE STUDIO. My hopes soar, then take a sharp nosedive and splat on the pavement. "Mars, I can't—"

"You don't have much time," Mars interrupts. "You're going to have to find a dress off the rack that needs very little tailoring. Otherwise it'll take months to arrive."

"How do you know that?"

Mars pinches my chin. "I may not have your mad skills, but you're not the only one who can do research."

A little lump lodges in my throat. "You know that I can't afford a single one of those dresses and I'm going to find something to wear in a secondhand store," I whisper as she leads me inside the boutique.

Mars squeezes my hand. "I know, but that doesn't mean you have to skip the bride experience."

We cross the plush carpet past four separate seating areas with sleek couches and round pedestals set before three-way mirrors. Hundreds of dresses hang along the walls. I'm afraid to even touch them. A woman in a navy pantsuit approaches with crystal champagne flutes.

"Hello, ladies. I'm Marybeth. Which one of you beautiful women is the bride-to-be?"

She must say that to everyone. I raise my hand. "Me. I'm Constance and this is my maid of honor, Mars."

Despite it being noon on a workday, I take the champagne. The bubbles tickle my nose when I take a tiny sip.

Marybeth leads us over to a tufted couch and we set our flutes on the glass table beside a silver tray of iced white petit fours. Mars immediately pops one of the desserts into her mouth.

"First things first," Marybeth says. "Constance, do you have a style you're leaning toward?"

"She envisions white or off-white, sizable train, accentuate her long neck and collarbones. Constance has a killer body so don't cover it up too much," Mars says with a hand over her mouth. "Forget mermaid, that's trying too hard. And she needs one off the rack. Her wedding is a little over a month away."

Marybeth looks to me. I say, "My fiancé likes traditional things. Maybe something with a sweetheart neckline?" Mars makes a face but I ignore her.

"Is there a budget?"

Mars holds up my left hand and jerks her head at my engagement ring. "The sky's the limit."

Marybeth smiles so big her pink gums show. "Then I'm sure we can find something that will work!"

I give Mars a look as Marybeth leads me to a dressing room, where I sit on a brass chair. A few minutes later she returns with an armful of dresses. With her help, I slip into the first one, a Madison James ball gown in organza and tulle that makes me look like I'm heading to Cinderella's ball. I walk out to show Mars.

"Too much pouf." She waves me back toward the dressing room then pops another sugary treat.

Next up is a simple gown in ivory with a sweetheart neckline and no beadwork or sparkle. Hayden would love it. But do I?

Marybeth fastens the tiny buttons on the back then twists my hair into a loose chignon and pins it. I'm not someone who regularly studies herself in a mirror, but I take in my reflection and see a young woman with delicate bone structure, big eyes, a sharp jawline, and a slightly puzzled look . . . in a wedding dress. *I'm really getting married.* Marybeth leads me out to Mars, who doesn't even let me stand on the round pedestal in front of the three-way mirror before she sends me back to try the next dress. It's a beaded Maggie Sottero long-sleeve dress that gets a hard *no* from Mars even though I love the pockets.

"It's really comfortable," I say.

Mars makes a disgusted face. "That is *not* a priority."

I ask, "Who's the bridezilla here?"

I try on a dramatic high-low shirtdress that stops at midthigh and then falls into a ruffled train in the back just to make Mars laugh and we both crack up. Forty minutes later I've tried on twelve dresses, none up to Mars's standards, even the one with crystal stars woven into a sheer ten-foot train.

"We need to head back to work," I tell Marybeth when she brings in another dress.

"Just one more." She unzips an opaque plastic dress bag. "It's a sample we just got in from Margaux, and a steal at $999. I didn't even know we had it. Your friend Mars found it in the back." The excitement of trying on wedding dresses has worn off and I'm a little sad. I've been given a taste of what's possible, except it's not possible for me.

Marybeth slips a silk sheath over my head. "Cali takes old-fashioned wedding dress designs and updates them but preserves the romanticism," she explains. "This dress needs to be tailored. The cowling in the front should rest just below your collarbones and then it's open in the back and drapes to the base of your spine. Notice the gold stitching and that the ivory color has a faint rose hue." She sucks in a breath. "Whoa! I can't believe this fits you so well. But what do *you* think?" She spins me around to face the mirror.

I've been staring at a spot on the carpet and slowly lift my eyes. The dress is soft, romantic . . . and the cut accentuates my collarbones and curves while the pale pink perfectly complements my skin tone. My eyes fill.

Marybeth grins. "I thought so. Let's go show your friend."

I stand on the round pedestal in front of a three-way mirror and can't believe it's me. This is my dream dress, and I didn't even know I had a dream dress.

When I turn, Mars swipes at her eyes and says, "It's perfect."

"It is."

Marybeth steps forward and attaches a crystal tiara and lace veil to my head. "They're beautiful," I say, "but I'm going to wear wildflowers in my hair."

And then the clock strikes midnight. I force a smile and thank Marybeth. "I'll think about it. But right now we need to get back to work." I change and zip the dress back in its plastic cover. Marybeth tells me she can hold it for twenty-four hours before she takes the dress away. I tell myself Hayden wouldn't have liked it but don't feel any better.

Mars waits by the front door. "Thank you," I say and hug her. "That was really fun."

When Marybeth comes over to unlock the door and let us out, the dress bag is still draped over her arm. "I hope you have a beautiful wedding," she says and extends the bag.

I take a step back. "Oh. I'm sorry. I can't—"

"Don't expect a wedding gift, too," Mars says and takes the dress bag.

I'm totally lost. "What are you doing?"

Mars kisses my cheek. "I'm supporting your dream by using my travel fund to buy my best friend her wedding dress."

I start to say there's no way I can accept such an expensive gift, but recognize by the set of her jaw that I won't get anywhere. Voice catching, I say, "This is the most generous gift anyone has ever given me."

"If Hayden is truly what you need, then I'm ready to hold your bouquet while you say *I do*." Mars blinks so hard a tear squeezes onto her lashes.

On our way back to the office, a pigeon poop hits my shoe. "Disgusting!" Mars says with a look of horror.

I laugh. "Bird poop is considered a sign that mysterious plans will come to fruition. But I agree, it's pretty gross."

When I've cleaned my shoe and am back at my desk, I check Instagram. My friend request to Lydia has been approved and she's DM'd me:

Constance, I'd love to help the shelter's animals. Let's meet! Let me know time and place and I'll be there.

Chapter Fourteen

Brock is in court the rest of the afternoon. Mars skips out early for a dentist appointment and I can't stop thinking about James, Anna, my ring, and whether there will be another note waiting for me, so I wrap up, text Hayden that I have to work late at the office but will meet him at Delilah's for game night.

Molly waves me over to the library's information desk. "Constance, quick question."

"Yes?"

"I ran into Hayden the other day and he told me the game night regulars are invited to your wedding. So exciting! Is it a formal affair?"

"Wear whatever's most comfortable. It's in our backyard."

"Such a pretty space—love, love, love the xeriscape."

How does she know about Hayden's old backyard? "It's grass, actually."

"Oh. Huh. That's weird. Hayden was never big on gardening. Always said there were better things to do." Casually she adds, "I helped design the yard when we dated so we could spend our time cooking and going to wineries. Hayden loves a hearty cab and has great taste!"

I never knew they dated. Why wouldn't he have mentioned that to me at some point? And the Hayden *I* know would never spend a lot on a bottle of wine. I keep my voice light. "We foster dogs so the grass comes in handy."

Molly chuckles. "Dogs? Plural? That's weird. I never knew Hayden liked animals."

If she says *that's weird* one more time my head might explode. I pin on a smile. "Will you be able to make our wedding?"

"I wouldn't miss it!"

I hear my name as I walk toward the stairs. Veronica sits in the café, named Hemingway's, to the left of the atrium, with Chester and the surfer guy in the Berkeley sweatshirt he never takes off. She waves me over.

"Take a load off." She gestures at the large French press on the table and pours me a mug of coffee.

I don't want to be rude so I slide onto a seat and dutifully sip the hot brew even though a coffee anytime after breakfast means I'll have trouble sleeping.

"I'm Travis," the surfer says with a handshake.

"Constance—and it's nice to meet you. What are you researching?"

"My thesis is on the biblical motifs in the early paintings of Raphael," Travis says. "What you're working on sounds way more interesting."

My stomach dips. "Have you read any of James's letters?"

Travis shakes his head. "I'm a month behind on my dissertation. My wife is already pissed."

"You're married?" He looks barely twenty-five.

"Yup—high school sweethearts. *And* we have twins. I wanted to hold off until I got my PhD and a teaching position, but Mai didn't. I do love the little monsters. But I wish we'd waited—it's total chaos at my place."

Veronica says, "Twins are a handful. In my first marriage, I had three kids spaced two years apart and they still drove me up a wall."

"Are you married now?" I ask.

"I have a partner. We've been together four years. Met her at the College of Marin. I teach eighteenth-century poetry—Alexander Pope, Samuel Johnson, and the like—and Diane teaches theater." Veronica beams. "Her students have the highest acceptance rate to Juilliard of any two-year college in the country. Diane would like to get married, but I'm not sure."

"Of her?" Travis asks.

"Nah. Love her to bits," Veronica replies. "It's just that I've been down that road before, thought it was a forever thing. It'd be embarrassing to try and fail again."

It could be as simple as that with Hayden—he's embarrassed that he tried with Lydia and failed. "Does Diane know you were married before?" I ask.

"Of course she does," Veronica laughs. "Even if I hadn't had children, I wouldn't have kept that a secret. Diane has to love me, mistakes and all."

I need to make it clear to Hayden that I love him, *regardless* of his past. But will the truth about my dad affect how he sees me? Our conversation from last night comes back . . .

You'd have to have done something truly unforgivable for me to break it off with you. Like killing someone. Taking a life is indefensible . . .

I didn't kill anyone, but I've supported Dad despite the horrible things he's done. What if Hayden insists I turn my back on him? It would be hard for me to turn away anyone I've let close to me, especially my father. I refresh my coffee to hide the shine in my eyes.

"You good?" Veronica asks.

I opt for a partial truth. "Just tired. I haven't been sleeping well. Reading about James and Anna and the war has crept into my dreams."

"I can only imagine," Veronica says.

Timidly I ask, "Do you think that you and Diane are meant to be?"

Her smile slips. "Yes. Can't imagine life without her, but she's getting tired of waiting for me to commit. Truth is, she's threatened to leave me."

I venture, "James wrote that he hoped he'd have enough time to truly know Anna despite the uncertainty of war . . . but we know that he died young."

"It's tragic," she agrees.

"I haven't finished the letters," I add, "but it seems like maybe you have a chance that James and Anna might never have gotten?" Now it's Veronica's turn to blink back the gleam in her eyes.

"I take back what I said about my twins," Travis interjects. "I'm glad they came when they did, despite the lack of sleep, dirty diapers, and that every surface in our apartment is sticky. Nothing in life is certain, I guess. So bring on the chaos."

"Well said," Veronica notes with a tiny nod in my direction that warms my cheeks.

Chester has been very quiet. "You doing okay?" I ask.

"I found my great-grandmother. She was separated from her three children when the ship carrying her and three hundred other slaves docked in Charleston, South Carolina. How could people do that to another human being?"

My gut roils. "I don't know."

Veronica glances at my left hand then says, "Can I ask you something?"

"Sure."

"Why's it so important to find out about your ring?"

I take another swallow of coffee. "My best friend thinks I'm looking for a distraction."

"From what?" she asks.

I hedge. "I guess getting married is stressing me out. But I'm also incredibly drawn to the story. I didn't grow up believing in epic romances, that there's someone who can start your life anew with a kiss like Anna did for James." I flush at sharing something so personal and add, "I don't really think that's possible, but it's fun to read about."

Travis chuckles. "Let us know if the hero ambulance driver and his hot nurse actually hook up."

A sparkler goes off inside me at the possibility. "Will do. Let's get to it," I say and lead the way back to Special Collections.

The old volume is in the same spot and I bring it back to the only empty chair, at the head of the table. Pulse accelerating, I open the book. Again, my note is gone, replaced by a blue one. I glance around to make sure my fellow researchers aren't watching as I slide the note free with tingling fingers and unfold it on my lap.

Dear Constance,

I've thought about the lies your fiancé has told. Perhaps he chose not to share his school experience because it was a painful one?

I also went to a boarding school—it was my choice. I didn't have a happy childhood home. There was a lot of fighting, some of it violent. My father was a functioning alcoholic . . . most of the time.

Boarding school turned out to be difficult, too. After a family visit went awry, I became the brunt of cruel jokes by the other boys. Those experiences, coupled with my early home life, led me to create a hard shell—one of the curses of being a child of an alcoholic. We learn to hide our emotions, avoid conflict, and suppress our needs because they were once treated as irrelevant.

You are right that we must take responsibility for our actions, but wounds from childhood do leave a mark. As adults we have the maturity and intelligence to decide whether to let those scars determine our actions or choose a different way of life.

As for your fiancé's previous engagement, men handle rejection in different ways. Some talk about it, some bury it to avoid embarrassment, and others feel ashamed of their failure. I hope that eventually your fiancé is brave enough to share his past with you. I can tell that you have an open, kind heart and would listen.

Constance, it would be remiss if I didn't ask, could your own unresolved issues and secrets be part of what's casting your engagement in doubt? Or is it more than that?

Best,

J

My body stiffens at the last two sentences. I focus on the part about being the child of an addict. It rings true for me, too. I learned early on that conflict resulted in cruelty and that asking for anything, even for my dad to stay, led to horrible situations, like his arrest. I tear a piece of paper free and write my response.

Dear J,

Thank you for sharing about your childhood with me. I am so sorry it wasn't a happy one and that your worst moments were met with unkindness. I, too, have experienced the nastiness of bullies. They find the most vulnerable place inside you and expose it to the world. The only good part, I think, is that experiencing cruelty creates the ability to empathize with others. Clearly, by the compassion in your letters, that is what happened to you.

My childhood was not great, either, and there are things I haven't shared with my fiancé. You're right that my own issues may be clouding my judgment. Maybe when we have ugly secrets, we become suspicious that those we love do, too, and I'm unfairly judging him?

One of my secrets is that my father was also an addict—both alcohol and drugs. My dad used to tell me he loved me and then he'd disappear for days, months, and sometimes years. My mother never wanted a child, told me this often, and walked out when I was eight. The lesson I learned was that if I don't ask for what I want or need, then the person I love won't have a reason to abandon me.

I continue to think about what you previously wrote—about not sacrificing what's important to me in order to be loved. But isn't love about compromise? If I were dating a man who couldn't walk, I wouldn't ask him to climb mountains with me. Isn't it worth giving up some of my passions to ensure a happy marriage?

Right now my life is accelerating and feels like it's veering out of control. My wedding date is in less than two months but I've found it hard to focus on the planning. My grandfather has dementia—he's the only family I can count on and he's slipping away. I have a best friend who I worry will never find someone to love because she doesn't believe it's possible. And the animal shelter where I work is going to be sold—the rescues will lose their home. There's nothing I can do to save them and I feel powerless.

Yours truly,
Constance

As I fold the piece of paper, a rich scent once again tickles my nose. It's tobacco. Travis sits a foot to my right. The smell must be from his clothes. I lean over and whisper, "Do you smoke?"

He makes a face. "Never even tried a cigarette. Why?"

My nose itches. "Don't you smell tobacco?"

He shakes his head then returns to work.

A chill dusts my shoulders. I tug on my sweater, sneak my note into the book, then withdraw James's next letter.

Dearest Olivia,

Tonight Anna confided that she was once married. Sebastian was a childhood friend terrified of going to war . . .

I lose myself as Anna tells James about her past without embarrassment or apologies. My imagination builds scenes and creates three-dimensional characters, and all the sights and experiences of James and Anna's world—her smile, his touches, the scent of sandalwood soap that clings to his uniform, the flowers Anna loves, and their undeniable attraction—come to life within me.

"Closing time," Colin calls out.

Dazed, I look up, so lost in James's letters that the afternoon raced by.

"Constance," Colin says as he approaches the table. "I know you're researching your ring and reading letters about the Great War and wondered if you'd be interested in additional material?"

"Like what?" I ask.

"My great-aunt Agnes was also a nurse in World War I. She was an incredible woman whose father didn't support her desire for an education. She was part of a team that went overseas to treat the wounded."

The desire to hear another voice from the past instantly blooms within me. "I'd love to read about her." Colin hands me a printout with links to several articles and books. "Thanks so much." He tweaks his paisley bow tie with a pleased smile then returns to his desk.

"Any more clues about your ring?" Travis asks as he packs up.

"No. But Anna told James she married a childhood friend before he left for the front," I share. "She wasn't in love with him, but he was afraid and needed to know someone back home was thinking about him. Sebastian was killed three weeks later and Anna became a nurse to care for young soldiers who were lucky enough to survive the fighting."

"She sounds pretty amazing," Travis notes.

"James thinks so, too. He wrote that they've already shared their fears and dreams; that falling for her feels *inevitable*."

Veronica leans in, pigtails swinging. "Is it mutual?" she asks.

I grin. "Definitely. Both of them felt like they'd met each other before, which isn't possible. She'd never been to America and he'd never visited France."

"Maybe they met in another life," Chester suggests.

"Seriously?" I ask. "You believe in reincarnation?"

"Yeah, I do," he admits. "My ancestors deserve another chance for something better."

"I buy it, too. The twins' *terrible twos* have to be punishing me for something I did in another life," Travis quips with a belly laugh.

As we walk out of Special Collections and down the hall I ask, "Do any of you believe in ghosts?"

"When I was a girl, I saw my grandfather sitting on a rocking chair on our porch," Veronica says. "He'd been dead two years. I told Mama and she washed my mouth out with soap."

Chester pulls a look of disgust then asks, "Did you ever see him again?"

Veronica nods. "The very next night. He told me about a stuffed bear named Bartleby that Mama stole from her best friend. Grandfather said to tell Mama that story and she'd never wash my mouth out again." Veronica giggles. "You should've seen the look on her face."

"I grew up in my great-aunt's house," Travis says. "After she died, her favorite book kept appearing on the kitchen table. We'd put it back on the shelf and a few days later it'd be right back on the table. Dad said it was her way of asking us to remember her." He turns to me. "Do *you* believe in spirits?"

"I do. When I was little, staying at my grandpa's for a weekend, I woke in the middle of the night and saw the ghost of my grandma Hazel." It feels good to be around people who won't judge me if I confess to believing in something otherworldly.

"Constance?"

I whirl. Hayden walks down the hall toward us. "What are you doing here?" I ask.

His smile fades a bit. "You sound like you're not happy to see me."

"I just didn't expect you," I say and kiss him. "Everyone, this is my fiancé, Hayden." There are introductions all around and then my friends take off.

"I thought you were working late at the office," Hayden says.

"I finished earlier than expected and wanted to do a little more investigation on my ring before game night. But why are *you* here?"

Hayden leads the way down the stairs, his back to me. "Robotics was canceled so I decided to use my free time to check out the library archives. They have some old photographs from World War I that I photocopied to bring the Flanders Fields poem alive for my students."

Something feels off. But that's probably because I haven't told him about the notes, which is not fair to Hayden.

"How was work?" he asks.

I grin. "Actually kind of amazing. Remember that divorce case I told you about?"

Hayden nods. "Younger woman, older guy. He cheated?"

"That's the one. They had a prenup that gave her very little."

"But she signed it," Hayden recalls.

As we cross the lobby and head toward the front door, Hayden's hand presses on the small of my back. I search for the same sensation James and Anna had when they touched, or the ethereal feeling that sometimes happens when I'm reading about them, but while I feel a deep connection to Hayden, there's no gravitational pull or hint of magic. I remind myself that's not what I want. Stability is more important to me than a head-over-heels-in-love ride that will crash or burn out.

Hayden repeats, "She signed the prenup, right?"

"Yes. But she was only nineteen. Anyway, she had her husband sign a postnup after he cheated for the first time that said if he had another child while they were still married, the prenup was void and she got half of everything." I take a big breath. "Today I discovered her soon-to-be ex-husband had a little boy during their marriage."

Hayden whistles. "How'd you figure that out?"

My grin stretches so wide my cheeks hurt. "I picked through his credit card receipts and followed up on a hunch. My boss was really impressed." We go through the revolving door together and step onto the street. I turn toward Hayden, anticipating a high five or congratulatory hug.

"It all seems kind of seedy to me," he says then finally gives me a quick hug. "It's not your fault. Sometimes people are just immoral all around. Hey, did you find anything new about your ring?"

The resentment that's been simmering inside me boils over. "No," I snap, "but I did talk to Molly." I wait for him to say something, but he doesn't. "She told me that you two dated?"

"Oh." He glances at his watch. "We should hurry if we want to make the first game."

I'm stunned that he's just going to ignore the question. "Did you drive here?"

Hayden shakes his head. "I took the bus."

He follows me to my Vespa, climbs on, then says, "It wasn't a big deal."

I twist to face him. "How long did you date?"

"A year."

My body stiffens. "A year?" A police car races by, siren blaring, and I wince. "That's longer than us. Why'd you break up?"

"Different values." He reaches for my hand. "I was really young and, to be honest, I'm not proud of the way I ended things. Molly's a nice person, she just wasn't *my* person, and I never mentioned her because it was so long ago, okay?" He kisses my palm. "I love you, Constance. Always."

As I pull into the street, I recall what Molly said the day after our engagement.

Hayden is quite a catch. Word to the wise, though. Don't let him know that you know.

Hayden *is* a catch. But worry still digs sharp nails into my chest. Despite my desire to ignore it, I can't make it go away. Ellis's warning that it's what people don't say that tells the real story echoes through my mind and I vow to find out the truth about Hayden's past engagement when I meet with Lydia.

Chapter Fifteen

I'm shocked that Lydia is willing to meet at the shelter on Friday at 7:15 a.m., but she messaged that she was *super excited* to meet *ASAP* and *take photos for a cause!!!* Turns out she's *obsessed* with *early bird* hot yoga so it was a *no-brainer* to *swing by after class.*

In the midst of cleaning out cat litter boxes, stained coveralls over my work clothes, I hear the tap-tap-tap of Trudy's cane, look up, and see her leading a statuesque woman in black yoga pants and a gauzy white top my way. Lydia is even prettier in real life. A wave of insecurity rolls over me.

"Your influencer is here," Trudy says with a twirl of her cane. I suspect she's still not exactly sure how Lydia can really help us, but she's game to try anything.

I peel off my gloves and shake Lydia's perfectly manicured hand. "Let me show you around." I lead her through the cat room first, where she's taken with a black-and-white kitten.

"She'd match my Great Dane, Duke!"

I take the three-month-old out and put her in the crook of Lydia's arm. "Her name is Apple. She was left in an apple crate outside a putt-putt golf. Her littermates all found homes, but she's still available for adoption."

Lydia holds out her phone and takes a selfie with the kitten nestled by her neck, then hands Apple back. "I'll ask Ari. That's my husband."

"Does he like cats?"

"He adores *me*," she says with a little laugh.

As I put Apple back in her cage, Lydia notices my engagement ring.

"Oooh!" she gushes. "An antique ring! It's absolutely stunning. Mine-cut?"

"Yes."

"Wow. I love those ruby flowers. May I?" She takes my hand and examines the ring. "The etching is gorgeous. Clearly your fiancé has great taste."

Questions flit through my mind. Did he buy you a similar ring when he proposed? Why didn't you two get married? Did you break his heart? As we walk through the bunkhouse, Growler lets out a snarl that makes Lydia jump. "Sorry," I apologize. "That's Growler."

"With his manners it's going to be hard to find him a home," Lydia says. Still, she bravely stands at his gate despite the growls and takes a photo. "He deserves a chance, too."

We continue down the row of pens, with Lydia stopping to take selfies with the dogs. When she sits between two rambunctious border collies we've named Whitney and Houston, they both try to climb on her lap at the same time and the resulting video for her Stories is a laughing Lydia lying on her back while both cover her with licks. When she shows it to me I have to admit she's really good at this.

"I'd take these two home if my husband was game," Lydia

says as she stands and brushes herself off. "But I think they're a little too wild for him."

"Have you been married a long time?"

She stops to take a photo of Houdini. "Seven perfect years."

"Any secrets to a happy marriage you can share with me?"

Lydia holds up the stacked diamond-encrusted bands on her ring finger and grins. "Choose wisely. Just kidding. That's only part of the equation if you want it to last."

We wander outside to the larger play area and watch dogs playing fetch with the high school kids who volunteer before school. Lydia takes more videos.

"What'd you mean, exactly, by choose wisely?" I ask.

Lydia taps her perfect bow-shaped lips with an index finger. "Prewedding nerves?"

"I guess, yeah."

"You've come to the right person, then. I've been engaged four times."

"Four? How many times have you been married, if you don't mind my asking?"

She chuckles, "Only twice," then crouches to take a video of a white Yorkie named Sky leaping impossibly high to catch a red rubber ball. "The first man I was engaged to was *very* different from the guys I dated in college—all fraternity types. We went out for two years before he popped the question. I was worried he'd never ask and relieved when he finally did. He had all the right qualities, wanted kids, and we had similar interests."

"So what went wrong?"

"His parents didn't approve."

"Why?"

Lydia sighs. "My mom was single when she had me, worked

as a waitress in a diner. I had a degree from an okay college, some good work experience, but a lousy credit score. His parents didn't trust anyone from a different background. They thought I was a gold digger who only wanted his money. They tore me apart, then threatened to take away his trust fund if we married. I broke it off."

I don't know what to say.

"Not because of the money," Lydia adds. "I was young and stupid enough to think we'd be fine without it. I ended things because he didn't defend me. My mom only had a high school education, but she was life-smart, a damn hard worker, and taught me that I'm worth more than that."

One of the bloodhounds wanders over and Lydia hands me her phone. I take a photo of her holding the dog's ears in the air. She's very photogenic. "What about the second engagement?" I ask.

"My girlfriends and I went through a phase where we volunteered with various charities to meet guys. We worked with Habitat for Humanity for about a year—shirtless dudes swinging hammers," she says with a wicked grin.

Hayden used to volunteer for Habitat. We walk out of the pen and head back into the shelter. "So you met your next fiancé at Habitat?"

She nods. "But it turned out he didn't have the desire to be upwardly mobile. He worked hard, but it was a dead-end job. Despite loving him, I didn't find that attractive."

I wince. Poor Hayden. No wonder he kept the engagement a secret. But I'm also relieved. I can understand that his ego was bruised. And in time hopefully he'll share what happened. I no longer feel the need to push this. Still, I have to tell him about my dad. A tremor runs through me. What will I do if Hayden tells me I have to let Dad go? He was never a perfect father, but he's the only one I have, and he's worked really hard to get clean, better himself.

We wander into the washroom where a volunteer bathes a Rottweiler mix. Lydia snaps several photos then says, "You'll need to give me all the names and fun facts about each dog for my posts. I'll do one a day until the shelter closes."

Dread pools in my belly at the thought. "Of course. So how'd you meet your husband?"

"First, I dated then married a successful stockbroker. He couldn't keep it in his pants so we divorced. A year after, a friend set me up with my current husband—she's married to his brother. Ari is twenty years older than me. He's wealthy, generous, and freaking fun. And, I'm wife number three. He doesn't want to go through another expensive divorce."

I can't stop myself from asking, "Do you love him?"

"Of course." She tosses her hair, still perfect from the last blowout despite hot yoga. "There is only the happily ever after we make." She cackles. "I probably read that in a fortune cookie."

"Can I ask how many children you have?"

Her right eye twitches and she quickly rubs the skin beneath it. "None. Ari had two with his first wife and three with the second. He didn't want any more."

Everything is a trade-off, I think, and then wonder if I'm becoming as jaded as Mars.

After Lydia leaves I head to Growler's pen. He's wedged in the back corner and curls his upper lip. I open the plastic bag I brought, wave a chunk of hot dog in the air so the smell reaches him, then toss it into his pen and take a small step back. He doesn't move. I take two steps . . . and Growler creeps forward to eat it. "I know you were dealt a bad hand," I say softly. "But we don't have a lot of time left. I can't save you if you don't help me."

Chapter Sixteen

Brock is on a conference call with the partners, so I have a few spare moments and send animal bios and fun facts to Lydia then decide to search for a photo of Anna so that I can imagine her more clearly the next time I read James's letters.

Since I don't know her last name, the best bet is to contact the American Hospital of Paris in the hopes that they kept some sort of class photo of their nurses along with a record of their full names. I find their website and email the Department of Communication then return to my guest list for our wedding to make sure I haven't forgotten anyone.

It's so soon. In a week we'll send out the wedding Evites Hayden chose—a Scrabble-themed card with the words WE'RE GETTING MARRIED on a game board along with RING, LOVE, and FATE—some of the words we played on our first date. The memory that the word LIAR was also on that board jostles me, and I worry about how I'm going to escape this un-nerving second-guessing about my future. I have to tell Hayden what I've been keeping from him before the invites go out.

My email pings. The American Hospital of Paris has already replied. Quickly I scan the short note. There was a flood at the hospital in 1940. All of the photographs and records from World

War I were destroyed. Without Anna's last name, I'll never have a photograph of her.

"You look bummed," Mars says as she rounds her desk and drops onto the chair.

"Just hit a dead end trying to find a photo of Anna," I say.

Mars frames her face with both hands. "Guess you'll just have to imagine her as me, then."

It's very Mars to want to be the star of Anna and James's love story. "Maybe I want to be the glamorous war nurse," I joke. But we both know I'm more of a supporting character—the leading actress's buddy.

"What else is going on? I feel like I never see you out of the office anymore," Mars says.

I know she wouldn't say that unless it was really bothering her, and it's true that we haven't seen each other often recently. "I'm sorry I've been so busy. With the shelter closing and wedding planning I haven't had much free time." I wasn't going to tell Mars, didn't want to admit I was spooked, but in an effort to get my best friend to like Hayden more, I add, "I met Lydia."

Mars launches from behind her desk and plops onto mine. "HOW?"

The look of shock on her face makes me laugh. "She's an influencer. I DM'd asking if she wanted to help us try to place animals before the shelter closes."

Mars studies my face. "Wow. I didn't know you had it in you. Pretty sneaky—I'm so proud."

I chuckle then explain, "Lydia has over a million followers."

Mars crosses her long legs. "Not the point. You wanted to meet her. So you *are* having doubts." She blinks hard. "Did you ask her about Hayden?"

"In a roundabout way. Turns out she met Hayden at Habitat for Humanity. She loved him, but he wasn't *upwardly mobile* enough so she broke things off. My guess? It devastated him."

Mars considers. "That's pretty brutal."

Hopeful, I add, "You can see why he didn't tell me about her."

"Yeah. I guess. So your doubts?"

"Are gone," I say with a bright smile. But that's not true. I still worry a little that Hayden felt the need to lie to me about boarding school and that I haven't met any of his friends or know more about his parents and their rift. I also recognize that if I don't find the courage to ask for more compromise about how we spend our spare time my passions will completely fall by the wayside. But most of all, I'm afraid Hayden won't want me when I tell him that I have a father in prison.

Mars slides off my desk and returns to hers. She spins her chair around in dizzying circles. "How's the wedding invite coming along?"

She's trying to be supportive so I read it aloud:

"'Please join us as Constance Sparks, granddaughter of Ricky Trumble, weds Hayden Whittaker, son of Grier and Whit Whittaker, on May 28, 2022, at 171 Texas Avenue, San Francisco, California. Vows at 4:00 p.m., followed by Jack's tacos, sangria, and dancing to Radio Paradise. Dogs and children welcome.'"

"You're not using your parents' names?" Mars asks, her tone flat.

"I was worried that someone might recall the name Gary Trumble." Even though Dad's crime was thirteen years ago, it was front page of the *San Francisco Chronicle* and picked up by the AP—his victim was young and full of promise. Googling him would certainly yield results. There's nothing to find under

Ricky Trumble. Grandpa's name is actually Richard and that's the name used in all the articles about Dad's crime. I double-checked. Defensively, I add, "It's appropriate to have Grandpa's name on the invite. He's the one who stayed."

She sighs. "You still haven't told Hayden."

"I've tried."

"I get that telling him is a big deal. What I don't get is why you'd want to be with someone who wouldn't love you *regardless* of your parents. Constance, you're the best person I know."

"You don't know that many people," I try to joke.

Mars rolls her chair over to me. "Why can't you see what I see?"

If you ever want to be loved, then shut up, take off that ugly dress, and go to bed.

I croak, "How do you get the voices from your childhood out of your head?"

Mars takes my hands. "I tell them to fuck off. Seriously. If I listened to every stray man my mother brought home who told me to scram; if I believed my mom when she said I wasn't smart enough to go to college; if I thought I deserved what her asshole husband number two did to me when Mom wasn't home? Then I'd believe I don't deserve a best friend like you, or to take all the wild adventures I do, or that I have the right to enjoy the men and women who come into my life." Mars squeezes my hands. "I tell those voices to fuck off because I'm the only one who gets to decide if I'm worthy. And if Constance Sparks is my best friend, I damn well am."

J wrote that as an adult I get to pick whether my wounds determine my life or choose a different way. In this moment, I desperately want to believe in myself like Mars does.

Mars hugs me tight.

"Hey, are you going to bring the older guy you're dating to my wedding?" I ask.

She pulls away. "Nope."

She's been so secretive about him. Mars is only that way when she thinks her choices are particularly egregious. "He's not, um, married, is he?"

Mars rolls back to her desk. "He's going to leave her but he's super committed to staying in his kids' lives."

"Oh." I watch the muscles along her jaw work.

"Say it."

I shouldn't. "It's just . . . We both know how it feels to come from a broken family."

Mars scowls. "If he's unhappy and wants a divorce, that's not my fault."

Gently I say, "But if he cheated on her—"

"Then he'll cheat on me, too? Sorry my relationship doesn't meet your high standards."

She gathers several files and heads for the door.

Every muscle in my body seizes as she prepares to walk out. "Sorry," I call out. "I'm happy if you're happy."

When Mars turns her eyes gleam. "He does love me."

"How could he not," I say, my voice thick. "Do you love him?"

"I have for a long time."

She's putting herself in an impossible relationship. But I love her enough to let it go. "I'm going to tell Hayden about Dad."

"When?"

"Hayden has parent conferences tonight and won't get home until late. Tomorrow night. I promise."

Reception buzzes. Mrs. Tarroway has arrived. Her husband

is already seated with his lawyer in the large conference room. I grab the binder of credit card receipts from Martin's Amex, each Snips and Snails charge circled in red. Brock hasn't told Laura what we've discovered. Sometimes, desperate people do desperate things that screw up our work.

I steel myself for the high-stakes emotional battle we're about to face and can't help but compare this moment with telling Hayden the truth about my family. Just like what Brock's about to do in the conference room, I, too, am going to drop a bomb. The difference is that I have no idea who will be destroyed when it detonates.

Chapter Seventeen

Through the glass wall of the conference room, I see that Martin Tarroway is seated on the far side of the table, a silver-haired lawyer named Daniel Flint to his right. Brock said Daniel is the top divorce attorney in the city and he looks the part in a perfectly tailored gray suit, red tie, and flashy cuff links. We file into the room, Brock first, then Laura, then me, and take our seats across from them. I study Martin—white button-down, blue suit jacket, jeans, close-set brown eyes, a narrow nose, and thin lips. He's well-preserved for his age, but his closely cropped brown hair has the helmetlike look of a dye job.

"Thank you for joining us," Brock begins.

"This isn't necessary," Martin states with the air of a man used to commanding attention. "I'm prepared to be more than generous with my wife."

Brock smiles. "Why don't you lay out what that means for Mrs. Tarroway?"

Daniel puts a hand on his client's arm. "We'd rather you fire the opening shot."

"We'd rather not," Brock says, still smiling. "After all, your client is the one suing for divorce."

Daniel clicks open his sleek leather briefcase, withdraws some paperwork, and slides it across the table. "As you can see, Martin will allow Laura to stay in the family home *instead* of selling his half, until the children are eighteen. She can keep her Mercedes *and* the minivan, and he'll pay substantial child support, plus add a fund for any *domestic* vacations she may want to take with the children, pending his approval."

"Domestic?" Laura asks.

Daniel ignores her and continues. "And, as stated in the original prenup, Laura will receive alimony for five years."

Laura looks from Daniel to Martin. "We've been married almost two decades. I left college before graduating, had our children, supported your business. I *loved* you." There's anger in her voice, but also a deep tone of hurt and betrayal.

Martin crosses his arms and says, "And I provided a *very* good lifestyle."

Brock lightly touches Laura's hand. "That's quite generous," he says to Daniel, "but Mrs. Tarroway would prefer to have *half* of *all* the assets."

"If wishes and *but*s were candy and nuts, we'd all have a Merry Christmas," Daniel remarks with an unctuous smile. "Let's be reasonable. Your client signed a prenuptial agreement. I'm the one who drafted it. There are no loopholes."

"Except for the postnup," Brock says.

"Against my better judgment," Daniel agrees. "But when a client is in love there's no stopping him. Regardless, that won't come into play."

"This doesn't have to be high drama, Laura," Martin drawls. "Things didn't work out for us, but we had a great run. It's time to move on. I wish you the best, honey. Sincerely."

Brock pulls out a folder and slides it across the table.

"What's this?" Daniel asks.

"Why doesn't your client tell us?" Brock suggests.

The photographs taken by the private detective Brock hired are inside. Martin sighs like we're wasting his valuable time, then opens the folder. I slide to the edge of my seat and Laura does, too. Martin's hand starts to shake as he goes through each shot: his little boy at the park in a shirt with a Snips and Snails logo on the front pocket; eating a cupcake in his mother's grocery cart; walking into a Montessori school; and having lunch with Martin Senior at McDonald's. The child is, indeed, the spitting image of his dad.

"You have a son?" Laura asks, like she can't quite believe it.

"Martin Junior," I say.

Laura presses a hand against her stomach like she's just been punched and then bit by bit sits up straight, squares her shoulders.

"Your former assistant, Rebecca, didn't want to talk to our detective at first. But once she understood that the child support you give her is far less than she's entitled to, she was a regular chatterbox," Brock explains.

Martin's face has gone a dark red that can't be healthy for a man his age. "I'm paying you four hundred an hour," he says to Daniel through gritted teeth. "Say something."

"Why don't we meet again in a week to talk about the division of assets," Brock suggests. "Mrs. Tarroway plans to be reasonable about stocks, homes, paintings, and insurance policies. In the end, her biggest concern is making this as smooth and painless a transition as possible for her daughters."

Laura leans in. "I'd like to say something to my husband."

Martin rolls his eyes, but she doesn't let his obvious disdain stop her. "You said you loved me, and I believed you. But what you said never really aligned with what you did." Color rises to her cheeks. "It's not just your fault, though. I let what I wished for blind me. But I won't make that mistake again. I do plan to be reasonable, Martin, for our girls' sake. But don't confuse my love for them with softness or vulnerability on my part. I *will* take half of everything we've built together. I deserve it."

After they've left, Laura thanks Brock profusely. "I'd like to take the credit," he says. "But it was Constance's attention to detail and hard work that led to the discovery of Martin's son. She didn't give up—she took charge and I just followed her lead."

There have been instances when Brock or one of the partners complimented me on a job well done. But this is one of only a handful of times I've actually felt truly proud of my work at the law firm. Laura wasn't entirely a victim but she was definitely the underdog, and I'm a big part of giving her a chance to begin again.

Laura's eyes glisten. "You've both changed my life—my daughters' lives, too. Thank you doesn't seem like enough."

I walk her to the elevator and press the down button.

Laura blows out air like an athlete getting ready to race. "Now the hard work begins. I have to figure out who I am, and the person I want to become—for my girls *and* me. I should've taken the time, done that first."

When she's gone I lean against the wall to steady myself. Am I racing down the same path Laura once took? I'm going to tell Hayden the truth about my family. But five, ten, or twenty years from now will I look at what I've given up to make Hayden happy, like my work at the shelter, which he clearly wants to curtail, or the mountain biking that was always my refuge, and resent him? Worst of all, will I have turned into someone I don't recognize?

Chapter Eighteen

The rest of the day goes by in a blur of calls and paperwork. That night Hayden has his parent-teacher conferences so I spend a quiet evening printing out the articles Colin suggested and discover that his great-aunt was part of a group called the Women's Oversea Hospitals Unit, which was supported by the National American Woman Suffrage Association. They staffed hospitals in France during World War I. I drift off reading about how the goal of this band of women was not only to help the war effort, but also to prove that they had the same courage, abilities, and intelligence as their male counterparts. They wanted to be treated equally in their profession and to gain the vote.

When the alarm on my phone goes off in the morning, I discover that Hayden has piled my papers on the coffee table, slipped off my shoes, and covered me with a down comforter. I hear him rustling around in the kitchen.

"Hey there," he says and steps onto the back porch carrying two steaming mugs. He hands me one. "You were sleeping so soundly that I decided not to wake you when I got home."

I sit up on the couch and gratefully sip the coffee. He's added a drop of vanilla almond milk, his favorite. My brain still feels a little fuzzy. Once again my dreams were filled with images of

World War I battlefields, mixed in with Lydia dressed like Little Red Riding Hood complete with a basket bizarrely filled with kittens. She wore my engagement ring and Dad, in a wolf's costume, was chasing her to get it back.

Hayden nods at the pile of papers. "Work?"

"Actually, I went down a rabbit hole reading about how US suffragists sponsored a group of women to help wounded soldiers in France during World War I."

"Wow," he says with a little laugh.

"Did you know that in the early 1900s only about six percent of US physicians were women?"

Hayden sits down beside me. "I did not."

"They were only allowed to treat women and children and the US War Department wouldn't hire women doctors. But the French were so desperate for help that they let female surgeons operate on their wounded soldiers. That changed how women were seen in the world."

"Super cool," Hayden says then takes a swallow of coffee. "So the parent-teacher conferences went well last night. Although Meryl Falton's mother was a piece of work and asked me to change her grade."

I feel a scratch of annoyance. He's not at all interested in my research, didn't even ask me *why* I was doing it. But is that fair? Teacher conferences are a big deal and it's not like we have to be fascinated by the same things. Still, I can't help but think about Laura Tarroway and how after almost two decades she now has to find herself again. I glance at the clock. "Crap. Gotta get dressed or I'll be late to the shelter."

"Be late and I'll make waffles," Hayden wheedles. He wraps an arm around my waist and pulls me close. Blueboy trots over from his bed to get in on the cuddle, but Hayden pushes him away with his foot then kisses my neck. "We didn't get to spend last night together."

I know Hayden wants me to stay; there's a tension just beneath the surface and I feel the tug of his desire. Normally I'd give in, but today of all days it's not possible. And he's not being fair. I slide free and head to our bedroom, calling over my shoulder, "Sorry. Trudy needs me."

"Lucky for me I won't have to share you with her for much longer."

His words sting even though I'm sure he doesn't want the shelter to close.

Hayden pops his head into the bathroom. "I'm really sorry. I didn't mean—"

"I know," I say and manage a smile around my toothbrush. After quickly dressing, I rush into the front hall to the wooden cubbyholes I asked Hayden to build for us. Before I moved in, there was a bench strewn with his wallet, keys, and articles of clothing and he was always searching for something. Now everything has its proper place. Hayden was also very happy to have me organize his pantry so everything he needs to cook is now labeled in plastic containers, including his spices. Blueboy and Samson trail behind me as I take my coat off a hook then slide my keys and backpack from the allotted spots.

Hayden meets me at the front door and helps slip the backpack straps over my shoulders. "You look nice," he says.

"Thanks. My usual stuff was in the wash." A sweatshirt and jeans are my go-to for Saturday dog walks but today I'm in a red jersey skirt and a camisole beneath an off-white sweater with the outline of a polar bear painted in black on the back that

Mars finds particularly egregious since it looks like a six-year-old did it. She doesn't understand that's what makes it special. "What're you doing while I'm at the shelter?"

Hayden wiggles his eyebrows. "A secret project."

I frown. I'm not a fan of surprises, either.

Hayden holds up both hands like he's being arrested. "It's not a crime, promise! It's a gift. You doing all right?"

"I'm good." The truth, though, is that I'm the one who's doing something wrong. But tonight he'll know everything. My insides drop like I'm inside a plummeting elevator.

Hayden presses, "You seem a little . . . preoccupied. Usually on Friday nights we download our week. Sorry we didn't have the chance last night, but was yours okay?"

I consider telling him about Laura Tarroway and the result of her divorce case. But he wouldn't be excited for her, or my part in that success. I remind myself yet again that he's entitled to his opinion, but it does bother me that I can't share my wins with him. "You're right," I admit, "I am distracted. Sorry. It's just hard to stop thinking about the animals at the shelter and what's going to happen when it gets sold. And Grandpa is slipping, saying strange things." I wait to see if Hayden will jump in. But he just hugs me and holds on a few seconds longer than usual.

"Are you good?" I ask.

Hayden tucks an escaped lock of hair behind my ear. "You're going to think I'm being ridiculous," he says, "but sometimes I'm afraid that the rug will get pulled from under our feet; that I'll lose you."

In this moment I realize that he's afraid of being abandoned, too, and that vulnerability makes me love him more. "I'm not going anywhere," I promise. "But tonight we need to talk about some stuff."

"You sound worried." Hayden squeezes my shoulders. "Talk now?"

I'm halfway there. But it's the second part that might end us. "Can't. I'm already late. But I promise we'll talk about it tonight." A quick kiss and I'm out the door.

I ride my Vespa to the BART station at Civic Center, park, then take the Red line to El Cerrito, transfer to a bus, and get off at Francisco Boulevard East and Main Street. From there it's a short walk to my final destination. The entire journey takes one hour and forty minutes, but I arrive in an alternate universe.

San Quentin is just north of San Francisco. When I first heard that was where Dad would serve his sentence, I researched the place and was shocked to learn that it was actually built by the inmates, who slept on a ship at night until the prison was completed. Now it houses almost four thousand men on a peninsula that overlooks the bay. Inmates can see the outside world through the bars—cars, office buildings, sailboats, barges, apartments, and homes—but they might as well be on another planet.

I was twenty-one the first time I passed through San Quentin's gates and arrived at the monolithic yellow facility with dirt-brown accents, surrounded by thick walls and barbed razor wire. Grandpa came with me. He barely looked at his son, spoke in monosyllables, and didn't hug him hello. I held Dad's hand the whole time to make up for it. And I hugged him extra hard at the end of the visit after Grandpa walked away without saying goodbye. My grandfather never came to the prison again, but for eleven years I've visited Dad three times a year.

Inside the prison, I wait in line for the metal detector behind a mom with three children—a teen, tween, and toddler, all dressed their best. There are a lot of rules to follow when you visit an inmate. Visitors aren't allowed to wear blue denim because that's the color of the inmates' clothes. We also can't wear sage green, camouflage patterns, or tan shirts because that's what the guards wear. Bras can't have underwire as visitors could sneak the wire to a prisoner to be used as a weapon. That's why I have a camisole on under my white sweater. And my long red skirt adheres to the rule that women can't expose more than two inches above our knees when we stand.

When it's my turn, I put ten dollars in quarters into a plastic bin and pass through the metal detector. Then a female officer directs me to hold out my arms and stand with my legs wide. This part always makes me feel violated, even though I know the inmates go through much worse.

Dad waits in a green plastic chair at a table for two that's bolted to the white linoleum floor. The room is already filled with people visiting. Inmates in blue hold babies, laugh with their wives, girlfriends, mothers, fathers, brothers, and sisters. If it wasn't for the guards scattered through the room and the gates, barbed wire, and bars, it could be a scene from lunch at a shopping mall's food court. Dad pops to his feet when he sees me. He looks older every time I visit and his hair, threaded with gray, has receded farther. There are bags beneath his eyes and when we hug I can feel his rib cage.

"Constance! You're a sight. Pretty as a painted pony." He gestures to a chair and we sit.

When I was seven, Dad took me to the county fair. He played games to win prizes—a goldfish we named Bill, and a stuffed panda. We ate cotton candy, corn dogs, and saltwater taffy. He let me ride the carousel atop a beautiful black pony with a green saddle and called me *pretty as a painted pony* before he stepped off the ride. He watched from a bench as I spun in circles. Nausea nibbles at me.

"Do you remember the fair?" I ask.

"'Course I do. I won a goldfish and then you rode that carousel. Couldn't get my girl off that thing."

The truth, long buried, creeps into the light despite my desire to keep it locked away. I wanted to get off that ride after a few minutes but was afraid to climb down from the moving horse. Dad didn't respond to my frantic waves each time the carousel whirled by. After I threw up, a nice lady helped me off the ride.

Dad squeezes my hand. "I remember all the good times, especially your ballet shows at the YMCA."

One summer Grandpa put me in dance classes. He bought me pink ballet slippers, a black leotard, and white tights. The slippers were used, but I thought that made me look like I'd been dancing longer than the rest of the kids. Dad came to one of my recitals. A trickle of sweat slides between my shoulder blades.

"You okay, hon?"

I hold old memories at bay and chuckle. "I was a terrible ballerina."

Dad chuckles. "Yeah. But you tried harder than the rest of those brats."

"Do you want a coffee and some food?"

"Please."

I use my quarters to get several packages of chips and cupcakes from the vending machine then wait behind a gray-haired woman with a stooped back to get coffee. She has trouble figuring out how the machine works so I help her then return with two cups of weak coffee and watch Dad take a careful sip. "You look thin," I venture.

"Just off my appetite with the hearing coming up. Can we go over it again?"

A few months ago he went through the process, but I understand how badly he wants to do everything right. "Sure. There will be six members of the parole board. One member of the victim's family will be allowed to speak. Someone from the prosecutor's office can also give a statement," I explain. "Then the board will read my letter and it'll be your turn to make a statement about why you should be paroled. They'll want to know that you've accepted your guilt."

"If the boy hadn't gone for his phone, I wouldn't have tried to grab him," Dad says.

The muscles along my neck instantly knot. "That's not—"

"I know, I know. I have to say the damn words. I've been practicing. Take a listen?"

Inside I squirm. "Sure."

He folds his hands on the table and leans in. "Thirteen years ago I was an alcoholic and drug addict and my only thoughts were about how to catch my next high. I was a selfish and very mean man when I was running dry—that's what addiction does to you.

"In February of 2010 I went into the Quik-Mart in Oakland to grab some money. Carter Mitchell was the cashier that day. I had a small knife and demanded what was in the till. The poor kid was terrified and pulled out his phone to call for help. I leapt over the counter to stop him. I was so messed up with the drugs, so desperate for a way to buy more, that I launched too hard. Carter Mitchell's head hit the counter and it killed him. *I* killed him."

Dad's eyes fill with tears and a surge of hope buoys me. At his last parole hearing he didn't clearly admit his guilt, instead claiming, like he did at trial, that Carter's death was an accident.

"Carter didn't deserve to die. And I should've been found guilty. I've worked hard to be a better man in prison, attended Alcoholics Anonymous, gotten my chips, and taken anger management workshops. I'm in a prayer group, and I'm proud to share that I've gotten my college degree, despite some learning disabilities. I also try to give back by working in the prison infirmary to help those even less fortunate than me.

"As the parole board, I know that your number one priority is to protect the public from convicts. I swear to you that I understand that addiction and a tough childhood led to my crime and that I'll stay clean and never reoffend should you grant me parole."

"That's really good, Dad."

He beams. "Here's the part I left out last time."

I tense.

"My daughter loves and supports me and she has committed to doing *everything* necessary to make my transition successful, including housing, transport to meetings with my parole officer, and rides to my job."

All the oxygen has been sucked out of the room. There's no way I can provide the kind of financial support he'll need if he gets out, let alone a place to live and transportation. And Hayden would never be okay with any of it. I grip the sides of my head. "Dad, we need to talk about—"

"Holy hell," he suddenly shouts. A guard takes a step closer and Dad gives an apologetic wave. He reaches for my left hand and examines my engagement ring. "That is one *fantastic* ring!"

Crap. I'd turned the diamond to the inside but it spun to the front. "Thanks."

"That diamond is gigantic!"

"It's not real," I hear myself say.

"Shame. Maybe when I get out, hopefully damn soon, your man and me can do odd jobs together so he can afford the real deal."

I smile but my face is numb. We pass the next hour going over his statement again and eating stale chips and pretzels.

"How's your gramps?" Dad asks when I return with his third cup of coffee.

"Good."

"Still living the high life with that family?"

"It's not exactly the high life. Rosa and Marcio have a small home and take care of other people, too."

Dad takes a swallow of coffee. "I just wish the old man would forgive me."

We have this conversation every visit. "He loves you in his own way."

"He's not gonna live forever," Dad says with a sad shake of his head. "We'll both be sorry if, on his deathbed, we haven't made peace."

The bell that ends visiting hours rings and we quickly hug then I join the line of visitors filing out of the room. They give last waves to their loved ones and some of the children cry. I watch Dad join the prisoners being taken into a room to be strip-searched for any illegal contraband brought in by visitors before returning to their cells. *Will he be out in a month or two?* Fear gnaws at me, but it's not Dad's fault I haven't told Hayden the truth. Time has run out. Hayden will know everything tonight. *And then?*

On the walk back to my bus, I fall in step with a woman carrying a toddler.

"Good visit?" the woman asks as she shifts the baby to her other hip.

"Yes."

"Your man getting out soon?"

"My dad. His second parole hearing is coming up."

"What're his chances?"

My pulse quickens. "Hard to say."

"My boyfriend has his third parole hearing in five months. Truth be told, I don't want him to get out."

We cross the street together. "Why not?"

"He's a mean drunk with a nasty right hook. Had to call the cops a bunch of times."

"Then why do you visit?"

She gives her baby a cracker to snack on while we wait for the bus. "When he's on the inside he's sweet as pie. He tells me he's a changed man, but I'm no fool. First time I say *no* to money, sex, whatever, he'll paint the floor with my face."

"So if he gets out?"

She kisses the top of her child's head. "I'll have our bags packed."

Chapter Nineteen

It's only a few blocks from the BART station to where I parked my Vespa. If I hurry, I can still go to the shelter, give Growler a treat, then walk a few dogs before heading home. I round the corner and discover a river of water flowing down the gutters and a clot of maintenance workers in orange vests. A water main must've broken.

"You'll have to walk around," a slightly built young guy says. He points to the left and I turn toward a narrow street.

"Off you go now," he calls as I walk away.

The phrase reminds me of something, but when I look back to figure out what, the man has already rejoined the rest of the maintenance team and they stand in a tight knot taking a smoking break. I shiver despite the warm day, then focus on getting to the shelter. Halfway down the block, a square sign with elegant script hanging over a red door catches my eye: WESTCOTT & SONS ANTIQUE AND ESTATE JEWELRY. I'd forgotten all about the calls I'd made to the jewelry store, since no one ever returned them. A silver bell jingles as I enter the small shop. The carpet underfoot is lush, and the walls are painted black. In the center of the shop are glass cases, all containing sparkling jewels—

emerald, sapphire, and diamond rings, chokers, necklaces, and pendant earrings, each spectacular.

"Can I help you?" an elderly man in an immaculately pressed white collared shirt and dark slacks asks as he emerges from the back room.

"I've left several messages."

"Never check the machine," he admits. "I'm eighty-three and a Luddite. Plus, nothing compares to seeing our pieces in person. That's what my father and his father before him always said and it's true." He holds out his hand and we shake. "I'm Anthony Jerome Westcott."

"Constance Sparks. I called to ask you about my engagement ring." I hold up my hand and the diamond and rubies catch the light.

"Aha! You're the lucky lady," Anthony says with a big smile. "That's one of my favorites and your young man was so tickled to buy it for you."

I smile. "Do you know much about it?"

His smile dips as he nods. "You want to know the four Cs?"

"The what?"

"Color, cut, clarity, and carat," he explains. "Older diamonds might not have the razzle-dazzle of the factory-cut gems, but I assure you that your ring is the highest quality. I understand that some women need to know for themselves, though."

Instantly I blush. "I don't! I was just wondering if you knew anything about Olivia Edwards Arnaud and how she ended up with this ring?"

He shakes his head. "I'm sorry, young lady. I know the ring came from her estate, but with antiques many times it's difficult or impossible to know the story behind them. Does Mrs. Arnaud have any living relatives?"

"Not that I've found." I've done several Internet searches, but it's not like Olivia ever submitted her DNA to one of those companies that provide detailed family trees. "She did have a brother, James Edwards, who died during World War I," I add. "I'm researching whether he had anything to do with the ring, but so far nothing has come to light."

"Can I show you anything else? Maybe earrings?" he politely asks. Food smells waft from behind the curtain at the back of the shop. Clearly I've interrupted his lunch. "No. Thank you for your time." I walk to the door and the bell jingles again as I pull it open.

"Wait," Anthony calls. "Did you say James Edwards?"

I spin around. "Yes."

"Who fought during the Great War?"

I'm holding my breath and let it out. "He did."

"Did you know that there's a fund to honor that man? It's called the Hero's Scholarship. The only reason I know about it is that the daughter-in-law of an old friend is a recipient. You can ask her about it."

Hope fizzes in my chest. What began as a search to find out about my ring has turned into a longing to know more about both James *and* Anna. "Do you have that daughter-in-law's number?"

Anthony shakes his head. "But her warehouse is five blocks east, same street. My friend says she's a workaholic so she might be in today. Just swing by. Can't miss it. There're arms and legs in the windows."

He ducks behind the curtain before I can ask anything more,

so I head east, a nervous anticipation churning inside me. A broken water main led me to the jewelry store and now fate is directing me to this woman . . . though I don't know why.

You're still just looking for distractions, Mars interjects.

I ignore her. Beyond my desire to know James and Anna better, I can't shake the feeling that there's something I need to discover that will put my worries about Hayden behind me.

Anthony was right, there's no way I could've missed the warehouse. It's a massive gray building that runs the entire block, with arms, legs, hands, and feet made from all different materials dangling in its plate-glass windows. The door is made of steel. After knocking several times with no answer I try the handle and it slides open.

Inside is a giant laboratory—concrete floors, metal tables covered in wires, steel, plaster, and every imaginable machine from lathes to drills to giant 3D printers to high-tech devices I can't identify. Red plastic electrical coils hang from the ceiling over rows of blue soapstone lab tables. Scattered about are elliptical and Nautilus machines, hanging ropes for climbing, free weights, and even several underwater treadmills, one of which has a set of prosthetic legs hooked to an overhead frame running inside it.

I follow the sound of voices, winding through more workbenches and floor-to-ceiling plastic drawers labeled with words like Thumbs, Ankle Joints, Toe Bolts, and Blades, as well as every size screw, washer, wrench, and screwdriver, and tools I've never heard of before. When I round a corner there's a young boy running on a treadmill, one of his legs, from the knee down, made of what looks like carbon with a high-tech silver blade for a foot. A gray-haired woman in a white lab coat crouches beside him watching the prosthetic as he races faster and faster. Two people, who I assume are his parents, stand a few feet away. The man beams while his wife laughs through her tears.

"Okay, take a break, bionic boy," the woman in white says then stops the treadmill. "I want to make a few changes." She detaches the leg and the boy hops off and over to hug his parents, his grin a mile wide.

"Excuse me," I say and the woman, the leg balanced in her hands, turns.

"Can I help you?" she asks.

Despite pixie-cut gray hair, her face is unlined with a sharp chin and large brown eyes. "I'm so sorry to interrupt. Anthony Westcott suggested I stop by, but I can come back another time?"

"Walk with me," the woman says as she strides toward a workbench. She slides open a drawer of tools and goes to work on the prosthetic. "How can I help you?"

"I'm Constance."

"Ruth Leiter."

"Anthony said that you're a recipient of the Hero's Scholarship?"

Ruth fiddles with a screw then searches for a different tool in the drawer. "I am."

"I've been reading a compilation called *Letters from My War*—"

"That book!" A giant smile breaks across her face and suddenly she looks twenty-five, not midfifties. "I was a kid with a single father who worked a factory job. No money for college. Thought I was destined for some version of that life. Senior year

I did a paper about US volunteers in World War I and found James's letters in the Special Collections room at the Old San Francisco Library. The woman who compiled the letters, his sister, Olivia, started the scholarship. A tony old law firm ran it for a while, but now the United Way is responsible. Anyway, that's how I knew to apply."

"It's been around a long time, then," I say.

"Part of the deal is that recipients give back to the fund if we find success."

"How do they hold you to that?" I ask.

She meets my gaze. "They don't have to."

"And the other part?"

"To get the scholarship we have to commit to doing something to make the world a better place." She refocuses on the leg and uses a cylindrical tool to tweak the angle of the blade. "The Hero's Scholarship paid for my bioengineering degree from MIT. After I began this company I started giving twenty percent of my net profits to the scholarship. Plus I donate free prosthetics to kids like Benji," she says with a nod toward the boy now laughing with his parents.

"Why prosthetics?" I ask.

She sets the leg down and leans against the table. "My father lost his leg above the knee in a motorcycle accident. The transtibial prosthetic he could afford was crap. Even the most expensive ones at the time weren't great. Plus, below-the-knee amputees have an easier time rehabilitating and my father never really got back on his feet, as it were. I wanted to make the lives of amputees easier. If my dad were still alive, he'd have one of my designs."

"Anthony said you're a workaholic."

Ruth laughs. "Anthony and his best friend, my father-in-law, are old-fashioned men. They think I belong at home, barefoot and in the kitchen when I'm not having babies." She expertly spins the tool in her hand. "Why are *you* reading James's letters?"

"I'm searching for clues about the history of my engagement ring," I say.

"How does James or the scholarship tie in?" Ruth asks.

"I'm not sure about the scholarship, but my ring was from James's sister's estate, so I'm hoping his letters might mention it."

She cocks one brow. "You haven't finished them?"

I shake my head. "I've been busy, but also part of me doesn't want to reach the end."

Ruth glances at my ring, starts to say something, then nibbles her lower lip. "Those letters were a powerful experience." She meets my gaze. "I didn't want to finish them, either."

I struggle to put my emotions into words. "James's relationship with Anna, their bravery and dedication? It's made me question so many things. I'm searching for clarity anywhere I can find it, I guess." I don't tell her that I'm unsure about my fiancé or that I'm writing to James's ghost. She'd probably call the police to get the unhinged lady out of her lab.

"The scholarship wasn't the only thing that changed my life," Ruth says. "Reading James's letters changed *me*. Growing up, I never saw a healthy relationship up close. When I read about James and Anna, how much they loved each other, their selflessness, the way James treated Anna and also how devoted she was to both him and her work . . ." Ruth sighs. "Notwithstanding what happened, those two became my model for career, love, and marriage."

"Can I assume you're happily married?" I ask.

"We have four teenagers," she replies with a laugh. "But yes, Lars and I are mostly happy *despite* them. He's been a stay-at-home father and I'm the breadwinner. Works for us, not so much for Lars's father, but the trick there is to limit our exposure," she adds with a wink.

Ruth gestures at the lab. "This place is part of James's legacy. My life, my husband's, our children's, and the countless people who use the prosthetics I design are also part of that legacy. We're the silver lining to his short life." Ruth puts a light hand on my arm. "Maybe you're reading those letters to figure out how you can be, too."

Her words don't provide any real answers, but do spark something deep inside me. Instead of heading directly to the shelter, I'm drawn back to the library, filled with even more questions and also the desire to see if there's another note from J waiting for me.

Molly, for once, is nowhere in sight as I climb the stairs to the Special Collections room. Colin nods as I slip on gloves. "I read about the Women's Oversea Hospitals Unit," I share, "and how female surgeons and nurses treated thousands of soldiers and civilians but also had all-women teams of plumbers, mechanics, drivers, and electricians who renovated old buildings and turned them into hospitals."

Colin beams. "All of those women faced grave threats and some died, posthumously awarded the highest honors. While serving, they developed new medical treatments, saved countless lives, and even built coffins to lay to rest those who succumbed to their injuries." His eyes meet mine. "I do find, no matter what we're researching, understanding history imparts the gift of perspective in our own lives, too."

A cold draft slides around my shoulders and the fine hairs on my arms lift. "Have you seen anyone else read *Letters from My War*?" I casually ask.

"You're the first I can remember," Colin says.

Again I feel incredibly relieved to know that if there's a letter awaiting me it doesn't have a worldly explanation. After I retrieve my book, I head to the table. Veronica and Travis aren't there, but I take the empty seat next to Chester.

"How's it going?" I whisper.

"I discovered that two of my great-grandmother's children were sold to the Stagville Plantation in North Carolina. The Bennehan-Cameron family owned about nine hundred people."

"That's beyond horrific."

Chester rubs his face. "Slavery is right up there with some of the very worst things people can do to another human being and I feel all sorts of ways about it." He blows out a breath. "We think if we don't get the girl, or a promotion at work, or have some bad luck, things are tough. But my ancestors fought for their lives, for their right to be seen as human beings, *every day*. They were more powerful than any superhero because all they had was their bravery, resilience, and intelligence." His eyes shine and a tear escapes then slides down his cheek. "It makes me really proud."

I give Chester a big hug and he holds on tight. His research puts my own in perspective. I can't begin to imagine the complexity of his feelings. All I can do is my best to support him.

"When I first met you I didn't think we'd become friends."
I pull back. "Why's that?"

"What do a guy researching slavery and a gal digging to find out about an expensive engagement ring have in common?"

"You tell me."

"Besides hoping for answers, surprisingly, empathy. You know just what to say or do when someone is lost, like Veronica the other day, or sad, like me. My mom always said that I had the ability to relate to others' pain, and that's you, too. You must've had some tough experiences that made you that way."

"Well . . . I have." My cheeks grow warm. "But usually I stay on the periphery of things with people," I admit.

"That's a shame," Chester says. "Glad you made an exception for me, that we're friends."

"Anytime." A little smile tugs at the corners of my mouth as he returns to his research. When I open James's book, there's a note on blue paper waiting for me. The world around me flashes brighter as I slide the note below the table.

Dear Constance,

While I don't know how it feels to have a mother and father abandon me, I do understand why you're afraid to ask for what you need. But if you never show the real you, how can you trust anyone's love? How can you trust yourself to make the right decisions?

What you wrote about love being about compromise is, in part, true. But if you were a mountaineer, would you choose a husband who couldn't share that passion? It would be one thing if he did, then fell from the mountain and lost his ability to climb. That is where compromise would enter. You might forgo mountaineering for something you could enjoy together. It's another situation entirely if mountaineering is what makes your heart sing, and you choose a man who doesn't appreciate, support, or share that passion. You can exchange your own desires for his—this does work for some couples. But ask yourself, while there's still time to make a choice, is that what you truly want?

I'm so very sorry to hear about your grandfather. I believe that the people we lose only fade if we fail to herald their accomplishments and pass on their love and wisdom. There is a poem by a war surgeon named John McCrae called "In Flanders Fields" that eloquently explains that the living must carry the torch for the dead. That is how you will ultimately show your grandfather that he isn't forgotten.

That's the poem Hayden read to me. I flinch as my two worlds almost touch.

I believe that life, at its essence, is about the people we have touched with acts of service and kindness. That is not to say that I was always a good man. I tried and sometimes failed those I loved. You wrote of compromise and that was not always my strong suit. In the end we must all choose what we are unwilling to lose—be it a dream, a passion, a person, or ourselves. And what informs that choice most of all is discovering a raison d'être.

My life's purpose was once myopic—to be financially successful and esteemed by those I respected. But that changed as the world opened around me. I realized that acts of service made my life worthwhile, and that finding my soul mate, someone who believed not only in me but also in herself, whose work I could be proud of, whose touch sparked a fire and the desire to be a better man, was my true dream.

Constance, what is your raison d'être? Is it marriage and children, the animals you care for, or have you yet to discover it? There is no right answer—as we evolve, that purpose will, too. The important thing is to surround yourself with people who will allow you to grow despite life's challenges and devastations, like the red poppies that covered Flanders fields.

Warmly,

J

I reread the part about showing my real self and a trickle of nervous sweat runs down my back. Before I can edit my thoughts in any fashion, I respond . . .

Dear J,

You are right about showing the real me . . .

I wrote that my dad took off during my childhood. Some of those disappearances were about drugs and women, but some were prison sentences—he stole a car and sold heroin. Now he's serving fifteen to life for second-degree murder after killing a young man in a robbery.

My fiancé believes my dad is dead. It's a lie I've hidden behind most of my life. All the taunting in school and the reactions of past boyfriends showed me it's hard, if not impossible, for most people to separate a man who committed murder from his daughter. The day Dad took a life forever changed the way I'm perceived by others. Still, I've always believed that by allowing him to stay in touch with the outside world through my visits and our phone calls, I could help him to do better.

Dad has a second parole hearing very soon. He's asked me to write a letter to tell the parole board he's a different man who has paid his debt to society. But my grandfather believes his son should remain in prison; that he ruins everything he touches. I think Grandpa is wrong. Still, I'm uncertain about writing that letter.

Regardless, tonight I will finally tell my fiancé the truth. You're right: If he doesn't know all of me, I can't trust his love, or my ability to make the right decision about our future. And my own secret will taint how I perceive him.

As for my raison d'être . . . I've never asked myself what it is. As a kid, I wanted to be a veterinarian, but once Dad was arrested for murder, I had to get a job quickly, make money to pay his legal fees, and now I'm supporting my grandfather's care, too. The latter is an honor, but none of this gets to the heart of your question. I need to think more about it before I respond. No one's ever asked me before.

Warmly,
Constance

I fold my note, glance surreptitiously about to make sure no one is watching, then slide it into the book and withdraw James's next letter.

June 1917

Dearest Olivia,

Anna and I have been assigned to the same base hospital! On the long drive there, she rode in my ambulance's passenger seat, drenched from the rain but uncomplaining. She is one of the unsung heroes of this terrible war. Nurses work in hospitals shelled by the enemy and risk their lives but are only paid roughly four dollars a day for their sacrifices . . .

The unfairness makes me sit back in my chair. I understand Anna wasn't a nurse for the money, but still!

"You okay?" Chester whispers.

"I'm going to ask for a raise."

He gives me a funny look. "Okay."

"It probably won't be," I quietly explain. "There's a salary cap for paralegals at our firm. But I skip lunches and work overtime whenever my boss needs me. Capping my salary isn't fair. Plus I've been reading about what women did in the 1900s to practice medicine and to gain the vote. The least I can do is stand up for myself."

Chester grins. "Go get 'em."

I smile back then return to James's letter.

The rain finally stopped in the early evening, and the hillsides shone emerald green, adorned with the ruby-red poppies that are Anna's favorite. We stopped for the night in a small village and Anna and I stole away to a farmer's field . . .

My insides heat up as what happens next unfolds. After finishing the letter, I carefully return it to its envelope.

Chester asks, "Any luck about the ring?"

"No, but Anna and James are falling hard for each other . . . and they made love in a field beneath the stars." I've never called sex *making love* and blush.

I want to keep reading, but it's time to head home and talk

with Hayden like I promised. As I descend the stairs, I check my phone for messages—my ringer has been off since the prison. Rosa has called seven times. Hayden has called four. Rosa never calls unless something is wrong. Mouth suddenly dry, I call her number.

"Hello?" Rosa says.

"Rosa, it's Constance. Is everything okay?"

"Sweetheart, your grandfather had another heart attack. The ambulance took him to Oakland Hospital."

My world stops spinning. "Is he okay?"

"I don't know."

I take the stairs two at a time, sprint across the atrium and out the door, and race down the sidewalk to my Vespa. "Please, please, please let him be all right," I say over and over again as I speed toward the hospital. "Please . . ."

Chapter Twenty

Hayden is already at the hospital when I arrive. He hugs me and I hold on tight. "How did you know?"

"Rosa couldn't reach you. I told her you were at the shelter."

Did Hayden call the shelter's landline? "My ringer was off and—" Mars runs through the sliding front doors, saving me from more lies. She's in sweatpants and a button-down and her purple hair falls in wild curls.

"I called her," Hayden says. "Hope that's all right?"

A rush of sudden tears makes them both appear blurry. "Yes. Thank you." I haven't been a great friend to Mars lately, but she came anyway.

Mars hugs me. "Is Gramps okay?"

During college, Grandpa always invited me to bring Mars along when I visited him for a home-cooked meal. When Mars had the flu, she even stayed with Grandpa and he made soup, watched her favorite movies with her, and did her laundry— things her mother never would've done, if she'd been around and not living in Las Vegas with her latest husband. Grandpa has been a surrogate dad for both of us.

"What if he's not going to be all right?" I ask in a tiny voice.

Hayden says, "He's on the sixth floor, resting comfortably.

They did an angiogram, found the blockage. They'll put a stent in later."

"Open-heart surgery?" Mars and I ask in unison.

"No. They'll go through an artery in his groin. Not as invasive but still has its risks," Hayden explains.

We head up to see him. Each ding of the elevator scrapes my already raw nerves. Grandpa has always been my compass, even as he's started to fade. *Without him I'll be lost.* Hayden reaches for my hand. Mars takes my other one. When we get to the sixth floor, Mars and Hayden take seats in a small waiting room while I head down the white linoleum corridor to room 601, my sneakers squeaking with each step.

Grandpa lies in a narrow hospital bed, his eyes closed. Machines surround him. At Rosa's he's usually in a brown terry cloth robe that hides the bony shoulders and the sharp jut of his collarbones. In the thin hospital gown he looks frail. I quietly place a metal chair beside the bed and take his hand.

His eyes flutter open. "Constance . . ."

Grandpa devolves into coughs and I pour water from a plastic pitcher into the beige cup on his rolling table and guide a straw into his mouth. "You gave me a scare."

He sips slowly then clears his throat. "Sorry. But you know . . . old men don't . . . live forever."

My eyes fill. "Don't say that."

His eyes lose focus and he stares out the window of his room. It's windy out and the clouds race across the sky. I hesitate then say, "I saw Dad today. He asked about you. He wants the chance to make peace."

"I once read about a man who had a pet boa constrictor," Grandpa says. "Raised it from an itty-bitty thing. That snake was useful at times—kept the house free from mice, was good company 'cause the man didn't talk much. One night it slithered into his bed and choked him to death while he slept."

My skin itches. "Dad isn't a snake."

A nurse comes in to record his blood pressure. "I know Gary is up for parole again," Grandpa says after she leaves. "The prison wrote me. Are you going to send a letter to the board?"

He wants to make things up to me. "Yes."

Grandpa rolls the edge of his blanket between fingers with painfully swollen joints. "I'm an old man now. I won't be able to protect you."

"Dad wouldn't hurt me."

"He was always a rotten apple." Grandpa's eyes pierce. "He killed that poor kid for a few bucks."

My conversation with the woman who was visiting her boyfriend at San Quentin returns . . .

He tells me he's a changed man, but I'm no fool . . .

So if he gets out?

I'll have our bags packed.

After Grandpa dozes off, Mars tiptoes in and kisses his age-spotted forehead. When he's wheeled out for his procedure, Mars, Hayden, and I go to the cafeteria for dinner, but I can't get anything down. My best friend and fiancé make small talk, trying their best to distract me. It's nice to see them on the same side. Once Grandpa makes it through having the stent put in, I ask Hayden to head home to feed the animals. I'll spend the night in Grandpa's room. Mars stays for the rest of visiting hours and we sit beside his bed while he sleeps.

"What does he think of Hayden?" Mars whispers.

"He doesn't really know him," I say.

"Maybe the thing about his previous engagement doesn't matter. Hayden called me, came to the hospital, stayed with you. That counts."

Tears prick my eyes. "How's *your* guy?"

"Still married," she quips. "If someone I loved was in the hospital he could only show up if he figured a way to sneak out of the house."

She *does* want more. "You should have someone who supports you *all* the time."

"I have you, right?"

We link pinkies. "Always." I tell her about James's latest letter, the drive to the hospital, and that James and Anna made love. "He thinks destiny brought them together," I share.

"We don't believe in fairy tales," Mars reminds me.

Grandpa moans in his sleep and I adjust his blankets to make sure he's warm.

Mars changes the subject. "You were at San Quentin today?"

"Yes. Dad's nervous about his parole hearing." I think about the boa constrictor story and my chest squeezes. "I was going to tell Hayden about him tonight, before this happened. I'll do it first thing tomorrow. Swear."

Mars nods. "He's a good person."

That's the first real compliment she's ever given him. "Hayden and I had a conversation about what's nonnegotiable in a relationship," I say softly. "His was murder, and he doesn't believe in rehabilitation or forgiveness."

Mars's eyes widen, but to her credit she says, "It's easy to make moral judgments when you're not in the situation. In the end it won't matter."

For the first time, I realize that if it does I'm not sure whom

I'll choose. Not because Dad deserves my loyalty—because I shouldn't have to choose.

"What's nonnegotiable for you?" Mars asks.

Hayden has never asked me that question. "I'm not sure."

Mars meets my eyes. "If your fiancé kicks you to the curb, I'll marry you. It'd be a shame to waste that wedding dress."

I chuckle. "That would seriously cramp your lifestyle."

Mars flashes her million-watt smile. "Yeah, it would. But I'd do anything for you." She digs in her pocket and pulls out a penny, gives it to me. "Just found it today. Make a wish."

I close my eyes and wish for Grandpa's survival, and to figure out who I am, besides the daughter of a murderer and a mother who quit, Hayden's fiancée, and, according to Mars, a woman who can never say no. Then I wish for Hayden's continued love and understanding. Just when I think I'm done, a final wish lands like a light kiss on my forehead and I wish to be a part of James and Anna's legacy, like Ruth is, in some small way.

Chapter Twenty-One

Very early Sunday morning, once the nurse tells me Grandpa is stable and will sleep much of the day, I head home. Before I climb onto my Vespa, I dig the penny Mars gave me out of my pocket and toss it on the sidewalk so someone else has the chance to make a wish.

Hayden is still snoring when I climb into bed. He rolls over, spoons me. In the safety of his arms some of my worries slip away, but the ones that remain leave me with the overwhelming exhaustion that accompanies treading water for far too long. First thing in the morning I will tell Hayden the truth. We're sleeping soundly when his iPad buzzes. He fumbles, opens it, then mutters, "Skype?" Half-awake, he clicks on the green accept button. An elderly man and woman materialize on the screen.

"Mom? Dad?" Hayden asks, "Is everything okay?"

I leap off the bed and pull on a white turtleneck dotted with tiny red ducks, followed by jeans, and frantically comb my fingers through my hair. I'm about to meet my future in-laws.

His dad asks, "How are you, son?"

"We haven't spoken in a week," his mother adds.

I thought they were estranged. Did Hayden reach out about

our wedding? I stay off camera but can still see his parents' faces. Grier has gray-blond hair that slices along her jaw, green eyes a shade darker than Hayden's, and razor-thin lips. Whit's receding hair is salt-and-pepper and he's retained the boyish good looks of his son. Both are dressed in button-down shirts, hers white, his blue. In this moment everything is possible. I envision Christmas dinner, taking them to Fisherman's Wharf when they visit to see their grandchildren, game nights, and a real friendship.

Whit glances at his wife then says, "A few nights ago we saw Austin Wilmers at the club."

Hayden hesitates then asks, "How's Austin?"

"Fine. But he had some interesting news," Whit says. "Seems you're getting married soon and he's the best man. Your mother and I did our best to hide the utter shock."

Whit sounds hurt. I'd initially hoped they were calling because their son had decided to tell them about our wedding and they wanted to meet me. Acting on instinct, I slide next to Hayden, determined to fix this. "Hello, Mr. and Mrs. Whittaker, I'm Constance, Hayden's fiancée. I'm really glad to meet you and we'd be honored if you'd come to our wedding."

"Good to meet you," Grier says, her eyes bright.

My voice has a warble. "You, too!" *Please like me. Please don't have this be the end.*

Hayden puts an arm around me. I can feel the thud of his heart against my side. Why is *he* so nervous?

"How long have you two dated?" Whit asks.

"Eight months," I say.

Grier adjusts the scarf draped around her neck. "A wedding this soon is quite rushed. Are you pregnant?"

I flinch. "Me? Um. No. We're just ready for the next step."

Whit gives a curt nod. "I'm sure you are."

I look from Whit to Grier. "I love your son very much."

"You're a paralegal?"

How did she know that? "Yes. But it might not be what I always want to do."

"That's a job that requires you to be good at research?" Grier asks.

I nod and smile, like some sort of wind-up doll desperate to be claimed from the shelf. "That's part of what I do."

Grier shoots Whit a look then says, "We hired a detective. What we found out about your past shocked us."

Hayden actually laughs. "There's nothing shocking about Constance. She's an open book."

Grier grimaces. "Son, you don't know this young woman."

Hayden's arm tightens around my shoulders. My body has gone very still. I'm an animal that knows it's in a hunter's scope, isn't sure which way to run.

"Her *real* last name is Trumble and her father, Gary, is a *convicted murderer*," Whit says. "He's at San Quentin. He killed a boy for fifty-three dollars. *And* he's up for parole. That animal could be free very soon."

I feel the bullet strike. He even has the amount right. Hayden looks at me, mouth agape.

"How could you?" Grier demands. "After your sister."

"What is she talking about?" I ask. But Hayden won't even look at me.

Whit says, "Hayden's sister, our daughter, Elizabeth, was raped and murdered on her way home from school. She was sixteen and beautiful and the light of our lives. The man who did it is on death row but continues to appeal when he should've been dead a decade ago."

Now I understand why murder, to Hayden and his parents, is an irredeemable act. "I'm so sorry to hear what happened to Elizabeth."

"Are you sorry for the parents of that young man your father murdered in cold blood?" Grier asks.

I wait for Hayden to say something like *Constance isn't responsible for her father's act.* But he doesn't. My voice shakes as I say, "I am very sorry for my father's victim, and his family. My dad has tried to become a better man in prison. It's all he can do."

"Leopards don't change their spots," Grier snaps.

Hayden gives a reflexive nod and my insides shrivel.

"What's more," Whit adds, "your *fiancée* visits that murderer. And, she's *clearly* looking for someone rich to marry. She has no savings and hasn't even managed to pay off her college debt. Pathetic at her age."

Grier's eyes bore into me. "If you think you're going to touch Hayden's trust fund, think again. We will cut him off without a penny before we'd allow that to happen."

A piece of the puzzle silently slides into place and I hear Lydia's voice . . .

They tore me apart, then threatened to take away his trust fund if we married. I broke it off . . . Not because of the money. I was young and stupid enough to think we'd be fine without it. I ended things because he didn't defend me . . . I'm worth more than that.

Hayden was Lydia's *first* fiancé.

He finally hits the red disconnect button and the screen goes black. Hayden still can't look at me. My ears fill with static as the panic fully takes over. I've waited for this moment all my life—when I have *everything* to lose and my worst fears come true. But the memory of sitting across from Hayden at Farley's returns and it cuts through my dread. He told me that we want the same things—marriage, family, and a partner who doesn't run when things get tough. Hayden isn't the kind of man who will turn his back, walk away. He knows Dad's past has nothing to do with me. He loves me and even though this situation is really awful, we'll work through it.

"Why did you lie to me?" Hayden finally asks.

Tears sting the back of my throat and it takes a full minute before I can respond to him. "I learned early on that no one wants to date the daughter of a murderer. But I was going to tell you. I tried again and again—"

He glowers. "But you didn't."

"I was afraid. But I planned to last night, and then Grandpa ended up in the hospital. Ask Mars, I was going to tell you today."

Hayden nods slowly like he's trying to digest this situation. "You can understand how they feel. Elizabeth was the golden child. I loved reading and poetry, always wanted to teach, but my sister was a genius with numbers. Dad hoped she'd follow in his footsteps, make him proud. They've never gotten over the pain and grief of her death. What your dad did? That's anathema to our family and too much of a reminder of their own loss."

He's defending them. I scramble for something solid. "Why didn't you tell me that you came from a wealthy family?"

"It was the best way to ensure you loved *me* for *me*."

The chaos coalesces. "You didn't trust me?"

He grimaces. "I didn't want history to repeat itself."

In this moment I actually pity him. "Lydia didn't end things because your parents were going to cut you off. She ended things because you didn't defend or trust her." I reach for his hand but he pulls it free.

Hayden's cheeks burn bright red. "How the hell do you know about Lydia?"

"Mars found out you'd been engaged before. And then you lied about your high school, plus I didn't know your friends, had never met your family—"

"So *you* didn't trust *me*?" he interrupts. "That's ironic."

I consider throwing Mars under the bus, but that wouldn't be fair. "I just needed to make sure."

"Did you research my family's money, too?"

"What? No! Hayden, I don't care about their money. I planned to happily live in this house, on our combined salaries. I've never wanted to fly on a rocket ship. I love *you*."

He finally meets my gaze with ice-cold eyes and says, "You're not who I thought you were."

"I'm the same person I've always been." As I say this he slowly shakes his head. "Why'd you tell me you were estranged from your family?"

Hayden looks away. "I didn't want to give them the chance to ruin us."

I can hardly speak around the lump wedged in my throat but manage to croak, "They don't have to."

"They already have."

I find a duffel bag in the closet. Blueboy has been sitting by the open door with his ears flattened. He whines as I pack, then dribbles on the floor. There must've been a lot of fighting in his old home. Quickly, I grab a paper towel and clean up the puddle on the floor.

"Where are you going?" Hayden asks.

"I'll send someone from the shelter to pick up Blueboy and Samson."

"You don't have to leave right away."

"I do." I take off my engagement ring and put it on the nightstand. "I'm truly sorry about your sister."

I grab my duffel and run down the front hall. Hayden watches from the steps as I bungee my bag to the seat then climb onto my Vespa and drive away. The final blow hits hard enough to take my breath away. He doesn't try to stop me. He never steps off the stairs while I drive away from everything we shared.

Chapter Twenty-Two

If I keep crying, I'm going to have an accident. I drive to Mars's apartment on Russian Hill and ring the bell. She doesn't answer. In desperation I ring it again and again until her voice comes over the intercom.

"Who is it?" She sounds half-asleep.

"It's me—" I start to cry. Mars buzzes me in.

When she opens the door, dressed only in an oversized blue-and-white pinstriped button-down shirt, it's clear I've woken her. "I'm so sorry. I didn't have anywhere else to go."

Mars leads me into her small one-bedroom filled with an eclectic mix of antique and modern furniture and throws the clothes on the red velvet couch to the floor to clear a spot. I sink into the cushions and she grabs a paper towel from the kitchen counter so I can blow my nose and sits beside me.

"What happened?"

I tell her everything.

Mars leaps up, paces the room, eyes filled with fury. "I was worried something like this might happen."

"What?"

She hesitates then sits back down. "After I found out about the engagement, I did more digging."

"Why?"

"You're my best friend. I couldn't help myself. Whit Whittaker is a big finance guy. He runs a multibillion-dollar hedge fund at a firm his grandfather started. But since Hayden didn't seem to have much money and you said he was estranged from his family, I figured they'd cut him off for some reason. And I read about Elizabeth. It was tragic."

"Why didn't you tell me any of this?"

She tugs at her curls. "You made me promise not to do any more research! Hayden wasn't what I wanted for you, but you were happy. When he called me after your grandpa's heart attack and showed up at the hospital to support you, I made my peace with him."

"Why did you hate him so much at the start?"

"He struck me as fake, even before I knew about the family money. And the way you bent over backward to always do what he wanted. It was like watching my best friend disappear bit by bit."

A sob hitches in my chest. "I guess now we know how he could afford my ring."

Mars looks down. "You gave it back?"

I stare at my bare finger and start to cry again.

Mars heads into the kitchen, pours me a glass of water, then grabs a diet soda from the fridge, takes a few gulps. "Sorry, hung over. My brain needs a caffeine hit to make sense of this."

I finally notice the empty wine bottle and two glasses on the coffee table. The pile of clothes on the floor includes Mars's dress and a man's suit and black dress shoes. "Shit, you have someone here."

"It's not important. What do you want me to do? I can go over to Hayden's and tell him lying about Gary was my idea."

I shake my head. "It wasn't."

"Then fuck him and his snooty parents. You're better off. Remember that woman I dated, Ferris? The minute she cheated on me, there were no second chances. And I was really into her."

I wish I could be like Mars, easily discard someone the moment they disappoint me. But I love Hayden, despite everything that just happened. I'm struggling to believe he really didn't defend me to his parents after everything they said about me. I know he was shocked, disappointed I hadn't confided in him . . . And his lies? Mine were bigger. A fresh round of crying hits and my tears soak through the shoulder of Mars's shirt. The light scent of cologne clinging to the fabric tickles my nose. I sneeze. "Can I stay here until I find a place?"

"Of course. I just need to—"

"Get rid of last night's date?" I ask.

"Yeah. He's taking a shower. Go grab a coffee on the corner and I'll send him packing."

The bedroom door opens and a man in briefs toweling his hair dry steps out and says, "Mars, let's grab some breakfast before I take off."

I recognize the cologne, then his voice, and finally his face. *Brock.* All the facts line up—the nights I lied to Reagan when my boss was out for a scotch before heading home, the times Mars couldn't go to lunch or grab dinner coinciding with Brock's appointments or court time. Mars's face has gone completely pale.

I ask, "How long?"

"Shit," Brock says, finally registering who's sitting on Mars's couch. "Constance, we—"

"Almost a year," Mars replies. "It started right after you moved into Hayden's place."

She's been lying to me for almost a year. "Are you going to leave Reagan?" I ask my boss. He looks away. I grab my duffel bag and head to the door.

"Where are you going?" Mars calls out.

"Anywhere but here." I turn to Brock. "I was going to ask for a raise because I deserve one, but I quit. Effective immediately."

I drive to the only place left. Trudy takes one look at my tear-stained face and leads me to the apartment at the back of the shelter. It has a tiny kitchen along the far wall, twin bed, love seat, and small television. She stays there instead of her town house in the Castro when an animal is sick or if she works late.

"You can stay here until the developer who buys this place takes over," Trudy says. "After that, you're welcome to the couch at my place. Whatever happened, you don't deserve it, kiddo."

I start to cry, even though I should've run dry by now. Hayden's parents were awful, he was awful, but if I hadn't lied they couldn't have blindsided him. "It's all my fault."

Trudy gives me a hug. Her scapulas jut out like tiny wings and she smells faintly of orange blossoms. It's the first time she's hugged me and we've known each other for close to a decade. I set my duffel bag on the floor and sink onto the bed.

"Do you want to talk about it?"

"Not really."

She fills the kettle and puts it on the stove then pulls two mugs from the cabinets and tea bags. "Peppermint okay?"

"Yeah."

"Did I ever tell you that Bert and I separated once, early in our marriage?"

"No."

"The boys were young: eight, seven, and five. Bert started to come home later and later, always with gin on his breath. Turned out he was having an affair with a coworker." The kettle starts to whistle and she pours hot water into our mugs then dunks the tea bags and wraps the strings around the handles. She brings them over and sits down beside me.

"You separated because of the affair?" I ask.

"There were several factors, but that was the last straw." She blows on her tea. "You and I were raised in different times. I never considered college, took a two-month typing and short-hand course then became a secretary for a plumbing business. I met my future husband at thirty-two—long in the tooth for a woman in my day. I'd thought I might end up a spinster. Then along came Bert and I was so relieved. He was a good man, though he had his weaknesses, and he wanted children as much as I did. I quit my job the moment we said *I do*, and got pregnant." Trudy takes a tiny slurp from her mug. "The affair was a gut punch. I thought I was doing everything right—a hot dinner on the table every night, I never let myself go, despite the exhaustion of three kids, and I kept a neat home."

"Did he end it after you found out?"

She shakes her head. "Not sure where I found the gumption to kick him out. I never thought I could make it alone. Got another secretary job, but I was a single working mother with three little boys. Back then, alimony wasn't guaranteed and during the process of separation and divorce Bert wasn't required to help me out. He did, but if my mom hadn't stepped up, watched the kids so I could work, I still would've drowned."

"I always thought Bert was a great guy."

"He was and he wasn't—people are complicated, much more so than our cats and dogs. While we were separated, I let Bert visit the boys, never fought with him, and just carried on. I've always loved animals, especially the discarded ones who need us most, and started dreaming about this shelter, researched possible locations, found these buildings, and figured out how to make enough money boarding pets to support my passion." Intensity sparks in Trudy's eyes. "Getting separated, learning how to make it alone, and starting this shelter changed me."

"How?"

"I realized that I didn't need a man to make me fulfilled or happy. I just needed to take care of my boys and save as many animals as I possibly could."

"But you ended up back with Bert."

She chuckles. "After about a year, he came home with his suitcases, stood on the porch, looking like a beaten dog with his head hung low, and asked me if he could come home."

"And you let him?"

She sniffs. "I locked the screen door and asked him why."

"What'd he say?"

"That our life had scared him—the overwhelming responsibility, and the fact that he wasn't my first priority anymore. He said he understood that we had small children and they needed to come first, but he missed the attention so he got it elsewhere." Trudy finishes her tea. "I asked why not stay with his mistress and he said *she's not my family.*"

"Hayden didn't cheat on me," I say quietly. "He learned

something about me and decided he didn't want me anymore." I swipe at my leaky eyes. "Why'd you take Bert back?"

"If it had just been me, I would've divorced him. But back then I thought that the boys needed a father. Now I realize I would've been enough. Probably even better, given that I was the glue that held us together in the tough times. But we can't change the past."

Trudy pats my hand. "Once you've thought about Hayden's part in your breakup, will you want him back?"

All my insecurities flood in and I'm drowning. If Hayden apologizes, will I forgive him? I struggle for clarity. He's everything I want—solid, dependable, committed to marriage and children. Our future is mapped out and he's my safe place. For a split second I try to evade the truth hurtling toward me, but there's no escaping it.

"I thought Hayden would always be kind, loving," I croak, "but the side he just showed makes me unsure of who he truly is and whether I can trust him." A sob hitches in my throat. "Were we ever truly right for each other or did I just want things to work so badly I forced it?"

"Only you know that answer," Trudy replies.

I consider how she pulled herself out of a tough situation, found her raison d'être, and about all those women in World War I who risked dying to prove that we're capable of more. "I deserve better than how Hayden just treated me," I finally say. "If I have to, I can stand on my own."

Chapter Twenty-Three

Over the next few days, my life begins to take on a new pattern that I'm surprised to find is comforting in its routine. Now that I live at the shelter, I don't need to speed through my morning work and I spend the days walking dogs, snuggling the old ones who need it most, and playing with the cats. In the evenings, I help the other volunteers feed the animals, make sure their water bowls are full and the pens clean. Trudy and I spend several hours each day contacting people who have fostered and adopted our animals in the past. Most days we strike out.

When calls come in from Dad, I take them and just listen, go over his parole hearing again and again. I don't think about how life will change if he gets out. It doesn't matter anymore. Every day is another slog through mud. I manage to visit Grandpa at the hospital, and then at a rehab facility he's sent to when it's clear he's too weak to go directly back to Rosa's. I don't mention Hayden. Grandpa has enough to contend with.

Trudy must've told Ellis about my breakup and that I need space because he doesn't show up to help out or walk the dogs. I find myself looking for him, but know that's just me trying to distract myself from the glaring fact that Hayden has walked away from our relationship without a backward glance.

There are times when I do consider calling my ex, usually after a few glasses of red wine. But I don't. He hasn't called me once. The part of me that's overwhelmingly disappointed with his choices is a little relieved not to rehash things; relieved that he's made the decision for both of us. But the other part is still heartbroken that I've lost him and my dream of our life together. Love doesn't just vanish, regardless of the circumstances. It takes time to wither away.

I skip going to the library, unable to drag myself beyond the shelter for anything that's not essential. At first, Mars called every day, but I never called her back and eventually she stopped. I still love her, but can't work up the energy to fight for us. Trudy brings takeout every other night and we watch whatever series interests her on Netflix. Her favorite is a show called *Alone* where outdoorspeople are sent to a remote location without support and compete to survive the longest and win half a million dollars.

Growler has become my biggest focus. I sit on the concrete floor outside his pen for most of my meals and toss him treats. At first he wouldn't eat them while I was there. Now he'll boldly walk within a few feet of me to retrieve a treat then slowly back up, his eyes trained on me like I'm going to reach out and take the food back, or worse. He never stops growling, but the decibel level has lowered. I ignore it and talk to him. Trudy thinks we should have the vet come euthanize him before the shelter is sold and he's sent somewhere else. She worries that the people who run the next place he lands won't be as kind to him. But I fight for more time. A dog that's been so obviously abused deserves as many chances as possible. Plus, he's become my confidant.

A few weeks into my self-imposed exile, I'm sitting in front of Growler's pen with my lunch, avoiding the eye contact that sets him off. "I understand what it's like to have people who are supposed to love you also hurt you," I share. "My mother walked out when I was eight—didn't even leave a note. Never called. A few months later she was found dead in a motel room."

I trace the outline of a heart on the concrete floor. "Mom once told me a psychic said she'd die suddenly from a broken heart. I was always afraid that if I did something *bad* it would kill her. When I heard she'd died, I thought it was somehow my fault. Little kids take things very literally—" My voice catches. "But I didn't have anything to do with her death. It was just a clogged artery."

Growler has gone silent.

"You and I both had rough childhoods. But we reacted differently. I tried harder to earn love to fill up the empty space inside me. And I was afraid to ask for what I needed for fear it'd push people away." I meet Growler's eyes. "You decided love was dangerous and to protect yourself with aggression so no one could hurt you again. But deep down we both wished for the same thing—to love and be loved."

A line from one of J's letters returns . . . *You must not give up the things that are important to you in order to be loved.*

"I used to mountain bike—you'd like those trails in the woods," I tell the dog. "And I loved spending time with my best friend, Mars. She's a wild ball of fun. But I pretty much stopped biking, chose Hayden every time over Mars because they didn't like each other and I was afraid to lose him. I would've eventually given up most of my time at the shelter to follow Hayden's passions. And the rescues I did bring home would've ended up in a kennel in the backyard instead of a house. I was wrong, though. You can't live in fear or give up what's valuable to make people love you—it just leaves you unsure of who you really are and emptier."

Growler has crept halfway to me.

"You think acting ferocious is your only option. But there's another way. Please let me show you." I put a small piece of chicken in my hand just inside the gate. He might bite me. Still, I keep my hand there. "What happened before you came here is not your fault. What happens from now on is up to you." Growler is only inches away. Gingerly he takes the chicken from my fingers. Elation bubbles through me. Every animal at the shelter should get a second chance, a good life no matter what happened in their past. It wasn't their fault. And it wasn't my fault, either.

Over the next week, the heavy weight on my chest begins to lift. Growler continues to take food from my hand. I start feeding him his entire meal that way—breakfast, lunch, and dinner, one piece of kibble at a time. He no longer snarls at me. Trudy watches but says nothing. It's progress but he's still not a dog that could easily be adopted. Still, I refuse to give up on him.

Tonight, I eat take-out Vietnamese beside his pen, handing him his kibble dinner every other bite. "I've stopped checking my phone to see if Hayden called," I confide. Growler cocks his ears. "I should've told him the truth, right from the start. But Hayden lied, too, about his past and family. That wasn't right, either." Growler scoots forward and licks my hand.

The next night, after we've had dinner, I reach up and pet Growler for the first time, my fingers gliding over his smooth gray fur. He doesn't pull back so I scratch the white blaze on his chest and his tail thumps. Slowly I open the gate, crawl inside. Growler watches me but doesn't run away. Instead he curls on the floor then shuffles forward and rests his muzzle on my thigh. Relief tastes sweet. "Good boy. We're both learning how to do better."

Later, I curl up on his dog bed. It takes a while before he joins me, but he only puts his head and one paw on the cushion. I drift off. In the middle of the night I wake to discover Growler pressed against my stomach. A rush of love for this broken creature that has found the courage to trust again overwhelms me.

I sleep in Growler's pen for another night and then, after everyone has left the shelter for the evening, I open his gate and he follows me back to the apartment and lies down on a fleece pad beside my twin bed. Our eyes meet. "You're going to be okay," I promise. "I'll find an apartment I can afford that allows dogs. I'll be your forever home." Growler reaches up with one paw like we're making a pact. We both drift off . . .

I walk along a forest trail. There are glimpses of blue sky above when the wind parts towering trees and the air is cool and smells of wet earth and pine. The path winds to the right and a man is waiting. I recognize him as the old man I met on the steps of James and Olivia's childhood home, but he's got a full head of dark hair, wears riding britches and a dark sweater, an unlit cigar tucked behind one ear. There are two saddled horses beside him. One is butterscotch, the other chestnut with a white blaze on her chest. I pet the chestnut and she nuzzles into my shoulder.

The man gestures to the horses and asks, "Ready?"

Fear twists my insides. "I've never been on a horse."

"Just because something scares you isn't a reason to avoid it."

"What if I fall off?" I ask as he helps me onto the saddle.

His narrow-set brown eyes sparkle. "What if you do?"

Growler nuzzles my palm. I come fully awake with the knowledge that I've wallowed long enough.

Chapter Twenty-Four

In the morning I take a shower then forgo the gray sweats I've been living in for comfy jeans and a pink sweater. I find Trudy in the office with her readers perched on the tip of her nose.

"Look what the cat dragged in," she says.

"I need to get a job." My savings are almost gone and Grandpa's bills are starting to add up.

Trudy adjusts her glasses. "What are you thinking?"

I consider what J wrote—how acts of service made his life worthwhile, and how I felt when I was able to help Laura despite the odds stacked against her, and her husband's money and power. Memories of another atypical case the firm took on—a young man who'd suffered due to a doctor's negligence—return. We were able to ensure that his ongoing medical needs would be met for the rest of his life.

"I'll always volunteer at animal shelters, but also need to make a living," I reason. "Something that really counts. I never wanted to work in law, but it turns out I'm really good at it. There are parts I do love, but I'm tired of working for the Goliaths."

"You could get a job as a paralegal for the state," Trudy suggests.

My conversation with Ruth flashes back to me . . . *My life, my husband's, our children's, and the countless people who use the prosthetics I design are part of James's legacy. We're the silver lining to his short life. Maybe you're reading his letters to figure out how you can be, too . . .*

"I want to focus on helping the people who need me most—the underdogs who don't have a voice, and victims of crimes," I think aloud. "I'd like to work for the state . . . but as a lawyer for the district attorney's office so I can help *lead* the fight." My words have weight and feel like a raison d'être. I've never considered myself a leader, but after reading about all those incredibly brave women in World War I, I want to be more like them.

"Then figure out how to make it happen," Trudy says with a sharp nod. Her eyes track from my wet hair to the clean clothes I finally put on. "And it's good to see you ditch the sweats and step back into the land of the living," she adds then looks away, but not before I catch the shine in her eyes.

"How are *you* doing?" I ask.

"The shelter has been given a death sentence and there's nothing I can do to commute it," Trudy replies.

Frustration clogs my throat. "It's not fair."

"Nope."

When Ellis first told me about the sale, I suggested a fundraiser. Raising nine or ten million seemed no more possible than flying to the moon. But law school feels out of reach, too, and I'm still going to do everything possible to make it happen.

"Trudy, what if we try to raise the money to buy the shelter and boarding buildings?"

Her forehead creases. "It's not just the shelter and pet boarding buildings, it's the entire city block. There are other warehouses on the land that the owners lease out, too. There's no way we could afford it all. Constance, sometimes the good guys just don't win."

She's right. But that doesn't mean we shouldn't try. "You created and have run this shelter for almost forty years. You have relationships with so many people in the community and some have pretty deep pockets. I can set up a nonprofit—I've done it at work, easy as falling off a log. You cull through your database and make some calls, solicit donations."

"We don't have much time," Trudy says skeptically.

"What have you got to lose? If we get some big pledges, you can present them to the owners and then ask to postpone the auction. If we prove what's possible, they might just give us the time we need to raise the rest of the money."

Trudy wrinkles her mouth side to side. "At least we'd go down fighting," she remarks with a glint in her eye.

"Let's manifest the dream," I say and reach out my hand. "We get the money, buy the shelter and those other buildings, and the rent from them can keep this place running forever." Trudy's grip as she shakes my hand is surprisingly firm.

"Now get out of here," she says, "and figure out how you're going to swing law school."

After all the animals are cared for, I return to the apartment and begin my research. First I Google the tuition for the University of San Francisco School of Law. It's $52,580 a year and that doesn't include books, food, or lodging. Even with financial aid, there's no way I can swing it. I do more searches. There are more affordable law schools in other states, but I need to be near Grandpa.

I click a random link to a blog written by a young woman named Samantha who couldn't afford law school. She became a lawyer *without* ever attending graduate school. I read further and learn that California is one of the states that grant licenses to practice law under the Law Office Study Program. Prospective attorneys have to study under a practicing attorney's supervision for eighteen hours per week for four continuous years. Pass the First-Year Law Students' Examination. Receive a positive moral character determination. Pass the Multistate Professional Responsibility Exam and the California Bar Exam. Surely, I've already met the first requirement with eleven years at HDB.

"It's not going to be easy to study for those exams if I'm working," I murmur. But still, I need to make a living so that's really the only option.

Since I don't want to return to Hollister, Duckwall & Berger, I Google "paralegal salary, District Attorney, San Francisco" and discover the pay is about what I was making at HDB. I dial the main number for the DA and ask for Human Resources.

"Susan Jones, how may I help you?"

Suddenly nervous, I clear my throat twice then croak, "My name is Constance Sparks. I'm a paralegal looking for a position with the district attorney's office."

"Let me check to see if any positions have been listed."

"Thank you." Unable to sit still, I pace the tiny apartment.

". . . It looks like the only position currently on file is for an applicant enrolled in law school. Are you currently in law school?" Susan asks.

"Um. I was planning to do the Law Office Study Program?"

"Hmm. Then I'm afraid we have no positions available," Susan says.

Hope slips through my fingers. "Thanks for your time." I prepare to hang up, but something Mars said stops me . . .

I'm the only one who gets to decide if I'm worthy.

"Wait! I've worked for eleven years at Hollister, Duckwall and Berger as a paralegal. I can get excellent references and, while I'm not currently a law student, I bet I know more than they do based on experience."

"That's probably true," Susan admits. "But I'm sorry, you're not qualified for the position."

"Did anyone ever give you a break in life when you needed it the most?" I press.

". . . Yes."

"I need this. Just give me the chance to interview. Please. After that it's up to me to prove that I deserve the job." I hold my breath.

"Be at the San Francisco DA's office at three thirty tomorrow afternoon. You'll interview with Ellen Galloway. She's the deputy district attorney looking for a new paralegal. Word of warning, that woman hates to waste time and she's going to be pissed off that I let you through."

I pump a fist into the air. "Thank you. I'll be there." For the first time in forever, I see a light shining at the end of a dark tunnel. When I slide into Growler's pen to tell him the good news, he covers my face in wet licks. "I'm going to make you proud," I promise my dog.

Part of what J wrote, about finding a soul mate, someone who believes in herself, whose touch sparks a fire, returns to me as I sit beside the dog on the cool ground. The memory is bittersweet. Mars and I have always known that life is never going to be perfect. I kiss Growler on the nose and he licks my chin in return. A feeling of contentment rolls through me. Even if I don't get the happily ever after of childhood dreams, that doesn't mean I can't be fulfilled. There are mountain bike trails to ride with my dog, opportunities for exciting adventures, new friendships to forge, and a career to pursue that will not only give me a raison d'être but make a difference in other people's lives.

The urge to return to the library to read James's letters to Olivia hits hard. It's no longer about my ring. James's experiences have truly broadened my horizons. He had the bravery to cut ties with his father's expectations, go to France to find himself, risk his life to help others, and he lived in the moment with Anna despite the war raging around him, as did Anna. The dive into researching my engagement ring has shown me that I wasn't living *my* life to the fullest and I plan to change that.

My bruised heart gives a squeeze. I've been so adrift that I never even considered a note from J might be waiting for me. Now I can't get to the library fast enough. I want to tell him what's happened. That I've lost my fiancé but found my raison d'être.

The moment I step into the library's atrium, Molly launches toward me from behind the information desk.

"Constance. Hang on!"

I keep walking, desperate to avoid rehashing my breakup. I've moved on, but that doesn't mean my heart isn't still tender. She catches me halfway up the first flight of stairs.

"I am *so* sorry to hear about you and Hayden. He told me at game night. Asked me to keep it from the rest of the club—he's not ready to share the news." She lowers her voice and adds, "Hayden didn't tell me much, but if I'm being honest, I'm not shocked you two didn't make it."

"Why's that?" I ask, my tone sharp.

Molly holds up her hands. "No offense, but it seemed to me you're from different worlds."

She's right, just not in the way she thinks matters. While Hayden and I were still together, it felt disloyal to ask Molly any details about their relationship or breakup, but that's no longer an issue. "Can I ask why you and Hayden broke up?"

"He's a good guy, but he likes to pretend he's not from money. A friend I went to Columbia with knew his family. I mentioned it. It was a while after he'd had his heart broken by a gold digger named Lydia and he was still overly sensitive. TBH, the way he dropped me was kind of insulting."

Our eyes meet and I say, "Yeah. I get that."

Molly's smile kicks back in. "But it all worked out for the best. I recently met a very accomplished man. Nothing's happened yet, besides helping him do research for a book he wants to write." She lowers her voice. "His job is so hectic he doesn't have time to come during normal hours. The things we do in the hopes of finding love," she adds with a wink. "I'm working up the nerve to ask him out. How about you?"

"I think it's better for me if I stay single."

There's a new librarian at the desk inside Special Collections— a woman in her midsixties with salt-and-pepper hair scraped into a low bun. I show her my library card, stow my backpack, then head into the stacks to retrieve the book. When I reach the table, it's half-full already, mostly new faces but Chester is there. He sports a recent haircut and smiles when he sees me.

"How's it going?" I ask.

"A little better," Chester says. "I discovered that one of my great-grandmother's children escaped to freedom and became a teacher. That's what I do—teach fourth grade. My adoptive parents are both venture capitalists. Now my career choice makes sense. *I* make sense . . . if that makes sense," Chester says with a bittersweet smile.

"It does," I say. "We all want to figure out how we fit into the world." Maybe that's another reason why I've kept returning to find out about James and Anna's love story and to read J's notes. I'm trying to find *my* place.

"Where have you been?" Veronica whispers as she emerges from an aisle with a pile of books balanced in the crook of her arm.

"Vacation," I reply.

She takes in my recent weight loss, nine pounds the last time I checked, then nods at my bare hand. "Where's your ring?"

I manage to keep my voice steady. "We broke up."

Veronica's smile crumbles. "I'm so, so sorry, dear."

"It's okay," I say. "I think it was for the best." She places a gentle hand on my shoulder and then moves along with her pile of books.

I open *Letters from My War* for the first time without an engagement ring on my finger. There's a sense of loss, but also of freedom. My ring led me down this path, and it's shaken up my life. I've always been a planner, but it's less terrifying and more exciting than I expected to have a blank slate, to know that the rest of my story is entirely up to me.

Right away I notice that the last note I wrote to J is gone, but there's no new blue note. I'm submerged in waves of disappointment. I needed more words of encouragement from him. Has the spell been broken? Dejected, I slide several of James's letters to Olivia free and begin to read.

July 1917

Dearest Olivia,

   *The base hospital is housed in an old chateau surrounded by wild
gardens. My days are a whirlwind of transferring wounded soldiers
from the aid station, shelling from the enemy a constant threat, while
Anna works tirelessly to treat their horrific wounds. She is indomitable. I
know it is fast but I have fallen head over heels in love with Anna and
told her so . . .*

My heart overflows for them. When I open the next letter,
I'm shocked that it's addressed to James's parents.

Dearest Mother and Father,

   *I have found clarity amidst the violence and destruction of this
terrible war. My life is filled with purpose and, though I was not looking
for it, with love . . .*

My eyes burn as I read on. Once I've finished and collected
myself, I eagerly share what I've learned with Veronica and
Chester. "James told Anna he's in love with her and she's in love
with him so he wrote his parents to ask for their blessing to
marry."

"So dang dreamy," Veronica gushes.

"Shhh," a bald guy at the end of the table says with a finger
to his thin lips.

Chester whispers, "What about the ring?"

My world dims a tiny bit. That's what happens when you let
go of a dream. "I still haven't found any mention of it in the
letters."

After Chester returns to his research and Veronica heads into the stacks to find another volume, I pull a pencil from the jar on the table and, despite the absence of J's note, write him anyway.

Dear J,

A lot has happened . . .

My grandfather had a heart attack. He's alive but weak. He was my friend when I had none, confidant when I couldn't find the words, and my soft place to fall. I don't want to think about what life would be like if I lost him.

My fiancé and I have ended our engagement. His parents dug into my past and told their son about my dad. They also accused me of only wanting to marry him for his money. My fiancé was shocked, about everything. I don't blame him, but he let me walk away without an explanation. And he hasn't tried to get in touch—that says more than anything. He doesn't trust me or think we can move beyond my past.

At first, I desperately wanted him back. But looking back and trying to be more honest with myself nowadays, he wasn't proud of who I am once he knew everything, or the work I find meaningful. He also wasn't willing to share my passions as I did his. I thought that the only way I could be loved was if I gave bits of myself away and never said no, but in the process I almost lost myself. I don't want to do that anymore.

You challenged me to figure out my raison d'être. I've realized that while law didn't start out as my passion, fighting for people who have no voice actually gives me a sense of worth and accomplishment. I'm going to pursue becoming an attorney with a focus on victims' rights. I've also convinced

Trudy, the woman who started the animal shelter, to try to raise enough money to buy it. Regardless of whether we're successful, she'll know that she did everything she could to fight for her life's work.

Finally, while I do admire that part of your own raison d'être was to find your soul mate, I don't believe that exists— at least not for me.

Warmly,
Constance

PS I missed your notes

I glance around the room to make sure no one is looking, then slip my note into the front sleeve of the book with a silent prayer that J will read it.

"Turn that frown upside down," Veronica says when she returns from the stacks with a new book.

I didn't realize I was frowning and dig up a smile.

"Party at my house on Friday!" She scribbles down the address for Chester and me. "Nothing fancy. Just bring yourselves and an appetite."

The idea of meeting new people is appealing after shutting myself away at the shelter. It's also a step toward creating my new life. "I'll be there," I promise.

Chapter Twenty-Five

Ellen Galloway is tall, whippet-thin, wears a navy pantsuit, a gray silk blouse, and a scowl that starts with the deep grooves in her forehead and finishes at the severe droop of her mouth.

"I'm sorry you were told that this job was open to paralegals when I *clearly* wrote in the job description that I'm looking for a second-year law student."

It's hard not to fidget under her glare. I avoid adjusting my slightly wrinkled white blouse and rest my folded hands on the black pleated pants Mars hates. "I have eleven years of experience at Hollister, Duckwall and Berger."

"This isn't a straight paralegal job, it's designed to be a mentorship," Ellen explains. She shuffles the files on her desk. "It's my hope that it will lead to employment as a lawyer with the district attorney's office."

Inside my nerves thrum but I calmly reply, "I plan to be a lawyer."

"Yet you're *not* in law school," Ellen snips.

My cheeks grow warm. "I can't afford it. So I'm going to do the Law Office Study Program."

Ellen glances at my resume. "You've worked in a practicing

attorney's office for more than four continuous years, but you were not enrolled in the Law Office Study Program. Nor have you studied under an attorney and taken the required periodic exams. In addition, the California Bar has a passage rate of less than fifty percent and that shrinks to below five percent for exam takers who didn't graduate from law school. What makes you think you can be in that five percent?"

My hands tighten into fists. This is going to take longer and be more difficult than I first thought, but I'm still going to do it. "My mother abandoned me when I was eight. My father was a drug addict and alcoholic who was convicted of second-degree murder and sent to prison. But I worked my way through college, spent a decade helping the partners at HDB win big cases. I'll be in that five percent because I have incredible attention to detail. I'm really smart and determined to succeed."

"Why not just work for another big law firm while you study?" Ellen asks. "If you do pass the bar, they'll give you a job and you'll make a hell of a lot more money than working for the DA."

"I've never wanted to make a hell of a lot of money. My goal is to find work that's meaningful and help take care of the people and animals I love."

"You said your father is in prison?"

"Yes."

"Would you have prosecuted him?"

I don't even blink. "Yes. He was guilty and the family of the young man he murdered deserved justice."

Ellen nips at her lower lip with very white teeth. "You know, sometimes cases aren't that clear-cut. Even on our side they can still break your heart."

I consider that. "Do you believe in the value of what you do?"

"Yes."

"Then it's your job to prove to me that working for the DA matters. If you do that, you'll be mentoring a future lawyer for the district attorney's office."

She sits back in her leather chair, long fingers folded on the desk. "You may never pass the bar."

"I will."

"Why did you leave HDB?" Ellen asks.

"I inadvertently discovered one of the married attorneys was having an affair with a paralegal and decided it was time to resign."

Ellen notes, "Workplace affairs happen."

"True. But from that point on, I'd never know if I was getting promoted or demoted for the right or wrong reasons."

"Did you tell anyone?" she asks.

I shake my head. Ellen's brown eyes meet mine for a long pause.

"Assuming your bosses at HDB confirm you're qualified," she finally says, "you start a week from Monday. Go see Susan in Human Resources to fill out the paperwork. And tell her that I'm pissed at her."

I practically skip to my Vespa and sing under my breath the entire way back to the shelter. As I walk through the doors, there's a moment when I miss coming home to the warmth of Hayden's bungalow, the delicious smells always emanating from the kitchen, the backyard where I played with the long-haulers while he worked in his shop. But I don't want to go back. That's something.

After dinner—a burrito for me and kibble for Growler—I

let him out of his pen and together we double-check that all the animals have fresh water. He follows me around the same way he used to follow Lucy. Suddenly Growler lets out a low snarl and I spin to see Ellis slowly backing away, his hands in the air.

"Don't be afraid. If I think someone is okay, he's willing to grudgingly accept that person." I walk over to Ellis and Growler follows and sits down at my feet but still gives him the side-eye.

Ellis whistles under his breath. "I can't believe the change in him. How'd you do it?"

I consider the question. "I told him the truth. What're you doing here?"

"My last surgery finished sooner than expected."

"I hope that doesn't mean you killed someone," I joke.

"I muddled through," Ellis says with a mischievous grin.

"You haven't been around."

"Glad you noticed."

Heat creeps up my neck.

"Mom said you needed some space; that things with your fiancé ended?"

It doesn't hurt as much to hear someone say as it did a month ago. "Yes."

"Some guys don't know they've got it good," Ellis notes.

I force myself to meet his gaze. "How do you know he had it good? You don't really know me very well."

Ellis doesn't look away. "You can tell a lot about a person who rehabilitates a dog everyone thought should be euthanized."

I fill Houdini's water bowl, kiss the top of his head. "You're wanted," I remind him then move on to the next pen. "I got a new job today," I share. "You're looking at a paralegal for the district attorney's office."

Ellis gives me a high five. "That's great!"

It actually seems like he means it. I add, "My plan is to work while also doing the Law Office Study Program. When I'm ready I'll try to pass the bar without having to attend law school. Not many people actually pass," I admit, my excitement faltering a bit.

"You will."

For once, his eyes are sincere instead of mocking.

"How about a drink after we finish here?" Ellis asks. "I need to drown my sorrows."

"What are you sad about?"

He hangs his head. "Mom is still bent out of shape at me."

"She might be in a better mood soon."

"Why's that?"

"I convinced her to let me set up a nonprofit to solicit donations to buy the shelter and land. Trudy is reaching out to supporters and community members to ask for pledges. Maybe we'll even raise enough to keep the shelter going in perpetuity. It'll be your mom's legacy."

Ellis gives me a strange look. "You're something else."

I think about how James's last letter to Olivia was truly all about living in the moment. It's high time for me to try that. "One drink." Despite my newfound determination to steer clear of men, a single butterfly takes flight in my belly. We get back to work side by side checking water bowls and cleaning pens. Ellis tells me about his day—four surgeries, including an appendectomy on a seven-year-old girl he used the teddy bear trick on.

"And the lollipop?"

"Of course. I keep them in a desk drawer now."

I chuckle. "You're good with kids after all."

"Turns out, they're my favorite patients," Ellis admits. "They don't ask tough questions and candy is all that's needed to get a smile."

"You've found a new raison d'être," I say.

Ellis's eyes glitter. "I have." As we put the supplies away, he asks, "So what do you do for fun now that you're a single woman?"

"I used to love biking in the Headlands and on Mount Tam. I'm planning to get back to it . . . after the shelter is sold. How about you?"

"I kitesurf off Crissy Field in the Marina."

Anytime I ride over the Golden Gate Bridge I always notice the kitesurfers. They look like brightly colored birds riding the waves. But the bay has a strong current and is filled with barges, tankers, and recreational boats that make what they're doing seem risky. "Aren't you afraid of the barge traffic or getting sucked out under the Golden Gate?"

"Says the girl who mountain bikes." Ellis reaches out and rubs a smudge of dirt off my cheek with his thumb.

My skin tingles where he touched it. One of Mars's favorite expressions—*the best way to get over someone is to get under someone else*—runs through my mind. But I'm not Mars, and there's no way I'm going to let things go further than one drink. I return Growler to his pen with a promise to get him later, then Ellis comes back to the apartment. Trudy left some beers in the fridge and there's a half-empty carton of Thai food from my last meal.

Ellis chuckles. "Cook much?"

"Not anymore, if I can avoid it."

"Same." He pops the tops off the beers and hands me one. "Cheers."

We clink bottles then sit on the small couch together. Suddenly I'm very aware that he's only inches away, the way his Adam's apple bobs as he swallows, the clean scent of soap that wafts off his skin. I take several sips of beer. "So, why kitesurfing?"

"It's like surgery," Ellis replies.

"How so?"

"Both require intense concentration. I could teach you how to kite?"

I'd really like to try. But a memory of the first time I gave up going for a ride to take a cooking class with Hayden returns. It was the beginning of giving pieces of myself away.

"Penny for your thoughts?" Ellis asks.

"It'd be fun to learn to kitesurf," I reply, "but first you'd need to go mountain biking with me. It's a sport I'm never going to give up again." My stomach lurches. Did I just ask him out? I take another swallow of beer and realize I've drained most of the bottle.

"Why mountain biking?" Ellis asks.

"My grandpa and I used to do it together. When we were in the woods, trying to find our way or racing down a hill, the outside world went away."

"And you needed that?"

I'm at the edge of a precipice. In the past I've always backed away. This time I jump off it. "My mom walked out when I was eight and died a few months later from a heart attack. My dad is in prison. He robbed a convenience store and killed the clerk in the process. It might've been an accident, but I'm not sure. So yes, I needed an escape."

Ellis doesn't look away. "That must've been hard on you."

"Sometimes. My childhood wasn't like yours with Bert and Trudy."

"Mine had its ups and downs."

I can't seem to find my footing. "That's all you're going to say after learning about my parents?"

"Unless you want to talk more about them?"

I hesitate. "Another time. And maybe you could tell me about the ups and downs . . . if you want."

"I'd like that." Ellis launches off the couch. "So mountain biking. It's a deal."

I blurt, "But it's not a date."

Ellis teases, "Did you want to ask me out?"

"No," I snip. But a tendril of heat winds through me.

"Another beer?"

After sharing the truth about my parents I could use one. "Okay."

"Want to hear a secret?" Ellis asks.

Suddenly I'm back in the sixth grade at a party, picked by the spin of a bottle to play *two minutes in the closet* with John Jensen, unsure what happens next. "Um. Sure."

"When I was a kid," Ellis says as he pops the tops then climbs over the back of the couch with our beers, "my folks used to make us work summers at the shelter. I hated this place."

"Why?"

"Well, no kid enjoys scooping poop. But also it seemed really sad, warehousing all the animals."

"A lot of them find new homes."

"Yeah, that's true. But the ones who don't—they watch the others leave with new families and that seemed cruel."

"Your mom would say the animals leaving is what gives us hope."

"She's an eternal optimist. Anyway, one summer Mom insisted that I take care of the *special* dogs. The ones with health issues that needed shots, and others that required retraining. There was this one poodle that terrified me—"

"A poodle?" I giggle.

"Don't shame me while I'm baring my soul," Ellis quips. "Her name was Georgia and whenever I turned my back she'd try to bite me in the ass. I started wearing canvas pants that she couldn't bite through."

"So what happened?"

"I lived in this apartment with her. Fed her every meal by hand. Took her for long walks. Mom said her former owner had hit her. Obviously I never did. Eventually Georgia stopped trying to bite me. One day she climbed on my lap, on this very couch. After that, we were best friends. Actually, our family adopted her and she slept in my bed every night."

I take a swallow of my beer. "And the moral of that story?"

Ellis meets my gaze. "Good things are worth the hard work and the wait."

Another butterfly joins the one still fluttering inside my chest. When he gets up and walks to the door, I think about calling him back. Maybe I'm more like Mars than I thought.

Ellis turns at the door. "See you soon, Constance."

I get to work finishing the framework for the nonprofit. When I'm done, I retrieve Growler from his pen and he follows me back to the apartment and curls up on the couch beside me.

I listen to the dog's snores and think about Ellis. There's more to him than I thought, and it's clear he cares about his patients, loves Trudy—and he's good with animals. I'm a little shocked that I told him the truth about my parents . . . but also proud that I'm doing things differently this time. And he didn't run when he found out about Dad or ask me to give up my favorite sport for his. My nerves jangle. We're going mountain biking together—and it *might* be a date. I drift off thinking about how much I wanted Ellis to kiss me . . .

Chapter Twenty-Six

In the morning, Growler follows me around the tiny apartment, unwilling to let me out of sight. He even sits outside the shower waiting for me to finish. I peek around the curtain. "Is this what our life together is going to be like?" In response he thumps his tail. "Works for me." A text pings and my insides jump at the idea it might be Ellis. But when I check my phone it's Mars. I'm relieved to hear from her and ready to talk.

MARS: Meet at Smiley's Diner by the office?

ME: I can be there at 8

I throw on tan corduroys with green vines sewn down the sides that are dotted with tiny pink, red, and orange smiley faces, a light blue sweater, and sneakers, leave Growler in his pen with a rawhide, then stop by Trudy's office.

"You sleep okay?" Trudy asks.

I take a seat across from her. "I did."

Trudy focuses on the paperwork in front of her. "Did my son behave?"

I blush. "Yes."

"He *is* a good man," Trudy says.

"Ellis told me you're mad at him."

"Did he say why?"

"No."

Trudy harrumphs. "Have a nice morning. Don't forget you're helping make calls to Washington, Idaho, and Oregon shelters at noon. I'll drive every single fur-ball to whatever no-kill shelter is willing to take them."

"I sent the nonprofit formation documents to your email. Just print them out, sign, and get them back to me so I can file them with the secretary of state for you. Have you identified people to call for pledges?"

"Yes." For the first time in weeks her smile reaches her eyes. "Don't worry, I'm preparing for the worst but I won't give up without one last fight."

Mars leaps to her feet the second I walk through the front door of the diner. "Constance!"

I didn't realize how much I missed my best friend until this moment. We haven't gone more than a few days without contact since college. Even when she'd fly off with a new crush, she'd at least text. She's changed her hair color from violet to sapphire blue. It suits her, but there are gray shadows beneath her eyes.

"I'm sorry," we both say in unison. And then we hug each other tight.

"Has Hayden called?" Mars asks as we take our seats.

"No. But I haven't called him, either. It's over."

Mars purses her lips. "Are you sure?"

"You were right. I was giving too many important parts of

myself away. And even then, he didn't stand up for me with his parents."

"Asshole," Mars growls.

I shake my head. "They're all entitled to their opinions. But Hayden and I aren't a good fit. And even though I tried, I do still hate cooking." Neither of us laughs, but maybe someday we can find some humor in what happened. I tell her about Trudy and my hopes we can raise enough to buy the shelter, my success with Growler, and the latest letter James wrote to Olivia but skip the part about writing J—it's no longer about embarrassment, maybe it never was. The truth is that I can't risk her practical nature somehow breaking that magical connection. I need him.

Mars asks, "Where have you been staying?"

"The shelter."

A look of pure horror crosses her face. "What? No. Come stay at my apartment."

"Thanks, but Trudy has a studio there that I'm using until I find a place."

Mars shakes her curls. "I don't want you living with all those unwanted animals."

"They're not unwanted, they just haven't found their forever home." But Growler has. His home is wherever I am.

"What are you going to do for work?"

Sudden shyness hits me out of the blue. I'm not embarrassed by my choice, but we've spent the last decade poking fun and complaining about our bosses. "I got a job as a paralegal at the DA's office. I'm doing the Law Office Study Program. In four years, I'll take the bar."

Mars's mouth falls open. "You want to be a *lawyer*?"

I laugh at her reaction. "Turns out I do. But not for the corporations our firm usually represents. I want to fight for underdogs."

"Of course you do." She twists her mouth side to side, like she's processing my reveal. "That might actually give me the kick in the butt I need to figure out what I really want. Medicine is out—the long hours would crush me. But maybe I could figure out a business. Be my own boss?"

My chest swells a little bit that she's actually considering following *my* lead. "You're Mars. You can accomplish anything you want."

Her brows draw together. "You really think so?"

I'm not used to her showing any hint of insecurity. "I'm sure of it." Finally, I ask about the elephant in the room. "You and Brock?"

Mars pours another packet of sugar into her coffee cup. "He's not going to leave Reagan and the kids. I've always known that. I'm fine with it."

I consider letting it go, but she's entitled to better from me, even at the risk of losing her. "You watched your mom get rejected over and over again. Choosing people who can't really make a commitment is your way of protecting yourself. But I know you want more or you wouldn't go to events like yoga speed dating. And I also know that you're better than an affair with a married man."

Mars's eyes gleam and she gives me a small smile as she leans in across the table. "When did you get so wise?"

"I'm working on it."

"Noted." She grabs a Kleenex from her purse and quickly blows her nose. "Did you get all your stuff from Hayden's?"

"I don't want to go back there," I admit.

"Then I'll go after work today."

I launch from my chair and give Mars another hug. I've missed her so much. "Thank you for not letting me go."

"Never," she whispers in my ear. "Want me to give Hayden the evil eye?"

I chuckle. "Do you remember *all* my superstitions?"

"The ability to cause misfortune with a glare would be a true superpower," she replies with a grin.

"True," I agree. "But no evil eye. Hayden's been punished enough that he's lost me."

Her eyes gleam. "Don't you dare make me cry again."

I give her another squeeze then step back. "A friend is having a party tonight. Come with me?"

Mars's smile is watery. "I wouldn't miss the chance to hang out with you."

We hug again on the sidewalk, then I hop on my Vespa and drive to the library to read more letters before helping Trudy make those calls.

When I step through the door to Special Collections, I spy the usual suspects at the long table along with some new faces. With a nod at Travis, who's sporting a red Berkeley sweatshirt today, I head into the stacks, round the corner to retrieve the book of letters, and freeze. A man on tiptoes reaches for it. From the back I see he has brown hair and wears a gray fleece over loose Levi's. *Hayden.* His hand hovers over the volume. Without any wavering doubt, it hits me that I don't want it to be him. He touches the spine then moves three down to pull out a different book. As he turns, my stomach flips. But it's not my ex. By the time the man passes me, he's cracked open his book and is engrossed. I remember to resume breathing, then climb the step stool and retrieve *Letters from My War*.

As I settle in at the table an unexpected sense of gloom descends. At the end of this collection of letters, James dies. I've gotten so caught up in his love story with Anna that I'd almost forgotten it ends with tragedy. And what about my notes to J? Will they end, too? To banish the darkness, I quickly turn the pages. My note is gone, replaced by a familiar blue slip of paper.

Magic dusts my skin as I slide the new note onto my lap . . .

Dear Constance,

    I'm so sorry about your grandfather and also the end of your engagement. Learning about your father from his parents must've been quite a shock. Isn't it sad how sometimes the people we love disappoint us? The tough part is to figure out if they're worthy of forgiveness. Is there a chance you two can work things out?

    Concerning your father and the difficult decision you must make about writing a letter supporting his release . . .

    When I was a little boy, I was frightened of my own father. He was loud, sometimes angry, and prone to take a belt to my backside (mostly when he was inebriated). My mother tried to protect her children, but sometimes failed. Our neighbors, a childless couple, would see my tear-stained face and invite me over to play.

    Yasmin loved to garden. She'd let me pick green beans off the vines, pop cherry tomatoes warm from the sun into my mouth. Arthur and I would sit on the porch swing and he'd listen to me, hanging off every word as only a man who loves children but isn't able to have his own does. He made me feel like I wasn't a burden but a privilege. And that changed the way I saw my father. It was his job to make me feel special, like Arthur did, and he'd failed. He wasn't worthy of my love.

I am pleased that you have discovered your raison d'être, but concerned that you do not believe that there is someone out there that can love you the way you deserve to be loved. Take your time, prove to yourself that you are truly worthy, but then I believe you should open your heart. Love is a gift, not a curse, regardless of how long we get to hold on to it. Ask anyone who has been given the chance if they would have preferred to have never met their twin flame. They will reply with a resounding NO. To live without that kind of love is to deny oneself life's greatest joy, accomplishment, and pleasure.

Warmly,

J

PS I've missed your notes, too

He missed me. I'm elated to read it and feel energized as I pull a sheet of paper free from my notebook and start my own letter.

Dear J,

Just now I thought I saw my fiancé in the library, about to pull *Letters from My War* from the shelf, and my first thought was that I didn't want him to be the man writing to me. While there are moments of loneliness when I miss parts of our life together, it's over.

I will consider your kind words about love, but if I choose to open myself up to it, this time I'll make certain it's not the only thing in my life. That's something I've learned from the woman who founded the animal shelter. She discovered her purpose—saving animals—when her husband had an affair.

And, along with caring for her little boys as a single mother, it changed the way she saw herself. She's older now, and I worry about what will happen to her if our fundraising efforts fail and the shelter is still sold at auction. Her son thinks that her raison d'être should be her grandchildren, but I don't think anyone can decide that for someone else.

I understand what you were saying about your father and my own. That it's not my responsibility to prove to the parole board that he's worthy of release. It's his responsibility to prove that to them, and to me. But once Grandpa is gone, Dad will be my only remaining family. People are complicated, some more than others, and not all good or bad. Shouldn't I extend the man who gave me life some grace?

What scared you most in life?

Love,
Constance

My heart bumps hard against my sternum. I signed the note *love.* But it's true. I love everything about J even though a relationship with him is impossible. I slide my note into the sleeve, then withdraw James's next letter to Olivia. My pulse picks up speed as I read.

Mother and Father have refused to give the blessing for Anna and I to wed . . .

Disappointment chokes me before I can continue. I envision James crumpling the telegram in his fist. Every fiber of my being wants him to march into the hospital, find Anna, and, despite his parents' refusal, fall to one knee and propose . . .

> *I found Anna in the recovery ward and shared the telegram. She was crestfallen but quickly collected herself. She is not the kind of woman who would want a man who could be so easily swayed by his family. I tore the thin missive to shreds and then dropped to one knee. Bedridden soldiers erupted in cheers. Anna asked if I was certain and I explained that she is my family now . . .*

It's what every woman wants to hear from the man she loves. I pinch away the tears in my eyes, read several more letters, then peel off my gloves.

"Any luck?" Travis asks.

Veronica and Chester look up. "James asked Anna to marry him, despite his parents' disapproval, and she accepted."

"Woo-hoo!" Veronica shouts and is instantly shushed.

"That's not all. Olivia is in love with a French man named Louis who she met before the Great War began," I whisper. "Their parents don't approve, but James told her to follow her heart; that he'd help her—" My voice snags with emotion at James's devotion. I always wished for a big brother to protect and defend me, someone who could show me what was possible.

Veronica pats my hand. "You doing okay?"

I summon the kind of familiar smile that no longer feels like a total act. "I'm putting one foot in front of the other."

"See you tonight," Veronica says with an exaggerated wink that makes me think she's up to something big.

As I leave the library, I make a call to the only wealthy influencer I know.

"Constance, how are you?" Lydia says. "Did you find more homes for those poor little fur-babies?"

"Some, but not enough," I reply. "Remember when you told me how much your husband loves you?"

"Of course," she says with a musical laugh.

I take a steadying breath. "Enough to help save all those animals you saw at the shelter?"

Chapter Twenty-Seven

Mars shows up at the shelter in high-waist navy culottes and a crop top, a medium-sized cardboard box of the things I'd left at Hayden's house in her arms. She sets it down on an end table then looks around the small studio. "No wonder you're depressed."

Growler lets out a low rumble, gets up from the couch, and pads over to sniff her. With no fear, Mars crouches in front of him and gives the dog a friendly rub on his chest. His tail twitches then wags and he licks her on the mouth. "You're my kind of guy," Mars says with a giggle.

Growler's reaction to my best friend is proof that animals are great at judging character. "Thanks for getting my stuff," I say. It's stunning that almost a year with Hayden can fit into a single box and makes me wonder if I always knew that things were never quite right.

"You doing okay?" Mars asks as she curls up on the couch with my dog.

I plop down beside her. "Was Hayden there?"

"Yes."

My stomach muscles clench for the gut punch. "Did he say anything?"

Mars hesitates then replies, "That he misses you."

It still feels like a punch to the gut. But I'm less winded. "I'm going to return the wedding dress."

"Don't," Mars says with a hard shake of her curls.

"I want to get your money back."

She yanks off her shoes, puts them on the coffee table.

"What are you doing?" I ask.

"Inviting fate to take over and bring you the love you deserve," Mars says. "So one day you'll *definitely* need that dress."

I burst out laughing. "You don't believe in happily ever after," I remind her.

Mars gives a half shrug then looks me up and down. "Is that what you're wearing to the party?"

I've chosen tan overalls and my porcupine T-shirt. "Why don't you pick something out for me," I offer and Mars darts to the closet, Growler at her heels. She chooses skinny jeans and a flowered blouse she forced me to buy nine months ago that I've never worn since and ankle boots she gave me last year for my birthday, again, never worn. I'm not entirely comfortable but Mars deserves a win.

We leave Growler in the apartment with a peanut butter–filled Kong and climb into Mars's bright red Volkswagen Bug. She drives us over the bridge to Mill Valley, where Veronica lives at the end of a narrow street in a super-cute Arts and Crafts–style home complete with whimsical stained glass and wind chimes hanging from Japanese maples. When we knock on the etched-glass front door no one answers, so we follow the sounds and a flagstone path to the backyard.

The party is in full swing. Bluegrass music plays from speakers on the back deck, and people mill around or talk in small clusters. I spy Veronica with her arm around a woman who must be Diane. Her partner has long silver hair and wears a gorgeous gold-embroidered tunic and pale green linen pants. I've never seen Veronica in anything but a baggy sweater and a skirt, but tonight she's in a flowing dress a shade darker than Diane's pants.

"Constance!" Travis calls out. Chester, beside him, waves.

Mars and I grab a beer and a plate of appetizers from the outdoor bar before heading over to say hello.

"Who is that gorgeous man?" Mars whispers as we approach.

"Chester," I reply. "And slow your roll. He's taken." I try one of the appetizers and a burst of incredible flavor floods my mouth. "Holy hell, these are good."

Mars tries one and a look of pure delight crosses her face. "Un-fucking-believable," she gushes. "I'm in love with whoever made these!"

"Constance," Travis says with a smile. He's changed out of his usual sweatshirt and wears a button-down blue shirt and fleece vest.

"I didn't know you owned anything but Berkeley sweatshirts," I joke.

Travis chuckles then points to his legs where two toddlers, their cheeks and pudgy hands sticky with whatever they just ate, cling. "I keep a few sweatshirts in the car for when I go out in public," he explains. "With these little monsters into everything, they're the only clean things I own." He nods at the pretty woman by his side. "This is my wife, Mai."

"So you're the woman researching her engagement ring," Mai says. "I love hearing all the stories about James and Anna. It's so dreamy! I'm up to my eyeballs in poopy diapers so when Travis comes home I demand all the details. Can I see the actual ring?" Travis elbows her. "What?" Mai demands.

"It's okay," I tell Travis then turn to Mai with a soft smile. "I gave it back. But I'll keep the stories coming for as long as I can."

"And this is my girlfriend, Isa," Chester pipes in and puts his arm around a statuesque woman who looks like a supermodel.

"Of course she is," Mars murmurs.

"We teach together," Isa says. "I've been at it for five years and Chester was hired at our elementary school last year but is already a student and parent favorite." She beams at him. "I've never seen someone take to teaching so fast. It's like he was born for it."

Chester and I share a look. Veronica wanders over, her arm linked through a younger woman's. "My daughter would like to talk to someone her own age and not my old fuddy-duddy friends," she says. "This is Scarlett and she's the genius who prepared all the food."

"The appetizers are unbelievable," Mars says and everyone voices their agreement.

"Scarlett is a brilliant chef," Veronica says. "Right now she's putting in her time, working as a sous-chef at Red's in Sonoma. But one day she'll have her own restaurant."

"And Mom will do all my PR," Scarlett adds, her cheeks pink. "Obviously."

I notice that Mars has sidled closer to them. Scarlett is

gorgeous—with long hair that frames her round face in soft curls and enormous brown eyes.

"How'd you learn to cook?" Mars asks.

"I went to cooking school in France, then worked in Hong Kong, Greece, France, and Spain," Scarlett explains. "Basically whatever food inspired me, I went to that country to learn how to make it. I've been back in the US for a year and Mom's right, eventually I do want to open my own place, but that's a ways off."

She takes a step even closer to Mars and my friend actually touches her arm and says, "I love to travel, too . . ."

I can literally feel the attraction rolling off the two women. In all the time I've known Mars, I've never seen her so obviously show her hand. Everyone around them notices, too, and we all slowly move away with mumbles of more food, another drink.

Fifteen minutes later, Veronica taps her wineglass and the crowd falls silent.

"Welcome, friends and family," Veronica says. "Diane and I are so happy you could join us. I'm especially thrilled that my daughter, Scarlett, who has graciously provided all the delicious food, could attend. While my sons haven't quite embraced that their mom is now a full-fledged member of the LGBTQIA+ community, I have hopes that one day they'll come around." Veronica's voice catches and Diane steps closer and takes her hand.

"My better half," Veronica says with a grateful smile. "Anyway, Scarlett has prepared a seafood paella that smells divine, but first I have a surprise."

Diane cocks her head. "What's going on?" she asks.

"Many of you know that I was married before . . . to a man," Veronica fake-whispers and there's a ripple of laughter. "Diane and I have been together for four blissful years. Truth is, I didn't even know I liked women *in that way* until I met her!" Veronica turns to face Diane, takes both of her hands. "Diane taught me that love is about the person, not the wrapper they come in. And she's patiently waited for me to come to terms with my divorce and some of my children's reactions to our relationship." Veronica takes a steadying breath then states, "Diane, recently I've been reminded that not everyone gets the chance we've been given. You are the love of my life and I don't want to waste another moment." She creakily drops to one knee.

"What the heck you doing?" Diane asks.

"Proposing, you silly goose," Veronica replies and pulls a sparkly diamond ring from the pocket of her dress. "Diane Mary McGinness, will you marry me?"

"Of course I will!" Diane helps Veronica to her feet and they dance around like schoolgirls. "You just name the date and I'll be there," Diane adds with a giddy grin.

Champagne bottles are uncorked and we all toast the newly engaged couple then sit down at folding tables covered in bright pink cloths to enjoy Scarlett's incredible meal. A river of contentment runs through me as I watch Veronica and Diane kiss.

Mars is very quiet on the drive home. "What's up?" I finally ask.

"I'm going to end things with Brock," she says without taking her eyes off the road.

I turn to study her. "Why?"

Mars grips the steering wheel. "My best friend is Constance

Sparks. She's courageous, brilliant, and loved by everyone who matters. I want to be more like her."

The compliment turns my heart to mush. "Does this have anything to do with Scarlett?"

"I'm not exchanging one for the other if that's what you mean. Scarlett is way too cool for that. But I'm ready to be available when the right person does come along."

I'd be lying to myself if I didn't admit to a new surge of worry for her. "You might get hurt like I did."

Mars glances over at me. "You're bouncing back."

"I am." We link pinkies as she drives. It's a silent promise that we're both determined to do better. "By the way," I say, "I'm going mountain biking with Ellis."

Mars squeals, "You're going on a date with Trudy's hot hunk of a son?"

"It's a *deal* we made, not a *date*." But the butterflies in my stomach still take flight at the mention of his name.

"Do you want it to be more?" Mars asks. She gives me an intent look while waiting for my answer.

I can't stop the flush creeping across my cheeks. "I just broke off an engagement."

"Over a month ago. And you know what I say about the best way to get over a guy—"

"That's a bad idea. Ellis was born to flirt and he's the kind of guy who probably only wants what he can't get. Now that I'm single, he'll back off." But if I'm honest, I'm no longer so sure that I want him to. In fact, I can't chase away the sense of connection I feel around him, so much so that I long to get to know him better now.

"Come on, Constance, live a little," Mars wheedles.

I chuckle. "I'm not you. But I am willing to have more fun and try dating again." The memory of kissing Ellis in my dream returns and this time there's no guilt attached, just a smoldering heat that's impossible to ignore.

Chapter Twenty-Eight

A re we visiting someone before we go home?" Grandpa asks as our Uber turns into Rosa and Marcio's driveway.

"This is just where you're staying while your house is being renovated," I reply. After his surgery Grandpa had trouble regaining his balance, so a social worker insisted on a rehab facility. Insurance only covered part of the three weeks there and dread at the forthcoming bill eats at the lining of my stomach. Somehow I'll swing it.

Grandpa tugs at the gray sweater that hangs off his bony shoulders. "I want to go home, Denise."

That was my mom's name. "I'm Constance, your granddaughter."

"You're not a bad mother, but you need to hug Constance more, tell her you love her."

Since the heart attack, Grandpa has been more confused. The doctor said he's exhausted from the procedure and rehab, but also that it's expected as his dementia progresses. His doctor agreed with Rosa, that I should just roll with whatever Grandpa says and not challenge or try to correct him. Otherwise he'll get agitated and scared about what's happening to his mind. It's brutal, but I can do it for him.

"Okay, Ricky," I say and kiss his wrinkled cheek. "Promise." I get out of the car, run around to his door, and help him out. We slowly walk the stone path.

Rosa opens the door. "Welcome back, Ricky! I baked your favorite muffins."

"I don't live here," Grandpa tells her. "I'm just staying until my house is ready. Then I'm going to help Denise take care of Constance. Her dad's back in jail and she needs some extra love."

I look away so he doesn't see my wet eyes.

"Let's get you settled for a visit, then," Rosa says with an easy smile.

Once we're seated at the kitchen table, Rosa pours two mugs of coffee, decaf for Grandpa, and puts blueberry muffins on a plate. She kisses the top of my head as she leaves. I butter Grandpa's muffin and try not to notice that he can barely keep his coffee from spilling.

"Constance, where's your ring?" Grandpa suddenly asks.

My throat tightens and I cough to clear it. "I gave it back."

"That's good." He takes another bite of his muffin.

"What was wrong with Hayden?" I ask.

Grandpa says with his mouth full, "He told me that you were the woman of *his* dreams but when I asked what *your* dreams were, he had no idea." He harrumphs. "Why'd it end?"

I wipe a crumb onto my napkin. "I didn't tell him about Dad."

One of Grandpa's bushy eyebrows lifts. "How'd he find out?"

"His parents."

"Huh. Why's it their business?"

"I guess they thought Hayden needed protection."

"From Gary?"

"From me. And Hayden passively agreed."

Suddenly Grandpa slams his fist down on the table and the coffee in our mugs sloshes. Other than when I was a little kid and he fought with Dad, I've never seen him get angry or even raise his voice.

"Hayden should've defended you," Grandpa thunders, "and dammit, Gary ruins everything he touches. They should never let him out of prison."

I rest a hand on his arm. "Like you said, Hayden didn't know my dreams. So it's for the best."

"I'd put the world on a string for you if I could."

A tear slips down Grandpa's cheek and I wipe it away. "Can I ask you something about Grandma?"

Grandpa instantly beams. "Hazel? She was the prettiest lady in the world, smart as a whip, too. Made me so proud she picked a dope like me. Never touched a drop of alcohol in my life, but I was addicted to her, from the first kiss to the last. Smashed my heart to bits when she died."

"Are you sorry you met her?"

Grandpa looks at me with genuine horror. "Even if I'd known about the car accident, that I'd lose her so young, I would've chosen to marry her every day, over and over again. Time with Hazel was a gift from God."

I can still see the secret in her smile as she sat at the foot of my bed. "I wish I'd known her."

"She would've loved you, Constance," Grandpa says.

"Why?"

"Hazel danced to a different drummer, from the way she dressed—she was a fan of very big hats—to the adventures she planned for us. That woman always surprised me, even if it was just a bicycle ride by the water or a love note hidden in my pocket. Hazel was devoted to her family, friends, never met a stray animal she didn't want to keep, and she was kind from the top of her head to her toes. You're two peas in a pod."

My heart warms at the comparison.

Before I leave, I help him to the recliner in the TV room and it soothes me to see some normalcy as he settles in to watch a rerun of *The Price Is Right*.

Over his shoulder he calls, "Denise, children who aren't loved right grow up thinking they have to prove they're worthy to every Tom, Dick, and Harry. I don't want that for my girl."

That's true, I think as I walk down the front path. But now maybe it's *my* choice on what I deserve from the people I keep close.

My phone rings. It's Lydia Sproule. "Hey, Lydia. What's up?"

"I can't talk long but wanted to let you know that Ari has agreed to pledge five hundred thousand."

I can't feel my feet. "Dollars?"

"What else?" She laughs. "I told you my husband loves me."

I do a happy dance and a passing car honks. "Lydia, you are the absolute best! I'll send you the paperwork. Thank you so much."

"Pleasure. Gotta go, my facialist is here."

Quickly, I dial Trudy's number. When she answers, I blurt, "I just got a $500,000 pledge!"

"What? From whom?"

"Lydia, the influencer."

Trudy chuckles. "Well, young lady, I've made half a dozen calls and so far my grand total is $1.2 *million*."

Hope goes off like fireworks. "Should we call the owners, ask for more time?"

"Give me a few more days; at this rate I can get a lot closer to their number. That'll have the most impact."

My feet barely touch the pavement. "We're doing this," I say.

"We really are," Trudy replies.

Chapter Twenty-Nine

When Ellis knocks on the shelter's apartment door my insides leap like I'm a teenage girl. I'm excited to spend the day with him, and even more excited that he asks questions about our bike ride all the way to the trailhead, like he's a kid, too, and thrilled to spend time together, try something new.

"Will we go through any creeks?" Ellis asks as we unload the bikes.

I laugh. "Only if you fall off a bridge."

"Are there stunts, like teeter-totters and jumps?"

"Not on this trail, but if you like this ride and want to try some there are other trails we can check out."

Ellis grins. "Oh, I'll like it."

I check the tires to hide the pink in my cheeks then make sure his seat height is right. "Ready?" I ask.

Ellis hops on his bike and says, "You lead and I'll follow."

I try not to notice how good he looks in his mountain bike shorts or the way his shirt clings to a muscular but lean torso. I'm wearing tan bike shorts and a pink shirt with rabbits on the hem and can't help but wonder if he thinks I look good, too.

Since Ellis has ridden a road bike but is new to mountain biking, I choose an intermediate trail.

"Any last words of advice?" he asks, pedaling close behind me.

"Try not to fall."

He cracks up. "Will do."

We don't talk much, just take in the scenery—wildflowers are in full bloom and the fields are speckled with violet grass widows and bright yellow clumps of wild parsnip. We start to climb up a narrow dirt trail that winds between old-growth trees. When we hit a rocky section I hear Ellis's tires slip. I glance back to see him use a tree to push off and regain his momentum. "Nice!" I offer him a little more encouragement and keep pedaling. "This next section has some big roots. Center your weight over your seat so your wheels don't spin out. If your back tire gives, slow your pedals until it regains purchase." He makes it over the roots and lets out a tiny whoop that makes me laugh out loud.

"Is that Aussie shepherd still at the shelter?" Ellis asks a few minutes later.

"Helen? She is," I say. "Why?"

"I'd like to take her."

"I thought you didn't have enough free time for a dog."

"I can hire a dog walker during the day," Ellis explains. "And I'll be there mornings and nights, and can take her for adventures on the weekends. She'd probably love these trails or time at the beach. If a better option comes along for her, I'll let her go."

I'm shocked but thrilled. "Have you told your mom that you've developed cardiomegaly?" I joke. "It might help her forgive you for whatever you did wrong."

"It'll take more than adopting a dog," Ellis says.

"Her mood is definitely brightening. I got a pledge for half a million dollars," I share. "And your mom has pulled in $1.2 million."

"Wow. That's unexpected. But still," he ventures, "that's a long way from nine or ten million."

"Agreed. But we only just started."

"You have less than a week."

"But if we show the owners we have the ability to raise a lot of money in only a week," I explain, "our hope is that they'll postpone the auction, give us the time we need to raise the rest."

The trail cuts left, across a hillside of emerald-green grass dotted with orange and red California poppies. I draw in a lungful of the sweet air and listen to the birds and the sound of our tires crunching and feel . . . a sense of overwhelming peace for the first time in forever.

"How was bringing your grandfather home?" Ellis asks.

"He thought I was my mom part of the time. And he got really mad at one point, which isn't like him."

"It's hard to watch the people you love lose bits of themselves. At the end, my dad changed. The meds made him hazy and the pain brought back aspects of his personality I hated growing up."

The trail forks and I stop on a flat area to give Ellis a break. "Like what?"

He leans on his handlebars. "A lot of anger. It made me feel like I was a little boy again, desperate to escape." He takes a swig from his water then asks, "What's your grandfather angry about?"

"Part of the equation is Hayden."

"What actually happened with him? Or is that too personal a question?"

It is personal, but I actually want to tell him. "Hayden's parents found out about my dad. Their daughter was murdered and they didn't want their son to marry the child of a convicted killer. Plus, they thought I was a gold digger." I take a swig from my water bottle. "I had no clue Hayden came from money. Grandpa was furious that he didn't defend me to his parents."

Ellis scowls. "He should've."

I agree, but I'm at a good enough place now that I can shrug and move our conversation on to something else. "It doesn't matter now. And Grandpa didn't think the two of us were the right fit anyway."

In the shadow of the forest Ellis's eyes are an even more intense green. He asks, "Why's that?"

"He told me that he didn't think my ex knew any of my dreams for my life. But that's partially my fault. I tried to fit into his life but really never asked for the same in return. Though in fairness, Hayden did try at times, especially with the animals I brought home."

"So the other part of the equation that made your grandfather angry?"

Anxiety prickles but I stick with the truth. "My dad is up for parole. Grandpa doesn't want him to get out."

"Do you?"

My nerves ping. "Ready to ride more?" I wait for Ellis to stand up then use a tree to push off and start pedaling. "It wasn't always bad. Dad came to my ballet recitals, took me to the fair." My stomach churns as I talk about him. "So the answer is that I don't know."

When we reach the top of the trail there's a wonderful viewpoint—a panorama of the Marin Headlands, Golden Gate Bridge, the sparkling bay, and the city of San Francisco.

"This is incredible, Constance," Ellis says. "Thanks for bringing me here."

We pull water bottles from their cages and sit on a flat rock close to each other. Ellis shares the bag of figs he brought. "Having fun so far?" I ask.

"Definitely."

His smile makes my insides melt. We lie back on the rock and watch a cluster of sparrows chase after a peregrine falcon. "It's called mobbing," I say.

"Why do they do it?" Ellis asks.

"They're defending themselves and their nests from a perceived predator."

Ellis rolls onto his side, head perched on his elbow. "How do you know that?"

"From an animal behavior class I took in undergrad." He's so close I can see the tiny chip on his front tooth and smell a heady mixture of sweat and soap. I can't take my eyes off his lips. The air between us is suddenly charged. Ellis leans in and I close my eyes for a kiss . . . that never happens. Instead, he gently pulls a twig from my braid. This is clearly *not* a date.

"Let's get going," I say. "Take your time on the downhill. There are a few big drops and some narrow bridges and logs that you can stop and walk or climb over if you don't want to ride them. If you lose sight of me, just remember to take every right turn." Without looking back, I hop on my bike and take off.

No matter how fast I descend, I can hear Ellis behind me. He doesn't get off his bike, survives every obstacle . . . until he doesn't. I hear the crash and hit my brakes then turn. Ellis tried to ride over one of the narrow bridges and fell off it. Heart in my throat, I dump my bike on the side of the trail and run back. His bike is upside down, tires still spinning, and he's curled on the ground five feet below the split-log bridge in a dry creek bed. "Ellis! Are you okay?"

Slowly he rolls onto his back, wiggles his fingers and toes, and then sits up smiling, his helmet lopsided. There's a smear of dirt on his forehead. "I'm good. Damn, that happened fast."

I scramble on my butt down to him. No blood, and from the way he's moving nothing appears to be broken. I pull him to his feet a bit too fast and Ellis wraps an arm around my waist so we both don't go down. Our bodies press together. Right away it feels like his body fits every curve of my own. Every spot where our skin touches instantly feels more alive. I break away and try to pull myself together as I begin to climb up the embankment. Ellis grabs his bike and follows.

"What's going on, Constance?" he asks when we're back on the trail.

"What do you mean?"

"Your mood. It changed at the lookout."

My face blazes red. I'm such an idiot. "It's nothing. Just . . . I thought . . ."

A slow smile tugs at the corners of his mouth. "I'm trying to be a gentleman," he says. "Give you time to find your footing. Like I told you when we had beers. Good things are worth the hard work and the wait."

A guy hasn't surprised me, in a good way, for a very long time. It's intoxicating. Flustered, I say, "How about you go first and control our speed?"

"Nah," Ellis replies with a cocky grin. "The view from behind is better."

A delicious heat spirals to my core. I busy myself getting back on my bike.

"Why'd I fall off that bridge?" Ellis asks.

"Mountain biking is all about looking where you want to go. The bike follows naturally," I explain.

"Sounds like life," Ellis notes.

He's right about that. "Were you looking ahead or down in the creek anticipating a fall?" I ask.

"In the creek," he admits. Then he wheels his bike back up the hill to try the bridge again.

"Hang on," I call. I grab a handful of yellow flowers and run them in a line at the far end of the bridge. "Once your front tire hits the log, look for the flowers, okay?"

"Okay!" Ellis shouts and then he rides back down to the bridge, this time with less speed, and bumps his front tire onto it.

I watch him look for the flowers, which draw his eyes to the right place, and he easily clears the bridge then swerves to a stop beside me. His grin is immediately contagious. "Way to go!"

Ellis hops off his bike, picks up one of the flowers he didn't crush, and tucks it behind my ear. He's so close that I draw in his exhaled breath. Despite being wildly distracted, we make it down the rest of the trail without any more falls.

"Next time I want to see if I can ride it clean," Ellis says as we load the bikes into his Sprinter van.

"Next time?" I ask. Ellis reaches for my hand and a jolt of energy shoots through me.

He smiles his sexy, pirate smile. "If you want to invite me?"

This *was* a date. And Ellis wants another one. Mountain biking. A sport *I* love to do. Every nerve in my body zings. There's no question in my mind that he's someone I want to get to know better. "How about next week?"

Chapter Thirty

After a quick shower and a game of catch with some of the dogs, including Growler, who doesn't like to share me but tolerates it with only a few grumbles, I head over to the library and climb to the third floor to find a book Colin mentioned. A library employee in her midtwenties, dressed in an olive-green jumpsuit, her curls cut short around a heart-shaped face, is in the stacks shelving volumes from a pushcart. I find *No Man's Land: The Trailblazing Women Who Ran Britain's Most Extraordinary Military Hospital during World War I* by Wendy Moore and pull it from the shelf.

"What's that one about?" the young woman asks, hazel eyes inquisitive behind red cat-eye glasses.

I read the synopsis on the back of the book then summarize. "Two doctors from the United Kingdom," I say, "Louisa Garrett Anderson and Flora Murray. During World War I, the British government wouldn't let them treat men, so they went to Paris and established a military hospital to care for wounded soldiers. They were so successful that the British Army later asked them to run a large hospital in London. It was called the Endell Street Military Hospital, nicknamed Suffragettes' Hospital, and the all-female staff treated more than twenty-six thousand wounded soldiers."

"I'm Amelia," the young woman says with a nod at her name tag. "You writing a paper on those women?"

I shake my head. "Constance, and nope."

Amelia crouches down to replace a book. "Going to war sounds pretty risky."

"It was. But you and I have so many more rights because of the sacrifices women like them made. Big change takes bravery."

"You trying to get something specific out of reading that book?" she asks.

I consider the question. "Yes, I guess so. I'm working on a new way to live, so inspiration helps." When Amelia stands, our eyes meet and I see longing in hers and recognize a kindred spirit.

"Maybe I'll check that book out when you bring it back," she says then pushes her cart down the row.

It's a different time of day than I usually come to Special Collections and the main table is filled with people I don't know. Quickly I retrieve my book, find a seat, and open *Letters from My War*. My note is gone, replaced by a now familiar blue slip of paper. The world around me dims as I drop the note onto my lap.

Dear Constance,

You asked what scared me most in life. Two things. Not making a difference. And that I didn't have the ability to find lasting love, have a successful marriage and a family.

I was a selfish man in my youth, focused only on my own pursuits. But then I met a woman who challenged me, and it made all the difference. I wanted to be a better man and to defend and protect her. But I learned that was not always possible. In my life I faced many challenging situations, tried to find ways to make everyone involved happy and fulfilled. But sometimes you can still lose what's most important to you.

My scalp tightens. What's he talking about?

Be kind to yourself, Constance. You will make the right decision about whether to support your father. Perhaps you will find a way to do this on your own terms and in a manner you can live with regardless of the outcome. The way he chooses to live, once he is, indeed, a free man, reflects only upon him, not you.

What scares you most? And what is your vision for the future?

Love,

J

He wrote *love*. Despite the impossibility of a relationship with a man who lived one hundred years ago, and my growing attraction to Ellis, there's a joy to reading the words I hoped he would write to me. I grab a pencil from the jar on the table and write back . . .

Dear J,

What scares me most has always been losing someone's love. That's why deciding whether to write the letter for my dad is so hard.

The truth is that my father was an incredibly selfish man. He's worked the past few years to change and has earned

another chance for freedom. I don't want to stand in the way.
But I also don't want to be the reason he gets out and hurts
someone else. The responsibility I have in this situation
weighs heavily on me every day.

As for your fear of not being able to connect deeply with a
woman, you've been a confidant and good friend when I needed
one the most. I don't know what I would've done without you.
You are right that it's impossible to make everyone happy, but
I can't imagine if they knew your heart, that they didn't
forgive you for whatever offense you believe you committed.

You asked about my vision for the future . . . In the next
few years I hope to have a law degree and work for the district
attorney finding justice for those who need it most. In my free
time, I'll volunteer for animal shelters and foster as many dogs
as possible.

I don't know if I'll ever find a partner. But if I do, I hope
he's like you were and makes a difference in the world,
whether it's large or small; has the ability to empathize; is
kind, smart, and wants to be a father. As long as I'm indulging
in this fantasy, if my grandpa is still alive then, I'd want him to
live with our family, so that I can take care of him the way he
cared for me when I was small.

Eventually, my dream is to live outside the city where the
long-haulers I foster would have the freedom to explore and
my children could climb trees, build forts, and discover who
they want to be. I'd make certain that they know they are
always loved and wanted and that nothing they do could ever
change that.

At night, after everyone's asleep, my husband and I would
lie on a blanket in the backyard and share stories, our dreams,

but also be content in the silence. And in the morning, amidst
the delicious chaos of a large family, there would be no one
else I'd rather have at my table.

What were your dreams?

Love,
Constance

I slide my note into the sleeve, then withdraw James's next
letter to his sister.

August 1917

*Last night I surprised Anna with the enclosed drawing of an
engagement ring—platinum with a center diamond and on the
sides red rubies in the shape of the poppies she loves. Please use funds
from my account to have the ring made and the inside band inscribed
with: À la maison pour toujours. "Forever Home" is what Anna is
to me . . .*

I study the drawing. It's the exact ring Hayden gave to me.
James designed it for Anna. Mystery solved. A pang for what I
thought I had with Hayden runs through me. But he's not like
James and I wasn't his Anna. Now I know the provenance and
owner of my former engagement ring. But my original question
remains: How did it wind up in Olivia's possession?

"How are our lovebirds?" Veronica asks as she slides onto the
chair beside me.

I show her the drawing of Anna's engagement ring.

"Whoa," she says. "It was yours!"

I nod. "Anna said she'd be happy with a string on her finger but James insisted."

"So the mystery is solved and you're done with the research?"

"I still want to finish the letters, find out if James had the chance to give the ring to Anna . . . before he—" My voice catches.

Veronica touches my arm. "I know you're caught up in the story. But remember it happened a long time ago." She nods at the gold band on her own wedding finger. "Life is for the living."

"You got married already?" I exclaim. Instantly a woman at the end of the table shushes me.

"You reminded me that life can be short and nothing is guaranteed," Veronica says.

"That was James," I say, correcting her.

Veronica shakes her head. "It was *you*, kiddo. Thank you for going out on a limb for a foolish old woman you didn't even know that well. That was brave."

"You're not old or foolish."

She laughs. "I don't mind the gray hair or wrinkles. I've never felt luckier."

The idea that my sharing James and Anna's story with Veronica helped her finally commit to Diane makes my heart swell.

"Despite royally screwing up in my first marriage and putting my relationship with Diane in jeopardy, she believed in me," Veronica adds. "Hopefully I won't mess things up." She dabs at her eyes then opens the thick volume in front of her.

I pull out James's next letter and start reading.

August 1917

Dearest Olivia,
    This morning Anna and I were married in the garden of the
hospital by an aumônier—one of the fighting priests who have joined
the Great War with a rifle in one hand and crucifix in the other . . .

I whisper to Veronica, "Anna and James just got married, too!"

Veronica's eyes light up. "What'd she wear?"

"An ivory silk dress with a crown of wildflowers in her hair. And her ring arrived just in time. James is sending Olivia a photograph of the day so she can feel a part of it." I move my chair a little closer. "Anna is pregnant. They're overjoyed."

Veronica's smile dims. "Can I say something to you that I'd tell my own daughter?"

My nerves do a little jitter. "Sure."

"When I first came to Special Collections to research poetry for my class, it was in part as a way to escape the upset that my sons didn't support my decisions and the pressure I felt about Diane. This was my place to hide. Now I set an alarm—two hours tops, then I go home." She pats my hand. "Maybe . . . ask yourself if there are things you're avoiding and then make a plan to deal with them so you can live life *outside* these walls to its fullest."

I think about how the one thing I'm still hiding from is the letter for my dad, and what J wrote about finding a way to support him on my own terms. I lean in and kiss Veronica's soft cheek. "Thank you. And congratulations. You won't mess things up with Diane. I believe in you. And she matters too much to you."

I pack up my things. I'm meeting Mars for dinner, but instead of heading right to the shelter, I grab a coffee at Hemingway's café, pull out my iPad, and open a new email.

Dear Parole Board,

I'm writing this letter as a character witness for my dad, Gary Trumble, who is seeking parole for his crimes.

Thirteen years ago, my father was addicted to alcohol, opiates, and probably other drugs I don't know about, when he robbed a convenience store and caused the death of Carter Mitchell. His addictions do not excuse his actions that day. He is guilty of taking a life and no amount of time served can make up for Carter's death and the Mitchell family's loss.

Dad has spent the past three years participating in the Alcoholics Anonymous program, working through anger management training, and has earned his AA chips. He also volunteers in the prison hospital. I do not know if he has remorse for his crime, but I hope that these choices reflect that he wants to be a better man.

Should my dad be paroled, I cannot provide him a place to live. I also do not have the financial means to cover travel, medical, or insurance needs. Dad has a father, but they are estranged and my grandpa is in poor health and lives on Social Security and Medicare, so he will not be able to provide help, either.

Gary Trumble will need government assistance to reenter
society, transitional housing, and help finding employment
so that he doesn't succumb to the pitfalls of the recently
paroled. I sincerely hope he gets this support and that he
succeeds in the outside world.

Sincerely,
Constance Sparks

My finger hovers over the send button, but a rush of fear
makes my hand tremble. Maybe I wasn't ready like I thought I
was. Checking the time, I know I'll need to rush to make it to
meet Mars.

Before I leave the café, I save the letter to my drafts folder.

Chapter Thirty-One

Mars and I order take-out Chinese food and when it arrives we eat at a picnic bench while Growler, Houdini, and a handful of other dogs race around the shelter's yard. "Careful," I say when she leaves her chopsticks poking out of her bowl of rice.

Mars sighs dramatically. "I don't remember this one. What, pray tell, will happen to me?"

"Crossed chopsticks represent death." A chill dusts my body. I'm almost through with the letters James wrote to Olivia. He *will* die soon. While intellectually I've known that all along, the truth makes me horribly sad. I have the feeling that the letters from J will stop, too, when I read about his death. I'm relieved when Mars pulls her chopsticks out and sets them on the table.

She asks, "You do realize that superstitions are your way of trying to exert control over the world?"

I give her the side-eye. "How'd you get so smart?"

"I was born this way. Kidding, not kidding," she jokes. "So tell me what else is going on with you?"

I think about telling her details of my ride with Ellis, but decide to hold back until I know if it's going to turn into something. "I read about Anna and James getting married," I share.

"You're still reading those old letters? Why? The history of that ring doesn't matter anymore."

"I'm living vicariously. Anna and James met their perfect match, got married. Now Anna is pregnant."

"Was," Mars points out with a hard blink.

My chest tightens. "I know they're dead."

"Then let it go and spend your free time in the *real* world. Here."

Somehow the thought of leaving James and Anna behind doesn't sit right . . . and I worry about how it will feel when I'm no longer hearing from J, that it will leave an enormous hole in my life. "I will. Soon. I've almost reached the end."

Mars takes a bite of her hoisin tofu then asks, "So what's your takeaway from all those letters?"

Heart dangling from a string on my sleeve, I admit, "I want what James and Anna had together."

Mars snorts. "You don't believe in—"

"Soul mates? I do want to believe in them," I confess.

Mars squints like she's trying to see me better. "What happened to the woman I knew who was looking for comfort and safety; a worn-in sneaker for a partner?"

I meet Mars's piercing gaze. "She decided she wants more."

"Hmm." Mars tosses a ball for Houdini and the little dog scoots off to retrieve it. "By the way, I asked Scarlett to go for a walk next week."

"A walk?" That's not Mars's usual wild style.

She actually blushes. "Maybe I want more, too."

When my phone rings the ID reads: San Quentin. I put the call on speaker—Mars will demand a recap so this is easier.

Dad says, "Hey, honeybunch."

"Hi, Dad."

"Only a few days until my parole hearing."

"I know." Mars blows up several of the balloons we keep on hand to play with the dogs and bats them to Growler, Houdini, and a pug named Bacon.

"Thing is, the prison staff just notified me that they haven't received your letter," Dad says. "That's a mistake, right?"

". . . A lot has been going on."

"What could be more important than your old man getting out of prison?"

The slight edge to his voice turns me into a little girl again. "I'm sorry. Hayden and I . . . we broke up."

"No! That's a damn shame. I'm really, really sorry, kiddo. But I bet you'll find someone better next time. A guy who can actually afford a real diamond would be nice, right?"

I'm irritated to hear that's what he thinks of me. "That never mattered to me."

"That's because you're a truly decent person," Dad says. "Have I told you lately how proud I am of you?"

"Thanks."

"All I want is the opportunity to be there for you when things like this go down." He blows out air audibly. "Constance, do you know what *backdoor parole* means?"

"No."

"It means dying in prison. I'm getting old. Afraid that might happen if I don't get out of here soon."

Mars is watching me, her lips pressed together. For some reason she's never believed that my dad could change. But people do deserve a second chance. I need to consider rewriting my letter to the parole board, support Dad's bid for freedom. "I'll send the letter today."

"Good girl. I'll call you right after the hearing. Hopefully with good news! Wish me luck. Love you to pieces."

I hang up, then watch the dogs chase after balloons, afraid to look over at Mars and see her feelings written across her face.

"You don't have to write it," she finally says.

"He's been in prison thirteen years."

She scowls. "For a crime he committed."

"But he's served most of his sentence; worked hard to change."

Mars blinks hard. "I'm just going to say it. No matter how you want to remember things, he was a *shit* dad."

"He tried." And he wants the chance to do better.

Mars's hands ball into fists and she stomps her feet. "I can't do this anymore."

"What are you talking about?"

"I can't watch you beg for scraps from a guy who consistently lets you down. It didn't matter as much when he was in prison, but now the stakes are too high. You're finally getting your life together. The last thing you need is for Gary Trumble to blow it apart."

I shake my head. "He didn't *always* let me down." And I want to have family in my life, even if he's late to the role. At this point, he and Grandpa are the only relatives I have.

"Remember when I had the flu and your grandpa took care of me?" Mars asks.

I want to look away but her eyes hold mine. "Yes."

"He told me the *truth* about the ballet." Mars blinks hard to punctuate her words.

Before I can stop it, a memory claws its way out of the recesses of my mind where I buried it . . .

I'm five and it's my first ballet recital. Grandpa is seated in the front row in his best suit and a pink tie he found at Goodwill that matches my tutu. The music swells and our gaggle of ballerinas leap across the stage in the clumsy way kids do. Lavonia Johnson forgets where to go next and I grab her hand and pull her into the right spot. And then it's my turn to do a plié, pirouette, and arabesque at the front of the stage. Grandpa's face is tipped up, drinking me in, and I'm so happy . . .

There's a loud noise in the back of the small theater. Dad bursts through the doors and they slam shut behind him.

"Sorry, sorry," he calls out. "Sorry I'm late."

He trots down the aisle in ripped jeans and a stained T-shirt, backpack slung over one shoulder, and sits a row behind Grandpa. I try to do my part, forget the arabesque and one leap, then fade back into the group. Dad talks too loud to the people next to him. Grandpa turns, says something.

"Relax," Dad shouts. "I'm watchin' m' honeybunch dansh."

Distracted, I forget the rest of the routine and end up alone on one side of the stage as the rest of the ballerinas leap away.

"Wait fo' m'girl," Dad shouts.

I start to cry.

"Don't be a crybaby! Connie, jus' follow the other brats. It's not that fucking hard!"

Mars watches as the memory crashes over me, her jaw set. The shame of that moment returns. I wanted to run out of the auditorium and never come back. "You're right," I admit. "I buried a lot of the bad stuff. My dad was a terrible parent at times. And he committed a horrendous crime. But what I grapple with is, does that mean he should *never* be given the chance to get out and do better?"

Mars's shoulders slump. "Why do you have to be such a good person?"

I meet her gaze. "I heard you. Promise."

After Mars heads home, Growler and I make sure all the animals have fresh water and then return to the studio apartment. Growler curls on his cushion beside my bed. But the hours pass and I'm not any closer to falling asleep.

I grab my computer, move to the couch, open up email, and pull up the draft of my letter to the parole board. Why haven't I sent it? "I'm afraid he won't love me . . . or stay once he's out," I murmur. "I'm afraid that he'll hate me." But why does that matter so much to me? When the female surgeons in World War I first arrived at hospitals in France the male doctors ridiculed them. Yet they didn't care if they were wanted. They knew their value, focused on what mattered, and earned respect. Isn't that how I want to live my life, too?

"I'm not going to let Dad manipulate my emotions to make me feel bad for him anymore," I tell Growler as he sleepily climbs onto the couch and rests his head on my thigh. The weight of his presence steadies me. "He might not forgive me," I tell my dog. But I can't be responsible for someone else's choices anymore. It's up to *him* now.

I hit send.

Chapter Thirty-Two

In the early morning light Hayden waits by my Vespa holding two cups of coffee from Farley's. I'm certain one is my favorite—a vanilla soy latte. His shoulders are hunched from the cold, hair a bit too long and wind tussled. A red flannel shirt hangs beneath the hem of his down jacket, and he has on the same canvas pants and worn boots he wore the first night we met. Hayden rocks from foot to foot to stay warm. Sensing my presence, he turns.

"Constance."

I feel so many things in this moment—a longing for what I thought we had, anger at how he treated me in the end, sadness for the dream's demise, and the remnants of love.

Hayden holds out the coffee and asks, "Can we talk? Preferably somewhere warm?"

"Here is fine." I take the cup and sip.

Hayden clears his throat. "I should've called. Right away."

"But you didn't."

Grooves crease his forehead. "I wasn't sure how to fix things."

Weight presses on my chest. "Maybe that's not possible."

Hayden takes a step closer. "I should've told you about the money, my sister, and Lydia."

"Why didn't you?"

"Things were so good between us. I didn't want to ruin it."

"Same reason I didn't tell you about my dad. But I shouldn't have lied about my parents."

He nods. "And I wish I'd defended you with mine. I was just so . . ."

"Shocked?"

"Yeah. I thought that I knew everything about you." Hayden's voice is filled with gravel. "I *wanted* to think that I knew everything about you, that we were indestructible. But that wasn't fair to you. I'm so very sorry."

Despite everything, I inch closer. "I'm sorry, too." He reaches for my hand and I don't pull away.

"I'm also devastated that Grier and Whit won't accept you," Hayden says. "It's irrational, I know, but the pain and grief from Elizabeth's murder will never fade for them."

There's a quiet inside me like the held breath before a wish. "You'd give them up?"

Hayden blanches. "What? No, I couldn't do that. I'm the only child they have left." He holds my hand tighter. "But we don't need to get married. We can continue to live together and I'll keep my relationship with them separate."

He's still not choosing me. I leave my hand in his, but it's gone numb. "When I was a kid, my dad would show up days late for special events, forget to call for Christmas, disappear for weeks or months at a time and then explain his absence by saying that I was loved but not always wanted." I struggle to speak around the invisible hand clenching my throat. "And that's what you're saying to me right now, that you love but only want me *some* of the time."

"That's not true. I love you and want us to be together *despite* my parents. Remember the words on our Scrabble board that first night we played? FATE. LOVE. RING. It all came true! We were meant to meet, to be together."

I don't point out that the word LIAR was also on that game board—we both know it. Mars asked me if I believe in soul mates. I'm not sure. But I do know that I want more than the unstable foundation Hayden and I had together. I want to be with someone who'll extend grace, and support me through the hard times life deals out.

"Maybe fate played a role in our relationship," I admit. "The idea that the universe had finally granted my biggest wish—to find my person—I desperately wanted that to be true. Probably because the people in my life who were supposed to love me mostly fell short. But I get now that fate isn't some mystical force that brings us together and guarantees a happily ever after. It's what happens next—what people *do*, how they treat each other day to day, in the good and bad and truly awful times, *how* they care—that matters more."

"You can't just walk away from us," Hayden implores.

I feel the invisible weight of Growler's head resting on my lap, his smooth fur beneath my fingers the first time he decided to trust me. "Ultimately, fate isn't what happens *to* us. It's what we *choose*." I slip my hand free. "And we've chosen different things."

"Constance." Hayden exhales my name like a prayer. "Please reconsider. We both can have almost everything we want."

"Take care of yourself, Hayden." He watches me get on my Vespa and drive off. Again he doesn't try to stop me, but I no longer want him to.

Chapter Thirty-Three

San Francisco Bay in May is sunny but cold as surfers slice through the water attached by long lines to orange, yellow, blue, and green kites. It's Sunday so there are dozens of them out there playing in the waves. I sit on a bench, warm in a down vest, cream-colored sweater dotted with black paw prints, and leggings, and watch as a kiter comes close to the shore. Ellis, in a black wet suit, his hair slicked back with salt water, hops off his board, lands his kite in a fellow kiter's hands, then jogs over. My pulse speeds up as he nears.

"You made it," Ellis says.

I grin. "That was a pretty impressive showing."

"That's what I was hoping you'd say." He nods at his van parked nearby. "Give me a sec to change and then we'll start your lesson."

I eye the blue-black water. "It looks cold out there. But I'm game."

Ellis laughs. "I love that you're willing to get in the water, and without a wet suit, which is very bold, but we'll start with a trainer kite on land."

He changes into jeans and a flannel jacket, covers his wet

head with a green wool hat, then unfolds a tiny red, crescent-shaped kite and attaches long lines to a handlebar. Ellis steps back and gives the bar a snap, and the kite lifts into the air. He shows me how to move the kite across the sky by applying pressure to the bar.

"Your turn."

I twist my hair into a bun so it stays out of my eyes then nervously take over and the small kite jerks and tugs. Ellis gets behind me, puts his hands over mine, and shows me how to direct the kite. It zips around, moving in spurts like an angry hornet, and then crashes to the ground. He launches it again and we work together to keep the kite in the air. When it almost tugs me off my feet, he wraps an arm around my waist to keep me on the ground.

"You ready to solo?"

I nod and Ellis steps back. It's mesmerizing to watch the kite race against the sky. When I move it too quickly and it lifts me onto my tiptoes Ellis is right there to pull me back down. Once my neck gets tired of staring up at the kite I ask him if we can sit on the grass and am surprised but definitely pleased when he settles behind me, my back pressed against his chest. Together we watch the kite float across a sky now banded in purples. When the wind tapers it flutters to the grass.

"What'd you think?" Ellis asks.

His lips are so close that the sensation of his warm breath tickles my ear. Uncomfortable at just how much I want to stay in his arms, I slide free and sit beside him. "It's been a long time since I've tried something new."

Ellis plucks two clovers from the grass and twists them

together to make a four-leaf one. He holds it out to me. "That's cheating," I say, but take it anyway. "*Real* four-leaf clovers are supposed to offer magical protection against bad luck."

"Good to know." Ellis makes another one and tucks it in his own pocket. "I could use some extra luck. So why haven't you done anything new in a while?"

"I really liked flying that kite."

Ellis waits a beat then lets me off the hook and asks, "Enough to do it again?"

"Definitely. I want to get in the water next time."

He chuckles. "Safety first, but I'll get you in there soon—in a wet suit and life vest. How was your ride?"

This morning I went over the Golden Gate Bridge and into the Headlands. Once I start working for Ellen I won't be able to take morning rides so I'm making the most of it. "Great. I didn't see another soul on the trail and it gave me time to think."

Ellis tucks a loose lock of hair behind my ear, his fingers lingering, and asks, "About what?"

I fight the urge to lean in to prolong our physical contact. "What I want."

"Does it involve your ex?" Ellis asks.

"In a way. He showed up at the shelter."

"Why?"

"To plead his case."

Ellis's smile fades. "Ah. So he's willing to defend you to his parents?"

I shake my head. "Hayden's parents wouldn't know."

"What'd you say?" he asks.

"Remember I told you that I've been reading letters sent home by an American ambulance driver from the Great War?"

Ellis asks, "James Edwards, right?"

"Exactly. His parents refused to give their permission for him to marry Anna. But he did it anyway. I want someone who picks me, who makes me his family like James did with Anna."

"That's how it should be," Ellis agrees. "Any idea how to make it happen?"

I hesitate, uncertain how much of the truth to share. Then I make a choice. "Hayden used to call me *constant* Constance. I always said yes, met his needs and everyone else's. I want to be there for my friends, family, and ultimately a partner, but now I get that my own desires have to be part of that equation."

"Wise words," Ellis says.

As the conversation drifts off, we lie back on the grass and watch the sun set. Silence stretches between us and it's comfortable. Like we've known each other forever.

We meet for dinner at a sushi place seated side by side at a table for two. Ellis compliments the green short-sleeve sweater I wear that has a tiny koala printed on the neck. I found it at a flea market and my squeal of delight caused Mars to threaten disowning me.

"My best friend thinks my sense of style is . . . odd," I admit.

"You seem to lean toward animals and flowers," Ellis notes.

"They make me smile."

"Me, too," Ellis says with a little grin. "And I like that you're honest and natural," he adds.

"Well, this honest woman has no idea what to order," I admit.

"I've got this, then, if that's okay?"

I nod and he orders his favorites. When the fish comes it melts in my mouth. We drink hot sake, talk about Grandpa and Trudy and how much they matter to us, our favorite places,

the biking trip to Portugal that's on my bucket list, and how
Ellis wants to go to Fiji to learn to surf. We make plans to bike
somewhere new. And then Ellis kisses me. When I kiss him
back the most delicious heat spins through my body. He's a sexy
guy, but it's more than that. I have never, ever experienced a kiss
like this—it's like being drawn into someone's gravity and takes
everything to break free.

"Why now?" I ask.

"What do you mean?" Ellis asks.

"You've known me for years."

He takes another sip of sake. "Part of that time I was married."

"Part of it you weren't and I was single."

"It's taken me a while to grow up," Ellis confesses. "But I
was lurking at the shelter for months, trying to get to know you
better before I asked you out, but—"

"Then I started dating Hayden," I finish. We stare into each
other's eyes and I no longer want to look away. I can handle the
feelings he provokes in me.

When he kisses me again his lips are more insistent and
desire ignites within me. It's an epic kiss . . .

"Will you come to my house?" Ellis murmurs.

I want to. His hands have slipped around my waist, finger-
tips gliding beneath the hem of my sweater. With his lips on
mine, it's gotten hard to think straight. In the past, I've tum-
bled fast into every relationship. Mars is right that I've been a
pushover, wanting to please, putting my needs aside. Hal did
steal my mattress and I let go of things that gave me joy for
Hayden. If I want whatever is happening with Ellis to be different, then change has to start with me. I pull back from our
embrace. "I need a little more time."

Ellis's eyes smolder. "I can wait, but let's get out of here while I can still walk without risking a ticket for indecent exposure. Dinner Wednesday at my place?" Ellis asks once we're on the sidewalk. "I want to cook for you."

"You hate to cook," I tease.

He laughs. "I'll plate the takeout and we can watch a movie. And bring Helen."

Stunned, I sit back. "You were really serious about adopting her?"

"You thought it was just a line?" Ellis asks, his tone mock offended. "Already bought her a bed, toys, and the kibble you feed at the shelter. I have a dog walker lined up, too. I'll be able to take her for a morning run before work, but she'll get another trip to the park during the day with a few friends. If I have an emergency surgery my neighbor has agreed to help out."

Happiness pops inside me like a champagne cork. Helen is getting a forever home! "Then I'll bring her Wednesday . . . if you're really ready?"

Ellis pulls me in for another kiss. "Constance, I'm ready."

As I walk to my Vespa, I wonder if this is how Anna felt after her first kiss with James. Like every color is brighter, every smell more intoxicating. Did she imagine the moment when their kisses would lead to more? On the drive home it feels like I'm flying. Even though there's no safety net below I'm willing to take the risk of crashing because there could be something worth it ahead of me.

Chapter Thirty-Four

Over the next few days, Trudy and I manage to place four cats in forever homes and two dogs in foster ones. We do believe we have a chance to avert the sale, but still need to plan for the worst. We also spend time calling more possible donors. To date, we have almost $4 million pledged. Neither of us can believe it, but people respect the work Trudy's done for the community, and they want to be a part of saving the shelter and its animals. Still, we're running out of time.

It's stressful as Trudy and I scramble to make calls, but I need the distraction. Dad's parole hearing is today and the board votes right after and then hands down the verdict. Dad could be on his way to being a free man by this afternoon. My heart and head play tug-of-war. But it's up to the board, not me.

"I'm taking Helen to Ellis's tonight," I mention.

"My son does love animals," Trudy admits, but doesn't smile.

"You're still mad at him?" Before she can answer, Mars pops into the office. I jump up and give her a hug. "What are you doing here?"

Mars whispers in my ear, "I figured you'd need some moral support."

"Thank you," I whisper back.

She holds up a bag from El Rinconcito, our favorite food cart. "I brought lunch."

"Trudy, you remember Mars," I say.

"Of course. Why don't you young ladies enjoy your meal while I shuffle this mound of paperwork on my desk," Trudy says. She adds, "Just remember, there's no such thing as perfect."

"What's she talking about?" Mars asks as we head back to my apartment, Growler at our heels.

"Maybe Ellis?" I venture. "He's cooking me dinner tonight."

Mars slings an arm around me, smiles as she squeezes tight. I called her when I got home after our sushi date and recounted the epic kiss. The moment we sit down on the couch and unwrap our burritos, my phone rings.

"This is a call from San Quentin State Prison from inmate number 12759. Do you accept the charges?"

Every muscle in my body clenches. "Yes." I put the call on speaker.

"Constance?"

"Dad. How'd it go?"

"You really gonna ask me that?" he demands.

I wrap my arms around my torso and hold on tight. "What happened?"

"The family showed up again. Carter's mom pled with the board to keep me in prison, said she's still on antidepressants, can barely get outa bed. Still! His dad called me dirt. Men get shanked for less than that in here. His sister blubbered that Carter would never meet his niece and nephew 'cause I murdered him in cold blood. It was a fucking accident. That's why I didn't catch first-degree murder charges."

Given that Dad was high at the time it would've been harder to prove intent. The prosecutor went with second-degree murder to ensure a conviction. "Dad, they—"

"The woman that ran the parole board meeting asked me all sorts of questions," he interrupts. "I was rattled on account that I had no one there to support *me*. No one had *my* back. But I told her about my volunteer work, the anger management meetings I attend, and my associate's degree and how I take care of inmates in the prison infirmary, change filthy sheets, empty bedpans. Then one of the men on the board asked me to define the difference between *remorse* and *regret*. Who the fuck knows that?"

"Regret is an emotional reaction to your past behaviors—wishing you hadn't done something to avoid punishment. Remorse is admitting and taking responsibility for your actions, feeling sorrow and guilt," I explain.

"You should've gone over that with me!" Dad shouts.

I wince. "I didn't know that they would ask that question."

Mars leaps to her feet, paces the small apartment, Growler at her heels.

Dad continues, "And then they read your letter."

"Dad, I—"

"They gave me a copy." He shuffles sheets of paper then reads, "'Should my dad be paroled, I cannot provide him a place to live. I also do not have the financial means to cover travel, medical, or insurance needs.'"

My nerves are wound so tight they might snap. "I told the truth so that you could get the appropriate level of support once you were paroled."

"You don't tell the truth to the parole board! And you *are* going to support me when I'm on the outside. You're *my* girl."

There are bright red spots of anger on Mars's cheeks. "Hang up on him," she hisses.

I ask, "What about the part of my letter about Grandpa? That he's in poor health."

"What about it?" Dad snaps.

The last piece of the truth lands not with a painful crack but a wet thud. "You don't care about him at all."

"I'd do anything for my old man. I love him to bits. Same goes for you."

Dad's words and his actions have *never* aligned. I always knew that, but I wanted a father so much I wasn't prepared to accept it—until just now. Quietly, I say, "Goodbye, Dad," then hang up. When he tries to call back I block the number.

"Are you okay?" Mars asks.

"Yes," I say, and I'm proud to realize it's true.

Chapter Thirty-Five

Helen has lost her mind. Ellis filled a wicker basket with toys, just for her, and now she's pulling them out one by one, tossing each into the air, then diving back into the basket for more. She finds a stuffed panda, brings it over to him, then goes back to discover the next new toy. "You're going to spoil her," I laugh.

"Isn't that what you're supposed to do?" Ellis replies.

I imagined Ellis lived in a condo—all leather, concrete floors, and glass surfaces. So I was stunned to find his house is in the Presidio, a parklike setting with enormous trees that sits high above the Marina. The area was once a US military base until the federal government took over, created the Presidio Trust, and converted the old officers' quarters into private rental homes. Ellis's kitchen is modern but has warm blue soapstone counters and the floors are reclaimed wood partially covered with Persian carpets. There are a few leather couches, but they're worn and the art on the walls is mostly photographs of ocean waves, mountains, and forests with massive redwoods or golden aspens.

"Not what I expected," I admit once he's given me the tour. "I thought you'd live in a steel-and-glass tower."

"I've always believed home should feel comfortable," Ellis says as he plates tapas from Bellota, a Spanish restaurant on Brannan Street that I've walked by but could never afford to try. Helen happily curls up on one of three plush beds he's bought her, a red chew toy between her front paws. "Are you sure you're up for the challenge of a two-year-old Aussie?" I ask.

"I have someone coming next week to put in a dog door and an outdoor run," Ellis says, "just in case Helen needs to go outside while I'm at work. But hopefully a morning run with me then two hours with a dog walker during the day will suffice."

We sit down at a table built into the corner of the kitchen with padded benches and windows all around. Suddenly I'm nervous and flounder for conversation. "So, um, how was work?"

Ellis passes me a plate. "The little girl I told you about came in for a follow-up."

"Is she okay?" I slide some of the tapas onto my plate. The dish slips and I almost **drop** it then nearly knock my wineglass over.

"She's doing great," Ellis says. "Are *you* okay?"

I laugh then admit, "I'm nervous."

"Why?"

It takes a moment to untie my tongue. "Because I haven't been in a new guy's house in almost a year."

Ellis grins. "It's casual. Just dinner and a movie."

He's dressed informally, in jeans and a light blue shirt, and I'm in my daisy sweater and Levi's, but when he hands me a plate and our fingers touch, I don't want to take my hand away and the desire coiled inside me is anything but relaxed. We neglect our dinner once Ellis leans in to kiss me, and I think about what James wrote after his first kiss with Anna, how his whole world exploded and began anew. My face flushes with heat, but I'm not embarrassed for Ellis to see how much he affects me.

"What's happened in your world since we kissed?" Ellis asks with a sly grin.

I blush again. "We rehomed a few animals, or at least found fosters," I share. "And we've raised over $4 million in pledges to buy the shelter."

Ellis whistles. "I'm impressed."

My insides glow at the compliment. "On the less bright side of things, my dad had his hearing. Parole was denied."

"I'm sorry," Ellis says.

"I'm not," I admit. "He called me, furious."

"It's not *your* fault."

"It is in part. He'd asked me to write a letter to the parole board saying that he deserved a second chance, and that I'd be financially responsible for him when he was released." I take a sip of the delicious wine Ellis poured. "But I don't know if he's been rehabilitated and I can't afford to support him. So I wrote that."

Ellis refills both our wineglasses. "Sounds like you were honest."

"I was. But he may never forgive me."

"Given his bad acts, isn't it his responsibility to prove that he's worthy of *your* love?"

The skin on the back of my neck prickles. "I have a . . . a friend who once said something like that, and also that the wounds from childhood leave a mark on us. I guess writing the truth to the parole board is my way of choosing who I want to be, *despite* the past."

We clink our wineglasses, and I toast silently to a brighter future for the both of us.

"I get where you're coming from," Ellis says. "I told you that when Dad got sick, I didn't want to spend time with him. Showing up every day, changing soiled sheets, even reading to him was my way of choosing the person I wanted to be, regardless of how he'd hurt me in the past."

"Did you ever tell him how you felt as a kid?"

"Before he died we had an honest conversation. But it wasn't really necessary. I was already free."

"I hung up on my dad then blocked him," I confess. "It'll take time to sink in, but I think I'm free, too."

Ellis clears the dishes and brings on the dessert—warm, sugary churros. We demolish the entire plate and in the silence the sexual tension between us builds. Side by side we clean the dishes, our hands, elbows, and hips brushing. Each touch sends off sparks. When we finish, Ellis rests his hands on the counter on either side of me, only a few inches between us, and asks, "Movie?"

I kiss him. Within seconds his hands are in my hair, my own on his waist. It's hard to breathe as heat swirls in my belly. Ellis runs his thumb along my jaw, then my lower lip, and I pull him closer, feel how much he wants me. Our kisses intensify and my knees actually grow weak. Ellis's hands slide beneath my sweater and everywhere they touch they leave an invisible imprint. He lifts me onto the counter and my legs automatically wrap around him.

Helen barks.

"I think she needs to go out," Ellis says, slightly breathless.

We grab our coats and head into the cold night. A full moon

shines down as Helen races around the trees, thrilled to be outdoors and off leash. She spins in tight circles then takes off again. It's pure joy to watch her. A rabbit darts from beneath a bush. Its white coat is silver in the moonlight. Helen spies it and gives chase but luckily the bunny escapes. I murmur, "Rabbit-rabbit."

Ellis asks, "What's that for?"

"If you say it the first day of the month, before saying anything else, you attract good luck."

"It's the end of the month," Ellis points out.

I laugh. "It can't hurt."

Once Helen has tired herself out we head back inside. I'm suddenly awkward again, uncertain of what to do next.

"Movie?" Ellis asks. "I have an old favorite picked out, but you can veto it."

We settle on a soft couch and Helen hops up between us. Ellis laughs. "We have a chaperone." Gently he leads the Aussie to her fleece dog bed and gives her a rawhide to chew. She happily sets to work on it.

"What are we watching?" I ask as Ellis turns on the TV.

"Okay, you might as well know this about me," he says with a shy smile. "I'm a Trekkie." He pulls up the movie—*Star Trek: Insurrection*. "Be honest. Do you want to go home?"

Delight ripples through me. "And miss Data malfunctioning and Captain Picard stopping the Son'a from displacing the peaceful Ba'ku?" I innocently inquire.

Ellis's eyes bulge. "Seriously?"

"Mars turned me on to *Star Trek* during college. And, just so you know, Jean-Luc Picard is *the* sexiest man alive."

Ellis holds up his hands. "No arguments here." He starts the movie, then reaches for my hand. His touch reignites our spark and we don't even get through the opening credits before Ellis is trailing kisses down my neck. I slide onto his lap and we kiss until my lips are tender. Ellis's hands press against the small of my back and our hips move as if they're meant to fit together. And then he stops.

"What is it?" I ask.

Ellis admits, "I don't want to be your rebound."

I consider. "I can't promise anything. Only that I want to be here, now, with you."

"Is there anyone else?" he asks.

There's J. "No one who's real," I say.

Ellis gives me a funny look, then picks me up and carries me into his bedroom. The moon gives the room an ethereal glow as we slide onto a king-sized four-poster bed. Ellis slowly begins to undress me, starting with the buttons of my sweater. His kisses fall lower and lower. Each touch sends off a shower of white-hot sparks that seep beneath my skin. When he slips off my bra then unbuttons my jeans, I slide them free then help pull off his shirt and pants. And then we're lying side by side, only the scrap of my lace undies and his boxers between us.

"What do you want?" Ellis murmurs, his fingers tracing the curve of my hips.

I pull him closer.

He slides his hands between my legs and his thumb finds my most sensitive place and moves in slow circles. He murmurs, "I want you to say it."

"Please keep touching me," I gasp.

"How?" Ellis asks.

It is the first time in my life that a man has completely

relinquished control; made everything about this moment *my* choice. And so I tell him and he slips my panties off and slides between my legs. The first touch of his tongue arches my back. He starts slowly, making me wait for each brush of his lips, then moves more quickly as my hips rise up and the heat tumbles inside me, until my fingers are in his hair and I'm consumed and cry out and then reach for him, wanting the feeling to go on and on.

"We can stop," Ellis says as he kisses me, his hands on my breasts, fingers brushing my nipples until desire burns even hotter.

"I don't want to," I say then slide off his boxers. Sex has never felt so intoxicating with a man before—playful at times, intense, and incredibly intimate. After, we're both so tired that we curl up together and I drift off still smiling.

I sleep without dreams. And when Ellis reaches for me again in the middle of the night there is no road map, just our mutual desire.

In the early morning, we take Helen for a walk then have a quick coffee before Ellis leaves for work. He's on call for the next few nights so we say our goodbyes in the driveway.

"If the auction still happens, Saturday will be a really hard day for your mom. Are you going to be there?" I ask.

The muscles in Ellis's jaw clench and unclench. "I'm not sure I can get away from work."

A trickle of disappointment runs through me. His mom is going to need all the support she can get if we're not successful. "Well, hopefully you won't need to. Trudy texted this morning that we've now raised $4.2 million, and she's still making non-stop calls."

Ellis focuses on a robin as it lands on a nearby tree branch. "Regardless of what happens, on Saturday evening we could drive to Sonoma, spend the night, do some mountain biking, and then go to a winery?"

I start work next Monday at the DA's office so a weekend getaway, especially if we're celebrating saving the shelter, would be fun. "Sounds like a date," I say with a little smile.

Ellis's phone rings. He apologizes but takes the call. "Hey, Rey . . . I thought we'd decided . . . Well, Matthew would have to if you sided with me . . . Can we talk about it? Seriously? You're both making a huge mistake." Less than a minute later, Ellis hangs up. Despite the sun shining through the trees it feels like we're standing beneath a gray cloud that's emerged from nowhere. "Everything okay?" I ask.

He shakes his head. "It's just . . . I made a mistake and don't know if I'll be able to fix it."

I kiss him. "We can talk about it on our weekend away, figure it out together. Okay?"

". . . Okay," he agrees then pulls me in to his chest again.

But Ellis's next kiss doesn't feel as carefree as the one that came before it.

Chapter Thirty-Six

Trudy and I sit at her desk, frozen. We're both beyond nervous to call the owners' lawyer, but time has run out. We've raised $4.8 million, more money than we ever imagined possible, but will it be enough to prove we can raise the rest? "We just have to hope they're realistic about price, and that they're good people," I say. "I mean, who doesn't want to save animals?"

Trudy harrumphs then makes the call. She's put on hold and we listen to Muzak—"Lucy in the Sky with Diamonds"—played with violins.

"Lawrence Antoine speaking," a deep voice finally says. "Is this Trudy Winters?"

Trudy leans over her phone. "Yes, it is, and my associate, Constance Sparks, is also on the line."

"The auction is all set for Saturday. Do you have any questions?" Lawrence asks.

"We've been conducting a fundraising campaign to buy the shelter from your clients."

Lawrence asks, "How much have you raised?"

"We have $4.8 million pledged," I say.

"Ah."

"What does that mean?" Trudy demands.

"Frankly, it's too little, too late. The auction has been advertised and interest from developers is off the charts."

"But we can raise more money," I say.

"That's *pledged* money, not dollars in the bank. Donors are a fickle lot," Lawrence remarks. "One day they pledge half a million, the next they need that money for a down payment on a vacation home or Timmy's college tuition. My clients have instructed me that they aren't willing to take that risk."

Trudy mutters, "Of course they're not."

I'm a mouse in a damn maze again. This time I've made it to the end, but there's still no reward or way out. "Please. Is there *anything* we can do to change their minds?" I beg.

Lawrence sighs. "I'm sorry."

Trudy hangs up. We sit in silence for a few minutes. The reality that we've lost, that the auction will happen, spreads through my body like poison. Trudy's face is pale, her wrinkles more pronounced, and I wonder if I've made things worse by giving her false hope. "I'm so sorry."

"It's not your fault," she says. "I knew it was a long shot."

I pretend not to notice the quiver in her chin. She's an incredibly proud woman and her life's work has just been destroyed.

"Why don't you head out with Fudge? He's got a good foster home to go to. And there are also four cats to deliver."

I swallow the lump in my throat and refuse to cry. If Trudy can carry on, then I can, too. I load Fudge, a three-year-old bulldog, and the cats into her van and drive first to a home in Golden Gate. Jeff and Erin, a sweet couple who've already adopted a one-eyed Yorkie named Memphis, have agreed to foster Fudge. They will have their hands full. The bulldog can somehow maneuver his thick body beneath fences and also has the ability to open doors—with a running start.

I'm greeted at the door to their cute Victorian-style home with smiles and we go through the home inspection. Jeff has already put an extra lock up high on the front and back doors to keep Fudge's mischief at bay. We head into the backyard to make sure it's safe. "If you can just put chickenwire at the base of the backyard gate, that'll ensure he can't sneak out," I suggest.

"No problem," Jeff says and heads into his garage to find supplies.

My hope is that despite his naughtiness, they'll fall in love with the sweet bulldog and give him a forever home. Memphis is already showing him around the house and sharing her toys, so there's a chance.

"Bye-bye, Fudge," I say and give the furry lump a kiss before climbing back into Trudy's van. The cats are going to homes in the Castro, Marin, and Berkeley and it'll take me all day to deliver them and do home inspections. Hopefully their fosters will keep them, too, but it can be hard if there's already another feline in the home. A lot of cats refuse to share their space.

By the time I get back to the shelter it's dark. I'm exhausted both from last night and the emotion that comes with knowing the shelter will soon close and some animals won't be rescued in time. After toasting a veggie burger for dinner, I send Ellis a text that he might just be the *second* sexiest man alive, but he doesn't respond. I know he's on call, probably in surgery, but doubt wriggles under my skin. With effort, I remind myself that regardless of what happened, or will happen, between us, I'm going to be fine.

When I fall into bed, Growler climbs up and curls beside me. His warmth helps me find sleep.

I dream about walking through overgrown gardens, perfumed air in my lungs, the flowers otherworldly in the moonlight. After settling on a low stone bench, I raise one hand high. A star shoots down from the heavens trailing a glittery silver and orange arc into my palm. I make a wish and then . . .

My alarm jars me awake. I set it early so I could get to the library before taking another lucky dog to his new home. Given the disappointment that we couldn't save the shelter, I could use the distraction of James and Anna's love story. I also feel compelled to finish the letters, despite the sadness I know will come with James's death. My heart clenches. I'm not ready to lose J—his counsel, his honesty, and our connection have been invaluable.

When I pop my head into Trudy's office to tell her I'll be back in a few hours, she's hunched at her desk, staring into space. "You okay?" I ask.

She shrugs. "Not much choice. I forgot to ask, how'd Helen settle in at Ellis's?"

I blush. "She's in heaven. You didn't tell me he's a Trekkie."

Trudy flashes a tight smile. "He's a lot of things."

I call Mars on the way to the library and let her know that the auction is still on.

"You tried," she reminds me.

Sadness envelops me. "Yeah," I say, voice rough, "but sometimes the good guys still lose."

Mars changes the subject in an effort to lift my spirits.

"How was your dinner with Ellis? I called but you didn't pick up."

A memory of Ellis in bed flashes. "It was . . . a lot of fun."

"You slept with him!" Mars squeals, as always reading my mind. "How was it?"

"Incredible." I stop short of telling her Ellis might be my person. I don't want to rush it. But I'm falling hard for him.

When I walk through the front doors of the library, Molly is at the information desk. "How's the new guy?" I ask.

She makes a sad face. "I thought last night was *it*. He called late, wanted to meet here. A romantic evening in an empty library sounded like the perfect time to ask him out. I did . . . but he said there was someone else and apologized profusely if he'd given the wrong impression." She groans. "Truth is, he never even flirted with me, just needed access after hours to get some research done."

"I'm sorry."

Molly shrugs one shoulder. "Hey, the fantasy was fun while it lasted."

There's a new librarian at the desk when I sign in, but Veronica, Travis, and Chester are at the table, engrossed in their work. I grab a pair of gloves and retrieve James's book. When I open it, there's a note waiting for me and as usual, the outside world falls away.

Dear Constance,

Thank you for all of your kind words. Your belief in me shows that you are a truly empathetic person, but sadly it is unwarranted.

The future you envision for yourself is a beautiful one and I hope you will achieve all that your heart desires. I believe you can.

Remember, every choice you make will form ripples in your life and the lives of others and have consequences, some of them dire. Choose wisely.

A shot of adrenaline needles my skin. What does *that* mean?

Whoever you love will be beyond lucky. You are one of a kind and truly worthy of a devoted love in return.

James and Anna's story has almost come to an end, and so must our notes. It is time for you to live fully and for me to move on.

Love,

J

The fears of being abandoned, unwanted, not special enough barrel toward me. But a single thought stops them. J helped me navigate the most difficult time of my life. If I'm not grateful in this moment for that magic, then I wasn't worthy of his effort or kindness. I recall Veronica's advice that *life is for the living* and tamp down my jagged emotions. She's right, and so is J. Despite the loss that will linger, it's time for me to move on, too.

Dear J,

You have made an enormous difference in my life and I'm so grateful. You've inspired me to dream of more for myself, and the stories you shared helped me find perspective, courage, and my voice. I will always remember you.

Love,

Constance

I slip one of James's final remaining letters to Olivia free, determined to savor his words.

Dearest Olivia,

Last night we lay on a blanket in a field of lavender and Anna wished upon a falling star—that our unborn child would be a son we'd name Destin, which means fate. When the war ends, we've decided to live in Uzès, a small town in Provence, and will buy a farmhouse with land for all the animals Anna loves and enough bedrooms for the many children we'll have together . . .

My hands have grown sweaty beneath the white gloves as I worry that James doesn't have much time left. I can't stand to imagine the heartbreak that Anna will feel after his death.

September 1917

Dearest Olivia,

Anna is gone. Unbeknownst to me, she convinced a fellow ambulance driver to allow her to accompany him to a poste de secours. Anna believed she could save more lives that way. In the early morning hours a shell struck her ambulance. All were lost. Enclosed you will find Anna's engagement ring. I cannot bear to look at it.

All my love,
James

"No," I gasp. "No-no-no." Anna and her baby died. Only when Veronica's arms wrap around me do I realize that I'm crying. Chester rubs my back and Travis reaches for my hand.

"Anna died," I tell them.

"Oh no." Veronica's eyes fill. "And the baby?"

I nod.

"That's it?" Travis asks like he can't quite believe it, either.

Another sob hitches my shoulders. Anna's death and James's misery are devastating—it's like I knew them, like they had become a part of me . . . and now Anna and the baby are gone. And James? He's lost his soul mate *and* his son. Slowly I pack up my things.

"Constance, are we going to see you here again?" Veronica asks.

"I don't know," I croak. "I saw there's an afterword from Olivia, but I'm not sure I can bear to read it." James dies, too, and in this moment I can't bear to see that in writing.

Veronica kisses my forehead. "We're always here for you if you need us."

Chapter Thirty-Seven

The auction is held Saturday morning in the parking lot of the shelter. It's the kind of cold, windy spring that San Francisco is known for and charcoal-colored clouds promise showers. There's a small tent set up in case it rains and a crowd of about twenty people mill around the lot, there to either watch or bid for the property. I go as moral support for Trudy. Mars comes to support me as Trudy's life's work is dismantled and the animals' fates decided, and also because it was meant to be my wedding day.

A brisk wind blows and I zip up my fleece and rain jacket to stay warm. "Why not just list the property with a Realtor?" I ask Trudy.

She pulls on one of the crocheted hats she makes for anyone who'll take one. "The owners aren't dummies," she explains. "An auction creates a sense of urgency and a potential feeding frenzy that will up the price."

"Are they here?" I want the chance to make one final plea.

Trudy glowers. "Trust me. It doesn't matter."

I see Ellis and another man who could be his brother at the edge of the crowd. I wave and he nods but doesn't smile. That does nothing to help my deepening anxiety over where things stand between us.

Trudy follows my eye. "Just remember, they all make mistakes."

"What do you mean by that?" I ask.

"Attention, please," says the auctioneer, a tall woman with gray hair swept into a low bun, dressed in a long wool coat, leather gloves, and a sky-blue scarf, as she takes her place behind a small lectern. The crowd settles then quiets. "Welcome. I'm Patricia Jackson from Jackson, Gold and Vincent. We're here to auction off parcel 57, including all land and existing buildings. If you have a paddle that means you've been preapproved and received all the pertinent information about the property.

"The way this auction will work is that you'll raise your paddles each time you want to increase the standing bid. We will move in increments of $100,000. Once we conclude today's auction, the existing tenants will have one month to vacate their buildings. We have signed estoppels from all of them confirming their tenancy is month to month. Any questions?" She scans the crowd. "Okay, then. The bidding will start at $8 million."

Paddles fly as the price climbs from $8.5 to $9.2 to $9.4 to $10.0 to $10.2 all the way to $10.5 million. At first there are nine people raising their paddles, but at $10.8 million all but six drop out. A middle-aged bald guy dressed in jeans, a black leather jacket with shiny silver zippers, and motorcycle boots looks the most determined. "Who's he?" I ask Trudy.

"Yates Deckman. Biggest developer in the Mission—used to call me all the time asking when the property might sell. He did those ghastly modern condos a few blocks down."

Yates raises his paddle again and again, his weathered face expressionless, until the price reaches $11.2 million and only three other bidders remain. With each $100,000 I imagine the animals inside the facility being separated from their companions, shuffled to different shelters, afraid and alone. I reach for Mars's hand, hold on tight.

"Do I hear $11.5 million?" Patricia asks.

Only two bidders remain—Yates and a middle-aged woman, her red wool coat open over a tailored pantsuit. Yates is now glowering between bids, but the woman smiles each time she raises her paddle.

Patricia calls out, "Do I hear $11.7 million?"

Yates hesitates then raises his paddle. The woman immediately raises hers to bid another $100,000 on top of that.

I ask, "Who is she?"

Trudy hisses, "Another vulture."

"We're at $11.8 million," Patricia says. "Do I hear $11.9 million?" The crowd murmurs. "Going once, going twice . . . Sold to the woman in red for $11.8 million."

Several people offer their congratulations to the winner and the crowd disperses. Trudy walks over to the woman and holds out her hand. "I'm a tenant, Trudy Winters. Let's talk about your plans. There are a lot of moving parts to get my animal shelter emptied and we could use a bit more time than a month."

A gold charm bracelet on the woman's wrist jingles as they shake. "Ronda Green. We'll be in touch."

We watch her walk away, black heels clicking on the asphalt. It's over. Trudy has aged ten years in the past half hour. When I hug her she holds on like she's been tossed into the deep ocean with no idea how to swim.

"Mom," Ellis says.

Trudy turns. "I'm amazed all three of you aren't here."

"Matthew couldn't make it." Ellis turns to me. "This is my brother Reynolds."

I shake Reynolds's hand. He's a doppelganger for that *Shades of Gray* actor Jamie Dornan.

"Are you two happy?" Trudy asks her sons.

Reynolds tries to put his arm around her, but she moves out of reach. "In time you'll see this was the right move," he says.

Ellis's cheeks go ruddy. "Constance, can I talk to—"

"Mom, be reasonable," Reynolds interrupts. "Matthew and I have families to support. Plus, you're getting up in years. We want to be able to take care of you."

I look from Reynolds, to Ellis, to Trudy. "I don't understand."

"Oh, Constance . . . When I took Bert back, we worked together to buy the property from the previous owner. It was in Bert's name—that's how we did things back then. When he died, Bert left it all to our boys—it was a tax thing, and also a way to give them some extra income from the other buildings on the property," Trudy explains. "He never imagined they'd sell the shelter out from under me. Destroy my life's work, take away what matters most."

"Come on, Mom," Reynolds snaps. "Your kids and grandkids should matter most."

"My grandchildren have their parents and they're busy with their own lives and don't want to spend time with an old lady. You have your degrees and professions. The animals inside that building have *no one*." Trudy pivots and walks away, leaning heavily on her cane.

One thing is clear to me—I couldn't have been more wrong about Ellis. Anger burns through me. I don't know what will happen if I speak to him right now. Trudy was right, everyone makes mistakes, but this is unforgivable. How can he not have told me?

"Constance, can I explain?" Ellis asks.

"No." I turn and stride toward the shelter, Mars at my side. Ellis calls out, "I tried to—"

I slam the door behind me before he tells another lie.

Chapter Thirty-Eight

I can't stand to be at the shelter surrounded by all the animals and their uncertain futures, so I head to the library to finish what I started. At this point my day can't possibly get any worse.

There are two new people at the research table, no sign of my friends, and Colin sits at his desk discussing the rules with a young man in a blue tracksuit and bright white sneakers. I stow my backpack and pocket the key. When I pull the book of letters from its shelf it feels heavier, as if all that's happened over the course of James's time in France, the war, and the loss of Anna has made the small volume take on more weight.

Slowly, I leaf through the letters, recall the descriptions of France, the first time James saw Anna, their drive in the rain to the hospital, the night they first made love, James's proposal, the ring he designed, their wedding and joy at the news of Anna's pregnancy. James's and Anna's bravery, love, and devotion opened up my world. I'm beyond grateful and will never forget them.

Now it's time. I turn the page to Olivia's afterword.

My brother, James V. Edwards, was one of the ambulance drivers during the Battle of La Malmaison, where the French mobilized to capture Pinon, Chemin des Dames ridge, and Vaudesson. There were 12,000 casualties on the French side. James was one of them, injured on October 24, 1917, when a bomb exploded beside his ambulance. James died a few hours later with Wesley Caldicott, a classmate from Harvard, at his side. Wesley wrote that the moment before he passed, James murmured, "Anna, I'm coming home."

James's body was buried beside Anna's beneath the shade of a plane tree outside Uzès, a village in France where the two had once dreamed of living, and where Anna's family had laid her to rest. The three of them are at peace—James, Anna, and Destin.

Louis, by then my dear husband, and I visited Uzès after the Great War and I planted red poppies, Anna's favorite flowers, beside the simple quartz stone that bears all three of their names. I visit once a year to make certain that the stone is tended and the flowers still grow. They now cover the entire hillside.

In James's name I have established the Hero's Scholarship. My hope is that it will inspire people to help others and change lives so that my brother's legacy of bravery, dedication, and kindness can live on.

"Vivre sans aimer n'est pas proprement vivre."—Molière

(To live without love is not to live.)

Sincèrement,

Olivia Edwards Arnaud

When I leave the library it's still cold and windy, but the sun peeks from behind leaden clouds. For the next few hours I wander the city then drive to the Golden Gate Bridge, park my Vespa, and walk along the expanse, watching the waves roll beneath me and birds soar along invisible air currents. Several larks mob a hawk, driving him away, and the memory of my mountain bike ride with Ellis, how happy we were, returns. Rage burns inside my chest. I was such a fool.

"Would you mind taking our photo?" an elderly man asks. His wife's arm is linked in his and they wear matching tan slacks, white windbreakers, and red Fisherman's Wharf baseball caps.

I take his phone and they pose for the picture. "How long have you two been married?"

"Fifty-two blissful years," the man replies with a twinkle in his brown eyes.

"If you don't mind my asking, how'd you meet?"

His wife says, "It was fate. I was crossing the street and broke a heel. Edwin was behind me and caught my arm before I fell. We went on a date that night and married a month later."

"I don't know about the fate thing," Edwin says with a chuckle. "But once I met Beverly, I was determined not to lose her. Only a fool turns his back on true love."

My insides twist. Did Ellis and I have the chance for a love like theirs? Regardless, any shot we had is over. I steel myself to return to the shelter and help Trudy begin the process of dismantling her life's work. The good guys have lost. Now all I can do is find more homes for our animals with the short time we have left.

When I get back to the shelter the tent is gone from the parking lot. I find Trudy at her desk poring over a stack of papers. I expect to see the defeated woman I left a few hours ago, but she looks radiant.

"Constance! Come in."

"Did you place more animals?"

Trudy hands me an envelope. "I was asked to hand deliver this to you."

"What is it?"

She beams. "You'll see."

I slide the letter free and silently read . . .

Jackson, Gold & Vincent Law Office

San Francisco, New York, London

Patricia Jackson—Partner

Dear Ms. Sparks,

Please consider this an invitation to join the Board of Directors for the Mission Shelter Trust, established to hold my client Hayden Carrington Whittaker's gift of the property and buildings. Please contact me to discuss this further.

Best,

Patricia Jackson

I splutter, "I don't understand."

"I was given a similar letter," Trudy says. "Do you know what this means?" She barrels ahead without waiting for an answer. "We're still in business! And now the other buildings on the property will create enough income to support the shelter without my having to run a pet boarding business. And the donations we solicited can be used to expand and also do some long-deferred maintenance." Trudy reaches for my hand and squeezes. "Constance, you made me believe this was possible.

Hell, you set up the framework and then manifested it, *and* you're on the board."

It's hard to breathe. "But . . . but why would Hayden do this?"

She taps her temple. "I don't know. Maybe to win you back?"

Overwhelmed, I drive to Hayden's house, knock on the door. There's no answer so I pop the latch on the side gate and follow the stone path into the backyard. If we'd never broken up, I'd be in a wedding dress right now, my hand resting on Grandpa's arm as he walked me down the aisle . . .

Hayden sits on a bench set beside the buddleia bush. He wears the same ivory fisherman's sweater from our first date and there are gray half circles beneath his eyes that point to a sleepless night. He stands when he sees me.

"Why did you buy the shelter?" I ask.

"To apologize to you."

"That's one hell of an expensive apology."

Hayden rubs bloodshot eyes. "No one should ever make you feel unworthy of anything. I'm devastated that I did."

"This doesn't . . ." My voice snags. "It doesn't change anything."

Hayden lowers his head. "It was worth a last shot."

"Can you get your money back?" I ask. It would crush Trudy, but if Hayden did this with the expectation that we'd get back together, then it isn't fair to take his money.

Hayden shakes his head. "I don't want it back. My trust fund has ruined every serious relationship I've had. I don't really need it, so the money might as well go to a good cause."

Something inside me shifts as *we* settle firmly into the past. "Thank you doesn't seem like enough, but saving the shelter means everything to Trudy, to me, and all the animals."

"I didn't *just* do it to win you back," Hayden admits. "It was something you said to me last time we talked. About how fate only plays a small part in relationships; that what happens next— what people *do*, how they treat each other day to day, in the good and bad and truly awful times, *how* they care matters more." Hayden's smile is lopsided. "I want to be that kind of person who gives something of themselves in that way."

His sentiment leaves me stunned . . . and proud. Trudy was right. I did help manifest this. Finally, I notice the new bench's curved lines and polished wood. "Did you make that?"

"Yes," Hayden says. "It's mahogany—found it at a shipyard. It was once the deck of a sailing ship from the early 1900s."

"It's beautiful."

"It was supposed to be your surprise wedding gift." Hayden kicks at the ground with the toe of his boot. "I still love you . . . but can't desert my parents. They've already lost one child and they're my only family."

Despite everything, I take one last moment to mourn the loss of our relationship. I search for a way to honor what we did have. "You used to call me constant Constance," I begin.

"It was what we both wanted," Hayden says. "A stable, loving relationship with no surprises. That's what you needed, after everything that happened in your life. Me, too."

"I get why you crave consistency; why you're afraid to take risks. Your sister's murder was an unimaginable tragedy, and your past relationships have left deep scars. And you're right— for obvious reasons, that's how I was, too."

Hayden's body tenses. "Was?"

"I've realized that a life *without* soul-searching, new experiences, surprises, and risks isn't enough for me," I say. James never would've met Anna if he hadn't been searching for his raison d'être and clarity. They never would've fallen in love if they'd played it safe.

"I've never been a daredevil," Hayden admits.

"I'm not saying you should take up base jumping. Just allow for other people and the possibilities they bring into your life. Maybe," I gently add, "don't try to fit into your parents' version of the world; create your own?"

"It's not their fault," Hayden interjects. "They lost *everything*."

His words are hard to digest; they don't sit right with me. "They still have *you*. And you're more than enough. You don't have to keep proving that to them." I lace our fingers together one last time. "I hope you find your match, Hayden Carrington Whittaker, and have a wonderful life." He hugs me tight, then releases the hold bit by bit, like he's still hoping I won't let go. I step free, head toward the gate.

"Wait." Hayden scrubs a hand over his face then says, "You should know that the shelter trust wasn't my idea. Trudy's son came to see me."

I grip the gatepost. "What do you mean?"

"Ellis was in a bind. He'd tried to convince his brothers not to sell the shelter, but they wouldn't budge and he couldn't raise enough money to buy out their shares. He told me you tried to buy it, too, created the financial structure and solicited donations but came up short. I was clearly his last resort. I asked if he was doing it because he had feelings for you and the answer was obvious."

I shake my head to try and clear it. "What? Wait. I don't understand. *Ellis* asked *you* to buy the shelter?"

"Yes. He contributed his share and I put in the remaining two-thirds of the money."

The phone call he took in his driveway comes back . . .

Hey, Rey . . . I thought we'd decided . . . Well, Matthew would have to if you sided with me . . . You're both making a huge mistake.

"When I told him that I still loved you," Hayden continues, "that if I bought the shelter it'd be in part to win you back, Ellis didn't hesitate."

My brain might explode. I'm beyond furious that Ellis and his brothers thought it was their right to destroy Trudy's work, shocked that Ellis would turn to Hayden, risk whatever relationship we'd started, and proud that he'd go to such an extreme effort for his mother's sake.

"What will you do now?" Hayden asks.

"I don't know." Before I climb onto my Vespa, I have a call to make.

Chapter Thirty-Nine

"What are you going to do?" Mars asks.

We're seated on a bench at Crissy Field. The beach is mostly deserted—it's chilly and dark clouds have once again eclipsed the sun and promise more rain. "I don't know. What Ellis did? It's a giant red flag, right?"

Mars tosses one of the stones she collected on our beach walk into the midnight-blue bay. "Maybe."

"Seriously? Ellis had so many opportunities to tell me that he and his brothers owned the land and shelter. Instead, he said it was time for Trudy to move on, that she was like an old weight lifter—"

"What?" Mars interrupts.

"It doesn't matter. The point is, Ellis thought she should spend time with her grandkids, not rescue animals any longer."

"He's allowed to have an opinion."

"The shelter is Trudy's raison d'être. And he lied. Repeatedly." She blinks hard. "There's a vast ocean between Ellis and Gary."

"We're not talking about him," I snap. "The worst part is that I was falling for him. We had sex—"

"Incredible sex," Mars points out.

"That only makes it worse." It means I trusted him.

Mars tosses another rock and it skips twice on the water's surface. "The way I see it, you have two men in love with you—"

"Ellis isn't in love with me."

Mars sighs. "Okay, Ms. Literal. You have two men willing to give up a fortune for you. So what are you going to do about it?"

I take one of her rocks and throw it as far out to sea as possible. "Hayden and I are over."

"And Ellis?"

"It wasn't a little white lie, Mars. It was a HUGE one. Just because he helped save the shelter doesn't change that fact."

"I'm not asking about facts. And for the record, Ellis didn't actually lie to you. He just chose to keep a family matter private." She reaches for my hand. "Jeez, you're freezing. Remind me again why we couldn't have done this in a coffee shop, or better yet gotten doughnuts?"

"This felt more appropriate," I say.

"So misery wanted miserable company?" Mars jokes.

I half smile. "Yeah, something like that."

"So what do you want to do about Ellis?" she asks again.

It starts to drizzle. "Find out *why* he didn't tell me."

"Then what are you waiting for?" Mars hops off the bench and starts to walk back to the parking lot.

"That's it?"

She turns. "You're Constance Fucking Sparks."

With her encouragement, I take out my phone and dial Ellis's number. It goes straight to voicemail. I know he has the day off, so I leave a message. "Hi," I say. "I know what you did. We should talk. I'm down at Crissy Field. I'll wait for you here." I pull up the hood of my jacket and watch the waves batter the sand. It rains for a bit, then a weak sun peeks out and a few families brave the beach, their dogs chasing balls and Frisbees, kids digging in the sand, making ephemeral castles. A couple jogs by, long legs perfectly in sync. Four men decked in matching rain gear spin expensive bikes down the path. The sun falls lower and lower in the sky. It gets colder. I check my phone to see if the ringer is off or if there's a missed text. It isn't. There's not.

My growing doubt, held at bay for the past few hours by my own anger, lunges forward. Maybe Ellis is angry at the way I treated him at the auction. Maybe he's having second thoughts about giving up his share of the profit from the sale. It is millions of dollars. Maybe he was *never* that into me, and buying the shelter was entirely about Trudy . . .

You're Constance Fucking Sparks, Mars's voice reminds me.

The cold day has seeped into my bones. To get enough blood flow to feel my hands, I run back to my Vespa then drive to the Presidio. At this point my thoughts are so muddled that I have no idea exactly what I'm going to say to Ellis. But this needs to happen face-to-face.

I find him behind his house throwing a ball for Helen. She races through the trees, tail madly wagging, retrieves an orange ball, and drops it at his feet. Ellis hears me walk up and turns. He looks worn-out, his eyes bleary.

"I called you."

He fiddles with the zipper of his blue rain shell. "I know."

"Why didn't you call back?"

Ellis scrubs a hand over his face. "I had some things to take care of . . . and then I was trying to collect my thoughts before we spoke."

"Like I said, I know."

His face pales. ". . . About the shelter?"

"And Hayden."

"Ah. He was the only solution I could find. But I still wasn't sure it'd work out until he called after the auction to let me know that woman was bidding for him."

"And you're giving Hayden your share of the sale?"

Ellis nods. "I had my lawyer draw up a promissory note an hour ago, signed, and sent it to him."

I force the lump in my throat down. "Why didn't you tell me?"

"I did try."

"When?"

"In the driveway of my house, after we spent the night together. That's when my brother called and I realized that I was powerless to stop the auction; that I needed to go to plan B, reach out to Hayden." Ellis tosses the ball again and Helen races off. "I had no idea what he'd say, but Hayden agreed to try . . . in part to win you back."

I recall Ellis's words that morning—*I made a mistake and don't know if I'll be able to fix it.* And then I kissed him, the same way Hayden kissed me whenever I was about to tell him about my dad, like he sensed I was going to drop a bomb and was desperate to keep our world from exploding. I did the same thing to Ellis. That doesn't absolve him, but my anger deflates as quickly as it rose up, leaving me bruised and sad. "But if you'd told me from the start—"

"That I was one of the owners forcing Trudy out, taking away her life's work?" Ellis interrupts. "Despite believing at the time that I was doing the right thing, you never would've given me a chance."

It's true. "Because you were wrong."

Helen races back and drops the ball at Ellis's feet. "I get that now," he says. "So I did the only thing I could think of to make things right. And I lost you in the process." He tosses the ball again and Helen bounds off. "So you and Hayden are back together?"

"That was a big risk you took," I reply.

"It was."

"Hayden and I are over for good."

Ellis meets my gaze, his eyes intense. "Why?"

"He's not my person." He closes the distance between us but doesn't reach for me. Still, I can almost feel the electric heat of his touch. It feels good just standing this close to him.

"I was wrong about my mom. She needs the shelter; the work she does matters and the rescue animals are beyond fortunate to have her. You helped me see that. I'm ashamed of my part in almost taking the place away from her. And I was wrong not to tell you that my brothers and I owned the property after inheriting it from our father. I'm sorry." Ellis takes a deep breath. "You have every right to walk away and never speak to me again. But I've fallen for you, Constance."

"Why?" I demand.

"You're smart, kind, and brave. You stood up for my mom, fought to save the shelter. I'm proud of how honest you are about your family and the way you handled the situation with your dad. And you're fearless. Hell, you were ready to attach yourself to a powerful kite and get into the bay without a wet suit. That water is fifty degrees."

"I thought it was warmer," I admit.

He takes my hands. "Constance, when I'm with you, there's

nowhere else I'd rather be. When I'm not with you, you're all I think about. Can you possibly forgive me?"

Ellis was wrong to keep the truth from me . . . but he owns that. I think he would handle it all differently if only he had the chance. And I feel the same way about him. "No more lies?" I ask.

Ellis's eyes light up and he pulls me into him. I can hear the quick thud of his heart through his jacket as his arms hold me tight. Slowly, I relax into his embrace. When I tip my head back for a kiss, Ellis is staring off into the woods, his jaw muscles clenched. My stomach slowly sinks, and I wait for him to muster the courage to tell me whatever he's been keeping held back.

Chapter Forty

Ellis, I need to hear you say it. No more lies?" I repeat. Ellis drops his arms and all the warmth leaves my body. Helen has brought the ball back but he doesn't bend to pick it up so she wanders off to sniff around. I wait for the blade to drop, uncertain what he'll say but somehow sure it will mean the end of a second chance for us.

Ellis takes a ragged breath then meets my eyes. "I'm J."

For a second I have no idea what he's talking about—like I'm looking out the wrong side of a pair of binoculars and can't make sense of the tiny image in the distance. And then the truth rushes in and a silent bomb detonates. In the wreckage, I'm left mortified and furious.

Ellis is J. *My* J. Emotions threaten to overwhelm my brain so I focus only on logistics. "How?"

His brow creases. "That's all you—"

"How is that possible?" I repeat. "I asked the librarians in Special Collections and they said no one else signed out *Letters from My War.*"

"There was a woman who helped me. She let me in after hours. I told her that I was doing research, that my job didn't allow me to come when Special Collections was open."

"Molly." I recall our conversation about her meeting an *accomplished* man whose job was so hectic he didn't have time to come to the library during normal hours so she let him in after it closed. Molly had said to me, *The things we do in the hopes of finding love.*

"Yes, Molly," Ellis admits.

"She thought you liked her."

He grimaces. "I feel bad about that. I had no idea she thought that. I never meant to mislead her."

"Just me." The humiliation I've been trying to hold at bay chokes me. "Is this all a game to you?"

Ellis's look is pure misery. "No. I've always been obsessed with reading about adventures, expeditions, and war history. When you told me about James's letters, I felt . . . compelled to read them, too. And then I found your note."

"And decided it'd be a great idea to pretend to be James's ghost?" I demand. He takes a step toward me, but I back away.

"That was *never* my plan. You *assumed* I was James's ghost—"

"Because you knew about the dog who bit me!" I explode. "I've never told anyone about Axel. How the hell did *you* know?"

His eyes widen. "You told Trudy about Axel during your volunteer interview. When I realized I wanted to know you better, started trying to find out more about you, Mom told me that story."

My mind sprints back eight years. Trudy asked me a million questions before she allowed me to volunteer, said if I couldn't handle myself with all different animal and owner temperaments, that even though she needed me, I'd be a liability. I can't recall telling her about Axel . . . but obviously, I must have.

"I expected you'd figure out right away that it was me," Ellis admits. "That maybe we'd talk more, get closer when you asked me if I'd written the note. And then you didn't." He rubs the five-o'clock shadow on his jaw. "But it was obvious you needed someone safe to tell all the things you were afraid to say in the real world. You were dealing with so much pain and I wasn't sure you had anyone to turn to in that way, anyone you could really unburden yourself with. I wanted to help you, and the letters seemed to make you happy, so I kept writing."

My sinuses burn, but I refuse to cry in front of him. "I needed someone I could *trust*. Evidently that's not you."

Color rises in Ellis's cheeks. "I *never* told you to leave Hayden. I wanted to, but I didn't. If you think back over the letters, you'll realize I never wanted to get in the middle of your relationship, even though I knew I was developing feelings for you."

Frustration leaves my voice a mere whisper. "Did you enjoy making a fool out of me all this time?"

"You're no fool," Ellis says then reaches for my hand, thinks better of it, and drops his arm. "Everything I wrote about my own life was true. I went to boarding school. We're both children of addicts. My father's drinking and volatility did immense damage that I've had to struggle to overcome."

A tear escapes and angrily I wipe it away. "How can I believe anything you say anymore? Were you *ever* going to tell me you had written those letters?"

Ellis winces. "Yes . . . as soon as I could find the right time. Look, I should've told you the truth much earlier, but I got in too deep. I wanted to help you work out what you were going through, and then you ended up helping me see things in my life that were hard more clearly—my mom, the shelter, a way to keep Trudy's legacy alive, and what's most important. Constance, *you* inspired and changed *me*."

I think about all Ellis wrote as J about who he was, and the man he wanted to be. "You could've just talked to me anytime."

"You never would've shared anything personal—up until a month ago, you thought I was an asshole."

"I still do and now I feel betrayed that I ever trusted you," I say.

There are tears in Ellis's eyes. He grabs my hands, holds on tight. "I never intended it to go so far. But I couldn't stop reading James's letters, imagining the war and his and Anna's lives, wishing for a connection like theirs . . . and I couldn't stop writing you once you had left me the first letter. Constance, I don't want to lose you over this. I never meant to betray you in any way. I felt like we bonded when I wrote you that first letter and then I didn't know how to share the truth without destroying the possibility of anything between us. Can you please forgive me?"

I pull my hands free and the heat from his skin lingers but will soon dissipate. "I can't imagine I ever will."

Chapter Forty-One

It's easy to lose myself in my new life. Trudy offered to let me stay in the apartment at the shelter indefinitely, but I thought it'd be better for Growler to move on, and knew that I needed to take that next step as well. Mars worked tirelessly to help me find a ground-level studio apartment with a small fenced backyard. The neighborhood is Russian Hill—way above my pay scale—but it's a short run to the Marina beach for Growler to play in the sand and waves. In return for cleaning the lobby on Sundays and maintaining the planters out front, the building's owner was willing to discount my rent and even let me put in a dog door for Growler so he could go outside while I'm at the office.

Now every day I get up at five to take my dog for a run before heading to work. At lunchtime I race home so we can hang in the yard together, and after work we visit a nearby park before I spend the next few hours studying from a huge pile of law books that my boss, Ellen, lent me.

I did worry Growler might get lonely during the day, so a month ago I adopted Grumpy, a cat from the shelter who was always passed over by potential forever families because of the hisses he made when anyone petted him. I've realized those sounds were his version of purring. Grumpy hid under my bed for a few days, but now the two animals are inseparable. While I study late at night, Growler curls on his dog bed at my feet with Grumpy asleep between his front paws. When I finally fall into bed, exhausted, they cuddle beside me and I feel less alone.

On Sundays, I visit Grandpa. There are really good moments where we talk about how much fun we used to have riding our bikes together, bake his favorite sugar cookies in Rosa's kitchen, play abbreviated Scrabble games, or just watch *The Price Is Right*, both of us playing along with the contestants. The moments his mind wanders or he confuses me with my mother are sad, but I don't let them overshadow the fact that he's still here and loves me.

Today, as Grandpa and I sit at Rosa's kitchen table eating cookies, he tells me I should work less and focus on finding my person. "There's nothing more valuable and fulfilling than having a partner in life. Hazel wants that for you."

At first I assume he's confusing his dead wife with someone else and just nod and smile.

"She told me last night," Grandpa continues.

I consider telling him that Hazel passed long ago. Instead, I say, "She's kind to think of me."

Grandpa's eyes twinkle. "Don't patronize me, young lady. I know my Hazel is long gone, but she visits now and then, when it's important. And she wants you to prove to yourself that you're worthy and then open your heart."

The hairs on my arms lift. It's what J . . . Ellis wrote me in one of his letters.

Something flickers inside me then blows out. Ellis repeatedly reached out after our confrontation, but I never called or texted him back. His final note was handwritten, left with Trudy at the shelter. He doesn't volunteer there anymore, at least not when I have a shift. His note read: *I'm truly sorry. You're worth the wait.* I threw it in the trash. What he did was unforgivable.

"Will you consider it?" Grandpa asks.

"What?"

"Now who's losing their mind," he jokes.

"Someday," I promise just to make him smile. We finished our cookies and I head home to play with my furry friends and then study and prepare for work.

My new job has been overwhelming at times, even after three months. The DA's office is a beehive of activity, far from the carpeted halls and hushed voices at HDB. Work is fast-paced, sometimes chaotic, but my colleagues are passionate about justice, and that's exhilarating. Ellen is a tough but fair boss who expects the best every day, praises publicly, and admonishes privately. There's a lot to learn, but she's thrown me directly into the deep end. The cases I work on range from robberies to assault, vandalism and arson to a domestic violence situation that escalated into a homicide.

With the court date on the homicide only a few days away, we spend Monday afternoon preparing Ellen's case. I've compiled all of the domestic violence complaints Heather Roth made against her husband, Seth, over the course of their five-year marriage. There were eleven calls, but Seth was never arrested. This may have had to do with the fact that he's a police officer and in most cases knew or had a connection to the officers who arrived at their apartment.

I've also gone over all of Heather's hospital visits. Over the marriage, she had a fractured skull, broken left wrist, sixteen stitches, two broken ribs, and a ruptured spleen. There are photographs of her injuries, including one where her right eye is swollen shut. Bile rises in the back of my throat. "Explain to me again why we're charging this woman, who was obviously beaten by her husband, with *first-degree* murder?"

"What's the definition?" Ellen replies.

She keeps track of my studies and often quizzes me, so I'm ready. "The intentional killing of another person by someone who has acted deliberately or with planning."

"There are two classifications of first-degree murder. Felony murder—unintentionally murdering someone in the course of a felony—"

"And premeditated murder—the intent to kill and willful deliberation before the act." Ellen nods her approval and inside I shine. "But her husband was clearly beating her for years. The defense will show the jury all of her hospital records, they'll hear her emotional 9-1-1 calls, and friends and family will take the stand to corroborate that Heather was an abused woman."

Ellen nods. "And what they say will all be true. But Heather didn't kill her husband *while* he was beating her. She waited for him to come home. And when he walked through their apartment door she hit him in the head with a hammer—*from behind*. His skull was crushed."

"He might've threatened her before he came home," I say.

"We'll never know," Ellen admits. "But the law judges based on facts, not suppositions. And the *fact* is that Heather Roth lay in wait then murdered her husband. There were no defensive wounds on her body or signs of a struggle. He never saw what was coming and the coroner says the first blow was made with so much force that it probably killed him. She struck him four more times after that."

Ellen takes a sip of her Diet Coke, leaving red lipstick marks on the can. "I can see you feel sympathy for the defendant. The truth is, I do, too."

"So why charge her with murder?"

"Early on, I offered her public defender a lesser charge—manslaughter in the first degree—intentional severe injury."

"Why didn't he take it?"

"He's betting that at least one of the jurors will see those horrendous photos and vote *not* guilty. His goal is a hung jury. If that happens, the DA's office will be more likely to offer a sweeter deal to avoid the cost of a new trial."

"That bet is the difference between life behind bars and getting out of prison in time to see her youngest child graduate from high school," I point out. Despite their violent relationship, Heather and Seth have three small children.

Ellen's eyes glint. "Not my problem. My job is to get justice for Seth. And I'm going to win this case based on the law."

I sigh. "So one moment where a beaten woman fractures under pressure and fear will cost most of her life and leave her kids without a mother."

"I told you this job would sometimes break your heart. But the law doesn't take into account that people are fallible—that they make mistakes, some enormous and irrevocable. The law judges their actions in black and white. There are no gray areas." Ellen finishes her soda and opens another one. "Thankfully, real life is different or we'd hold everyone we love to impossible standards. Hell, my husband would've left me long ago if he held my worst moments against me, and vice versa."

"What if he'd done something unforgivable?" I ask.

Ellen looks up from her yellow legal pad. "You asking for a friend?" she inquires with a wink.

I blush. She knows I had a breakup a few months ago, but not any of the details.

Ellen says, "You once told me about that shelter dog you rescued."

"Growler."

"Why'd you give him a second chance?"

"I believed he was good deep down and shouldn't be judged solely by past mistakes; that if he was willing to work with me, eventually to trust me and prove he was trustworthy, too, he deserved another chance. But he's a dog," I point out.

Ellen cracks a rare smile. "They're not that different from men. Joking aside, if you love the guy, then give him the opportunity to prove he's worthy of another chance with you."

Over the past months lines from Ellis's notes have returned to me. I think of them as his words now, no longer James's. And there's a poignant nostalgia attached each time his letters come to mind. Ellis did a lot of wrong things for the right reasons. My brain tugs hard, but my heart gets in the fight. He believed in me when I couldn't, shared his own difficulties and what he'd learned, listened without judgment . . . until I finally figured out how to believe in myself. He lied, by omission, about the shelter property and that he was J. But Mars was right that he's not anything like my dad, who to this day hasn't truly taken accountability for his actions. And we don't live in a court of law. In real life people make big mistakes. I've made them, too.

"Do you mind if I take a quick break?" I ask Ellen.

"Five minutes," she says.

I duck into the copy room and dial Ellis's number. He picks up on the second ring.

"Constance."

I was expecting to leave a message and the sound of his voice throws me off. "Um. Hi."

"Hi," Ellis repeats.

My heart threatens to beat out of my chest. "I'm going biking on Mount Tam Sunday afternoon at two. If you want, you can join me."

"Do *you* want me to join you?" he asks.

"Yes."

"Then I'll be there," he says, his voice rough with emotion. "And I am truly so sorry for having hurt you."

"I know." I don't want to hang up, but the rest will have to wait until I see him in person. "See you Sunday." As I walk back to Ellen's office, I muse about the past year and all I've learned about seeking my own happiness. Life isn't a short and simple fairy tale. It's more like a novel. The reward that comes from hardships is the understanding that something better can be waiting in the next chapter if you work hard enough to create it. As I walk back to Ellen's office my steps are lighter. I'm not sure what will happen with Ellis, but he deserves another chance. We both do. Regardless, I'm worthy.

Chapter Forty-Two

18 MONTHS LATER

I open the box of keepsakes I've collected since letting Ellis back into my life. It's filled with handwritten letters, postcards, and mementos. I reread the first letter he ever wrote me as himself.

> Dear Constance,
>   Today you allowed me back into your life for a few hours. I'm grateful and hopeful that there will be more mountain bike rides together, more conversations about who we are and what we want in life, and the chance and time to build an honest friendship.
>
>   Sincerely,
>   Ellis

I shuffle through stacks of letters, read favorite lines, then pull out a postcard from an early guys' kiting trip Ellis took to Maui where he drew a cartoon picture of me on a kitesurf board riding the waves with him. The caption beneath it reads: *Can't stop thinking of you.* He surprised me and came home early so he didn't miss my birthday.

The first gift Ellis ever gave me rests beneath a dozen more letters. It's a photograph of Growler and Helen on a ride with us, both dogs filthy and smiling at the side of a creek. Ellis made it across that bridge on his third try and was wetter *and* muddier than the dogs but matched their ear-to-ear grins.

Beneath that photograph is a handwritten menu from the picnic basket Ellis prepared once I'd agreed to go on a *real* date with him a few months into our blossoming friendship. Quiche, green salad, and browned-butter ginger cookies for dessert, all from scratch. I later learned that the cookies took two attempts. He forgot the baking soda in the first batch. We had our first kiss, post breakup, our lips dusted with sugar, then watched the sun set over the bay, both dogs curled beside us. It was such a perfect moment that part of me wanted to run away before the dream once again shattered. I did, for about a week. Ellis waited patiently for me to return.

Smiling, I pull free a snapshot of Veronica, Chester, Isa, Travis, and Mai with us at a pop-up Thai restaurant. We're holding bottles of beer aloft, toasting Chester and Isa's engagement. Reynolds, Ellis's brother, was there, too. It was their first attempt to reconnect after the auction. It's slow going, but neither has given up. People are fallible, we all make mistakes, and both Ellis and I believe in giving grace when possible.

My fingers twist the chain of the locket Ellis gave me for our first Christmas together. When I opened it there was a tiny note inside: *I love you.* I knew those words meant something to him; that he backed them up with his actions. I told him that I loved him, too. We had Christmas dinner at Trudy's, and it was one of Grandpa's best nights in such a long time. He shared stories about meeting Hazel, how he told his buddy the moment he laid eyes on my grandma that he planned to marry her.

Inside this box of memories, there are plane tickets from our trip to Padre Island, Texas, where Ellis taught me to kitesurf in warm, waist-deep water then rented a Jet Ski to follow me around so I'd feel safe in the deeper water. I withdraw the train stubs from our weekend getaway in Montana. Trudy watched the dogs and we brought our bikes and rode and hiked in the mountains. At night we dipped into thermal hot springs and roasted marshmallows. We camped instead of staying at a fancy lodge because I'd planned the trip and it was what I could afford. I saw my first black bear that vacation and somehow managed not to run, while Ellis pounded our camping pots beside me until the big guy ambled off. Then we made love beneath the stars.

I sift through stacks of index cards that Ellis made to help me study for my first-year law students' exam. He gave up weekends of kiting, brought me coffee, lunches, and little treats to keep me going on the days I was exhausted from a full-time job but still had to study. Beneath the cards is a Polaroid of Trudy and Ellis standing under the new sign he had made: TRUDY WINTERS ANIMAL SHELTER. Trudy looks up at her son, beaming. They are closer than ever now, and Trudy is a combination of older sister and the mother I wish I'd had.

Wedged into a corner of the box are some of the date-night invitations Ellis surprised me with as our relationship deepened, many made from thick construction paper and cut into the shape of flowers. It's something we've both done for each other, despite long workdays and responsibilities, to keep the romance between us alive. My invitations have come in the form of scavenger hunts, and word puzzles he has to figure out in order to find the hole-in-the-wall restaurant or park I've picked for our date.

The final photograph is from the day Ellis proposed. We'd driven to Lake Tahoe to mountain bike on a trail that was too long for our dogs to join us. Unbeknownst to me, Ellis had gotten a buddy to drive Helen and Growler to the top of the ride. When we arrived at the summit, a grassy knoll dotted with pink and white sweet peas, they were waiting beside a bottle of chilled apple cider and a box of my favorite macarons—the French kind that melt in your mouth. Ellis pulled a plastic baggie out of his water bottle and dropped to one knee. I laugh at the selfie we took—the dogs on our laps, an emerald-cut diamond ring on my finger, Ellis's lips on mine.

There are so many experiences and adventures contained in this box, so much more time spent with Ellis than James and Anna were ever given. I'm grateful to them for showing me what love could be, and to the universe for giving me the time I needed to discover who I am, what I want, and how to trust and open my heart.

A knock on the door makes me jump. "Yes?"

"We need to hustle," Mars says.

"Come on in," I call.

The wedding is being held at Stinson Beach.

Mars is my maid of honor and as she adjusts the drape of the dress she refused to let me return, she asks, "Are you sure? If you're not, I'll drive the getaway car. We can be Thelma and Louise, but without the crash."

I giggle. "I'm positive."

Mars says, "Me, too," then blinks hard. Carefully, she places the pink-and-red flower crown on my loose hair.

I've never seen her more in her element, or happier. Her girlfriend, Scarlett, has made the meal we'll share with friends and family after the ceremony. She's an appropriate age and holds Mars's feet to the fire when the past reaches out with sticky fingers. They're talking about opening a small café together with Mars running the business side of things. She'd be a great partner for Scarlett in both business and marriage, if they choose that road. Mars is brilliant, and there's nothing she wouldn't do for the people she loves.

"Wait!" Mars reaches into her purse and pulls out a small velvet box.

"What's this?"

"It's from your fiancé. I told him you needed something blue, to baffle the evil eye."

I kiss her cheek. "Thanks. I'll take all the help I can get." Inside the box is a delicate blue enamel giraffe pin. Since we began dating again, Ellis likes to surprise me with animal and flower pins I can wear with the conservative clothing required at the DA's office. I have quite a collection and they always make me smile.

With Mars's help, I pin the giraffe to the white ribbon that's wrapped around my bouquet.

There's a knock on the door. "It's time," Grandpa says.

Mars gives Grandpa a hug then leaves us to make her entrance. She's dyed her hair pink for the occasion.

Grandpa, in a new pinstriped suit with a rose in his lapel, asks, "Ready, Constance?"

Today is a good day. I'm thankful whenever his disease gives us any of those. I take his arm. "Ready."

As we walk toward the beach, he asks, "Are you sure about this guy?"

"I am."

Grandpa's eyes shine. "Me, too. When he asked for permission I said only if he could tell me your dreams. And he knew every single one of them."

For now, we've bought a house with a big backyard for our animals that's down the street from Rosa and Marcio's so that we can see Grandpa for dinner every night. And he can come over whenever he wants. I asked him to live with us, but he said newlyweds need their own space. I kiss his soft cheek. "Thank you. For everything."

"It was the . . ." Grandpa's voice falters. "It was the biggest honor of my life."

I spy Rosa and Marcio on the beach. They've tied a white ribbon to the collar of their adopted dog, Blueboy, who is thriving with all the attention he gets in their home. They took Samson, too, and she loves to curl on Grandpa's lap while he watches his game shows. Veronica waves as I walk past, one arm wrapped around Diane's waist. Chester has brought Isa, who is pregnant with their first child, and one of the twins is perched on Mai's shoulders and the other on Travis's, making a mess of his white shirt. I smile at all the friends who have become my chosen family.

Trudy stands at the end of the aisle. She received a Universal Life Church minister certificate in the mail in order to marry us. My groom is next to her in a light tan suit, green eyes sparkling, his dark curls mostly under control, a pirate's sexy smile on his face. Growler and Helen sit to his left—the two dogs have become best buddies. I hug Grandpa then take my place beside my future husband. Growler noses my leg until I bend down and kiss his forehead.

"Of course he steals the first kiss," Ellis jokes and our friends all join us in laughing.

Ellis reaches for my hands then takes in my wedding dress. "No koalas, possums, or polar bears?"

A little giggle escapes. "I wanted to surprise you."

"I'm a fan of whatever you wear, but this dress? You look stunning."

"So do you. And I love the giraffe."

When it comes time for the vows, I go first. We've spent the past year and a half building our relationship from scratch, learning to trust each other with the truth, even when it's not pretty. There were a few twists and stumbles before we made it to this day. Sometimes it's difficult being the person you want to be, learning when to take a stand, how to let the little things slide, and the best ways to communicate. But we made it through each challenge stronger and more committed.

I've already said everything to Ellis that I need to in private, so I keep my vows short. "Ellis, I promise to show you the real me, always, and to continue to grow together and on my own. I promise to never bring more than three shelter dogs home at a time, to kite with you, and wait at the summit of every bike ride."

"She always beats me to the top," Ellis says to our friends and family and they chuckle.

"That's true," I agree then give his hands a squeeze. "A wise man once wrote me that life is a long road best traveled with someone who sees your light and helps it shine even brighter. For me, that's you, and I will always strive to help you shine brighter, too. Searching into the past changed my present and helped me figure out how I wanted to live each day. You've been part of that journey and I wouldn't trade our experiences for anything. We share a desire for adventure, a drive to help others, a love of animals, and the dream of creating a family. I can't imagine a future without you. You're my happily ever after, even in hard times, and I love you."

Ellis leans in and kisses me.

"Not yet," Trudy admonishes. "Your turn. Make it good."

"Constance, I promise to be honest, always, and to embrace all the animals you bring home, even the ones that eat my socks. I promise to learn to surf together in Fiji, but first to follow you to Portugal on our honeymoon and try to keep up on a bike. And even though you demolish me every time, I promise to continue playing Scrabble with you. To say you changed my life is a monumental understatement. I'm a better man because of you. And it's not just because you brought your grandfather, Helen, and Growler into my life—all of whom I love dearly. You lead with compassion, fight for those who need you most, value friendships, and always look for the bright side in every situation. We must all choose what, in life, we're unwilling to lose. I choose you and I'll continue to choose you for eternity. Home is wherever we are together. I love you."

"You may seal your promise with the rings," Trudy says.

Ellis slips a simple band of rose-colored gold on my finger and I slide an identical one on his.

Trudy says, "I now pronounce you husband and wife. You may kiss."

Ellis's lips find mine and as we're drawn into each other's gravity, our lives begin anew.

During our reception, Ellis and I steal away to the beach. Growler, unwilling to let me out of his sight, follows while Helen remains near the food table with hopes of treats. We settle on the sand and watch as Growler races at the waves, retreats, and then does it over and over again. He's a different dog now. We've both changed so much.

"I have a wedding present for you." Ellis pulls an envelope out of his suit pocket. "I thought we could open it together."

When I hold it I can feel there's a square of cardboard inside. "What is it?" I ask.

"I know you wanted a photograph of Anna."

"But the American Hospital of Paris was flooded."

"I wrote to every distant relative of Louis Arnaud that I could trace," Ellis explains. "One of them had an old box of photographs in her attic. She was kind enough to dig through them and send the photo in time for our wedding."

"How did she know it was Anna?" I ask.

"She said it's Anna *and* James on their wedding day. Someone wrote the names and date on the back."

"It must've been Olivia. James promised he'd send their wedding photo to her." I tear open the envelope and withdraw the photograph. It's a close-up of the couple at their wedding and hand-tinted. Despite the century that's passed, the colors are still vivid. The ring I once wore is on Anna's finger and a crown of pink, orange, and red wildflowers adorns loose auburn curls. She faces James, his back to the camera. I can just see a bit of his square jawline.

"It's incredible to see them together," Ellis says.

"It is." I study the wedding photograph of James and Anna again, look into Anna's midnight-blue eyes, the exact color of my own, take in James's jawline, similar to Ellis's, and the past and present have never felt closer. Love, I realize, is timeless, and its own raison d'être.

A cold breeze rolls off the ocean and brings with it the hint of tobacco smoke. I shiver then snuggle into Ellis's embrace and know I'm finally home.

When no one is looking in the Special Collections room, a few months after our wedding ceremony, I slip a note into the front sleeve of *Letters from My War*. I wrote it this morning, between my volunteer work at the Trudy Winters Animal Shelter and preparation for a court appearance where I will be assisting the state in a murder trial. It's a complicated case, but hopefully it will wrap up before my due date. I'd like to help find justice for the victim's family before I take maternity leave.

I slide the compilation of letters back into place on the shelf with a wish . . .

Dear Reader,

When I read these letters, I was lost. I had given away so much of myself in an effort to make everyone around me happy that I had nothing left. I'd relinquished my voice and direction in life. James's and Anna's bravery inspired me, and their connection and love for each other reminded me what I wanted in a relationship, and made me believe that true love existed . . . if only I believed that life offers that kind of lasting romantic love.

Finding myself took time. I had to embark on the unknown, acknowledge then let go of past wounds, accept that I couldn't change the people who were supposed to love me, and

understand there were others out there who would, indeed,
embrace me if I embraced myself and recognized my own
self-worth.

There's magic in James's letters, if you are willing to open
yourself up to it. When you finish with them, I ask you to
consider writing a note to leave behind for the next reader so
Anna and James's story of courage and true love can live on
and on.

All my best,
C

On my way out of the library I recognize the young library employee I met almost two years ago. Amelia sports the same short curls and cat-eye glasses, but she's thinner and there are dark smudges beneath her eyes.

"Excuse me," she calls.

"Yes?"

"A while ago you recommended a book to me. *No Man's Land*, about those female surgeons who volunteered in World War I."

"Did you ever read it?"

Amelia nods. "Big change takes bravery," she says softly.

"You okay?" I ask her.

"I'm kind of going through some stuff. Do you have any other book recommendations?"

"Yes," I reply with a smile. "I do . . ."

Acknowledgments

Dear Reader,

This is the part where I get to thank all the folks who made it possible for me to write this novel!

First, always, is my husband, Henry. H, you provide the love, adventure, friendship, support, and kindness that help make my writing career possible. Despite being a reluctant editor (you never want to hurt my feelings 😊), you're my first and most trusted reader. And you're the main character in the story of my life and vice versa. I have no idea how we were lucky enough to find each other, but I'm grateful every single day.

I would not have the opportunity to publish novels without the brilliance of my agent, Stephanie Kip Rostan. Steph, you give me the space to figure out the stories I want to tell and the direction to tell them better, and your wisdom, wit, and super smarts have provided the opportunity to dream bigger and bigger. Now on to the next one!! Thanks also to associate agent Courtney Paganelli at LGR Literary. I always love your smart feedback and really appreciate your time. And thanks to Debbie Deuble Hill, my film agent at APA, for all of your hard work!

During the process of crafting this novel about the power of a written legacy, I've thought a lot about my rock star editor, Kerry Donovan. Kerry, you helped me shape Constance's journey into a story about how letters that share hopes, fears, insecurities, dreams, and losses can travel through time, impact countless people, and help build a path to love and fulfillment. I'm incredibly grateful for the chance to create our own written legacy together and for the opportunity to work with you.

Huge thanks to the stellar Berkley Publishing roster, including the Penguin sales team, editorial assistant Mary Baker, senior marketing manager Fareeda Bullert, senior publicist Tara O'Connor, managing editor Christine Legon, production editor Lindsey Tulloch, and the rest of the Berkley team. Every book that gets published has all of your fingerprints on it, and readers wouldn't get to experience so many compelling, powerful, and entertaining novels without your diligence, expertise, and the time and commitment you apply to each novel you represent.

To my early readers, Henry Fischer, Laurie Forest, Dawn Weeman, Judy Frey, Sue Bishop, and Erin Burnham, thank you for your time, patience, and constructive input. To my folks, Jane and Art, thank you for your unwavering love. And to all my dear friends who are willing to go on dog walks, listen to story ideas, brainstorm, pretend to be tarot readers (Dawn, you're a star!), and throw a party to celebrate my book (Karen and Judy, you're the best!!), your kindness truly matters, and I feel so lucky to have each of you in my life.

To my cherished author buddies—what would I do without you? Writing is incredibly fun, but it's also pretty lonely at times. The opportunity to share our hopes and fears, crappy first drafts, the raves, and even some crummy reviews helps keep all this in perspective. Thank you for sharing the ups, downs, and milestones. I'll always be in your corner.

Bookstagram community, you're incredible! I love your gorgeous posts, creative reels, and how supportive you are of each other and authors. It would be impossible to list everyone, but I want to shout out a handful of Bookstagrammers who have posted amazing photographs of my novels, written lovely reviews, DM'd support, or left wonderful voice messages:

aymansbooks, bookbellas, bookapotamus, theliteraryllama, pnwbookworm, the_unwined, heyitscarlyrae, novelgossip, lesliezemeckis, love_my_ dane_dolly_, berittalksbooks, thebookend.diner, extrovertedforbooks, stacy40pages, linnareads, katieneedsabiggerbookshelf, read_with_steph, janinesbookcorner, hotcocoareads, bookmom22, foreverbookedup, sidneybookish, downtogetthefictionon, theurbanbookshelf, marchbeautyword, totallybooked, jamiseymore, ashleykritzer, readswithally, cassies_books_ reviews, wishful_reader_, books_teacups_reviews, booksfictionandlife, linnareads, somanybooksnotenoughtime, mamacappsreads, janinesbookcorner, amandasbookcorner, nikki_myreadingspot . . .

The following books and articles were part of my research for *The Book of Silver Linings*, including:

Books:

Friends of France: The Field Service of the American Ambulance Described by Its Members by Abram Piatt Andrew

In Flanders Fields: The Story of the Poem by John McCrae by Linda Greenfield and Janet Wilson

World War I (Eyewitness Guide) by Simon Adams, photographed by Andy Crawford

Articles:

Beck, Melinda. "Why Suffragists Helped Send Women Doctors to WWI's Front Lines." Mar 4, 2021 (https://www.history.com/news/wwi-women-doctors -suffragists-france).

"Women Physicians Going Abroad for War Service." *Evening Public Ledger*, May 4, 1918 (http:// chroniclingamerica.loc.gov/lccn/sn83045211/1918-05 -04/ed-1/seq-12/).

Finally, thanks to YOU, the reader, for turning the pages. The chance to let my imagination free, to devise plots and twists, bring characters to life, and dream up fictional places for you, is an honor. My hope is that Constance's journey will help someone find their way, and that you've discovered something within the pages of this novel that will ripple through your own life and beyond.

xo
Nan

PS: If you ever need a smile, visit an animal shelter and volunteer to walk a dog or cuddle a cat. And if there's a place in your heart and home, consider adopting an animal. They'll be forever grateful and fill your life with unconditional love.

The
Book
of
Silver Linings

Nan Fischer

Discussion Questions

1. Early in the story, Constance attends yoga speed dating. Have you ever attended a group dating event or blind date? Was it fun or a catastrophe?

2. Constance struggles with a low sense of self-worth stemming from her childhood. Did you have any childhood experiences that have followed you into adulthood and impacted your life?

3. Constance feels most at home with animals, and in particular, dogs that have been discarded. Do you have any animals, and if so, what do they bring into your life?

4. When Constance receives her first note back from J, who did you think was writing her, and why? Would you have written back?

5. In her relationship with Hayden, Constance gives up pieces of herself. Have you ever done this in a relationship, and if so, how did you reclaim yourself?

6. Hayden lied to Constance about his family and net worth. Do you think his actions were immoral, unfair, or justified? What about her lie about her father?

7. Inspiration and necessity lead to Constance finding her raison d'être. Have you discovered your own raison d'être, and if so, how did you find it?

8. Constance makes the difficult decision to cut ties with her dad. Have you ever had to end a relationship with a friend or family member to protect yourself?

9. This story, in large part, is about the far-reaching impact of a written legacy. Do you keep a diary or write letters? Has this story encouraged you to do so?

10. Do you believe it's possible that Constance and Ellis are reincarnations of Anna and James, or are their similarities just coincidental?

DON'T MISS

Some of It Was Real

AVAILABLE NOW!

One

Sylvie

The outfit is the easy part. It was chosen by a style consultant hired by my agent to create an image. I slip on a sleeveless black silk jumpsuit with crystals along the edge of a plunging neckline, fasten strappy heels and diamond hoop earrings, and slide a platinum ring whose sapphire stones form an infinity symbol on my index finger. On cue, my stomach cramps and I rush into the bathroom, grip the cold porcelain, and lose a late lunch. Moose whimpers then rests his blocky head on my shoulder. He's a 145-pound Great Dane, but despite his size, he's a big baby. "I'm good. Promise."

A kiss between Moose's eyes, swish of mouthwash, then I return to the mirror, sweep my dark brown hair into a glossy chignon. On goes a light coat of foundation, blush, eye shadow, dark gray liner, false lashes, and red lipstick. One final look confirms everything is in place. I swivel my chair and rifle through last-minute reminders. When the phone rings, there's no need to check caller ID. My agent always calls before a show. "Hey, Lucas."

Lucas crows, "We have a deal!"

The news shoves me back in the chair.

"Sylvie? Why aren't you jumping up and down and scream-ing? We've been working toward this for years."

"Are *you* jumping up and down?"

"I might've shot a fist in the air when Jackson phoned to say we had the green light. Syl, it's a guaranteed ten episodes, more money than we'd hoped for, bonuses, and if we get the num-bers, which I'm sure you will, we can push E! for a two-year run. This is *huge*."

"I don't know if—"

"I do—that's why we make a great team."

While we talk, I wander around the dressing room, past a long mirror, a chipped wooden table and mismatched chairs, and a dusty shelf with a drip coffee machine that looks like it belongs in a 1950s diner. My rider—a set of requests fulfilled by each venue—is pretty basic. I ask for a well-lit mirror, a pri-vate bathroom, a few bottles of water, and lots of coffee, but don't demand anything fancy, like an espresso machine.

"Sylvie?"

"Connections don't always happen. You know that."

"Then you build a bridge."

"When I started—"

"Syl, what you do? It's incredible. You make people feel bet-ter. There's no harm either way. I've told you that since the day we met. You're one of the good guys."

I rest my forehead against the cool wall to quell a nervous heat. "I'm not consistently filling theaters at the shows."

"Your numbers have been climbing fast."

"I've never been on TV."

"I negotiated approval for each episode."

"Who will I read?"

"A mix of celebrities and regular people. Sylvie, if you don't take this opportunity, someone else will. That's just the way things work in this business."

I run through my options. No family support. No real friends. No college education. *And this fits.* At first it was about survival, money, so I never had to go back home. But over the past few years, I've realized that this is the only thing that gives me some semblance of peace. "I'm in."

"Of course you are. It'll take a week for the lawyers to comb through the contract. When it's signed, we'll announce in *Variety*, Page Six, too. Sylvie?"

"Yes?"

"I believe in you."

The first time he said that was my third show after I moved to LA—just a basement club in Venice, but Lucas made sure it was packed and that a few small entertainment papers were there. I was on fire, hit after hit. Finally, I felt like I might be in the right place. After the show, he drove me back to the studio apartment in West Hollywood he'd rented for me. He turned off the engine and said, *I believe in you.* Then he added, *I'm going to make you a star.*

"You still there?" Lucas asks.

Moose leans against my leg and stares up at me. "Is Moose part of the TV show?"

"He even has his own contract."

I kiss the crown of Moose's head and his tail thumps. My first therapist was the one who suggested I get a dog. The young woman who took me around the shelter walked right past Moose, like he was invisible. He ran forward, put a massive paw on the chain links. I pressed my hand to his pads, can still recall their warmth. We chose each other that day. I kept Moose but let that therapist go. Lucas said I could hire a new therapist if needed. Even in the early days, he was aimed at the stars. Celebrities can be ruined by all kinds of past relationships and unethical practitioners. Lucas was determined to keep skeletons out of my closet. He also quickly understood that I didn't want to dissect a past that left me feeling like a disappointment.

Now Lucas is right again—a TV show *is* the next step. It doesn't matter how I fell into this profession. Before, I always felt like my shoes were on the wrong feet. This fits, despite my fears. And the bottom line is that what I do helps people.

There's a knock. "It's time," a muffled voice says.

I grab a black marker and slip it into my pocket. "Gotta go."

Moose mouths the enormous, stuffed fuzzy bone he loves and carries it out of the room. On the walk from the dressing room to the wings of any stage, I go through the guided imagery the last therapist I quit designed. It helps me overcome the anxiety that began when I first started going onstage and became crippling as my success grew. Today an image slips through the carefully constructed peace . . .

Pale sand beneath my feet, a blue-green ocean, foam nibbling at my bare toes. Behind me, a castle—ornate turrets dotted with pale pink shells, a drawbridge made from delicately curved driftwood, beneath it, a moat where tiny paper boats rock in the breeze. A wave gathers on the horizon. It grows taller and white horses gallop across its face. When the wall of salt water strikes, the castle will be destroyed and with it a treasure, something precious . . .

The vision disintegrates. Ghostly lips brush my cheek. I know what's coming next. A whisper I've heard intermittently my entire life. When I tip my head, the unintelligible slides away. I crunch an antacid to quell my burning gut then wait for the cue to step onstage and begin my show . . .

Two

Sylvie

Music flows through the theater's surround sound—a symphony of instruments that slowly builds. An intricate dance of multicolored laser lights traverses the empty stage then dry-ice vapor rolls across wooden boards and spotlights turn curls of smoke violet, azure, and emerald. The smoke dissipates, frenetic lights slow their search; the symphony strikes its crescendo. I walk to the center of the stage just as the last notes fade away, wait for the applause to thin and people to take their seats.

One hand on my dog's sleek, black head, I start. "Thank you for coming. I'm Sylvie Young and this handsome guy beside me is Moose. I get a bit nervous before each show and he helps with that, so I hope you don't mind him being here?" There are murmurs of encouragement. "Every psychic has an origin story that reveals when and how we first recognized our abilities. That might be when we predicted a grandparent's passing, delivered a message to the living only the dead could possibly know, or found a lost object, pet, or child. We must then choose whether or not to use our gift." My eyes scan the theater. Almost every seat is taken. "I never planned to be a psychic or stand on a stage. Sometimes where I've landed is overwhelming. Truly.

But what's most important is that when someone asks me to connect with those they loved and lost, I will do *anything* to make that happen."

I let this promise settle then continue. "My gift appeared when I was eighteen, living in San Francisco, and had just worked a double waitressing shift, food stains on my T-shirt, the smell of fried food in my hair. On the long walk back to a basement apartment, I stopped in the funky Haight-Ashbury neighborhood to rest on a bench. A few feet away, outside a magic shop named Abracadabra, a young guy read tarot at a rickety metal table. He was flying by the seat of his pants, but he had a gift for weaving stories. After a funny reading, I giggled. The tarot reader laughed, too; we chatted for a bit; then he scribbled a sign that read PSYCHIC $5 on a folded piece of cardboard and dared me to sit in the chair beside him. I took the seat, assumed no one would waste money on me.

"My first customers were sisters. The pregnant one was Bethany. I guessed she was almost nine months along—it wasn't a psychic thing, it was obvious that she hadn't seen her feet in a while." I wait for knowing laughter to subside then go on.

"Am I having a boy or a girl? Bethany asked.

"I rested my hands on the swell beneath the cool silk of her dress. The baby kicked and I jumped, laughed, and the mom-to-be did, too. To give Bethany a good show, I closed my eyes. An instant whooshing sound enveloped me, followed by a river of warmth that flowed around my limbs. The warm water cradled me and I felt my body slowly roll . . . but then something tugged, stopped me . . . The next thing I knew, the tarot reader was shaking me really hard. When I opened my eyes, Bethany was on her feet, arms wrapped protectively around her belly."

The audience is quiet, caught in the story's web. "*Why would you scare her like that?* Bethany's sister demanded.

"Confused, I followed her pointed finger. Scribbled across the inside of my right forearm were the words *I can't breathe.* I turned to the tarot reader. *Did you do that?* But his black marker was gripped in my hand and the writing was mine." Whispers float through the audience. "By then Bethany was crying." I tip my chin and look into the balcony section. "I should've apologized. But when I was little and in trouble, always with my mom, Dad would say that there was a plant that grew inside my belly called a *contrary tree.* Instead of backpedaling, I said, *She can't breathe.*"

I shake my head at the memory. "The sisters left. I eyed the water bottle that the tarot reader had given me. *What the hell is in that?* But it was only water. *What happened with Bethany exactly?* I demanded.

"He explained, *You grabbed my marker, started writing on your arm. I think you have the gift.*

"Of course I didn't believe him. The guy was leaving town and offered to sell me his table and chairs for ten bucks, put in a good word with the owner of the magic shop so I could still work in front of her store. He'd made a hundred and seventy-five dollars reading tarot in just two hours. After a full day waitressing, I'd only made twenty-eight bucks in tips. At that rate, I wouldn't make the month's rent. So I bought the table and chairs, figured I could try for a few hours after my restaurant shifts, vowed to keep things light and lovely, just play around.

"A few days later, I set up my table and nervously waited for customers. They actually came. After my anxiety burned off, it was surprisingly fun. I scribbled messages, hummed songs that burst into my head, and the customers were amazed. I still didn't believe the tarot guy, but I was a crap waitress and it felt good to be good at something, you know?" More than a few people in the audience nod in agreement. They understand that need to be recognized.

"Soon, there were lines just from word of mouth. People came to see *me.* Late one afternoon an old man named Arthur asked if I could contact someone who'd died. He looked so miserable that I agreed and closed my eyes . . . A red barn door materialized. It jumped into my head, like a kid in a classroom with her hand held high, desperate for the teacher's attention. I let the door swing wide and the tang of metal filled my mouth.

"Anything? Arthur asked.

"I felt a female energy cross the door's brink but couldn't see a face. The next thing I knew, I'd written a message in the crook of my elbow: *No rush. I'll be waiting. Take that watercolor class, old Tiger—M.*

"Arthur told me his wife's name was Maribel and she'd nicknamed him Tiger. She'd been dead six months, and he missed her so much, he wasn't sure he could hold on. After reading Maribel's message, he said that as a young man, he'd wanted to be a painter but had chosen accounting to support his family." The audience draws in a collective breath and I shyly smile. "Arthur kissed the bend of my elbow then walked off with light steps, like he'd sprouted wings." I lower my voice to share, "His smile has never left me."

Crossing the stage, I continue, "Six months later my business was going strong. I'd sprung for a black velvet tablecloth over the metal card table and I wore a midnight blue, sleeveless dress and used a metallic silver marker to draw stars, moons, and planets on the cheap cotton. It was pretty hokey, but I made enough to cover rent, eat more than ramen, and I'd quit waitressing." I admit, "None of this is very flattering, but it's important that you know that I didn't always believe in myself." Murmurs of disagreement ripple through the theater. Each time I reach this part of my origin story and the audience reacts with understanding and belief, I get a lump in my throat.

"One day a woman sat down across from me—pretty with dark blond hair. The man resting his hands on her shoulders had a baby on his chest in one of those trendy slings.

"*I'm Bethany*, the woman said. *You did a reading for me months ago, told me my baby couldn't breathe.*

"I apologized profusely for scaring her. She introduced her husband, Matthew, and I tensed, ready for him to tell me off, probably put me out of business.

"Bethany said, *I came home from your reading and insisted we go to the emergency room for an ultrasound. I was rushed into surgery. Grace's umbilical cord was wrapped twice around her neck. If I hadn't had an emergency C-section . . .* She started to cry.

"Matthew finished, *We wouldn't have Grace if you hadn't warned us. Thank you.*

"He gave me his business card, suggested I get in touch so he could connect me with people who might help.

"*Help with what?* I asked.

"*If you want to be a psychic for a living, do more than just this, then you need a talent agent. My friend Lucas Haughter is a big agent down in LA. I think he'd be interested.*"

I confess to the audience, "There was no plan. I just made that phone call. Lucas flew me down to LA and I did a reading for him. He signed me the same day and the rest, as they say, is history."

People have moved to the edges of their seats, ready for me to divulge secrets, solve mysteries, connect them to someone they lost, or turn back time so they can have a second chance. Finished with my origin story, I'm now ready to help as many of them as I can. They believe . . . and some of my story is even true.

Photo by Kelley Dulcich

NAN FISCHER is a two-time Oregon Book Award finalist for her novels *When Elephants Fly* and *The Speed of Falling Objects*. Additional author credits include coauthored sport autobiographies for elite athletes and a *Star Wars* trilogy for Lucasfilm. She lives in the Pacific Northwest with her husband and their vizsla, Boone.

CONNECT ONLINE

NanFischerAuthor.com
🐦 NFischerAuthor
📷 NanFischerAuthor

Ready to find
your next great read?

Let us help.

Visit prh.com/nextread